UNHOLY SEED

A Max Steele Thriller

Bob O'Connor

Unholy Seed

ICR Publishing
Atlanta, Georgia

ISBN: 1519687710

ISBN 13: 9781519687715

LCCN: 2015920206
CreateSpace Independent Publishing Platform
North Charleston, South Carolina

Printed in the United States of America
2015 – First Edition

Glossary of Terms & Codes

10-2 = loud and clear

10-4 = message received

10-9 = repeat

10-20 = location

10-23 = arrived; at location

10-76 = on the way

Signal 8 = meet

Click = distance, usually a kilometer

Mic = minute

NV = night vision

Perp = perpetrator

Satphone = satellite telephone

Sit Rep = situation report

TA = target acquired

UAV = unmanned aerial vehicle (drone)

Vic = victim

Chapter One

Memorial Hospital
Kingstown, Rhode Island

"No one should die alone," he said.

The ventilator gasped. It sucked air in, mixed it with oxygen, and pushed it through the tube into Nina Ondolopous Bente's lungs. The figure standing by her bed looked at the woman's mangled, misshapen flesh, and then at the tangled nest of tubes and machines. He watched the bed sheet rise and fall with each mechanical breath.

He supposed he should say something. What? Something sacred maybe. Can't they hear you when they're in a coma? He touched Nina's hand with gloved fingers. Cold met cold.

"You did the best you could," he said. "Married to the mob boss's kid. Had to be hell, but now it's over."

He would be quick. Had to be. The hole he cut in the plate glass window puffed the bottom of the drape. His Kevlar gloves were thick and stiff, but he could still feel the knife he held in his hand. His first cut would be the right carotid. He moved to the left side of the bed and severed it. Spurts of blood pulsed from Nina's neck. With the fluidity of a dancer, he hovered over Nina's torso and sliced the left carotid. Within seconds, he had severed the arteries on both wrists and both ankles. Blood sprayed like a garden sprinkler system.

The monitors wailed. He had seconds to make his escape. He sprang to the windowsill and yanked the repelling rope to test its anchor. Then, with one last glance at his handiwork, he jumped backward into the shadows outside the window. He repelled the exterior wall and was at the idling motorcycle in five long strides.

He felt the shot before the sound registered, felt it as he settled the helmet over his already hooded head. The bullet shattered the odometer in front of him. He ignited the engine and opened the throttle. The bike shot forward, its front tire lifting precariously from the pavement. He felt his heart thud inside the helmet, heard the scream of the engine beneath him, and wrestled the handlebars for control.

There would be no capture. There was only escape, or death by his own hand.

Residence of Dr. Maria Sanchez
Kingstown, Rhode Island

They made love the way artists paint, as if time were both urgent and irrelevant. The rhythmic lines floated along her canvas, punctuated by sharp, staccato dabs, and followed by long deep strokes along the seam. Her body splashed to life with bursts of color both bright and deep. She writhed beneath him, both caught by the stroke and overwhelmed by it. She sunk her fingernails in his back and he growled, painting feverishly now, with strokes dark, and mysterious, and pulsing with passion.

It was art birthed in fever and flame. She felt it build, wave upon wave, building, until the canvas gave voice to its secret in a burst of brilliant, pulsing flashes of white and red. The brush slashed and stroked until artist and canvas were one in a surge of sparks and flame. Detective Max Steele continued to paint, more slowly now. Maria arched her back and pressed her hips to keep him inside, as the brush weakened its touch into soft, pulsing petals, like a rose that quivers at the first splash of summer rain.

She rolled him onto his back, straddling him, and pushed herself up. Her wet, tangled hair fell like dark clouds along her face. “Oh God,” she said, barely above a whisper. It was so wrong. It was so right. And it was so dangerous, for both of them.

Mantisto State Prison
Kingstown, Rhode Island

Her tires spat rain like chaw from a toothless mouth. The sound reminded Sarah Stafford of the movie clip she’d seen while flipping channels. She had frozen, remote in hand, because it captured her with its horror. A woman was tossed into a pit of snakes. Their hiss rose to levels rivaling their victim’s screams. The snakes scattered when she hit the dirt, recoiled, and then returned. The woman clawed the wall, and jerked as fang after fang savaged her legs.

Sarah jerked and gripped the wheel tighter. Once seen, some things cannot be unseen, nor can they be scrubbed from the mind’s eye. They burrow into memory and come alive again at unexpected moments. She rolled up her window, and turned onto the access road for Mantisto State Prison. A long line of brake lights winked in the distance. It was a busy Saturday morning at the penitentiary. Visitors lined up like freight cars to get in.

Sarah shook her head. There was so much love in this line, and so much pain. And then there were the likes of her, Sarah, the seminary drop out. The sun breached the horizon. Ahead, it glinted off hundreds of feet of looping razor wire woven into the top several feet of the tall fence line. The light shone through the mesh of sharp metal, whose function was to shred the flesh of human beings who dared try to escape. It was beautiful, and it was terrible.

What was this place, really? And who were these people caged within miles of sharpened metal? Who were these human beings stuffed in metal boxes within these concrete buildings? And who were the people running this interminable and expensive timeout? For all her sophistication and knowledge, she knew nothing about penitentiaries, nothing of human storage units, nothing except that everyone paid a price for their existence.

As she inched closer to the fence line, the sheer volume of wire filled her vision. In the distance, the 20-foot gate shuddered and began to quiver. It slid slowly to the side, granting passage forward to a large white school bus. No sooner had it completed its slide open, than it reversed course and nearly clipped the rear of the entering bus as it closed.

Sarah continued to inch forward. Through the fence, she saw two gloved officers descend the shack steps toward the bus, now trapped between the outer gate through which it had passed and an inner gate. An officer was sliding something flat under the vehicle. Sarah's eye caught movement above. A dove was hovering over the smoked-glass guard tower, readying to land.

Coming to Mantisto State Prison was like passing through a veil into an alternate reality. There were scores of people here, but only a few were visible. Some were the watchers and some were the watched. Sarah leaned forward and craned her neck, counting. Four towers. Who were they watching? Me? The prisoners? Everybody? At any given moment, would there be a gun trained on her? Was there now? No doubt, visitors were among the watched. No doubt, the watchers were authorized to shoot the watched if circumstances dictated. She heard a loud whistle and her body convulsed.

An officer with a whistle between his teeth stood a short distance ahead next to a side road. She hadn't even noticed him. He motioned her to turn right. She turned and saw the parking lot several hundred yards in the distance. A dark building with mirrored glass stood just beyond it.

She parked and gathered her paperwork and identification. She followed the other visitors into the building. Inside, a uniformed man stood behind thick, meshed glass with a metal drawer protruding beneath and a circular metal speaker in the middle.

"Good morning, ma'am," the corrections officer said through the speaker when it was her turn. "Paperwork, please. License." He pointed to the drawer. Sarah complied, and the drawer slid into the wall. The officer scooped them up on the other side and disappeared behind a wall.

Sarah hugged herself and turned around. The large entry area was lined with plastic chairs, half of which were already occupied with people.

“Okay, ma’am,” the officer said behind her, and Sarah turned back. He slid the drawer, and Sarah collected the paperwork and a visitor’s badge. When she took the badge, she noticed her hand tremble. The officer noticed it, too, and looked up. “My first time,” Sarah said, and blew out a breath. The officer nodded and motioned her to the seats.

Residence of Dr. Maria Sanchez
Kingstown, Rhode Island

“I want more,” Max Steele said.

“Baby, that’s twice already.” She ran fingernails slowly down his chest.

“I want more between us,” he said, barely above a whisper. “I want to marry you.”

“Don’t start,” she said, and blew out a breath. “I thought you liked playing doctor.”

“You can’t resist me, Dr. Sanchez.” He pulled her down to him and nuzzled her neck.

“You can’t resist me,” she said, and buried her face into his chest.

“You’re right. I can’t,” Max said.

“Holy Mother of God,” she whispered into his chest hair, still sucking air through her mouth. This man, this man, this man. She’d prayed.

“God honey, I love . . .,” Max said.

“Shhh!” she said. It was sharp, and Max felt her head jerk. “Just shut up, okay?”

“You didn’t even know what I was going to say,” Max said.

She picked up her head. “I did.” She pushed away.

“What I ….”

“Don’t speak to me of love,” she said, sitting up.

“Nice,” he said. “Cut me off and toss me a line.”

“It’s James ….”

“James Fenton,” Max said, cutting her off. “I know. And this is why Bull told me never to date an intelligent woman.”

“You get the reference,” Maria said. “I’m impressed.”

“Don’t talk to me of love. I’ve had an earful...,” Max said, quoting. “Have you had an earful, Maria? I haven’t said a word.”

“I hear you speaking, whether or not your lips move.”

“What have I here? A naked mystic?” He felt her body jerk again and saw her head shake.

“Just a girl,” Maria said.

“You are a woman. Oh. My God.”

Her head wagged again. “I am. But when I am with you I am a girl, giggling, bubbling, sharing candy.”

“I love your candy.”

She leaned over and kissed his chest.

“So, little girl,” he said, stroking her arm, “You think I’m diminishing the powerful woman I see commanding orderlies in the ER?”

“Hardly,” Maria said. “She hasn’t gone anywhere. Let’s not get deep, not now, okay? And speaking of work,” she said, “we’re going to be late.” Maria lifted herself and stood. She paused at the edge of the bed and scanned his muscled torso. It was pocked with love marks. “You’re a mess,” she said.

“I am?” he said.

“Wait ‘til you look in the mirror,” she said over her shoulder. “I left you the towel.”

Max closed his eyes. Words of love and deities. It was another "Bull-ism," another phrase from the brother he would never see again this side of heaven. "You can set your watch by it Max," Bull had said. "Once you've gotten laid, out flow words of love and deities."

Was that all this was? This urge, this desire, to tell Maria he loved her? He mopped himself with the towel and stood. His feet led him toward the sound of water kissing Maria's body in the shower. The bathroom mirror had begun to fog, and he wiped it with the towel.

His eyes fell to his abdomen. "Good Lord, Maria!"

A soap-white head popped from around the end of the shower curtain. "What? Ooh," she said, and swished the curtain closed again.

"Oh my God!" he said.

"Oopsies," she said.

Maria shuffled into the kitchen wearing a terry cloth robe and trying to rub water from her long brown hair.

"I made you breakfast," Max said.

"You are going to make me late." She picked a slice of toast from the plate he pushed across the island, and crammed half of it into her mouth. "But I am starving."

"Clinic today?"

She nodded, chewing.

"What's the rush?" he asked. "We've got a little role reversal going on here."

"Early, um, appointments." She glanced at the clock and her eyes went wide. "And I'm late!"

"Okay. Run before I tell you I love you."

"Shhh," she hissed again.

"Whoa. Retract the claws, Cat Woman."

“You like my claws.”

“I do, he said, “but I don’t like being shushed, especially when I am trying to tell you I love you.”

“Don’t be stupid, Max.”

“Oh, now I’m stupid?”

She whirled on him. “We’re just fucking, okay?” She slapped a hand over her mouth and looked away.

“We’re done here,” Max said, and started for the bathroom door.

“Wait,” Maria said, turning toward him as he passed. “What’s that supposed to mean?”

“Means I’m done talking to you,” he said. “Getting in the shower.”

She followed him into the bathroom. He was bent over the shower faucets, his back to the door.

“I just can’t …,” Maria said. “I will be your mistress.” She tried to sound lighthearted.

He didn’t look at her, but she saw him flinch. “I’m not married.”

“Then I will be your woman.”

“I think you better go, Maria,” he said. “Weren’t you gonna be late?”

“I think you better look at me, Max Steele.”

He turned to face her with enough force that she took a step back.

“Look into these eyes, Max,” she said. “What do you see?”

“Tell you what I don’t see, or feel,” he said, “and that’s indifference. You aren’t just in this for sex.”

“I’m not,” she said, “but I can’t love you.”

“Then just what do you want?” He looked at the ceiling and blew out a breath. “Sorry.”

“What I want,” she said, stepping close to his chest now, “is for you to be happy and safe.”

"I am happy," he said.

"Then we're good here, yes?" she said. "That is, unless you let any more of that hot water escape down the drain without showering in it. Then it's going to be a cold shower and a bad day."

Max turned back to the shower, the towel dropped, and she watched muscles ripple as he stepped in and drew the curtain behind him.

One day it would end. She pursed her lips to stop the quivering. One way or the other, it would end. There was no living a lie, and also living happily ever after.

Crime Scene — Nina Ondolopous Bente's Room
Memorial Hospital
Kingstown, Rhode Island

Lieutenant Bert Higgins braced against the cold air rushing in through the hole in the window. He rubbed his hands.

"Ready to move the body, Lieutenant," the coroner said. He rubbed his hands together, too. "Colder than a witch's tit in a brass bra, as they say," he said.

"Not until Cap gets here," Higgins said. "Hey, can we get something up over this window?" He pointed toward two forensics techs in the opposite corner of the room.

"Can't touch it until photographs are finished," the older tech said. Yellow numbered tents littered the hospital room floor. Higgins watched the techs tiptoe between them in blue shoe covers.

"Dammit Lester," Higgins said, and squeezed his eyes shut. Lieutenant Sid Lester had been posted outside the door of Nina Ondolopous Bente's room. His instructions were to protect the patient and to restrict access to medical personnel only.

"I feel like shit already, okay?" Lieutenant Lester said, barely above a whisper. He squatted on his haunches in the corner furthest from Nina's lifeless body.

"Yeah okay," Higgins said. He walked to the hole in the window, and peered down the street. The area throbbed with strobes of red and blue. Crime scene tape bobbed and strained against the bitter Rhode Island wind. He felt the presence of his partner, even before a sound had been made or a word uttered. Higgins turned to see Captain Max Steele framed in the doorway. Max's eyes flicked from one numbered marker to the next. Higgins knew to keep his mouth shut until Steele finished collecting every detail from the room. He saw Lt. Lester pull his patrol hat lower over his eyes. The fingers of his gun hand drummed noiselessly on his thigh. Lester knew he was in deep shit. Everybody did. Higgins hadn't been where Lester was now, but he'd been close a couple of times.

Max blew out a breath and looked at his longtime friend, Dr. Harry Drine, Kingstown Coroner. "Give it to me slowly, Harry." Soft clicks and strobe flashes punctuated Harry's strides as he made his way to the door. "Let's step outside. Higgins, you too."

"Lester," Max pointed a wedged hand toward him, and the bustle of the room fell still in an instant. In the silence, Higgins saw his partner's hard, eagle-like stare soften. "Have you had your drug test?"

"Yes, sir," Lester said, raising his eyes to meet Steele's.

"Then go get the hottest cup of coffee you can find in the cafeteria, and wait for me there."

All eyes were on Lester, who looked younger to Higgins now than he had moments before. Lester rose and made his way to the door. Wordlessly, Max clasped a hand onto his shoulder as he passed. Higgins wondered if he would ever become half the leader, with half the heart, that he saw in Captain Max Steele.

"Higgins," Steele said.

"Sir?" Higgins said.

"Go with him," he nodded toward the slouched frame moving down the hall.

"10-4 Cap," Higgins said.

"Find out all you can," Max said in a low voice. "We've been burned before."

"Roger that," Higgins said with a nod. And then he was gone, hurrying down the hall to catch up with Lt. Lester.

Max turned to the coroner in the hallway.

"Do I need to see the body?" Steele said.

"Don't see why, Max." Dr. Harry Drine said. "Nothing you can't get from the pictures and the autopsy report. I'll try to file it in the next 48 hours.

"Did I hear you say 24 hours?" Max said.

"Killin' me Max," Drine said, and chuckled. "Guess I'll file that report in 24 hours. Thankfully for me it's not complicated." He fixed Steele with a look. "Not so for you."

"No?"

"As clean and professional a job as I've seen in my career," Harry said. "1, 2, 3, 4, 5, 6 arteries, and she was history. No way you're going to stop her from bleeding out."

"Any telltales? Trademarks? Clues as to who we're dealing with?"

"Just that it was overkill, if you'll pardon the pun," Dr. Drine said. "Severing both carotids would have been enough for a bleed out. This guy was making a statement. Definitely an execution."

"I see."

"By the way, I was about to give that boy of yours a sedative."

"Lester?" Max said.

Harry nodded. "We're all our worst judge. He skinned and hung himself in the meat locker over there in the corner."

"Screwed up and he knows it," Max said. "Twenty bucks says he left his post. Probably down at the nurse's station wiggling his dick."

"Said he might have winged the perp," Harry said.

"Higgins told me on the phone. They're looking for blood on the street."

The two men locked eyes, knew with a knowing that comes from years of processing and mopping up: nothing more to see here.

"I do want to see her for myself," Max said.

"Okay," the coroner said, "but you kick one of those marker tents, and they'll tear your ass up."

"Forensics? Screw 'em."

Harry snorted. "Say that now. Bump one of the tents and see whose asshole gets stretched."

Max returned to the room. He picked his way slowly through the blood spatters and tent markers. Didn't see anything interesting. Harry was right. The bed upon which Nina's lifeless frame lay exposed resembled a melted candy cane with alternating red and white blotches and stripes. A disconnected tube stuck garishly from her mouth. It was difficult to discern her face at all. Max had never met Nina Ondolopous Bente, but he felt he knew her. He had watched her on airport surveillance tape until his eyes crossed, looking for anything, any little thing that would help him take down the Bente Cartel. He had hoped one day to talk to her, held onto that thin thread of hope for a clue or two from her that would turn this morass of dead ends into one solid lead.

He took a last look at the body, lifeless and still, then he turned to the forensics team in the room. "All done here?" Max said. He heard them chuckle and murmur. It was a whimsical, ridiculous question, and everybody knew it. With scenes like this, they were never done in one sense. Still, with a professional hit like this one, they may as well have been done before they started.

"I'll be in the cafeteria," Steele said to no one in particular.

He found them in the furthest corner of the cafeteria. As Max approached, both men leaned back in their chairs. It was a reflex, an ingrained response to authority entering the room. Max pulled up a chair to the table and sat backwards on it.

How do you feel, Lester?" Max said.

"Do you really want to know, sir?" Lester said. "Or do you want to know how I could be such an idiot?"

Max looked at the young man in silence, saw the tears brim, patted himself for a handkerchief, and then pushed his frame upright and headed for the napkin holder. He snapped out a handful and returned to the table.

Lester was shaking his head.

"Nothing to be embarrassed about," Higgins said. "I've cried a couple of times just this year, right boss?"

Max nodded. "We both have."

Lester reached for the napkins and stuck a fist full toward his face. Held them there.

Higgins and Steele exchanged a glance and respected the silence that followed, while the proud young man struggled to regain composure. When Lester lowered the napkins, his eyes were unfocused and he appeared to be somewhere else.

"Are you seeing it again?" Steele said.

"Like it's on a loop," Lester said.

"Describe it for me," Max said softly.

"Happened so fast," Lester said, still not looking at Steele or Higgins, still seeing it. "I'm at the nurse's station," he said. "Figured what's the harm. I can see the room door from there and can be there in a couple seconds if anybody tries to get in. Or even if I see anybody coming down the hall, anybody coming in or out. Dammit, I was right there. Well, practically."

"And then you heard the monitors start to wail," Higgins said, focusing Lester back on the scene.

"We all did," Lester said. "And I ran for the room."

"Think very carefully," Max said. "Was there a moment, even a few seconds, when your eyes may not physically have been focused on that door?"

Officer Lester shook his head.

"Did anyone make friends with you?" Higgins said. "Maybe offer to help you out, you know, if you had to use the head?"

Lester had been shaking his head. Then he froze, and looked up into Steele's face. "We all gotta go, you know," Lester said.

"Look Lester, no one's after your hide here, so …," Steele said.

"Yeah right," Lester said, and looked at the table. "We all know about the witch hunt."

"The what?" Max said, a bit louder than he intended.

"We know," Lester said.

"You know what, exactly?" Steele said. Higgins watched the vein in his boss's neck swell. *Uh oh.*

"Nothing, sir, um, never mind," Lester said.

"You better spill it, young man, or it won't be just your job you'll be worrying about."

"Oh, we know that too," Lester said.

"Know WHAT, too?" Max heard his voice loud now in his own ears. *Red line, Steele. Slow the hell down.* "Sorry Lieutenant," Steele said, "for the tone I mean. I think we're all a little bit amped. Higgins, help me out." Max leaned back from the table. Took slow deep breaths. Waited.

"Sid," Higgins said, "You're telling us something important, and I want you to know we're listening. As God is my witness, we're both on your side." He watched Lester's eyes well again. "You're really scared, aren't you?" Higgins said.

Lester's words gushed out through the cries of the little boy inside. "We talk, you know, the guys? We know Chief Parker was a mole and now you're looking at us, everybody, wondering if we're dirty too."

"Okay," Higgins said. "That helps."

"And Parker got his parts blown all over the hillside the night you took Bente down."

"And you and the boys don't want the same thing to happen to you," Max said, "if suddenly we think you're working for Bente too. Am I getting this right?" He leaned forward.

"Right," Lester said, "and so everybody's walking on egg shells, know what I mean, trying not to mess up. And now," he spread his arms, "this."

"Shit, no wonder you're upset," Higgins said. "But I promise you it's not like that. You have my word."

Max watched his young partner in action as if he were seeing him, really seeing him, for the first time. What was he feeling? Respect. Yeah, but more than that. Higgins was coming into his own.

"Max?" Higgins was looking at him.

"Yep," he said, and cleared his throat.

"Lester says he's gonna try again to tell us, you know, all the details."

"Yes, please, Sid." Max liked the way Higgins called him by his first name. "We've got you at the nurse's station and you can see the door. And then we started talking about the restroom breaks."

"Yes, sir," Lester said. "I, you know, got to know the nurses on that floor pretty well. It was like we were all on the same team, looked out for each other."

"Go on," Max said. "Who covered for you?"

"Angie Davies mostly."

"She volunteered to watch things for you while you hit the head?"

Lester nodded.

"And by any chance, was she covering for you at the desk when the monitors went off?"

Lester nodded again and put his head down on the table.

Max and Higgins reached for their radios at the same moment. Max held up his hand, and keyed his mic.

"Steele to Base," Max said.

"Go for Base," the voice crackled through his handheld.

"Contact Kingstown Hospital. Have charge nurse, floor seven, hit me on my cell. Code 1."

"Copy," the dispatcher said.

"Okay Sid," Steele said, "that is a huge help, and I thank you. Now let's talk about next steps for you. You and I know you'll have to take a polygraph, okay? And Administrative Leave until we sort it out."

Lester was silent, his head still resting on the table.

"And they bagged your weapon," Max said. "You fired two rounds, you say?"

"Yes sir," he said through his arms. "Wish I'd shot that bastard right out of his saddle."

Miserericordia Clinic
Kingstown, Rhode Island

Miserericordia Clinic was located on a hillside near the harbor docks. A thriving Hispanic community had developed in the area as more and more demand for inexpensive labor attracted both documented and undocumented workers. Harbor work was difficult, the kind of labor no one but the desperate or the illegal would do. It was a poor community, and that meant poor hygiene and nonexistent healthcare. The clinic was founded as an outreach of Kingstown Memorial Hospital largely at the behest of one of Kingstown's Hispanic doctors, Dr. Maria Sanchez. The clinic's focus was prenatal care for pregnant women. Dr. Sanchez had been the driving force behind the project, and her willingness to volunteer twice a week in exchange for the hospital funding the mobile clinic, sweetened the pot enough to attract board approval. Maria refused the offer to fund support staff. She chose to run it by herself.

This morning, as she stepped from the car, her nose was met by the harbor's stench. Industrial oil, scum, and rotting food made the walk up the hill to the clinic a miserable experience. The exertion forced Maria to take large gulps of the fetid air. The packed dirt drive to the clinic at the top of the rise was pocked with deep ruts that made driving impossible. That was by design.

She nodded to the shadowed figure by the large live oak. She knew him only as Pablo, knew his protection services came at a price she didn't pay. He never spoke, never removed his sunglasses, night or day. She had never seen his eyes and wasn't sure she wanted to, because some eyes tell a story you do not want to know.

As she crested the rise, Maria glanced to her right and was met by a brilliant sun pulling itself from the edge of the Sound. She squinted back toward the trailer. To her left, she saw the line of bodies, beginning at the clinic door and stretching already around the end of it. The women, some with small children in tow, wore shawls to cover their heads. Thick, drab colored dresses fell to just above their sandaled feet. All but one of them was distended in the middle, giving evidence of their pregnancy. They greeted Maria with gap-toothed smiles. She wondered if even one of them had a full set of teeth in her head. The children were sleepy-eyed and withdrawn.

Maria moved quickly to the door and unlocked it. She knew many of these women would be anxious to be on their way. "*Todo está bien*," she said.

"*Todo está bien*," came the replies in a mash of murmurs and slurs. Maria smiled and returned the waves before slipping through the door. In one motion, she had the lights on and her lab coat in hand. There was no time to waste. Some of these women were carrying very heavy burdens.

She opened her briefcase and plugged in the laptop. It was already booted and ready for a retinal scan to unlock. She leaned down into the computer and blinked. After a moment, a blank screen appeared. She fished into the bottom of her purse for her lipstick and pulled open the bottom, extracting the miniature memory stick inside. Once she had plugged it into the port, the screen flashed and a spreadsheet appeared. Ready.

She slid open the cut in the clinic wall nearest the front door and called for the first patient. The woman who opened the door was great with child and climbed the trailer steps with difficulty. She was no stranger to the clinic and knew the drill. Maria looked up from the screen only long enough to nod and receive the code. The exchange was a wordless hand signal, one that the casual bystander or child would never even notice. The woman moved to the examination room, and Maria followed with the laptop in hand. She pulled the curtain behind them.

"*Inglés* o *Español?*" Maria said.

"English," the woman replied. "A little."

"Okay."

The woman undid buttons at the top of her dress and let it fall to the floor at her feet. Strapped to her belly was a rounded basket resembling half an enormous egg, the flat edge of which was tight against her middle. The exterior was covered with silicone to smooth it for those who might touch it through the dress. The rip of separating Velcro scratched like fingers on a chalkboard, but the woman was soon free of her burden. Maria held it for her as she detached it from her body, and then set it on the table.

"Scared to come here," the woman said. Maria took the packs of bills two at a time from the egg. It was filled to capacity.

"How much is here?"

"I don't know. They load it and help me put it on."

Maria barely heard her. She was counting money and logging it into the spreadsheet.

"So scared," the woman repeated.

Maria stopped and looked up. "What's your number?"

"Forty-six."

Maria nodded. "Been doing this a long time then?"

The woman nodded.

"You have family?"

The woman nodded.

"That's why you're here," Maria said. She touched her hand. "We're all scared, okay?" She looked into the woman's eyes. "Okay?"

The woman nodded.

"Let me finish and then I will load you."

Maria set the money in stacks and rows on the sheet covering the examination table.

"Do you need something?" Maria said, still counting. "Something to help you not be so scared?"

The woman nodded.

"A moment." She handed the woman the now empty basket to hold, and she folded the sheet into a tight bundle containing the money. She secured it with rolls of gauze and tape and dropped it into one of the laundry bags at the back of the room. Then she spread a fresh sheet on the table.

"A moment," Maria said, and held up a finger. She took the basket from the woman, who began to rock from one foot to the other. Nervous, Maria thought. Very.

She disappeared into the back of the clinic and fumbled for her keys. She unlocked the storage room. Supplies had been delivered sometime in the night, and the shelves were full to capacity with round shaped plastic bags. She reached for the respirator hanging on the wall and covered her face and mouth with it. A small bench protruded from the wall and Maria set the basket on it. She filled the basket with plastic pouches of white crystalline, and then backed out of the room with it.

As garish as she must have looked to the Latino woman, Maria returned with the filled basket still wearing the respirator.

"A moment," she said in muffled tones behind the respirator and returned to hang up the respirator and lock the storage room. She gathered a syringe and a small bottle of clear liquid on her way back to the examination room.

"Okay," she said, and blew out a breath. "Let's get you loaded."

"*Sí,*" Mule 46 said, and readied the Velcro straps. Maria guided the egg into place against the woman's midsection and secured the Velcro straps. With both hands, number 46 lifted the basket slightly while Maria tightened the straps.

Then Maria swabbed the woman's arm with a sterile pad and filled the syringe from the bottle.

"Deep breath," she said, and pushed the needle into the woman's arm. Mule 46 breathed noisily through a clenched jaw. And then it was done. Maria tossed her latex gloves on the table and reached for the woman's dress on the floor. She raised it over her as one would dress a mannequin and helped her with the buttons.

"*Todo está bien,*" Maria said.

"*Todo está bien,*" the woman said, and stepped heavily through the door.

Maria pressed the save key on the computer, then closed her eyes. All was not well. So, so not well.

She slid the cover open next to the door and called for the next patient.

Mantisto State Prison
Kingstown, Rhode Island

Time is the chief currency of a prison and everyone pays, including visitors. Sarah glanced at her wrist, then remembered her watch was locked up with the rest of her valuables. You wait in one place. Then they move you so you can wait in a new place. And then to another place. Until you are here, seated at a small table with a chair on the opposite side.

Surely, time is something the inmates think about, negotiate for, and calculate. Their timeout is their time in. The system calls it time served, but who does that time serve? Sarah blinked. There was too much time to think here, too much time to think about being here, to think about who else is here and why, to think about not wanting to be here, to ask yourself why you are here. Why are you here, Sarah? Are you here as the Christian do-gooder? To visit the downtrodden in their distress? Or is this visit personal? Did you just want to see his face one more time? Did you want to speak aloud the words that cycle through your head since that night? "Sonofabitch. Piece of shit low life scum. I don't sleep anymore, you asshole. Not one good night's sleep since."

As if on cue, the mind that does not forget, that cannot forget, cycles again, and Sarah is back in that car with Emil's hand trying to work its way up the inside of her thigh. She smells the putrid stink of his breath. She knows she will be raped in a matter of hours, maybe minutes, maybe now, and there isn't a thing she can do about it. And the hotel room. Vinnie pacing, Vinnie watching, Vinnie orchestrating the nightmare. And the knowing, the knowing that she cannot even die to escape it.

Sarah blinked and hugged herself again. Emil Bente, Jr. was dead. Vinnie Bontecelli was here, in a metal box somewhere in this place. Vinnie Bontecelli: part perpetrator and part savior. The only reason she had not been raped that night was because Vinnie had threatened to kill Bente if he touched her. But, the only reason she had been abducted in the first place was because Vinnie had allowed it.

So many words to say. *You won't say them, will you, Ice Queen? Won't spill all those words and be free of them, will you?*

She heard the rattle of his chains and looked up to see a corrections officer in the doorway escorting an old man in an orange suit. Chains stretched from wrist cuffs with a solid metal box encasing them, to ankle cuffs at his feet. She didn't feel her eyes well up until one emotional bandit made its way down her cheek. She swiped at it and sat up straight. The officer helped Vinnie Bontecelli into a chair on the other side of the table, and then took a position behind and slightly to the left of him.

Vinnie's eyes were cast toward his shackled hands. Sarah wondered if she would be able to hear past the thudding of her heart. He looked older, thinner, almost freakish, with his now bald head. He had had such thick, silver hair the last time she'd seen him. Suddenly, she wanted to run, run as fast as she could, anywhere. What did she think she was doing here anyway? Why had she come? Oh God.

Sarah felt parallel streaks of hot tears race from her eyes and splash onto her forearms. Her eyes met Vinnie's and Sarah looked away, then back again. There were words in her throat. She felt them.

"Thank you for writing," he said.

Sarah swallowed and nodded. "Thank you for replying." Sarah reached for a tissue in her purse, the one that always hung from her shoulder, except there was no purse. She had had to lock it up.

"I sent it to the cops, the letter," he said. "Figured they'd have your address, get it to you." He looked down. "Wanted to say something, say sorry for the way it all went down."

"The way it all went down? Is that what you call kidnapping?" She felt the heat in her neck. "How was it all going to go down, Mr. Bontecelli? Were you going to say, 'Sorry for your inconvenience? You're free to go now?' Is that what men like you do to people who've seen your face, who know your name, who can describe you to the people who want to put you away?"

"No."

"You were going to kill me," she said. "You'd tell yourself you had no choice. It's the breaks, right? I saw it that night in your eyes, heard it in your voice. You were going to take my life into your hands, and end it."

"Yes."

"You bastard," she said, her voice rising to a shriek.

Vinnie threw back his head and laughed. "And here I thought you'd come to save me." He laughed again. "Give me a Bible, tell me Jesus loves me, and you do, too, 'because he lives in me.'" He made the quote signs with fingers that rattled the wrist chains when he moved.

"Couple minutes left, ma'am," the corrections officer said.

"I'm done here," she said.

"But I'm not saved yet." Vinnie's eyes flashed, the mirth falling from his face like a collapsing building. He pointed his index fingers at her, now pressed together. "I said sorry, wrote it down. Wasn't personal."

"Life," she said, "is personal. It's always personal, you cockroach." She stood.

The guard stepped forward. "Please remain seated, ma'am, until the offender has been removed."

Sarah sat.

The officer tapped Vinnie's shoulder. Instead of standing, Vinnie leaned forward. "Why? Why bother coming? So you could curse me, call me a bastard?"

"I came to say I forgive you."

"Unless my hearing's gone off, you didn't."

"I didn't."

The corrections officer lifted Vinnie under the arm. The prisoner stood, laughing again. But it was a mirthless laugh. "Why don't you go sing some songs or chant some shit or do whatever you do to convince yourself how holy you are."

The officer had Vinnie halfway through the door. He jerked his head around, eyes glassy and blazing. "But you and I know better." He winked. "Don't we?"

Then he was gone.

"We do," she said to an empty room.

Chapter Two

Bureau Vehicle

Memorial Hospital Parking Lot

Kingstown, Rhode Island

"Next of kin?" Higgins said.

"Not that anyone knows, no," Steele said.

"I feel bad for her, you know?"

"You can't go there," Max said.

"You go there," Higgins said.

"Shut up." Max continued filling out his report on the laptop. "Lester's clean, my opinion."

"He's a good kid," Higgins said.

"Look who's talking, kid," Max said, and elbowed his young partner from the passenger seat without looking at him. "Hey, good job in there."

"Thanks Cap," Higgins said, smiling. "Lester's a little green, and a little light between the shoulders maybe, but he's okay …."

Max's cell phone chirped. "Steele …. Yes ma'am …. What time? Yes ma'am, I'll need a full description. And can someone pull her employee file? Yes ma'am, we're just outside." Max ended the call and looked at his partner. "Here we go, Higgins."

"Let me guess," Bert said.

"Back in there," Max said, and both men pushed the car doors open. They ran to the Emergency Room entrance.

"Guessing that was the charge nurse?" Higgins said as he held the door.

"Yep," Steele said, throwing himself through the door. When Higgins caught him halfway down the corridor, Steele said, "Angie Davies went home sick this morning."

"Imagine that," Higgins said.

"Exactly."

"What do you bet there's no such person as Angie Davies?"

"Damn well better be," Max said. "We need intel, something, anything."

Two more hallways and an elevator later, they were at the ICU nurse's station.

"Nurse Davies isn't answering her cell phone," the charge nurse said. "I'll take you to Human Resources."

"How long has she worked for you?" Steele said as they walked.

"I knew you were going to ask me, so I checked. Hasn't been long at all."

Max could feel the familiar stirring in his gut. *Not again.*

"She transferred in a couple of weeks ago," the charge nurse said, biting her lower lip.

"From?" Higgins said.

"That … I couldn't find," she said. "Another reason I want to go with you to HR."

"You call ahead to have them pull the records?" Max said.

"Of course."

Max quickened his pace. He knew his last question had escaped his lips with more heat than was necessary or appropriate. He would apologize later. Right now, he wanted to hit somebody. Anybody. His hand grabbed the handle to the Human Resources suite and he yanked.

"It's locked," the nurse said, and pressed the buzzer next to the door. She looked toward the black orb on the ceiling that concealed the camera. The door buzzed. Higgins was first to reach the handle.

"Easy Boss," he said in a whisper as Steele pushed past.

"Soon as we get the Social," Max said, "run it."

Her name was Velda Florida, but most people in Human Resources called her Mama. Already in her seventies, she was too loved to be forced into retirement. Right now, Mama had both feet squarely planted, her hands palm flat on the front counter, and she was glaring into the beet-red face of Captain Max Steele.

"And just what, young man, does Jesus Christ, my Lord and Savior, have to do with any of this?" Velda Florida said.

"Jesus Christ," Max said again through clenched teeth.

"There you go again." Both arthritis-gnarled hands moved to her wide hips. A bespectacled woman rushed up behind Mama and put a hand on her shoulder. "I'll take care of this Mama," she said in a hushed tone.

"Oh no," Velda said. "No, no, no. I'm staying right here until this man either tells me what Jesus Christ has to do with a missing file, or apologizes for his disrespectful and reprehensible behavior."

"Perhaps I can …." Higgins said.

"And you," Velda shot a finger toward Higgins, "can just stand down and wait your turn."

Her eyes returned to Max Steele, although the finger continued to point at Higgins. An eternal silence, that actually lasted no more than three or four seconds, rested upon the room. Higgins watched his partner wither under Mama's steady eyes.

"I am, um," Steele said, "I apologize." All eyes shifted to Mama.

"Captain Steele," she said. "On behalf of my Lord and Savior, Jesus Christ, your apology is accepted." She turned to the woman fidgeting next to her. "Now," Mama said, and took the woman by the back of the arm, her eyes still locked on Steele's, "just to be sure it wasn't misfiled, I'm going to check the files again. I'll also look in the files under the letters C and E in case someone missed when they were aiming for D. And Miss Kryder here will double check the database under every spelling of Davies she can think of, isn't that right, Miss Kryder?"

The bespectacled woman turned and was gone without a word. Likewise, Velda Florida turned and shuffled her massive girth around the corner.

Max felt air return to the room. He turned to his partner. "Head back to the vehicle," he said. "Run the name without the Social. It's probably fake. When the Lord's Ambassador returns, I'll ask if Davies registered a vehicle in the employee's parking lot."

Higgins nodded and slipped through the door.

Max caught up with Higgins at the vehicle. He dropped into the passenger seat and slammed the door.

"Davies is a ghost." Higgins said, looking at the side of Steele's face.

"Shocking," Max said. "Probably jumped on the back of that motorcycle after it rounded a corner, and …." He flexed open the fingers of his hand. "Poof."

"Emil Bente and his magic tricks," Higgins said.

"Think this is his handiwork?" Steele said.

"Don't you?"

"Do I think he did it himself?" Max shook his head. "But do I think he's enough of a shit pot to have his own daughter-in-law killed? Um, yeah."

"We had him, Cap," Higgins said, "once upon a time."

Steele nodded and fidgeted in the seat. "Had the Shark in deep freeze with his Number Two man. Had his daughter-in-law here with a guard posted 24/7." He grabbed at the gray-flecked bristles of his crew cut. "Now, NOW, Bente has slipped out a trap door in the best supermax penitentiary we've got. And mark my words, Higgins, he had help. Then, he arranges to have his own daughter-in-law assassinated before she comes out of her coma and talks." He scrubbed his scalp and blew out a breath.

"Your breath smells like a pig's butt," Higgins said.

"Oh, sorry," Max muttered reflexively, "and kiss my butt."

They grinned, and the tension eased.

"In your litany, you forgot to mention you got thoroughly dressed down by Big Mama in HR," Higgins said. "Another couple of seconds and she might've killed you. For righteousness sake, of course."

"Saw my life pass before her eyes."

"Bet."

"Bet you enjoyed that," Max said.

"I can neither confirm nor deny it, sir," Higgins said.

"She's got another bone in her teeth now, at least. When I left, she was hollering about a full-blown investigation into how files can up and disappear from HER department." Max's head snapped up. "Jesus, Bert."

"Good thing she can't hear you," Higgins said. Then, in his peripheral vision, he saw his partner's body go rigid and he glanced over. "What now?"

"Terrible thought just occurred to me," Steele said. "We still have one witness left."

"That's a terrible thought?"

"The terrible thought is that Emil Bente's a master at making people disappear." Max aimed a finger at Higgins's face, "If you were the Shark, who would be next on your hit list?"

"Only one I can think of is Vinnie Bontecelli," Higgins said.

Max snapped his outstretched fingers. "Bet you five bucks, he's next. We already know Bente left him like dog meat for the Dobermans."

"During the escape," Higgins nodded. "Vinnie's bound to be pissed."

"Ya think?" Max said. "Bente knows it. We need to split up."

"You realize it's almost dinner time."

"Your point, Agent Higgins?" Max said.

Higgins rolled his shoulders and cracked his neck.

"I'll need my own wheels," Max said. "Head back to HQ."

"You can have this one once you drop me off," Higgins said, starting the car. "I'll pull desk duty. I want to run backgrounds on every staff member who's been there nine months or less, and also on the HR staff. Somebody's got to know something about our assassin or his accomplice."

"Not necessarily," Max said. "But it's still a good idea." He looked at his partner. "For sure, the net we threw over that place had holes."

Higgins nodded. "Big enough for murder to happen under everybody's noses." He smacked the steering wheel and growled through clenched teeth.

"Temper, temper. Try to learn the good things from me, young man, not the bad," Max said.

Higgins took a deep breath and blew it toward the windshield. The two men sat in silence, both looking straight ahead at nothing. Finally, Higgins spoke. "Best two things you've taught me so far are that it's as important to think as it is to act, and that it's okay to care."

Max grinned. "Here I thought I was molding you into a trained killer."

"I was already a trained killer when you got me," Higgins said.

"Keep forgetting," Max said. "How many mixed martial arts titles did you hold?"

"Only one," Higgins said.

"Calling bullshit on that," Max said.

"It's the way we think," Higgins said. "MMA's hold only one title at a time, but hopefully it's a better title each time." He started the car and pulled it in a tight circle toward the hospital access road.

"Heard you had quite a reputation," Max said.

"Who said?"

"Secret agents," Max said, and grinned.

"Held the biggest title for five years," Higgins said, almost absently, as he drove.

"What was that one called?"

"Officially or unofficially?"

"The unofficial titles are more interesting," Max said.

"The Badass," Higgins said. "The real title was fancy, but if you were known in MMA circles as The Badass, that was something."

"Respect."

"Respect," Higgins nodded.

"Not a term of endearment," Max said.

Higgins shook his head. "Everybody wanted to kick my ass."

"I bet," Steele said. "Maybe I'll start calling you Lieutenant Badass."

Emil Bente, The Shark
Venice, Italy

Venezia. It was his postal address, as much as any man of his ilk had an address. It was a place to drive a stake into the ground, a place to call home. It was also the residence of his priest. And he had an appointment.

Surveillance and protection were always an issue and always somewhat of an art form. You must watch others without them having the knowledge, or even the inkling, that they're being watched. Same with protection. You must surround yourself with protection, without drawing attention either to yourself or to those protecting you.

Especially if you're rich. Or wanted. Or both. And especially if competitors lurked, looking for a chink in the armor, an opening, an opportunity to take your place.

It was the life Emil Bente chose, and it suited him. He adjusted his tie in the foyer mirror and reached for his felt hat, then put it back on the rack. He'd seen the FBI descriptions, knew the hat had become his trademark. He loved that hat, but it was time to retire it. How sad that, one by one, the things we love are put away from us, either by death or by the threat of it. For so much of his life, he had lived to be known and to stand out. Now, the game was to blend in. Be like glass, so perfectly translucent that people could look at you and never know you're there.

He took off his leather jacket and donned a peasant coat and watch cap.

"Better?" Emil said.

"I guess so," she said. "You don't look like my son, though, not like a Bente don. Your father, God rest his soul, would not approve."

"That's the point, Holy Mother," he said.

"I guess so," the woman said.

"Your birthday's tomorrow, remember, the big one," he said to the slumped figure in the wheelchair.

"Can't decide if it's a blessing or a punishment."

"Don't talk like that," Emil said. "When I'm out, I'll pick you up a present. Anything you want."

"I want you to outlive me," she said.

"Course I will. And I plan to put a hundred and fifteen candles on your cake in twenty-five years. Buys me a lot of time, Mother." He stepped from the mirror.

Mother Maria Bente waved a dismissive hand. "Every time you go through that door, I light a candle and pray to the saints, pray they preserve you, body and soul, until you come back to me. I had a dream…."

"Not the dream again Mother, please," Emil said.

"You can shush me all you want, but I know what I saw," she said, and rubbed her arms.

"It was only a dream."

She raised a gnarled finger toward him. "Or a vision." The finger trembled. "The snake bit you in the face."

"Enough Mother. I am alive and well." He flexed a bicep and grinned. "And strong."

She did not return the grin. Her lips were closed and pulled taut across her teeth. "I had to blow out candles for my grandson and my great grandson," she said softly. "I pray to die before I have to blow out yours."

"I gotta go," he said, and shuffled to the fireplace where she sat. "You got your bell?"

"I have. Light a candle and kiss your mother," she said.

He bent and kissed the top of her head, lit one of the votives on the mantle, and slipped through the door.

Tunnels. Despite being a city infused by water and waterways, Venice possessed a vast array of underwater tunnels. A work of engineering genius, the tunnels were as secret and as sacred as the relic bones of the saints that rested in the cathedrals. No one knew of the tunnels, and it was forbidden to speak of them. Select temple guards had been tasked to silence anyone suspected of whispering about their existence, and even a guard or two had been sacrificed to preserve the secret.

But Emil Bente knew the tunnels. His family built them for the papacy, generations ago when his great, great, great grandfather's brother was Bishop of Venice. Originally a means of escape, the tunnels became safe passage for Cardinals and Bishops, and for the family that made and maintained them. It was these tunnels that gave Emil the idea for his primary receiving and shipping facility in the Unites States. This morning, he used the tunnels to get to the cloisters without being seen.

Cloisters
Venice, Italy

Emil knelt before the man clothed in a full-length red cassock, and he kissed his ring.

"How is the Holy Mother?" Cardinal Nicolo asked as Emil rose and took a seat.

"She loves it that we call her that," Emil said, and grinned. "She's fine, Excellency. Turns ninety tomorrow."

"Ninety or twenty-nine? As I live, that woman is immortal," the Cardinal said, and nodded to his attendant to pour tea.

"That woman worries herself halfway to the grave," Emil said, and seated himself in the smaller of the two plush chairs.

"Oh, there's plenty of spark and vinegar left in her yet, if her confessions contain even a morsel of truth."

"Spicy are they?"

"Deadly is a better word. Her great grandson …."

"Something I need to know?" Emil said.

"Probably, but you know I can't tell you," he said. "The seal of confidentiality over the confessional is ironclad, immutable."

"Of course," Emil said. "But more than once, I have had to mop up the mess, as it were."

"I would refer you only to a hospital in the newspaper," the Cardinal said, looking into his teacup. He glanced up. "That's as far as I can go."

"United States newspaper, I presume," Emil said.

The Cardinal nodded.

"Thank you, Excellency."

The Cardinal nodded again and sipped his tea. "But you didn't come here to talk about her, now did you?"

Emil shook his head. "I came to make my confession and to bring my offering." He removed an envelope from his pocket and placed it on a tray between them.

"Your generosity to the Lord and his work is appreciated at the highest levels," Cardinal Nicolo said.

"Pity it won't get me into heaven, like in the old days," Emil said.

"The old days are gone, my son," he said, "but the millions you contribute to the Church still earn you a private suite with a view of the pearly gates, in my book."

"You provide me and my family a discrete complex within which to live, with round the clock protection by the Guard. I am grateful for that."

The Cardinal spread his hands. "Your family built it after all."

"Yes, but it is by your benevolence that we remain within its guarded womb."

"You are kind, Emil, but one could easily see it the other way around," he said. "I have been accused more than once of being a kept Cardinal, as one would keep a mistress."

"Nonsense, and you know it," Emil said, and sipped tea from his cup. "We are family. And you are my priest."

"And you are a ghost," the Cardinal said. "This is your home, but no one knows you live here except me and the temple guard. All of us have taken vows of secrecy and silence. And service."

Emil nodded, "If you please, Father, my time is short and my confession is long. May I make it now?"

"Of course."

"And may I make it here," Bente said, "within the sanctity and ... privacy of these walls, instead of the Cathedral's confession box?"

"You ask that every time," the Cardinal said, "and the answer is always the same. Yes. There is nothing sacred about two boxes joined by a wire mesh screen. I have always believed that confession ought to be face-to-face, flesh in the presence of flesh, when speaking about matters of the flesh."

"Thank you," Emil said. "It gives me no pleasure to speak of such things, but perhaps it will afford me some measure of relief."

"Are you suffering?" Cardinal Nicolo reached for his gold cigarette holder and the ashtray.

"I suffer because I do things that remind me who I am." He closed his eyes, and within seconds, he was back in the prison. "I betrayed my best friend. Left him to rot and die so I could get free."

"Tell me everything," Cardinal Nicolo said, "Do not pretty it up or hide what causes you shame. That is the cancer we will cut out of you, and we need to get it all."

Emil began to speak, and it was like being sucked out of time. He found himself swimming in dark water amid wreckage and debris, and he was drowning. It seemed only moments before that he had been at the helm of a magnificent sailing ship, a ship he had spent decades building and improving. It had exploded in less than a couple of hours that night. And now, he floated in a sea of broken and splintered pieces. His worst nightmare had come to pass: he was in prison.

At Mantisto State Prison, he told Cardinal Nicolo, he took nourishment through a straw because he clenched his jaw muscles so fiercely that moving them even to speak, let alone eat, shot sparks of hot pain through his face and down his neck. It was better to whisper anyway. It was the language of the prison. Shouting was for attention seeking, or for placing your ignorance on display, but it was not how real prison communication got done. Whispers, passed mouth to ear, were the way to communicate, and whispering happened wherever prisoners were allowed to gather: standing in line, at mealtime, or passing in corridors. The more artful whisperers were called mouth mules, and they were paid well by those whose solitary confinements made even whisper communications impossible to make personally.

Most covert operations in the prison were orchestrated by those whose voices were seldom heard publicly and whose faces rarely saw another inmate. Guards who participated in the Whisper Network, and there were many, were compensated handsomely for their complicity. To know a man's price, and to have the means to pay it, was to own him. Emil Bente owned Mantisto State Prison, or enough of it to assure himself that he would not be here long. It was by whispers that Emil had sealed his best friend's fate.

Emil continued to lay out his story to the Cardinal. He had learned quite a lesson the night he had been arrested in the field outside Kingstown, Rhode Island. He, Emil Bente, the Shark, had become arrogant, arrogant enough to underestimate FBI agent Max Steele. He had to admit, much to Steele's credit, that the man had not underestimated him. He had bested him. Round one to Steele.

Max Steele, at one level, was still not underestimating him. Emil had been placed in the prison's supermax wing. He was a sardine, and he was alone in the can. But Steele had underestimated Bente's network and miscalculated his reach. Blinded by his assumptions, Steele could not see the vast array of tentacles stretching in and through the system. And he seemed to know little about the Whisper Network.

When the police station chief, Parker, was compromised, he thought Steele would get a clue, and perhaps he had. But perhaps not, or perhaps not yet. That was why time was short and speed was critical. The Whisper Network had to function like never before if he was to escape.

That night, he had almost missed the soft scrape on the solid metal door. Emil Bente had squinted in the darkness toward the thin ribbon of light shining through the food tray slot. He saw the business end of a guard's ASP baton protruding just enough to crack it.

He knelt at the door, the posture of a man in the Holy of Holies and not in the unholiest of unholies.

"Yes," he whispered.

"Tonight," the voice whispered.

"It's already night," Emil said, "isn't it?"

"Yes."

"Soon then," Emil said.

"Yes."

"Be sure Bontecelli knows how …. Tell him I'm …. It isn't personal."

"I'll see to it." The ASP disappeared like a tongue returning to its mouth. The darkness yawned and swallowed him again.

It seemed to come within minutes, but he couldn't tell. Time was the precious commodity, next to freedom, and yet the place felt somehow out of time. As soon as he heard the locks begin to slide and click, he knew, without having to see it with his own eyes, that steps were being taken in another part of the prison. He knew that his blood brother and best friend, Vincente Bontecelli, was being set up to take the fall, so that Emil could go free.

It was all happening quickly now. Emil dropped to his knees and rolled flat on his back in the middle of the room to give them access. Three hooded men rushed in. One of them stripped off the top of his jumpsuit. Scissors sliced orange fabric up his legs and tore off the pants. Then his feet were free of the shackles. Then his hands. He stifled the urge to rub them.

Within seconds, he was dressed in other clothes and rushed from the cell. His feet insisted on doing the prison shuffle, as if his ankles were still shackled, and despite his commands to them to stride normally in the shoes. He knew it was about to get dark again. Very dark. Even as the thought traversed his mind, the prison went black and sirens blared. He heard a gate rumbling closed behind him. Behind him! He knew he was in the hands of pros. The emergency lights came up for two seconds, two long seconds, and then they too went black. He felt the night vision goggles forced onto his head and suddenly his vision returned, bathed in an eerie shade of green. He was on a loading dock. His escorts pointed wordlessly to a thick metal drum with biohazard stickers on it. He saw the oxygen bottles in the bottom and clawed for them, even as he was being stuffed into the drum. The lid was on and he knew the pounding was the metal hasps being buried under the lip to secure it.

He had about a minute, maybe two if he could control the panic, to find everything. His fingers reached the metal bottle and his fingers followed it to the narrow end, to the valve. He turned it and heard the quiet hiss somewhere near his ear. His fingers found the plastic tubing that led to nosepieces taped to the side of the barrel. He crammed them into his nostrils and inhaled oxygen deep into his lungs. After a few breaths, Emil felt the muscles in his neck begin to relax.

The barrel's linings made hearing impossible. All of his senses were on mute, but in his mind, Emil Bente didn't have to hear or see to know the script that was being played out. He wasn't going anywhere, not for a while, not until the prison had been restored to order and every crevice had been checked and rechecked.

No plan was foolproof. There was a chance they would pry the lid off the biohazard barrels and risk their own infection to ensure there was no one hiding within them. There was a chance the x-rays they'd take of the barrels would reveal that one was not like the others. He was rolling dice and he knew it, knew it was even too risky to try to buy silence at all levels of prison security. All he could do was say the rosary and wait.

His mind flashed back to the script, the script whispered across the network, telling Vinnie Bontecelli in his solitary confinement wing at the opposite end of the complex, that there would be a diversion but not to worry because Emil had arranged for his escape. Vinnie was coming along.

But he wasn't. He had been bait. Emil's instructions to Vinnie had been: "Let the ones who come for you drug you up so you can be carried out with the laundry." Emil knew Vinnie would trust him and do as he was told.

Emil opened his eyes. He met the Cardinal's eyes. Silence lay like a pall between them. The priest reached for his cigarette case, pinched one out, and lit it.

"Go on," he said, blowing a cloud of smoke toward the ceiling.

"There is no more," Emil said.

"Oh, I think there is a lot more," the priest said.

"Yes, Father, so much more," Emil said, as a sob lurched from his lips. "Sending my son away in the first place. I lied to him too, thinking he would tire of the fool's errand I sent him on. But I sent him to his death. It was a mistake, terrible and foolhardy. Emil slapped both hands over his eyes and wept. When he spoke again, it was through the gap in his hands. "I sent Vincente to keep him under control, but the boy was too wild. And I'm guilty of his death. I am a fool. I loved him."

Cardinal Nicolo let the man weep. Finally, he spoke. "Love and mistakes," he said to Emil, placing his hand on the man's knee. "It was how you were conceived, you and your brother. You want to talk about him?"

"I have no brother," Emil spat and swiped at his eyes.

"Oh, but you do."

"I have no brother," Emil said again. He felt his face flame. "My mother birthed a stranger from her womb. He has never been my brother."

"Have you seen him?"

Emil shook his head. "He vanishes for years at a time. The only reminder of his presence is the votive candle my mother lights for him. Please, can we leave him out of this?"

"Very well," the Cardinal said. """Another time perhaps." He removed his hand and fished in his gold case for another cigarette. "How is your jaw?"

"Terrible," Emil said. "I can talk, but I eat like my mother now. Shit she eats." He waved a weary hand.

"You suffer."

"Yes, Father."

"And are you ready for your forgiveness and absolution?"

"Yes, and my penance."

"Do you really wish me to assign a penance worthy of these sins?"

"Yes I do," Emil said, "or I will never walk as a free man again."

"You left one prison, and now you are in another of your own making." He took a long pull on his cigarette and blew smoke toward the ceiling. "If you would walk free, you must free your friend Vincente Bontecelli, one way or the other."

"One way or the other?" Emil said.

Cardinal Nicolo nodded. "You must break him out of that prison, then prostrate yourself before him and beg his forgiveness. Or, you must set his spirit free from its incarceration."

"By killing him?" Emil said.

"Do you know another way?" the Cardinal said, not expecting a reply.

"I feel I've already done it," Emil said. "Betrayal is a knife that plunges the heart again and again until there is only death."

"You are forgetting the healing balm of forgiveness, my son."

"It is unforgivable," Emil said. "He is my only real brother." He felt the tears well and burst the rim of his eyelids again.

"Kneel, my son," the Cardinal said.

Emil dropped to the floor like a man with a weighted barbell on his shoulders, his face to the carpet.

Cardinal Nicolo stood in front of Emil. "Incline your ear, wretched man that you are, and hear the word of the Lord. No one is beyond the reach of forgiveness. No one. Not even you. Not even me." He raised a wedged right hand in blessing, "May the peace of God, which passes all understanding, keep your heart and mind in the knowledge and love of God, and of His Son, Jesus Christ our Lord. And the blessing of God almighty, Father, Son, and Holy Spirit be upon you this day and remain with you always."

He raised Emil to his feet, and took him by the shoulders. "And one last thing. You must bestow another rosary."

Emil nodded.

Emil Bente took the long way home. The labyrinth of tunnels beneath the beatific city stretched for miles. Who would dream that beneath the waterways, along which lovers were punted by costumed men, and by which commerce was transacted boat to boat, barge to barge, and ship to shore, lay a whole other world? By God's mercy, almost no one.

He would have to talk to mother. But how do you approach a woman both frail in body and ferocious in spirit? How does the acting head of a massive operation speak to the actual head of it? How does he ask her in the most delicate way possible what she has done now? Add to the dilemma that the acting head is the actual head's son, and that the actual head has acted not from her position as the matriarch, but rather from the broken heart of a grandmother. He shook his head. And it was her ninetieth birthday.

The tunnels were masterfully appointed, well sealed and ventilated. The lighting was artificial, but it shown from original torch receptacles that once lit the passageways with fire. It had taken some electrical wiring magic to nest light fixtures within the torches in a way that threw enough light into the passageway to see by, without losing the sense that you were somehow teleporting in time to an Italy of old.

As a child, these tunnels had been a great place for Emil to play. Now, it was one of the few places he could go to think. And there was so much to think about. So much to forgive. So much to make right. But first, there was Mother Maria. The Holy Mother. The birthday girl.

Mantisto State Prison
Kingstown, Rhode Island

Back in the hole. Vinnie recalled the old movies, remembered bad guys being sent to the hole. In the movies, it was the fate worse than death. And here he was, in the hole. The inmates probably had a different term for solitary now. Whatever. It still sucked and everybody knew it, but not for the reasons most people assumed.

It seemed odd to him that isolation – separation from the noise and clatter and incessant blathering of other inmates – was considered the ultimate punishment. Most prisoners would relish it. All inmates were beset with the same malady. Vinnie called it the bullshit disease. To begin with, most inmates were full of it. It was their bullshit that got them here, and if it was bad enough, it might even get them killed in here. Trouble was that people who are full of bullshit don't like listening to, or hanging out with, others who are likewise brimming with it. People talking shit and acting like shit bags were a major irritant. But most people liked their own brand of bullshit. Worse, they were arrogant and ignorant enough to think others liked it, too. So they irritated the hell out of each other. The lucky few, who found they had bullshit in common, formed clusters. Some were gang affiliated, others not. Vinnie called these clusters shit piles or SPs for short. SPs could be useful. For jobs. He had them numbered. It made communication easier along the Whisper Network.

Solitary confinement isolated him from all of that. Couldn't see the bullshit or hear it. Perhaps they thought it a punishment that he also couldn't participate in it. They were wrong. The punishment, ironically, was the silence itself. Who knew that silence was so different from stillness, or the lack of noise? Silence was the land of demons, the Devil's playground, where torture was relentless and exhausting. Far from soundless, it was filled with voices, sometimes whispering, sometimes shouting, and sometimes screaming.

Most people might mistake the voices for thoughts. Vinnie knew they were not thoughts at all, but voices only the tortured could hear. They did not come from him, even though he was alone with them, hour after hour, day upon day. It was the worst punishment.

Most people on the outside didn't understand, couldn't understand, because the stillness they experienced never went on long enough to develop into deep silence. A few monks did, maybe. He figured they either kept the horror to themselves, or transformed it somehow. People on the outside could only sense it. It was why most people surrounded themselves with noise. Their radios were on in the bathroom, sometimes in every bathroom. The TV was on all day, in several rooms. People said they liked it for background noise. Really? Suddenly everybody needed background noise? Why? Perhaps somehow they sensed what Vinnie knew here in the hole, knew as only the isolated and the damned did.

It was to keep the voices at bay. Voices that accused you for everything that you have done wrong. Voices that deny your presence on this earth has any meaning whatsoever. Voices that screamed your worthlessness night and day until even you were convinced of it. Voices whose words pierced your soul until it deflated like a punctured life raft and you sank like the lifeless stone you had become.

Sometimes, Vinnie found himself standing in the center of his cell screaming one word over and over, until his throat was raw, and his voice failed, and spittle ran down his chin.

"Stop!"

"Stop!"

"Stop!"

Chapter Three

Hillside above Misericordia Clinic
Kingstown, Rhode Island

Carlos Guttiero raised the binoculars from the clinic and scanned the harbor. A crisp wind slapped his cheeks as it rose over the ridgeline. A lone tug pushed a flat barge piled high with barrels, guiding it toward a slip. He focused on a crane operator smoking a cigarette in his cab high above the peer, then brought his focus back to the clinic below. Pablo would be down there somewhere. Pablo was always somewhere nearby, and that gave Carlos a measure of calm.

He liked to be called C instead of Carlos or Mr. Guttiero, thought the boys ought to compare him to S, Emil Bente the Shark. Hey, why not? He knew some of the boys, behind his back, said the C stood for Creature because of his size, but he didn't care. Let the boys have their fun. They did what he told them to do. Always, and without complaining. That is the power of making examples of the first few who messed up or slacked off. It was a lesson his father taught him with a closed fist, and he never forgot it. Besides, everybody got paid on time and with bonuses for checking and double-checking to make sure mistakes did not happen.

He adjusted his stance in the back of the pickup, leaning against the cab to steady his view. Every muscle twitch made the view through the binoculars bounce. He thought of the bounce houses kids love, and his mind flashed to Carlos, Junior, and to that whore of a mother. He wondered where she was, and where she had hidden him when she took him and left. He didn't think she'd leave, thought she liked the money too much. He would find her, and God help her when he did.

His attention was drawn to movement at the clinic. Dr. Maria Sanchez was locking the front door. That meant the delivery was ready for them. No one had keys to the clinic except Maria, Pablo, and him, so the laundry bags were somewhat secure. The briefcase swung slightly in her hand as she headed down the rutted dirt driveway. He wanted to focus the glasses on that ass. So fine. He'd like to tap that some time. But there was work. He was there to be sure the drops were there and the pick up was made every Tuesday and every Friday when she ran the clinic. No mistakes.

He watched Maria's car pull away, watched until it was out of sight. Then he fished the radio from his parka pocket and keyed the mic.

"Base, this is Outpost One," he said.

"Go ahead for Base," a female voice said.

"The laundry is ready for pick up."

"Copy. Pick up van already *en route*."

"Copy that," Carlos said. "Outpost Three, you copy?"

"*Sí*," Pablo said.

They waited. Both were watching. Pick up and delivery were the two most dangerous moments of the week. Carlos glanced at the AR-15 nestled in a towel at his feet. The suppressor on it alone cost more than most people paid for their high-end rifles. The scope cost even more than the suppressor. Both were worth every cent the Shark had paid. The security and privacy of the operation must remain intact by any means necessary. He knew Pablo was armed too, but his AK-47 and 9MM lacked the stealth and precision Carlos had at his feet.

In the distance, he saw movement and focused the binoculars. A navy blue box truck with the words painted above the cab, "City Cleaning & Storage," made its way to the clinic. Like clockwork. He watched as the truck arrived and backed up to the mouth of the driveway. There it would stop and the men would drag the laundry bags of money down the hill on a sled. Except that something was off. The truck continued to back up the drive. It bounced in and out of the potholes and troughs in the hard pack where water had run off and did not come to a stop until it was at the top of the drive next to the clinic's harbor end.

Outpost Three, Outpost One," Carlos said into the radio.

"I see it," Pablo said.

Two men emerged from the truck and ran to the front door of the clinic. The second giveaway: running. Carlos trained his men never to run. Running attracts unwanted attention. The third giveaway was that the men went to the wrong door.

Methodically, Carlos removed the binoculars from his eyes and set them down in the truck bed. With his right hand, he lifted the AR-15 and cradled the tripod smoothly into place atop the cab roof. He popped the lens caps from the scope lenses, then keyed his mic.

"Outpost Three, standby for incoming."

"*Sí.*"

Slowly, Carlos snugged the rifle against his shoulder and flicked off the safety. Since he had sighted the scope on the clinic earlier, focusing on the man closest to the door took no more than a second. He let out his breath, paused, and squeezed the trigger with the gentleness one would use to tickle the chin of a baby. His target jerked and flew from view. Carlos steadied the scope on the second man, let out a breath, and squeezed the trigger. Missed! The second man was gone from his scope view. *Slowly Carlos. Breathe before you speak. Never know who may be listening.* He keyed the mic, "One bird is bagged," he said. "The other one flew."

"*Sí,*" came the radio response.

Carlos removed the AR from the cab roof and placed it gently onto the towel. Then he snapped up the binoculars. He saw the second man crab crawling toward the truck, and then a dark figure rounded the end of the clinic, arms extended in a shooting stance. The man on the ground jerked once, twice, three times, and then lay still.

"Base, this is Outpost One," Carlos said into the mic.

"Go for Base."

“Call the truck and check its location please,” Carlos said. “They’re behind schedule on the pick up.”

“Base is clear,” the female voice said. “Already attempted contact, but no answer yet.”

“Copy. That’s what I needed to know.” After a pause, Carlos keyed the mic again. “Outpost One to Outpost Three.”

“*Sí*,” Pablo said.

“Need assistance with clean up at your location?”

“No.”

“Copy. Standing by at my location. Base, you copy?”

“Base is clear,” the voice said, “Shall I arrange for another pick up vehicle?”

“Affirmative. I’ll stand by until it arrives.”

Through the binoculars, Carlos watched Pablo load the first body into the back of the truck and then the second. Then he used one of the empty clothing carts from the van and shoveled up the dirt where each body had been. Slowly, and with great precision, Pablo scoured the entire area, placing many things into trash bags for reasons only he knew. Carlos admired his thoroughness.

The replacement service truck arrived as Pablo was finishing up. He took a shooter’s stance once again as the men backed the truck to the end of the driveway and stopped. Obviously briefed by Base on the situation, they walked up the drive with their hands laced atop their heads. Carlos smiled beneath the binoculars. Better.

Pablo recognized them and lowered his weapon.

“All is well, Outpost Three?” Carlos said.

“*Sí*,” Pablo said. “I go.”

“Copy that, but wait until the laundry is loaded.”

“*Sí*.”

Dean's Residence
Ecclesia Seminary
Kingstown, Rhode Island

Sarah didn't know where else to go. She didn't want to talk to Terry Woodrow, her boyfriend, about it. He was always sure of the answers, and he was quick to tell her what to do. She could hear him, "Just forget about it, Sarah. Forgive Bontecelli, forget it, and move on."

Sure. Just like that. Why was it that people doled out advice like that? It was the Band-Aid offered to heal a gunshot wound. Seriously? "Oh, you fell off the roof and broke both of your legs? Here's a roll of Lifesavers. Suck on those." Oh, and her favorite nugget of advice: "Give it time." Sure thing. Time heals all wounds, right? If that's true, why are so many elderly people broken and bitter? And not just the elderly. Why are so many people filled with age-old hatreds, resentments, and unforgiveness? She knew so many people who looked, sounded, and acted more like steaming, burbling, cauldrons of hate than human beings.

Give it time. Such a load of unmitigated crap.

She pulled into the dean's driveway. The camper was gone, that giant roving home that still had no more than a few miles on it when she saw it last.

She sighed. Where was her head? She knew better than to come to this address. Reverend Tittle had retired as acting Dean of Ecclesia Seminary, and the board had appointed an interim dean. This wasn't his driveway anymore. It was Reverend Victoria Nile's driveway now.

Dean Tittle had moved to a campground on Lake Batam two hours away, drove the RV into a slot, and set up residence. The campground functioned more like a small village, with all the amenities. Sarah loved the name, "Lake Woes Beggone." Jeremy could use a little of that. Okay a lot. She missed him.

A soft tap on her driver side window startled Sarah so badly she screamed and rounded the back of her hand into the window hard. She hit it twice before she came to her senses, sucking air into her lungs and staring into the last face she expected to see.

The face of Rev. Jeremy Tittle smiled through the window glass at her. She rolled the window down as quickly as her arm would turn the handle.

"Jeremy! I mean, Dean Tittle," she said and felt her cheeks flame.

"Jeremy is fine, Sarah dear," he said. "Can't tell you how it pleases me to see you."

"How did you … know I …. I feel like I just conjured you," Sarah said. She grabbed her forehead. "I'm stammering like an idiot."

Tittle chuckled. "I came to get a couple of things from the backyard, and here you were sitting in the driveway. Sorry to startle you."

"Let me try again," Sarah said, "I came to see you and …" She felt them coming, and took a deep breath. No use. A sob barked from her lips and the tears overflowed the banks of her eyes. She laid her head on the steering wheel, feeling her body convulsing with wave upon wave. She tasted the salt on her lips. She felt his hand rest on the back of her head, felt something flow through her, and the waves began to slow. One word played like a tripping vinyl, again and again, through her mind. One word danced in the waves like a buoy tossed by wind and wave, but also anchored deep: mercy.

Sarah lifted her head from the steering wheel and ran a sleeve across her nose. "I came to talk to you, and then I remembered. I was missing you so much and boom, there you were."

"I think we had a divine appointment," Jeremy Tittle said. "How about we get a coffee? Okay by you?"

"Oh yes," she said, "I mean, can you? Do you have time?"

"Time?" Jeremy said, "I've got nothing but time. Lavish Lattes in 15 minutes. I'll grab these things and meet you."

Residence of Dr. Maria Sanchez
Kingstown, Rhode Island

At his knock, Maria opened the front door and whirled away from it toward the bedroom. "Just got home. Look like hell. Open the wine," she called behind her. "Nice to see you too," Max said, standing in the doorway. "I love the way you leap into my arms and plant a big kiss on my lips." He laughed and elbowed the door closed on his way in. He heard the shower come on and considered for one wild moment stripping off his clothes and joining her. Then he thought better of it. One thing he had learned about his girlfriend was that she hated surprises. Catch her off guard and you might be killed. He angled for the kitchen.

The wine was already on the counter, with the corkscrew beside it, and two wine glasses. Max wondered how she would appear from the bedroom tonight. Last night, he had heard the shower cut off and the next thing he knew, she was walking toward him in the kitchen without a stitch of clothing on, not even so much as a towel. They had had each other for dinner. And for breakfast.

But you never knew with Dr. Maria Sanchez. He smirked. Ironic that she specialized in being unpredictable, but demanded that he be just the opposite. He shrugged off his sport coat and untied his tie. He had heard that the greatest moment in a woman's day was when finally she was able to undo her bra and fling it across the room. He wondered if it felt half as good as undoing the top button of his dress shirt. Blessed relief.

The wine was red, room temperature, and full-bodied. He was on his second glass by the time he heard the shower turn off. Grinning, he leaned his back against the counter and waited to see what would appear. And waited. And waited. What appeared at last was a woman with perfectly appointed hair and makeup, wearing a tight fitting pink evening dress.

"Wow," he said, and pushed himself away from the counter. Their lips met in the center of the kitchen, and they drank deeply of each other. When they finally separated, both were out of breath.

"That kiss," Maria said, "was the only reason I waited to put on my lipstick."

Max laughed and handed her the other glass of wine. "Thank you, I guess," he said. "Probably would've been smeared all over my face."

"Without a doubt," she said.

"You look incredible," Max said. "We going out?"

Maria shook her head. "But you're going in. Later."

"Can hardly wait."

"In the meantime, I'll let you to enjoy what you see. And smell."

"Come here and let me smell you again," Max said, reaching for her.

She leaned into him and thrust her hips into his. Their lips locked and their tongues explored each other. His hands squeezed and stroked her through the dress. Then one hand slid up to the back of her neck and foraged for the zipper.

"Down boy," she said into his mouth, and kissed him hard one more time before breaking away. She brushed her hand along the bulge in the front of his dress pants, and then stepped to the counter. "Let's take this wine into the living room and you can tell me all about your day."

"Killin' me," Max said, reaching for her again.

"It's a lady's privilege to torture her man," she said, and walked into the living room.

Max pushed his hips off the counter and followed. "My day?" he said. "You're not going to like some of it," Max said, adjusting himself, and checking his zipper.

"Terrific," she said, easing herself onto the couch. Her dress slid up the black fishnet stockings tauntingly close to the panty line. She made no move to pull down the hem. "Who broke themselves out of prison today?"

Max stared at her for several moments, then shook his head and took a sip of wine. "You expect me to concentrate?"

Maria patted the seat beside her. "Do the best you can."

"Always do," he said, and sat as close to her as he could.

"Don't I know it," she said, looking at him over the rim of her wine glass. She stared at his face for a time, waiting.

"It's about your hospital," Max said.

"It's not," Maria said, sitting forward with a start.

"Is," Max said, "and it's a homicide."

"Max Steele, don't tease me," Maria said.

"Wish," he said. "Somebody murdered Nina Ondolopous Bente. Did it so perfectly that saving her was impossible, even if you got to her seconds after it happened. Somebody was making sure she wasn't coming back."

"Not possible," Maria said. "She was in ICU. Crash cart city, one on every corner almost."

Max shook his head. "All the crash carts in the world wouldn't have saved her. This guy, assuming it's a guy, knew exactly what he was doing." He explained as much as he felt he could about the crime scene.

Maria was quiet for a time. Her wine glass was pressed lightly against her lower lip, but she wasn't drinking from it. Max saw the faraway look in her eyes, wondered where she'd gone, almost asked but thought better of it. Best to let her process in her own way.

"You said you assumed it was a guy," she said finally. "Guess that means you didn't get him."

Max shook his head.

"So cruel," Maria said. "That poor girl."

"Bente is still mopping up, most likely," Max said. "Tying up loose ends, sweeping his footprints from the sand."

"And our poor little hospital," Maria said. "This is Kingstown, Rhode Island, for God's sake, not Miami or New York."

"Perfect place to hide in plain sight," Max said. "And I'm sorry, Maria, but we'll be tearing that little hospital apart looking for, well, anything that will help us get him."

"Be careful Max," Maria said. "I worry."

"Shark's the one who should be worrying," Max said. "His ass is mine. I'm going to wipe him and his entire operation off the board."

Maria stood, moved to the louvered plastic slats that covered the tall front windows, stuck a finger between two of them, and peered out.

"Expecting someone?" Max watched the back of her dress slide across her tight butt, scanned down past the hem to drink in perfect legs and small feet in high heels.

Maria turned from the window. "You make me nervous, is all." She was frowning when she returned his gaze.

"I make you nervous?"

"Yes," she said, "with all this talk of taking down a mob boss. You said yourself, he ties up loose ends better than anybody."

Max nodded, "Makes people disappear – poof – without a trace."

She returned to the couch and sat again with such force she nearly spilled her wine. "Yes, and did it ever occur to you, even once, that you are on his list of people to poof? Probably at the top?"

Max paused, and then reared his head back and laughed. "His poof list."

"It's not funny."

"The way you said it, it was funny," he said, and reached for her hand. She pulled it away and stood again.

"Dammit Max, you're pissing me off," she said.

"Come here, Baby." He reached a hand toward her.

"You piss me off," she said, and he saw her eyes flash. "You're on Bente's hit list and you're sitting here laughing about it. What's wrong with you, Max? Do you have a death wish?"

"I have a death wish alright. I wish that man dead, and I wish to be the one to kill him."

"Terrific," Maria said. "Bully for you, macho man. But what if he gets you first?"

"I got him first," Max said, "once." He felt his face flushing hot.

"My point," Maria said, smacking a balled fist on her hip. "And how do you suppose he feels about that? How motivated do you think he is to take you off the board?"

"Well, I'll be damned," Max said. "What's this now? Suddenly you care about me? This morning you said we're just fucking."

"So we are back to that, are we?" Nina kicked off her shoes. They sailed across the living room one at a time.

"We're back to that, yes," Max said. "I didn't like that."

"And I don't like this, Max," she said. "I can't respect a man who doesn't know when to be afraid, who doesn't know when to back off of a very bad man before that man kills him."

"Back off," Max said and snorted, leaning forward.

"Yes!" she said. "He'll kill you, Max."

Max barely heard the words. He was formulating his reply instead of listening. "Let me get his straight, so I make sure I am hearing you correctly." He lifted fingers to count. "We're just fucking." He moved to the next finger. "You don't even respect me. Have I got that right?" He didn't wait for a response. Lifted a third finger, "And I'm such a pussy, I'm gonna get killed by some sewer rat I've already busted once?"

"I think …." Maria began.

"I think," he said loudly, interrupting her, "you've got more respect for a two bit mobster than me. Maybe you should be fucking him."

Maria clutched her chest like she'd been shot, then looked down and dropped her hand.

Max wasn't finished. "I think it's you that you're worried about. Hang around me and you'll get killed right along with me, right?"

"You are shouting at me," she said, looking up, her voice rising, her eyes dark and hot.

"Afraid to be around a guy with a target on his back?" Max said. He felt his voice shake with an anger that alarmed him. "Afraid I can't protect you, being the weak little pussy I am?"

"I think you better go, Max," Maria said.

"I think I'm already gone." He took long strides to the kitchen and tossed his wine glass in the sink on the way to his coat. It shattered. Maria put her wine glass on the coffee table and stood unmoving at the couch. She watched Max punch his arms into his sport coat and swipe his keys from the counter.

"Maybe we can talk tomorrow," Maria called, as Max flung the front door wide to the night air.

He paused and she saw eyes that flashed with the ferocity of a raptor. "Maybe," he said.

"You know what?" she said. Both fists were on her hips now. "Just forget it. Good-bye Max."

He stepped onto the porch and pulled the door behind him.

She stood for several long moments, hiccupping air before collapsing onto the couch. "Be careful Darling," she whispered so softly it was like a breath. "You don't know him like I do."

Lavish Lattes Coffee Shop
Kingstown, Rhode Island

Rev. Jeremy Tittle insisted on paying for the coffee. He also insisted they both get something laced with chocolate and caramel and topped with whipped cream. While he waited for their order, Sarah found a vacant booth near the back of the shop.

"So," Sarah said, her eyes drinking in the delicious treat Jeremy placed in front of her, "do we drink this or eat it with a spoon?"

Jeremy laughed and slid into the seat opposite her. "It looks as sweet as your spirit."

Sarah stared at the man seated opposite her. "It feels like, well, a miracle, you appearing like that when I needed you," she said.

"The best gifts bless both ways," he said. "It's a gift to see you. I've missed our talks."

"How is life at Lake Woes Beggone?"

"I'm adjusting," he said. "Life is still good."

"What does that mean?" Sarah said.

He laughed. "You still don't miss anything, do you? Know just what to ask and when. I still think you'd make a terrific pastor." Then he closed his eyes, and opened them again. "It's a lot of adjustments, Sarah, a lot of change. From a big house to an RV half the size of a singlewide trailer; from a demanding job, to … silence, and plenty of it. I remember thinking, as a younger man, how great it was going to be when I didn't have the demands of my job anymore and could do whatever I want. Now that I have it, I'm not sure I want it anymore. I like having something to do, something worth doing." He paused and pursed his lips. Heavens, listen to me prattling on." He smiled and stuck a spoon in the melting whipped cream atop his coffee.

"Hardly," Sarah said, and sipped through her whipped cream.

Jeremy burst out laughing.

"What?" Sarah said.

"You have a whipped cream moustache."

Sarah grinned and reached for a napkin.

"Let me see if I can get one too," he said. He plunged his mouth into the side of the cup and came up with whipped cream all over his face.

Sarah burst out laughing. "Full beard," she said. "Bet you never got away with that at faculty dinners," she said.

"Ha," he said. "What a colossal waste of time those were. So much pretense." He shook his head. "That, I do not miss." He took another sip of coffee, napkin at the ready. "Enough about this old man. Tell me what's going on with you."

"I went to Mantisto today," Sarah said, "to see Vinnie."

"Bontecelli. I see," Jeremy said. "No wonder you're upset."

"Went to look him square in the face," she said, "and tell him I forgave him for what he did to me, for all he put me through."

Jeremy was silent. She looked into his eyes and saw – what – openness and acceptance.

"I couldn't do it," she said finally. "Told him I didn't."

"Good," he said.

"Good?"

He nodded. "You faced the truth in yourself, and you were authentic about it with the other person. What a gift for you both."

"Vinnie didn't see it that way."

"I suspect not."

"He mocked me," she said.

"And what does that have to do with you?"

"I know where you're going, but I still feel like crap, like he was right."

"Right about you?"

She nodded. "Being a hypocrite."

"I certainly hope so," he said.

"You do?"

"I do." He leaned forward and spoke in a soft voice. "We are all hypocrites, Sarah. All of us. No one is better than anyone else." He paused. "Forgiveness that asks you to be anyone other than the perfect gift you were formed and fashioned to be in the womb, is not Christ-like forgiveness. It is something else, something the church has made up. They've been at it for centuries: taking the words of Christ out of the context of the life of Christ."

"I may need to write that down," Sarah said. "Seriously, I think this is my biggest issue."

"It's most people's biggest issue," Jeremy said. "It's what's kept people from finding peace with themselves and love for themselves. It's also what's kept judgmental attitudes alive through the centuries."

"So I'm not a freak."

"You're human," he said. "So am I. It is in our common humanity, confusion and all, that we find the seed of real acceptance, of ourselves and others. And it's in our acceptance of ourselves and others that we find the seed of forgiveness. I call it the great 'Of Course.' Of Course, you do terrible things. Of Course, I do terrible things. Of Course, Vinnie does terrible things. It should come as no surprise."

"Yes," Sarah said, nodding. "Which is different from saying the terrible things we do to one another are okay. They are not."

"Of course not," Jeremy said. It is the other side of the great 'Of Course.' Of course, what Vinnie did is not okay, and no act, or decision, or words spoken by you or me or Vinnie will make them so." He took another sip of coffee.

"Okay," Sarah said, "so driving myself crazy thinking there is something I'm just not getting, or that I'm too much of a sinner…."

"Is just robbing you of peace," Jeremy said. "At least that's as far as I can get with it anyway. If anyone tells you they have the definitive answer to the forgiveness issue, ask them why folks have been fighting and splitting apart from each other over it for centuries. If they tell you it's because everyone else (but them) is wrong, or that those other guys are just haters, RUN!"

They sipped coffee and sat in silence for a time.

"Let's finish up and I'll follow you home," Jeremy said. "I've got a date with your roommate."

Sarah laughed. "Oh my God!" She fell back sideways in the booth. Fanned herself with her hands.

"What?"

"Oh my God!" Sarah laughed again. "Dr. Nettie Spruill is NOT my roommate," she said, still laughing. "And I live on the third floor of her house. As a tenant."

"More like a daughter," Jeremy said, "the one she never had."

"Awwww, I love her so much," Sarah said.

"She talks about you all the time," Jeremy said.

"I'm so lucky to have her in my life," Sarah said, and took the last swallow of coffee. "Freaks me out, though, when I think of you two … dating." She smiled.

"It does?"

Sarah nodded. "You're just … so … I don't know."

"Old?" Jeremy said.

"Oh God, I'm so embarrassed," she said. "I trust you so much, I just blurt stuff out."

"Why not?" Jeremy said. "Aren't we friends?"

"Oh yes," Sarah said, "Yes, yes! But, I don't know, I think of you as so much more than that, like a father almost." She had spoken into her empty cup, but the silence that followed caused her to look up. Jeremy's eyes had filled and his nose had gone red.

"I am … so honored," Jeremy said.

Sarah put her hand on his. "I hate it you are so far away now."

He smiled and brought a napkin to his eyes. "Now you sound like Nettie."

"Bet she doesn't like it one bit."

"I couldn't stay around here after I stepped down," he said. "Not fair to the new dean."

"I get that," Sarah said. "Can't Nettie move to you?"

"Whoa now, slow down," Jeremy said, picking both hands up from the table.

"I love it," Sarah said. "You get all flustered when you talk about her."

"Some things you never grow out of," Jeremy said. "When it comes to love, every man is still a young boy, and every woman is still a young girl."

Misericordia Clinic
Kingstown, Rhode Island

As if from another world, she heard the buzz of her cell phone, then heard it buzz several more times and then stop. Then it began to buzz again. Maria pushed herself off the couch and made her way into the bedroom. Maybe it was Max calling to apologize. She picked the phone off the dressing table, looked at the screen, and answered.

"You idiot," she said, and felt the rush of anger load her voice. "Don't ever call me on this phone."

"You better come back," Carlos said.

"I'm not home," Maria Sanchez lied. "I had to go into the hospital. Something happen?"

"You're damn right something happened," Carlos said. "You better come back. Now."

"What?" Maria said. "You did this? Are you out of your mind?"

"Did what? I'm talking about what you did."

"You better have nothing to do with this," Maria said, and ended the call. Carlos took the phone from his ear and looked at it. "What the…."

Maria dropped the phone. Oh Nina. Poor, poor Nina. Jesus, please don't let Carlos have anything to do with this! Surely not. But, if not, what was he on about?

She started to undress. She'd have to get back to Memorial and speak to her staff, remind them not to talk to the media. Then she could get out and call Carlos back. Maria reached behind her back and unclipped the red lace bra, shrugging it off even as she tugged down the matching thong. So much for romance. So much for love. She wished it were different. All of it. And she wished she had never been forced to meet Detective Max Steele.

Memorial Hospital
Kingstown, Rhode Island

Maria drove to Memorial, working herself into her lab coat as she hurried into the ER. The news, of course, was on everyone's lips. Homicide was front-page stuff. She wasn't ten steps through the door before her pager went off: all staff report to the Chief's office. Mercifully, Chief was too busy to speak directly with her and the others when they got there. One of his assistants wanted to make certain staff knew not to say a word to the media. Not one. About anything. Not about what they had for breakfast. Nothing.

Easy enough. She didn't know anything, and her staff in the ER didn't seem to either. The entire ICU was locked down tight. Maria knew she wasn't going to learn or help a thing for a while. What she needed was thirty minutes of uninterrupted silence, to think it all through, to figure out whether to risk making contact with the Shark, and what she would say. She plastered a smile on her face, gave Linda the charge nurse the "back in a few" signal, and retreated for the parking lot.

In the car, she grabbed reflexively for her cell. She punched in his number. "I'm in my car," Maria said into the phone. "Be quick."

"Come back," Carlos said.

"Why?"

"I will hurt you if you don't."

"I hate you," Maria said.

"That," he said, "is none of my concern. Come back right now."

"I'll be there in 10 minutes." She ended the call and slapped the phone onto the passenger seat. She reached into her purse and lifted the Smith & Wesson .380. She checked to make sure it was loaded and then took it off safety. "Let's see who gets hurt, *Puta*," she said, and put the car into gear.

She drove with one hand and held the gun in the other. It made her feel better. Max's face kept flashing in her mind. He would be so disappointed in her. She laughed without mirth at the thought. "And then he would arrest me," she said into the empty car. "What choice would he have?" And what choice did she have? She was going to have to do something, something she knew would ruin her life forever. "I'm sorry Max," she said.

Mantisto State Prison
Kingstown, Rhode Island

Vincente Bontecelli squeezed the rag in his massive fist. It was the same one they had stuffed into his mouth to silence his screams. He had saved it. Someone would pay for this, and he knew who. He held the man's face in his mind. Bente would regret the day. The one with the ring and all the rest, too.

That morning, he had been wakened by the sound of a lock turning. At first, it sounded a long way off, as if it were part of a dream. But then his eyes had blinked open, and he knew the sound was coming from his own cell door. Then he heard footsteps, fast, but moving away, fading. The air in his cell was thick and black, but there was a charged stillness about it. Vinnie swung his feet to the floor and stood. He wiped a hand across his scalp and onto his neck. Listened.

Listening. It was a favorite past time of the prison: listening to every sound, every scratch, every thud, every voice muffled by thick concrete and steel, every footstep. Listening for the difference in footsteps. Like a fingerprint, no two footsteps were quite the same, but like birds or trees or tones from an instrument, footsteps came in types, categories. There was the thick thud of jackboots that sounded the presence of a guard. There was the squeak and squish of the cafeteria worker who pushed the food cart along the hall, with trays clattering and wheels clacking. Then there was the softer swish and whoosh of inmate slippers, sometimes coming with the rattle of chains, and other times not.

Tonight, he heard Jackboots running, but running softly, tapping not thudding. Jackboots rarely ran, and when they did, the air was filled with shouting and bluster. Something was up. He heard his heart thumping loudly in his chest, and also something else. What was it? Something else. It was the laundry cart, and the whooshing of slippers. They were coming for him. Ha-ha! The Whisper Network had said the Shark was busting himself and Vinnie out soon and to be ready. He was so ready. Good-bye prison stink; hello fresh air!

The cell door slid. Two orange clad figures wearing blue latex gloves on their hands and black hoods over their heads, motioned silently for Vinnie to get into the cart. He could feel his face wide with a grin as he got in. They wrestled a foul-smelling sheet over him, and pressed his head forward between his knees. He felt fingers and arms shoving along his side and underneath his legs. Then he heard the scrape of a zip tie tighten behind his neck and in the under-crease of his knees. They pressed his head down into his knees. Tightened again. What? What! What the hell? He felt a prick at the base of his neck, and within seconds, he began to feel woozy. And then the laundry cart was moving. Quickly. Sounds assaulted him from every side, disorienting him. Where the hell? Oh yes, he'd been told he was going out with the laundry. He was gonna look like a wad of sheets. He felt the grin reappear on his lips despite the pain of the zip tie cutting into his neck and the fuzz in his mind.

The cart jerked and stopped. He heard whispers, but he couldn't make out the words. Then, very close to him, came a soft hissing whisper, "S says sorry." And the next moment, all hell broke loose.

Misericordia Clinic
Kingstown, Rhode Island

It was dark when she arrived, the last streetlight ending a couple hundred yards behind her. Maria walked up the dirt path to the clinic with only a small key chain flashlight to light her way. She kept her other hand on the gun in her lab coat pocket. The clinic door was ajar, and she swung it wide before entering. Carlos was reclining on the examination table, propped on one elbow.

"Tell me what this is about," Maria said.

"And it is nice to see you too, Dr. Sanchez," Carlos said without a smile. "Please come in."

"This is my clinic, and I don't need your permission to come in," she said evenly. "I can come in anytime I please." She brought the gun from her pocket. "You, on the other hand, are trespassing in a hospital clinic. State your business and get out."

"Such hostility from one so lovely," Carlos said. "Put that away before you hurt yourself."

Maria raised an eyebrow.

"*Sí*," a low voice behind her said. Maria turned and stared into the barrel of a 9MM pointed at her head. Pablo.

Her shoulders slumped and she lowered the gun.

"Make you a deal," Carlos said, sitting up and dangling his legs over the side of the table. "You place the gun on the table. I'll unload it for you, and give it back."

She stepped forward next to where he was sitting and placed the gun on the table. As soon as her hand was free, she swung, landing a vicious slap across Carlos's face. He grabbed for her, but she stepped back and he ended up clutching air.

"You son of a bitch," she said. Carlos jumped from the table and she swung again. This time he caught her arm and hurled her to the floor.

"Play time is over, girlie," he said, wiping the trickle of blood from the corner of his mouth. "Now, to business. Who were those men in the truck?"

"What men?" she said from the floor. "And I bet you've been beating up girls your whole life, you big strong man." She spat the words through strands of hair.

"There you go changing the subject," Carlos said.

"I changed nothing. What men?" she said, huffing air into her lungs.

"The men in our delivery truck. The men who weren't our men."

"How would I know, Carlos? Pick-up and delivery is your thing."

"True enough," he said. "And I figured I'd know by your reaction tonight whether you had anything to do with it. You pack a pretty good punch for a girl." Maria swiped at the hair in her face. Carlos looked across the clinic. "I say 'Not Guilty.' What do you say, Pablo?"

"*Sí*," Pablo said, and lowered the gun.

"Okay, I am going to step back over here with our friend Pablo, and you can get up and take your gun back," Carlos said. "See how much I trust you? It's still loaded." He joined Pablo.

Maria stood and pocketed the gun. "Talk," she said.

"Somebody took our truck, ditched our guys somewhere, and came here to pick up the laundry bags."

"Not our guys?" she said. "You sure?"

"Positive," Carlos said. "I was here."

"And these other guys are where?"

"Resting."

"Feds?"

"Not a chance."

"And our guys are …?"

"I don't know," he said. "Haven't found 'em yet, but by the looks of these *hombres*, I'm not …." He shrugged.

Maria blew out a breath and swiped a hand over her head. "Anybody but us finds them …." She looked around the clinic, not fixing on anything in particular. "And the laundry?"

"Pablo made the delivery," Carlos said.

"*Gracias*," Maria said.

"*De nada*," Pablo said, looking at the floor.

"Okay, we answered our question, and we solve nothing by standing around here tonight," Carlos said. "But Pablo did have one other thing before you go."

"*Sí Pablo*?" Maria said, and sighed.

Carlos answered for the man who continued to study the floor. "Pablo is too shy, but he thinks you may have been followed to the clinic this morning."

Maria fixed him with a long stare. "And tonight?"

"No," Pablo said.

"Who?" Maria said.

Mantisto State Prison
Kingstown, Rhode Island

Vinnie hadn't known what was to befall him. He had been bouncing inside the laundry cart as it whisked along one corridor after another. When it came to an abrupt halt, he assumed he would find himself in laundry or at a rear prison loading dock. But why the zip ties? Then he heard the whisper next to his ear, "S says sorry" and in the next instant, the laundry cart was tipped over and Vinnie tumbled onto the slab floor of the chow hall.

"What the hell!" Vinnie said between his knees. He felt cold steel against his neck and the zip tie released. He jerked his head up in time to see the gloved fist with the large, diamond-shaped ring rushing toward his face.

He didn't know how long he'd been unconscious. When he came to, Vinnie saw that he had been strapped to chairs atop a row of lunchroom tables, with slabs of C4 duct taped to his arms and legs. A note was taped to one of his feet. His head was exploding. Bolts of pain fired backward from his eyes into his head, and he had to squint to see down his outstretched legs. The note read, "If you move, this whole wing gets blown to shit. Tell them."

"Bastard," he said in a whisper. "You lying bastard." He looked again at the packs of C4 strapped to his arms and legs. So. This is what it looked like when they tied all their sins into your fleece and cast you from the city.

Scapegoat.

The metal plate in the middle of his cell door slapped open. Lost in the memory, the waking nightmare, Vinnie hadn't heard their footsteps.

"Stand," came the toneless command. "Face away from the door and back toward it, hands behind your back."

Vinnie's body moved as if on autopilot. Prison routine. It required no thought after a while. His wrists would be zip tied behind his back. Two guards would enter to shackle his legs. The zip tie on his wrists would be removed, and his wrists would be cuffed in front of him. A chain would slip through the metal box around his handcuffs, wind around his waist, and then be padlocked behind his back. Thus secured, he'd be ready to shuffle wherever they led.

"Where's the party today?" Vinnie said.

"You have a visitor," the taller guard said.

"I told you I don't want to see nobody."

"Let's go," the other guard said, and took Vinnie by the elbow. Vinnie shrugged out of his grip and shuffled through the door.

Vinnie was lying of course. Solitary sucked. Getting to see someone, anyone, was likely the highlight of his week. He watched the floor as he shuffled through locked door after locked door. Each one buzzed open with a slightly different tone. He bet the guards, whose world was so much bigger and filled with sound, never noticed. He snorted and kept shuffling. The sound level in the prison grew as he put solitary further and further behind him. One day would be the last walk, one way or the other. One last walk, either to freedom from Mantisto or freedom from his body in death. Once he avenged Emil Bente's betrayal, in full, he didn't care which way it went.

"Who's here to see me?" Vinnie said over his shoulder.

Silence.

"You gonna give me a hint?" he said.

Silence.

"Stop," one of the guards said. Vinnie stopped in front of a metal door. The shorter guard keyed the door open, and Vinnie stared into the face of Jay Caravanti, Esq., his lawyer. The guards placed him in the metal chair across the table from the man and his briefcase.

"Leave us, please," Caravanti said.

The guards retreated and closed the door.

For several long moments, the two men eyed each other in silence.

"How are you, Vinnie?" his lawyer said at last.

"Better than you, Caravanti," Vinnie said. "I'll see you dead."

"Even you know what a bad idea that would be," Caravanti said.

"Even me?" Vinnie's voice came hard and low across the table.

"Yeah, even you, dumbass, making noise on the Whisper Network how you're gonna kill Mr. Bente and his whole family and everybody else who set you up."

"Glad my message is clear," Vinnie said. "You tell Bente, too."

"Oh, he knows," Caravanti said. "Kidding me? I would advise you not to make yourself a target."

"Advise me from hell once you're there," Vinnie said.

"Okay, well, maybe we're done here," the lawyer said. "Maybe you get yourself a court-appointed lawyer, see how far that gets you, buddy." His face was flushed.

Vinnie didn't reply. He was the first to break eye contact and knew he'd lost. Again. "Okay," Vinnie said, and looked at the metal on his wrists.

"Okay," Jay Caravanti said, and snapped his shoulders to settle his suit jacket back in place. Emil could feel the lawyer's stare, felt it like prey feels when a predator locks onto him. "Look Vinnie. I'm not the enemy, okay?"

"Okay."

"Okay. Now let's talk about next steps." Vinnie heard paper shuffling but did not look up. It was his last act of defiance before submitting to the only person in the room who had any power.

"I hope these next steps include getting me outta here," Vinnie said, and looked up.

"The first step is to keep you alive in here, while we work on getting you out," Caravanti said.

"What have you heard?"

"I have heard," his lawyer said, "that you need to shut up. And quick. You know who controls Mantisto."

A tap at the door sounded and a guard poked his head through the door. "Five more minutes, Counselor."

"Make it ten and I'll go quietly," he said, and smiled. The guard nodded and closed the door. The smile faded and the lawyer leveled a steady eye on his client. "Look, nobody is happy about you being here, and everybody's working on it. Including me. Lucky for you, the court system is like a plugged up commode. Gives us time, for Phase Two."

"Is that what we're calling it now?" Vinnie said, and regretted the words when he saw the lawyer push back from the table.

"Alright," Vinnie said rattling chains as he lifted his hands. "Sorry, counselor. I'm, um, upset."

Caravanti's smile pasted itself again on his crocodile face. "Don't blame you, but let's get on the solution side of this thing, okay?"

Vinnie nodded. "What I gotta do?"

"Have the Feds been back?" Caravanti said. "They tell me nobody's been to see you, but I don't trust anyone here."

"I'm comforted to hear you say that," Vinnie said.

"You're comforted? Comforted?" Caravanti reared his head back and laughed. "What? You been reading novels or something?"

"Eh," Vinnie said, "I'm a classy guy." He chuckled, but it was mirthless. Playing along.

"That you are, Mr. Bontecelli."

"Don't remember any Feds here in at least a couple of weeks," Vinnie said. "Lose track of time in here."

"Bullshit," Caravanti said, not looking up from his papers. "Time is your pot of gold, and every day you're still in here, they take another coin. I know you count them."

"I am comforted to hear you say that," Vinnie said, and laughed for real this time.

He was met with raised eyebrows across the table. "Okay, I got word they're coming. Feds. They're all stirred up again."

"Yeah?"

"Yeah," Caravanti said. "Somebody killed a witness. Feds are pissed."

"Who?"

"Who – what?"

"Who killed a witness?" Vinnie said. "Emil?"

The lawyer shrugged and shuffled more papers, picked files up and dropped them again on the table.

"What witness?" Vinnie said. "I thought I was the only one left."

"Probably are," Caravanti said, and looked up. "But somebody was making sure."

Now it was Vinnie's turn to raise his eyebrows.

"The runt's bride, Bente, Jr.'s wife," Caravanti said. "In the coma at Memorial."

Vinnie shook his head. "She was never gonna come to. Mercy killing maybe."

"God knows," Caravanti said. "Nobody else seems to."

"Somebody knows," Vinnie muttered.

Jay Caravanti tapped the stack of papers on the table to straighten them. "I'll keep working on delays and stays. You," he paused until Vinnie looked up and they locked eyes. "You, say nothing. *Nada.* Not to the feds, not to the guards, not on the Whisper Network. We clear on this?"

"We," Vinnie said a little louder than he intended, "are clear, Counselor."

"And trust no one," Caravanti said. "Except me."

"Message received," Vinnie said.

Caravanti laughed. "There you go again. Message received." He snorted. "I'm expecting a simple, 'Okay,' and out of your mouth comes, 'Message received.'" He laughed again. "Sometimes I'm not sure who I'm talking to."

"I'm a mystery," Vinnie said.

Caravanti closed the briefcase just as the tap came and the door opened. "Right on time," he said to the guard. He stood and pointed at Vinnie, "Remember."

"I remember everything," Vinnie said.

The lawyer froze. "Don't you ever say that again. Never speak those words again," he said. "Ever."

"I don't remember anything," Vinnie said.

"Better," the lawyer said, and swept through the doorway wearing his crocodile smile.

Chapter Four

Residence of Dr. Maria Sanchez
Kingstown, Rhode Island

Maria hadn't slept much. Dawn broke with all the promise of spring, but daylight illuminated the shattered pieces of her life, and its only promise was another shift in the Emergency Room, another round of drama and trauma. Her breasts rubbed against the inside of the T-shirt she wore to bed. It was one Max had left a couple of weeks ago. It still smelled of him. She bent to pick up the pink pieces of the dress she had cut and torn from her body last night. She had bought it to wear for him, and now it lay shredded like the heart that beat beneath her swaying breasts. The knife lay in the middle of the living room floor, glinting in the morning sun. She recalled slashing the blade through the taut fabric between her thighs, heard again the ripping and growling of fabric as it tore, heard the sobs convulsing straight from her heart into the empty room.

She wondered how many tears were left, or whether she had cried them all out. She dared not break down in the ER. There were too many tears in that place already, and she needed to be steady and professional. Whatever that meant. It all seemed like so much bullshit and pretense this morning, when everything else in her life was breaking with the day.

Maybe she should call in sick. Was there a clinical diagnosis for a shattered heart? Was there a code with an empty box next to it that someone could tick with their pen? Was there a clinical diagnosis to reflect that essential pieces of her essential self were dying inside an otherwise healthy body and mind?

She dropped to her hands and knees, wadding cloth into her hands. And then, quite suddenly, her arms seemed to collapse beneath the great weight upon her and she lay flat upon the carpet, breathing into its weave.

How does one go on? Why does one go on? When it's all up for grabs, and no one's grabbing it, does it fall and get absorbed again for the next soul who gives life a go? Maybe the next one won't crash and burn so badly. Maybe the next soul will find what Maria reached for, but never possessed. Maybe they would let her watch from hell. If it is a real place of torment, then it will not be a place of flames and burning flesh. It will be the place where one sits forever, alone, in the frigid winter of their own regret.

Residence of Dr. Nettie Spruill, PhD
Kingstown, Rhode Island

They found her on her knees in the side yard. The powder blue stocking cap she wore was nearly hidden within the bed of roses. When she heard their laughter, Nettie extracted herself from the midst of the bushes and sat onto the backs of her shoes. She waved a muddied glove.

"Yes, Madam Gardner," Jeremy Tittle said with a smile. "I wonder if you could help us. We're looking for the lady of the manor."

"Oh, she's far too busy to see you now," Nettie said. "I do believe the Governor's come to tea." She batted a stray lock of gray hair from her face and managed to paint a stripe of mud across her forehead in the process.

Immediately, Jeremy went fishing in his pocket for a handkerchief. He wiped the mud from her brow, to the delight of a smiling Nettie.

"Aww, chivalry is not dead," Sarah said, "but I fear it might be on its last legs. I get after Terry about it."

"A lady ought not to have to demand it," Nettie said, "nor a gentleman have to be reminded."

"Indeed," Jeremy said.

"It's a new day," Sarah said. "Everybody's confused about what's expected of them."

"Love is expected of them," Nettie said, "just love." Her eyes closed and her face tilted toward the late afternoon sun.

"Don't get us going again on that subject," Jeremy said. "We sorted it all out over coffee."

"So that's what you've been up to," Nettie said.

Jeremy nodded. "While you labored in the fields, scratching the earth."

"Nonsense," she said.

"Speaking of love," Sarah said, turning with a wave, "I've got to get ready to see my love tonight."

"Have a nice time," Nettie waved to Sarah's back as she strode toward the back of the house. Stairs in the rear led directly to an exterior door to her cupola apartment on the third floor. Nettie and Jeremy watched her go.

Nettie turned and fixed Jeremy with an inquiring look.

"I told her that we were 'dating,'" Jeremy said, and made quotation signs with his hands.

"She nearly died."

Nettie looked at him, "Is that what we are doing?"

"Well … I, I mean, I guess so."

"You guess so? In matters of the heart, we never guess," she said.

"In matters of the heart, my dear, we are always guessing," Jeremy said. "And how is it that women seem possessed of the innate ability to make men stammer like idiots?"

She laughed and patted her gloves flat on her thighs. "It's a gift."

"Not to me," he said, but a grin had spread across his face.

"Here," she said, taking a glove off her left hand and raising it toward him, "help a girl up."

Jeremy raised her to her feet, and she turned into his arms until they were wrapped around her. She pecked him on the lips.

"I don't care what we're doing," she said. "I'm happy. Every time I see you, I feel happy."

"I, um, I, dadgummit!" Jeremy said, and Nettie laughed. She unwound herself from his arms and stripped off the other muddy glove.

"Carry your gloves for you, M'lady?" Jeremy said.

"Why thank you, kind sir, but won't you get mud on your hands?"

He took the gloves, gathered the gardening tools, and started for the garage. "I'll clean these up and see you inside."

"Take your time," she said. "I'm going to jump in the shower."

He felt her hand on his chest and opened his eyes.

"Must have dozed off," he said, and started to rise from the couch.

"Shhh," she said, and pressed with her hand until he was laying back again.

His eyes focused and he saw that her long gray hair had been pulled back in a ponytail. He saw earrings in her ears and makeup on her face, but she was still wearing a white terry cloth robe.

"You still dressing?" he said.

"Huh-uh," she said, fingering the buttons on his shirt. "All done."

He felt his heart skip and then pick up speed. "You got anything on underneath that robe?" he said.

"Huh-uh," she said, smiling but not looking him in the eye. She unbuttoned the top half of his shirt and slipped her hand inside, caressing his breast and teasing a nipple.

Her robe was loose at the top and he could see ample breasts rising and falling inside the terry cloth.

"How long's it been since you've been touched?" Nettie said. She was back out of his shirt and undoing more buttons.

"A long, long time. Nettie, I …." He heard his voice coming in a huff.

"Shhh," she said, and worked his belt lose from the buckle.

Jeremy was breathing through his mouth. He closed his eyes. In that instant, Jenny's face loomed before him. She was dressed in a silk gown. A shining silver boa encircled her neck. Her broad smile showed all those beautiful teeth, and her eyes danced. "My love, my life, my forever wife," he tried to say to her but no sound came out.

Jeremy felt Nettie's hot breath beneath his navel, felt himself beginning to swell beneath it. Jenny continued to smile but her image was fading, growing more distant, until there was a silent twinkle and she was gone. Jeremy sat bolt upright and his eyes shot open.

"What's wrong?" Nettie said. "Are you all right? Did I hurt you?"

Jeremy stood to his feet next to Nettie, who still knelt next to the couch. "No, um," he said, and zipped the fly on his trousers, and cinched his belt a hole too tight. "I'm fine. I mean, I'm not fine. I'm okay."

"You're pale as a ghost, is what you are."

Yeah, well," Jeremy said. He stopped short of telling her, but it was stuck on his lips and nothing else could navigate around it. "Look, Nettie," he said.

"I've done something wrong," she said. "I feel so foolish." She jerked closed the robe and stood.

"No," he said. "You've done nothing wrong."

Nettie's chin hung in the opening of the robe and she shook her head fast and hard. Her lips contorted. She slapped a hand across them and rushed from the room. Jeremy heard the bedroom door close. With force.

"I'm not ready is all, Nettie," he whispered. "It was Jenny. In Heaven. She …." He arced his arm in a full, slow circle. "She was happy for me, Nettie," he said, still whispering. "Us. Happy for us. I just need a little time. Is all. Nettie?" He took three steps toward the hallway leading to her room, and then stopped. He ran trembling fingers through the thin white strands on his head.

There followed a moment when time stopped. Several more moments passed before he could move again, before he could stop staring into the empty mouth of the hallway. His hands were drenched in sweat. He wiped them on his pants, turned, and made his way to the back door. He closed the door gently behind him. The tears came before his car key hit the door lock. He felt a great welling in his chest, and he hurried to get himself gone before he humiliated himself further.

The lines on the road blurred so badly before him that he had to exit into a rest area. Jeremy parked his car at the far end of the parking area near the woods. The phosphorous lamp over the restroom entrance glowed in the distance. He cut off the lights, and the darkness swallowed him. The welling in his chest breached its barricade, and he let it come, all of it. What gushed forth was more than tears, more than cries or sobs. Jeremy heard wailing, screaming. It was a terrible sound, a frightening, almost inhuman sound, and it was coming from him. His mouth was wide open and he was helpless to close it. Spittle waggled from his chin as he shook his head back and forth.

On and on it went, until he thought it might overtake him completely. This might be how it ends. He'd always thought he'd check into Heaven like it was a hotel. He'd wait his turn in line and then see if his name was on the list. But maybe Heaven's gate stood on the other side of Hell, and you had to crawl through first. Maybe you had to experience afresh every pain, every regret, every setback and cruel life reversal, every harsh accusation others hurled at you and every one you had hurled at yourself, every dashed hope and love lost. Maybe you screamed and sobbed until there was none of it left within you, screamed and screamed until the ears of Mercy heard your cries, and turned in your direction.

His breath came in short gasps, and his heart burned in his chest like it was on a spit. He saw it, torn and bleeding, a single wisp of smoke rising from it with every beat of his still beating heart. And then everything was nothing. The last thing he felt was his body slump against the steering wheel.

A woman wearing an Indianapolis Colts ball cap and walking her dog at the perimeter of the restroom light, heard the car horn blaring. Her German shepherd whined and tugged the leash. She peered down the empty parking lot to the darkened car at the end. Something was wrong. She grabbed the cell phone from her pocket and dialed 911.

Emergency Room
Memorial Hospital
Kingstown, Rhode Island

The State Highway Patrol found him slumped against the steering wheel, his eyes open and fixed, his lower jaw slack. He was breathing but otherwise unresponsive. Kingstown Fire and Rescue transported him to Memorial Hospital. When Dr. Maria Sanchez saw the name appear on her electronic clipboard, a sickness roiled her gut. An Emergency Room doc develops skin too tough for most things to penetrate, but it is different when you know the person. She knew Dr. Jeremy Tittle, knew him as the retiring dean of Ecclesia Seminary. She'd last seen him in the company of Dr. Nettie Spruill, smiling, his face radiating light. When she drew back the curtain of Examination Slip Seven, she saw a face and a frame she recognized, but without the person to give it life and expression. Tittle's eyes were unfocused, his shoulders hunched even in recline, and his jaw slack. Dr. Tatum was the attending physician, and he was looking him over when she arrived.

"What we got?" she said over Dr. Tatum's shoulder. "Stroke?"

"Won't know till we get the MRI, of course," Tatum said, "but I doubt it. Vitals are within normal limits, EKG, same."

"Let me see the strip." She examined the EKG readout, and handed it back. "Yep."

What, you checking up on me now boss?" Tatum said with a raised eyebrow.

Maria grinned and sniffed, "No, sorry. I know him. Not well, but …."

Dr. Tatum nodded. "He's next for an MRI, but in the meantime, I'm calling Psych."

"You think?"

He nodded. "My initial diagnosis: psychotic break."

Dr. Sanchez shook her head. "God I hope not. Brilliant man."

"Sometimes they're the most brittle," Dr. Tatum said.

"Most what?"

"Something my grandpa used to say, 'The brittle branches break the easiest.'"

"Excuse me," she said. "Got to make a call." She hurried to the break room and pulled out her cell phone.

"Max," she said when she got his voicemail. "I need a favor. Can you get Nettie Spruill's cell phone number and call me back with it? Dr. Tittle just got transported here. Call and I'll fill you in. Or text if you don't want to talk to me." She ended the call and wrapped her shoulders with both arms. It wasn't the hug she needed, but it would have to do.

Mantisto State Prison
Kingstown, Rhode Island

One of the supreme ironies was that time was everything in prison, yet no one doing time was allowed a watch or access to a clock. No one knew what time it was, and so everything that happened in an inmate's life was "some time".

And so it was some time, when Vinnie was in his usual state of sleeping wakefulness, that the food slot in the door slid open about an inch and a half. The tip of a metal ASP baton rested in the opening. It was the signal that a message was arriving from the Whispering Network. He rolled off his metal slab of a bed onto his knees and crawled near the opening.

"Yes," Vinnie said in a whisper.

The whispered message was spoken so softly, he had to strain to hear it. He knew if he put any part of his face too close to the slot, he would be jabbed with the ASP. He had tried to see the whisperer once, had put his left eye close to the slot, and had almost lost it. The jab had come hard and fast. It was only Vinnie's last second reflex that saved the eye, but it nearly broke the eye socket. The side of his face was black for a week. It was a lesson learned, and he never got close to the slot again.

"JD say we regroupin' and we gonna find and deal with the ones set you up. Don't say shit to no one. We deal widit," the whisperer said. Vinnie didn't recognize the voice. Someone JD sent and the guard escorted.

"Yes," Vinnie said. "Find the ring and cut off the whole finger. Send it to the Shark with my love."

There was a long moment of silence, then the ASP disappeared, and the slot slid closed.

Vinnie didn't know how long he remained on his knees by the door, but the pain finally brought him around. He went over each whispered word, squeezing every drop of news from it.

JD was the leader of the largest shit pile in Mantisto. Vinnie labeled JD's gang "SP1" and even told JD of the designation. Thankfully, JD loved it and even renamed his gang with that moniker, though he never told the members it stood for "shit pile". He let them make up their own meaning. JD was not his real name either, of course. It was his prison name: Junk Dawg, so named because his penis, his junk, was so big. He stood 6'8" tall and massive muscles stretched his black skin to the point of stretch marks. Four teardrop tats formed a line from the corner of his eye. He had killed, and he would kill again. He protected his men and they protected him. Not all members of SP1 were thugs. Many were model inmates, and that status had earned them privileged access to people and places in the prison that few other inmates could go.

Vinnie trusted JD about as much as he trusted anybody in here. He knew every man had his price, and any man could be bought if you had enough of what he wanted. You don't buy every man with coin. Some men you buy with power, or position, or reputation. Some men you buy with powder or pills. Vinnie was an expert at buying men. He had an instinct for knowing their price, and he kept himself well resourced so he could meet it.

JD was stacked with three life sentences for murder. He wasn't going anywhere and he knew it. Vinnie knew it, too, and used his cartel clout to cement JD's position as the prison's most powerful person. And because JD was beholden to Vinnie, in his pocket as it were, Vinnie had all the muscle he needed to exact revenge upon the prison minions who were part of setting him up. They would regret strapping him down to enough C4 to blow his parts into every corner of that chow hall. He could not identify any of the actors because of the orange jumpsuits and the black hoods, but one man made a mistake. A big one. He wore the jumpsuit, and the hood, and the latex gloves, but he forgot to take off the large ring on his right hand, a solid gold ring in the shape of a four-sided diamond that stretched against the latex covering the finger. It was an important clue as to how high up in the system this operation had gone. That man was not an inmate. Inmates were not allowed jewelry of any kind. Nor were the guards. That man was a prison official. He might also have been an outside guest, but Vinnie doubted it. The important thing was to find these guys, every last one of them, and to kill them in such a way that the message to Emil Bente was unmistakable: I am coming for you.

Bente had made two mistakes. The first was underestimating Vinnie's knack for self-preservation when he sent him along with JR, Bente's son, as his babysitter. Vinnie went, not just as a babysitter, but also as an entrepreneur. True, he had made a deal with the devil himself to do it, but the payoff was already huge.

If that whack job of a minister, George Fields, hadn't taken Bente, Jr. off the board, Vinnie's men would have. Those men haven't gone anywhere, nor has Vinnie's Rhode Island operation slowed one bit. Vinnie would have folded his entire operation into the Bente Cartel, at the appropriate time and for the appropriate price. That had always been his plan.

Not anymore. Emil Bente's second mistake was double-crossing him in the escape from Mantisto. It had always been the plan that they would get out together. He remembered everything. The ring. The words whispered in his ear, "S says sorry." Vinnie spat onto the cell wall. A large wad of spittle and snot oozed slowly down the wall.

Vinnie went back over the message from the Whisper Network. JD was regrouping. What did that mean? Had something happened to scatter SP1? Patience, Vincente, a voice in his head said so strongly he could have sworn it was spoken aloud. You never knew who's watching. At Mantisto State Prison, unless you were part of the cartel that owned it, you had to look over both shoulders at all times. Lesson learned.

Vinnie clenched and unclenched his enormous hands. *I am coming for you.*

The Library
Bente Residence
Venice, Italy

They were arranged in a perfect semicircle around his desk in the massive library. Ostensibly, the library had been constructed for use by the cardinal and his staff, but no one except Emil Bente and his people went in there. Through the years, the room began to be appointed with antique torture devices in addition to books, and so it became less and less of a place the clergy would want to go. Each chair in the semi-circle had an inverted five-foot sword clipped onto the back of it so that the point appeared to protrude from each woman's head. None had ever been detached from the chair, but the sheer optics made for clear communication.

The inner circle was small. The Shark liked it that that way. All five women sat perfectly still when he entered the room. Greetings and small talk were forbidden. Bente stood between his chair and the desk and made eye contact with each of them. Then he lowered his eyes to the desk and picked up the solid gold rosary that rested there in the shape of an S. All five women picked up a rosary from their laps. He began to say the Rosary, and they joined with him in unison. Their unified voice was strong and rhythmic. It echoed off the ceiling and walls, sounding more like chanting.

The rosary each woman held was heavy and ornate with protruding precious and semi-precious stones in brilliant arrangements of color. When they had completed saying the Rosary together, S and the others held the rosaries out in front of them so the cross hung perfectly straight at the bottom. Then, as one, they placed them around their necks. Emil Bente sat.

"*Mio Marias*," he began, "it is good that we are together in this sacred place. As always, it is a great risk for us to gather, and that is why we do it so infrequently. I trust you were careful?"

The woman in the middle seat pressed her wedged hands together and brought them in front of her face so that both thumbs rested under her chin.

"Yes Maria Milagra," Emil said, granting the petition to speak.

"I was questioned more than usual, Excellency, though my papers were in perfect order."

"It is a sign of the times, I'm afraid," he said. "Before terrorism became a household word, members of the clergy were considered above reproach. Now? They wonder if your habits are lined with plastique."

The words brought a smile to several faces.

"I must say," he said grinning, "it gives me great pleasure to see my top five assassins slip back and forth from this place, and in and out of your respective countries. Why? Because you are unarmed, you are women, and you are clergy. They are fools."

The woman seated in the far left chair raised prayer hands to her face.

"Yes Maria Yoka," Emil said with a nod.

"But we are clergy, my lord, and not in attire only," she said. "The world does not, and pray will never, know that the Temple Guard originally consisted of clergy only, and some of them were women. Nuns like us."

"Ahhh, indeed," he said. "It is their assumptions that maintain your anonymity." He raised a hand and began to count on his fingers. "Christian Clergy do not bear arms or employ weapons." Next finger, "Christian Clergy do not kill." Next finger. "Christian Clergy show mercy in the face of evil." Next finger. "Christian Clergy are never, ever, assassins." He smiled. "Of course, now you are managers and directors of operations, and that's why you are here. Beloveds, I need two things: production reports and distribution reports. Then I have a couple of assignments for you to pass to your people." He looked at his watch. "My pilots will be looking for me in exactly four hours. Let us begin, shall we?"

One by one, small laptops and handhelds appeared from within their robes. Once opened and powered, the women began lifting them to their eyes so the ocular sensor would recognize them and unlock.

The woman in the far right chair raised prayer hands and waited for permission to speak. It was the stillness that fell across the room that drew Emil's attention. He looked up from the spreadsheet before him and nodded, "Maria Novatska."

"Yes, Excellency. Thank you for permitting the indulgence," she said. "Before we begin with the numbers, would you brief us on family matters and, um, any pending situations?"

"Of course," Emil said. "Of course. We are of necessity so compartmentalized. I forget not all of you know everything. Besides, I was made aware of a new situation today in Maria Garza's territory."

He glanced her way and she nodded. He continued, "I have been able to touch base with her only briefly. Rhode Island. Again."

Maria Milagra raised prayer hands and Emil pointed to her.

"May we speak freely for a few moments?" she said.

"Yes," Emil said. "I'm always grateful for your respect, but yes, now let us speak together as brothers and sisters without the need for permission." He paused. "How foolish of me to jump right into the books, when perhaps this … this sharing … is the most important work we will do together today."

"Rhode Island continues to be a problem," Maria Milagra said. "A persistent distraction and a production nightmare."

"Amen," said Maria Garza. "Production is off. Shipments are down. Deliveries are increasingly dangerous."

"All of it since the FBI started … probing, shall we say." Emil said.

"Agent Steele," Maria Garza said.

"Agent Max Steele needs to go," Emil Bente said. He felt his still tender jaw clench, and he rubbed it, "But that's nothing new and not the new development I'm about to share." He looked hard at the Marias, who sat frozen, fixed on his face. "An assassin has struck in Kingstown," Emil said.

"Not one of ours," Maria Garza said, glancing to the others, "but a pro nonetheless."

"The target?" Maria Novatska said.

Maria Garza turned to Emil, and he nodded for her to respond.

"Nina Ondolopous, executed in a hospital bed, while still in the coma."

"Oh boy," Maria Milagra said.

"Not 'Oh boy', but all about 'The Boy,'" Emil said. He choked and looked away. "I'm afraid the Great Mother contracted out this hit."

"She suffers a broken heart, Excellency," Maria Milagra said.

"She does," Emil said softly.

"And so much hate," Maria Milagra said.

"Yes, our boy," Emil said. "My son, her grandson and now the woman, Ondolopous, who carried her only great grandson." Emil stood and moved to stand at the edge of a towering bookcase.

"Surely she can see that he was killed by that madman …," Maria Yoka said, and clutched her rosary. "Reverend Fields?"

He nodded without looking at them. "In her dreams, a priest jams a knife into her grandson over and over and over, until she wakes screaming and cursing God."

Maria Milagra nodded. "She tells me of the dream every time I come to see her."

"It's not her only dream," Bente said, barely above a murmur.

I've seen many people tortured in my life," Maria Yoka said. "The Great Mother tortures herself with things she conjures within her own heart."

"But he is dead, yes?" Maria Yoka said. "Why kill a woman so deep in a coma she will probably die anyway, and who has already lost the Holy Mother's great grandson from her womb?"

"God alone knows the heart when it goes black," Maria Milagra said.

"She won't speak about it," Emil said, "but knowing the soul of the woman as I do, she wanted to erase the woman who carried her great grandchild and denied her the privilege of ever holding it …." He heard his voice quake, as if from a great distance. "… in her arms." He felt it break, heard a snap somewhere in his chest, and then a roar of anguish rush from his mouth, vile and violent like a bull pierced a final time by the matador's spears. He shoved his arms into the bookcase, grabbed books, and hurled them into the room. He felt his arms reach for more and hurl them. He commanded his arms to stop, and they would not. The roar in his ears was coming from his own lips and he could not stop it.

He felt arms hold him as he heaved and sobbed, one set of arms and then another and another until he was surrounded. He felt their arms, and the press of their bodies against him, and the rosaries that hung from their necks. He felt the crosses pressing against him, pressing into him on every side. He saw them in his mind, saw them pulse and radiate.

He didn't know how long they stood holding him, but after a time, he raised his head. "I'm okay," he said from their midst. One by one, they released him with a squeeze. "And bless you, *mio* Marias."

Maria Papalous knelt and began to pick up books from the floor.

"Leave them," Emil said. "Time is precious and I feel I have distracted us terribly."

"This time is precious," Maria Milagra said, "just as it is."

He nodded, swiped at his face, and then returned to the desk. He pushed spreadsheets around distractedly while the Marias seated themselves.

"Excellency," Maria Papalous said, "I assume Maria Garza will clean up the, um, situation in Rhode Island. Can we assist?"

Emil Bente shook his head. "I'm going." He looked up and pressed a smile upon his face. "It will be my first return to Rhode Island … since my … release from captivity."

"Must you go?" Maria Milagra said. "I cannot think of anywhere more dangerous for you to appear."

"Must I go," Bente said, "to mop up the Holy Mother's mess? Heavens no. Maria Garza and her team are more than competent." He leaned back in his chair. "No, Cardinal Nicolo has assigned me a task. That's all I'd like to say about it, if you don't mind."

"I must see her," Maria Milagra said at the conclusion of the meeting. Emil looked upon the leader of the Marias and he felt a lump form in his throat. He coughed at it.

"She is suffering on the afternoon of her ninetieth birthday," he said. He looked to the rest of the Marias. "I assume all of you are coming to the Great Mother's birthday party this evening."

"Will she wear the habit for us?" Maria Garza said. "In so many ways, she is our mother and Mother Superior to us."

Emil Bente was silent for a moment. "I will ask," he said. "She still has all her clerical robes, but so far she refuses to wear them."

"But why?" Maria Garza said.

"Because of me," Emil said, and drew in a long breath, "and my brother."

Chapter Five

Mantisto State Prison
Kingstown, Rhode Island

Captain Max Steele drummed his fingers on the interrogation room table. He knew Vinnie might refuse to talk without his lawyer, might turn right around at the mouth of the door. Then the long drive out here would be for nothing. But Max was counting on Vinnie's anger to drive him.

A metallic tap sounded, and the door opened. Vincente Bontecelli shuffled in, escorted by a prison guard. His eyes met Steele's and he smirked. The guards seated him in the chair across the table from Max.

"You may leave us," Max said to the guards. "I'll knock when we're through." The door closed and the lock clicked into place.

The two men stared at each other in silence. At last, Vinnie tossed his head, leaned back in his chair, and grinned toward the corner of the room.

"Something amusing, Vinnie?"

"You must be desperate," Vinnie said.

"Yeah?" Max said. "How's that?"

Vinnie shrugged. "What time is it?"

"What does it matter? And you didn't answer my question."

"Time," Vinnie said, "always matters. It's the only thing that matters."

"Really," Max said. "What about pay back? Doesn't that matter?"

"Oh, hell yeah," Vinnie said and snorted.

"Maybe I can help."

"Not this again."

"He's out there," Max said, stabbing his finger toward the door. "You're in here. He got out. He set you up to be blown into a million bits. Shark chum. Now, you're rotting in here, and he's laughing at you."

"Yeah well, that'll …." Vinnie slammed his hands together and pointed with both index fingers, then froze. The muscles across his broad shoulders relaxed and he slumped back in his chair. He grinned.

"Will – what?"

"You know just how to push, don't you, Mr. FBI Man," Vinnie said. "Push my ignition and touch me off like a rocket."

"I think you've got a right to be pissed," Max said, "and a right to be scared."

"Scared?" Vinnie said. "Ain't scared of nothin'."

"No?" Max said. "Then you aren't very smart, either."

"Ehhhhh, you come here to insult me? That a new technique they teach you in cop school?"

"Not trying to insult you, Vincente," Max said. "Warn you maybe, but not insult you."

Vinnie sucked air slowly through his teeth and locked eyes with Steele. "Okay, I'll bite. Whatcha got?"

"All I've got is you," Max said. "You are the last witness, the last one who can testify against Emil Bente, and he knows it."

Vinnie fell silent, and Max continued in a voice barely above a whisper. "You're a smart man. I'm a smart man. You and I know damn well he nearly took you out INSIDE this place." Max swept his arm in an arc. "He couldn't have done it unless he's bought part or all of this prison. You following me?"

"Way ahead," Vinnie said. "But he don't own it all." Then he blew out a breath, "theoretically, mind you."

"Okay, theoretically works," Max said. "I'm not here to get up in your business, and knowing you like I do, you are formulating a plan in here as we speak."

"You're not as dumb as you look, Steele," Vinnie said.

"I'm not," Max said, "and you're not as dumb as I look, either."

"That sounded like respect," Vinnie said.

"It is."

"Then maybe this visit ain't a total waste of my time."

"Don't think so," Max said.

"What you offering?"

"What are you offering?" Max said.

"Do I need my lawyer in here to broker a deal?"

"You could go that way, if you want a complete idiot in here."

"Oh, so you've met him," Vinnie said, and smirked.

"I've met him," Max said. "But I come from the street. You do, too. We put together better deals our way."

"Yeah, right," Vinnie laughed, "You're such a thug, Captain Max Steele, FBI."

Max laughed and looked at his lap.

"What you offering?" Vinnie said.

"Keep you alive, to start," Max said. "Not because I love ya. Because I need help."

"I'm fine."

Max nodded. "I know how shit works in prisons. I know you got your people and all."

Vinnie smiled. "For the record, you don't … know how shit works in here."

"I know this," Max said. "I know, day to day, you live an awful long way from your people. Hell, solitary is in the supermax wing. How long did it take you to get here, to this room, from your cell? Ten minutes? Fifteen?"

Vinnie wasn't smiling anymore. His eyes fixed on the man across the table.

"Middle of the night," Max said, "guards paid to look the other way, to be in another sector. Video feed failure on the cameras for two minutes. They're in, they're out, and you're history."

"Let them try," Vinnie said, glowering.

"If I were a betting man, I'd say it's already in the works."

"Enough," Vinnie said. "What do you want?"

"I want to get you transferred out of here, to start," Max said.

"That ain't all you want."

"It's not," Max said.

"Listening," Vinnie said.

"All I want," Max said, "is an installment plan. Give it to me a bite at a time."

"You want me to narc on the Cartel."

"I want Emil Bente," Max said.

Vinnie was silent for a long while. Max held his breath, then breathed through his nose. *Close now. Wait for him to swim into the net.*

"Your passport up to date?" Vinnie said finally.

"Mine?"

Vinnie nodded and fell silent again.

Max waited, didn't even flinch, let alone utter a word.

"Italy," Vinnie said at last. "Start there."

"Where in Italy?" Max said.

"Venice."

"Where in Venice?"

Vinnie stared at him. "A bite at a time," he said. "How quick can you get me out of here?"

"Soon as we're done here, I'm in the Warden's office. You have my word."

"We're done here," Vinnie said.

Bente Residence
Venice, Italy

If you did not know what to look for, you would walk right by the elevator door and never see it. The hewn rock face that characterized the tunnel walls gave no hint that something lay behind them in places. Though there were no visitors, a visitor or intruder would see only stonewalled corridors punctuated by angled *faux* torches in the original hardware. Lives depended on secrecy and concealment, and no expense was spared in the camouflage. Each torch contained two nearly identical decorative crystalline rods parallel to, and clipped next to, the fixture plate. They were the size of small coffee shop stir sticks. One of them near the elevator to the Bente residence had code embedded into the crystal.

Emil unclipped the crystal rod, walked forward exactly seven steps, and then knelt. Near where the dirt floor intersected the wall was a small hole. Emil inserted the rod and withdrew it again. The section of wall to the right of him shuddered and then a large section sunk inward, withdrawing two and a half feet, pausing, and then sliding behind the section of wall to the left. It revealed a golden elevator door whose jam was bejeweled with precious stones, inlaid in an arched pattern. Two lights no thicker than pencils, mounted above and into the inner wall, were aimed so as to make the jewels sparkle as one approached the door.

Emil returned the crystal rod to its clip next to the torch and walked through the opening in the wall. There was no button to press to gain access to the elevator. One had to know which stone adorning its perimeter concealed the retinal scanner. One also had to know which stones to touch, and in which pattern, in order for the scanner cover to slide away. Emil touched three diamonds, an emerald, and two rubies. To his right, a medium sized jewel popped open, revealing the tiny scanner. He placed his right eye close to the scanner and tried not to blink.

He heard a faint beep, and the elevator doors parted. As soon as his feet touched the elevator's interior, the section of tunnel wall that had receded, slid back into place. Emil smiled. Technology. It was beautiful in itself. But when it was combined with other forms of beauty, like roughhewn rock and precious stones, it approached magnificent.

The interior of the elevator was appointed more functionally, except that the back wall was a thick sheet of glass. As it ascended or descended, one could see the various rock and soil levels, and the characteristically Venetian strata. It was as fascinating to him now as it was when he was a child, only back then the elevator shaft had been an intricate spiral of steps carved from the solid rock. All of it was an engineering wonder. It was such a shame that the world would never see it.

As the elevator doors slid shut, Emil submitted himself to yet another retinal scan. Then he glanced at the panel. There were only four buttons. Earth, Water, Fire, and Air. He pressed "Water," and the elevator began to move. Emil liked to check the sea level access area each time he used the tunnel. It was how he stayed in a state of readiness at all times. He knew exactly what he had, knew it was functional, and was confident he could rely on it. His mantra was, "Over Prepare," and he worked hard to instill this approach to life into his people. It was the reason he was still alive. It was why the Cartel was still thriving. He over prepared. He checked and double-checked, and he put redundant systems in place to ensure readiness in every circumstance and eventuality. He shuddered to think what might have been, had he not over prepared for the possibility of his incarceration at Mantisto State Prison. He would still be there.

He demanded over preparedness from every member of the Cartel, and ninety-nine percent of the time, they obeyed. So, why had it been so difficult with the members of his own family? His son – may he rest in peace – never understood. That boy's entire life had been characterized by impulsivity instead of preparedness. It cost him his life, and it had damn near brought the Cartel to its knees. Emil shook his head. He was still mopping up that mess.

And now the Holy Mother. What was she thinking? Why did she insert herself when she had handed the reins over to him once the multiple sclerosis struck? She could have asked him to take care of any situation or circumstance that troubled her. He would have prepared, and then he would've over prepared, and then he would've been successful in taking care of it without the need for a mop up operation.

The elevator chimed softly and the LED readout above the door read, "Water Level." The doors parted to reveal an underwater marina encased in a solid rock dome. No expense had been spared in its architectural and engineering design. To the left was a stationery crane. It was used to offload deliveries. Behind it and two stories up, he saw the windows to the main control station. Beneath it was Area B. It was the passage into the vaults. It was so heavily and covertly armed, that even Emil did not go near it.

To the right, and extending as far as his eye could see, were vessels as large as trawlers and as small as floating snowmobiles, as he liked to call them. On the near right wall was the dive area, complete with male and female locker rooms.

Emil snatched the handheld radio mounted in its charger on the wall next to the elevators.

"Emil Bente to all units, surprise inspection," he said. The radio came alive as post after post replied, "Clear." He waited for the Water Commander to join him, forcing a smile on his face. He wished he could visit and inspect every level here, and also every base of operations, but he was only one man, and he had lost his only son and had left his right-hand man in prison. And then there was Mother.

He would have to be quick. There was so much to do and so little time.

Bente Residence
Venice, Italy

Emil found his mother in the Garden. It was an area domed with opaque material designed to allow natural light to penetrate while still protecting the interior from overhead view. Combined with the misting system, it felt and functioned much like a hothouse. The area was over 5000 square feet. It contained two water features and over 9000 plants. One of the water features was also a Koi pond, and the fish had been carefully nurtured. Many were enormous and uniquely marbled. The other water feature was a four-fall waterfall. The top fall was near the thirty-foot ceiling, and the water cascaded from successive shelf rocks into shallow pools beneath. Because the area was enclosed, the sound echoed and reverberated throughout the space.

Emil found his mother at the waterfall. Her motorized wheelchair was parked perpendicular to the falls. The sound of the water this close to the falls was so loud that it prevented conversation. Emil walked to a table a hundred feet or so from the fountain, and sat, waiting for Mother to notice him and come to talk. It was their agreed way: he never approached her suddenly or interrupted her when she was alone with her thoughts and prayers.

At last, he saw the wheelchair turn and Mother approached the table. Emil shot to his feet, as one would when a queen entered the room. As Matriarch of the Bente family and Head of the Bente Cartel, Mother Maria Bente expected and received great deference, even from her family.

"Mother," Emil said with a slight bow. He walked to her, kissed the top of her bowed head, and then seated himself again.

"Come closer," Mother said. Emil skidded his chair across the huge porcelain slabs that covered the entire area. "I've been thinking."

"I have too, Mother," Emil said, "but you go first." She nodded. The water continued to rush and splash behind them, persistent in its journey to the bottom, and then its return to the top assisted by three enormous pumps beneath the water in the bottom pool.

"I want two things before I die," she said, and held up an arthritic hand to silence Emil as he opened his mouth to speak. "I want to write a memoir of my life, of our lives, and of the family. I want the stories to be told. I want the truth to be revealed in sentences, bound and stitched together in a book. Or two."

"Mother," Emil said. "You realize the danger, the risk, if such a book fell into the wrong hands? It would be the end of our lives."

She nodded slowly, locking her raptor-like eyes with her son's. "You fear the truth, don't you, my son? Your fear and your secrets will topple you."

Emil sat in silence, feeling the heat rise in his neck, knowing he must weigh his words carefully to such a great and powerful woman. "What you call fear, Mother, I call risk management. I manage the risks involved in operating a multibillion-dollar cartel. Advanced preparation to control eventualities and strict secrecy are two of my most powerful tools."

Mother nodded slowly, "Well articulated, Emil. I see your Oxford education was not wasted."

"But don't you see? That, too, had to be done in secret," Emil said. "What I would not have given to walk the streets of Oxford, to study in their hallowed libraries, and to throw around my neck the colors of my college. Instead, you had to have my Don's secreted into these cloisters to give me my instruction."

"It was necessary," Mother said.

"Yes, and that is my point, Mother. Secrecy is necessary. Privacy is paramount to our safety and security."

"Yes," she repeated, and Emil wondered for a flashing moment if she were mocking him or merely paralleling his speech, "but I'm damned if I will return to ashes and dust without some record of who we are and what we have built."

Emil put his hands to the sides of his head, and leaned back in his chair.

"Even if no one sees it except you, your brother, and the Marias, I want the Bente legacy recorded."

"I assume this is not a request I can refuse, Mother," Emil said.

"Think of it as my birthday present," she said.

Emil looked at the waterfall for a long time, as a noisy silence rested between them. At last, he rocked forward in his chair and took his mother by both hands.

"You know I will deny you nothing, *mia Madre*," he said. "You will ever be both my cherished mother and the Matriarch of this family."

"I wish you had known the Patriarch of this family," she said. "This memoir will paint the portrait of a great man and his legacy."

"Will you also write of his disgrace?" Emil said. His mother dropped his hands from hers.

"Truth is truth," she said. "I will write of his disgrace, and of my own." Her stare penetrated him, as it always had. His hands moistened with sweat and he heard his heart beat hard in his chest. "And perhaps I will write of your own disgrace, Emil Bente. Do you think for a moment, for even a moment, that any of us escapes one fall into disgrace after another? Like that waterfall over there." She waved her arm weakly. "We fall, and we gather ourselves, only to fall again. We gather ourselves again, until we fall again. And if we're blessed enough with time and years, we will be cycled around to fall again. No one can maintain themselves in a state of grace throughout a life lived with passion and courage. No one, my son."

Emil felt her power, felt it coursing through her shattered body, felt it coursing in his.

"My legacy, dear boy, and that of your father, is of the grace we found in our disgrace, for there cannot be one without the other."

"You miss him," Emil said, and he felt his eyes well with tears.

"Oh," his mother lurched in her wheelchair, "I miss him so. I tire of choosing each day to keep living without him. And even though writing the memoir will pick scabs off old wounds, I want to remember everything and have it live again."

"Yes, Mother, write your memoir," Emil said, "but may I request one thing?"

She had been looking again at the waterfall and turned her head back to her son.

"May I ask that you use one of the Marias to assist as your scribe?" he said.

She nodded. "Maria Milagra."

Emil nodded. "Maria Milagra."

"Is she here?" she said.

"Yes," Emil said, "and the others as well, except for one."

Her mother nodded and sighed, "You have a problem."

"I do," he said, "and I will fix it. Please let me fix it." Emil straightened in his chair. "And that brings me nicely, perfectly, to the thing that I wanted to talk with you about."

"But I said I had two things that I want before I die and we have only discussed one," she said.

"Mother, please," Emil said.

She folded her hands in her lap and nodded.

"Thank you," Emil said. "You know I promised you, when you turned control of the Cartel over to me, that I would handle things. Everything. We would still discuss it, but at the end of the day, I would take care of it." He felt his voice strengthening as he spoke. He recognized it. It was his authoritative voice, and it seemed to come on its own when he was directing the operation and he needed to communicate as the leader.

He cleared his throat. "Mother, I have learned of an action you took in Kingstown. At Memorial Hospital. Completely on your own and without my knowledge."

"I don't deny it," she said, and lifted a defiant chin toward him.

"Good. That's a start," he said. "Mother Maria, that was a grave error in judgment, if I may be so bold to speak to you in this manner."

"A grave error," she repeated.

"Yes, Mother," he said, "I knew nothing about it, and our people inside Memorial at the time were unable to contain the damage."

"What damage?" she said. "He did it. He got away."

Emil was nodding his head vigorously now, "Yes, an amateur, Mother. We had just about contained our exposure there, and now it has blown open again. Kingstown is one of our primary receiving and distribution hubs, as you know, because of the harbor." He blew out a breath. "I'm rambling, I'm so upset."

"Emil," his mother said, her voice raised and trembling, "look at me." He shot her a look with more heat than he intended. "Would you have killed that slut if I had asked you to? Would you? Would you have done that if I'd asked you to?"

The two stared at each other, and at last, Emil looked down in defeat. He shook his head.

"Right," she said, "so I did what needed to be done."

"Mother, it was too dangerous. I would have tried to talk you out of it. I would've asked you for time, time to let that woman wither and die on her own."

"She murdered my grandchild as sure as if she had stuck a stiletto through his chin and into his brain," she said. "She had to go, and I pray she went straight to Hell."

Emil stared at her for a long moment. "That kind of hate makes for bad decisions," Emil said.

"Good and bad are judgments made by people who have decided what is right and what is wrong," she said.

"I do not judge you, Mother."

"Oh, but you do."

"I am thinking of the safety of this family and our business," Emil said, "and I beg you, Mother, not to take any other actions without first discussing them with me. You put this operation in my hands for a reason, and I take it seriously."

"And you are a fine leader," she said, "but this was family business and I am still the head of this family."

"I honor that, and I honor you, *mia Madre*," Emil said, his head still bowed.

"See that you do," she said. "Now I must go light a candle." She pivoted her wheelchair. "Will I see the Marias tonight?"

"Yes indeed, Mother," Emil said, "at your birthday party."

"All of them, except the one," she said.

He nodded.

"I will let you deal with that one." She pushed the lever forward on her wheelchair and rolled from the room.

For several minutes, Emil sat in the chair without moving. His mind had gone blank, but his body was alive with something he could not identify, something that coursed and surged like the great tides. And then, as if he could hear the waves and taste the salt riding on the wind, he saw the small child standing at the water's edge, the little blue swimsuit bulged by the diaper beneath it. His face was toward the churning ocean. The waves surged, swelling with power as they approached. The child opened his arms, held them wide as the great wave neared. And then it swallowed him, like a beast who knows only hunger, and he was no more.

Warden's Office
Mantisto State Prison
Kingstown, Rhode Island

"I'm sorry," the bespectacled man said, returning the receiver to its cradle at his reception desk, "the Warden says he can't see you now. Would you like to make an appointment?"

"I'm sorry," Max said, mimicking the man's tone, "but this is the FBI and I will see the Warden when I damn well please." He marched past the man's desk and pushed the Warden's door. It was locked. Max whirled and shot a stare at the receptionist that would melt bronze. "You hit that buzzer to unlock this door in the next two seconds and I won't ram an ink pen through your eye and out the back of your head."

The door buzzed and Max was through it.

"You …," Warden Al Antonetti spluttered. A young woman wearing a very short, and very tight, skirt jumped from the Warden's desk where she had been perched. Too startled to catch herself and too constricted by the skirt, she sprawled onto the floor at the Warden's feet.

"No, you," Max said and shot a finger toward the man's face. "Matter of time until I gather enough evidence to blast your ass right out of that chair. In the meantime, don't think for a minute we don't know who you work for."

"I work for the State, the State of Rhode Island," Antonetti said, huffing air. He looked to the young woman who had gotten to her knees and was struggling for dignity as she attempted to stand. "Get lost," he said to her quietly. She stood and hurried past Captain Steele, disappearing through the door.

"Sorry to interrupt your work, you fat pig," Max said, and pointed to the door behind him. "She's young enough to be your daughter, you piece of dog shit."

"If you came here to insult me …."

"I came here for more than that, but now that I'm here, I find it irresistible. There's just so much material."

The Warden squared his rotund frame with his chair and sat back down. "What do you want?"

"For starters, I want no more funny stuff in this facility – from you or from your staff."

"Funny stuff?" the Warden said.

"Or I will launch a federal investigation."

"Look Steele, I don't know what …."

"The hell you don't," Max said, and leaned over the desk. "And by the way, every time you speak, I hear elephants farting."

The Warden glared and said nothing.

Max stepped around the desk, towering over the seated Warden. "I want Vincente Bontecelli transferred to another supermax out of the state. One within easy driving distance for those of us who want to visit. Given the cluster of states in the Northeast, that should be easy enough for you to arrange."

"You know I can't do that without a judge's order."

"Don't tell me your problems," Max said. "You have 30 days. Then I bring this whole house down around your ears." Max turned to go.

"Wait, Steele," the Warden said, holding up both hands. "I'll need 60 days." He paused. "But I'll get it done."

"Deal," Max said, "but in the meantime, I don't want to see or hear about a mark on Bontecelli's body, not even diaper rash. You got me?"

The Warden nodded but Max had already turned and walked out.

"Prick," Warden Antonelli said. He reached into his bottom left desk drawer and took out the lock box. He placed his eye to the retinal scanner and it buzzed. The lid unlatched and he opened it. The cell phone flashed, indicating a voicemail message. He dialed and entered the pass code.

FBI Headquarters, Northeast
Providence, Rhode Island

Lists, data, and reports. Nobody told FBI recruits that the majority of their job was administration and research. The administrative work drove Lt. Bert Higgins nuts. Lists and reports. But research was a different story. Research was like finding a story waiting to be told, if a clever agent could uncover it. He remembered the day, the moment, the phrase jumped into his head: the devil is in the details and that's good, because we are in the business of catching devils. He was in class and remembered scribbling it in the side margin of his notes. He'd never forgotten it, and remembering it transformed research projects from drudgery into adventure.

Max would be almost to Mantisto State Prison by now. It was good that they split up. Very good. Bert had been looking for an opportunity to do the "eyes only" research FBI Director Elizabeth Fenton had ordered. This research, though, didn't feel like embarking on an adventure. It felt more like betrayal, and it pissed him off to have to do it.

He pulled up the list. The name on the top of the list of Kingstown Memorial Hospital employees to investigate was Dr. Maria Sanchez. He'd been ordered by Director Fenton to conduct the background on Sanchez separately, in a separate and sealed file for her eyes only. If Max Steele learned of it .... Bert sighed. He couldn't even go there. The surface, professional part of Max Steele would probably understand. But the fact that his own partner hadn't discussed it with him first – even if he had been ordered to keep it to himself – would change their relationship. Maybe destroy it. This secrecy shit. It was like sucker punching your brother, mentor, and friend. But if he didn't do what he was told, he could lose everything. He'd worked hard to get into the FBI and to become a Special Agent.

But, on the other hand, Director Fenton was right. Dr. Sanchez's name did keep showing up in places that raised a legitimate concern, if not full-on suspicion. Bert opened the manila file in front of him and picked up the visitor log for Nina Ondolopous Bente. It was pages long, since every orderly, nurse, aide, and doctor were listed on it. Visitors from the outside were forbidden, but the officer stationed at the door had been instructed to take down full information from anyone who tried. That list was blank.

Bert's eyes scanned the list again and reached for his coffee. There was only one way to tackle a list this long: one name at a time. He remembered something his father told him growing up on the farm. Always tackle the crappiest jobs first and get them out of the way. He turned to the computer and typed in the name that had appeared three times on the visitor list: Dr. Maria Sanchez.

Director Fenton's question was on point. Why was her name on there at all? The ICU was not her department. She was an Emergency Room doc. So why three visits to that room?

Max had seen the list earlier when the two of them were at the crime scene. Higgins had seen his partner page through the list. He had to have seen Maria's name there, but he had passed the list to Higgins without a word. Why? Why wasn't her name a red flag for him? Was there something Max knew that he wasn't telling him? Or did he just assume his girlfriend was above reproach? He ran a hand over the top of his head. He reached for the pump bottle of hand sanitizer and spat the liquid into his hand.

It was probably nothing. He rubbed his hands, rubbed and turned each hand in the other. This whole thing. Probably nothing. He pressed the search button and the screen exploded with hundreds of Maria Sanchezes. Now, to narrow the search.

Bente Residence
Venice, Italy

The birthday celebration was held in the Garden. Emil would have preferred a live orchestra playing in the front left corner. It was a perfect spot for such entertainment. But secrecy dictated prerecorded music only. Everyone understood. All the Marias were in attendance, except for Maria Sanchez, and Maria Garza, whom Emil granted leave to return immediately to the base of U.S. operations in Rhode Island.

Mother Maria was the last to arrive. That was by design, so that the full complement of well-wishers would be waiting when she appeared. The room was a smattering of reds, whites, and blacks. Everyone was Roman Catholic clergy of one kind or another. The cardinals were in red and white. The Marias were in their black habits and flowing garments. Only

Emil Bente was clad in non-clerical garb. He straightened his black bow tie and snapped the coat tails of his tuxedo.

When she wheeled into the room, every person took a knee and bowed their head until she had positioned herself in the midst of them. Then, everyone stood and applauded. Mother Maria was clad in the white clerical dress of the Mother Superior that she had been. It was a last minute decision. Her wrinkled cheeks sagged over the rigid edges of her hood seams, and a pearl and diamond studded rosary hung from her neck.

The people in the room automatically queued to speak to her and to receive her blessing. One by one, they stepped before her wheelchair, knelt, took her hand, spoke their birthday wishes and received her blessing. For each person, she kissed the cross hanging at the end of the rosary around her neck and then made the sign of the cross with her arm outstretched.

Emil knew the line was long, and that Mother Maria's blessing was important to the people who stood in that line. He also knew his mother would be exhausted by the end of it. But all of them knew this might be the last opportunity to receive the blessing of the founder of this vast, and mostly secret, Order.

As head of domestic and foreign operations for the Cartel that this Order supported, Emil knew that most of the guests would also want to speak to him. He positioned himself in the back right corner across from the waterfall and received people after they had spoken with Mother Maria. Out of deference, the three Cardinals were shown to the front of the line and thus were the first to receive the Holy Mother's blessing. They were also the first to speak with him.

Cardinal Nicolo approached Emil, and the two men hugged.

"I need a cigarette," Cardinal Nicolo said, and the two men laughed.

"It's not worth the lecture from the Holy Mother," Emil said.

"Once a mother, always a mother I guess," the Cardinal said.

"You have no idea," Emil said, shaking his head.

"Oh?" he said. "New developments?"

"Yes Father," Emil said. "She is still like a caged tiger who knows how to pick her own lock: untamable and quite dangerous."

"It's what keeps her young," Cardinal Nicolo said.

"It's what keeps me hopping," Emil said, and laughed.

"Could be worse," the Cardinal said.

As the words left the Cardinal's lips, Emil noticed that a hush had fallen over the room. A man had entered the Garden dressed in khaki chinos, flip-flops, and a flowered Hawaiian shirt unbuttoned to the sternum. A wad of chest hair protruded like frayed wires. The person kneeling before the Holy Mother had just stood, and the man walked directly in front of the next person in line, and knelt before her.

Emil stood very still, as all eyes watched the Holy Mother and the man they all recognized.

Emil Bente watched his brother carefully.

The Holy Mother sat very still, gazing upon the man in the flowered shirt. Then she held out her hand. The man hesitated, then took her hand, and brushed his lips against it. She blessed him, he rose, and just as perfunctorily as he had arrived, he scuffed from the room without speaking or making eye contact with anyone.

"Speaking of worse," Cardinal Nicolo said. He moved off as the other two cardinals approached Emil.

At last, the final person in the line received the Holy Mother's blessing and stood. Emil excused himself from the small crowd surrounding him, and made his way to his mother. He passed by the refreshment table and grabbed one of the flutes of champagne.

"Some refreshment, Mother?" he said.

"The most refreshing thing," she said evenly, "would be to get the hell out of here, and out of these clothes."

"Now Mother Maria, don't be like that," he said. He handed her the champagne. She drank the entire flute in several large gulps. Her throat trembled with each swallow.

"What I need is a large snifter of cognac," she said, and her son laughed.

"I'll see what I can do," he said. "You are much loved and revered, Mother Maria."

"Do you know what the Marias said to me, each of them as they knelt?" She looked up at her son. "They thanked me for saving them."

"And so they should, Mother," he said.

"I'm not sure who saved whom," she said. "Remember when we first started gathering them? They were a scrawny troop of alley cats. Now look at them."

"They are strong and powerful women," Emil said.

"It was the least that a disgraced nun could do. They were a handful of young girls on the street, begging, whoring, doing whatever to survive. There were hundreds more. Pity we were only able to raise up a handful."

"And that handful let you know again tonight how grateful they are for the lives they have now," Emil said, "as am I, Mother."

She sighed, "Well, that's one of you."

"Ignore him, Mother," Emil said.

She looked at her hands. "Would you care to guess what he said to me?" she said softly. "Your brother?"

"I have no brother and I do not care what he said," Emil said.

"Oh, but you do, dear boy. He is your brother."

"By blood only," Emil said, and felt his lip begin to twist. He caught it and smiled.

She continued as if he hadn't spoken. "He said, 'I'm only here because I'd never hear the end of it otherwise.'"

"And we should be grateful that he graced us with his presence, right?" Emil said.

"Blood is blood, son," she said.

"He would do well to remember that his blood spills just like everybody else's."

"Please don't threaten him in my presence," she said.

"If he dishonors the name ...." Emil said.

"I'll not tell you again," she said, and the edge in her voice was sharp enough to sever an ear.

"Yes, Mother," Emil said.

"You are both my sons," she said.

Emil nodded and headed for the champagne. He caught the eye of Maria Milagra and motioned her to him.

"The Holy Mother would like a snifter of cognac," he said to her. "It's in my quarters, underneath the wet bar."

"Would you like to show me where it is?" she said, and looked at him with raised brows.

He clasped his hands, and whispered, "The last time I showed you where something was, we wound up showing each other a great deal more."

She whispered back, "As I recall, we forgot completely what we were looking for."

His voice was barely above a whisper, and he leaned toward her. "Perhaps both of us knew exactly what we were looking for." He shook his head and smiled. "You know I'd just end up having to go to confession, again, before I leave."

"Might be worth it," she said.

"You might need a swat, you bad girl," he said.

"I might like that too," she said and wandered away from him toward the interior of the house.

Emil willed himself not to follow her. And then lost his will. As he was making his way out of the room, Cardinal Nicolo intercepted him.

"Just the person I didn't want to see," Emil said.

"I figured," the Cardinal said, looking toward the now empty doorway into and out of the garden. "You Bentes are a hot blooded lot."

Emil nodded and laughed. "Two parts human, eight parts hound."

"I recommend celibacy," he said, "and cigarettes."

"Speaking of cigarettes," Emil said, "you must be about to chew on a ten penny nail," Emil said.

The Cardinal nodded, "Railroad spike. Now, you going to behave? Or do I have to stay here and babysit? Don't you leave in the morning?"

"Yes. No. And Yes," Emil said, and laughed. "Try not to light up until you get to the tunnel, Father." The two men hugged, and the Cardinal left.

Emil put his unfinished flute of champagne on the table, and stepped into a crowd of people. Presently, he saw a somber Maria Milagra return to the room carrying a snifter of cognac to the Holy Mother. While Mother and Maria Milagra were still chatting, he slipped from the room, made his way to his quarters, and locked himself in.

Celibacy. Didn't matter how many cigarettes he smoked, he never would have made it as a priest. But then, a lot of priests and nuns he knew didn't make it, either. The church had made it the forbidden fruit, but even the most disciplined disciples were vulnerable to its allure.

Chapter Six

Private Airstrip
Kingstown, Rhode Island

Porous. For all the money the United States socked into security and surveillance, their airports remained as porous as a cheap colander. They could strain out and catch the amateurs who attempted access, but the pros came and went as they pleased.

Emil smiled behind his oxygen mask. He felt the jet slow to taxi speed and knew that soon he would be in the hangar. He owned the plane, but it wasn't in his name. He owned the hangar, but that wasn't in his name, either. For all the assets at his disposal, Emil Bente was a paper pauper. On paper, he was an undocumented minnow; in reality, he was the Shark. He owned and controlled almost everything.

The flight paperwork showed transport of cargo only and no passengers. They had closed him into the specially lined wooden cargo box in Venezia and loaded him onto the plane. Now, they would unload and truck him to the back of the self-storage facility on the outskirts of Kingstown. His customized transport box contained two bottles of oxygen, one primary, and the other a backup bottle, in case one failed or delivery was delayed.

In moments like these, he thanked God he wasn't claustrophobic. The seal on the box was so tight, and the box was lined with so many jamming and cloaking layers, that the only sound inside was the soft hissing of oxygen as it passed through the plastic tubes to the cone covering his nose and mouth. It was larger than the hazmat barrel that carried him out of Mantisto State Prison, but not much.

He reflected, not the first time, how much this method of transport resembled being buried alive. He also considered how vulnerable he was in these moments. Someone wanting to eliminate him would have an easy time of it. There were lots of ways to kill a man sealed in a box. That's why so many precautions were taken and only the most loyal people were involved. It is amazing how careful people are when they know that even the appearance of placing him at risk would result not only in their death, but also in the death of every family member. Even the pets.

Emil considered himself a tolerant man, but every man had his limits. And every woman hers. He thought of his mother, that pillar of strength, who had ruled the Cartel with a fist that was still strong, despite her age. There was no doubt in anyone's mind who was in charge. She had earned her place. She had earned respect. He wished the world knew what a dynamic leader his mother had been in her life. It was a powerful life, but it was anonymous. The world would never know his mother's greatness, and he wished she would make peace with that. He would let mother write the memoir, and as soon as she breathed her last, he would erase it from the face of the earth.

He snuffed into the mask. What the world saw with its eyes, and heard with its ears, was theater. It was the highest form of deception, and the Bente Cartel was one of the international forces that kept it that way. But the entire system was dependent upon three interrelated things that were not negotiable. They were like the points of attachment a spider makes for its web, the anchors. One was that the Name must never be dishonored, and it didn't matter whether you were a blood relative or a complete stranger. If you dishonored the Name, you were erased, along with every trace that you ever existed. Another was that you must be an asset and not a liability. If, by your action or inaction, you placed the Cartel at risk, you were eliminated. Carefully and completely. And the last was loyalty. Divided loyalty was no loyalty at all. It was this connection point of the web that had Emil most concerned.

One of the Marias was compromised, or was about to be. He had promised to give Maria Garza a chance to handle it, but then he would take over.

The box jostled. He was being moved. The truck was next. He focused on his breathing and said the rosary he clutched in his hand. It was as essential to him in these moments as the oxygen he breathed.

Self-Storage Warehouse
Kingstown, Rhode Island

"Carefully," Carlos said to Gregorio, his younger brother. "Better yet, let me open it." Gregorio stepped back from the box. Within minutes, Carlos had the top unsealed. He motioned for his brother to take the other end. They lifted the top and set it aside. Emil Bente sat up and snapped the oxygen mask from his face.

He smiled at Carlos and then at his brother. "Water," he said. Carlos had a large bottle of his favorite brand on a chair. This was not his first time, and he knew what Emil Bente expected. He had explained it to his brother until both could recite it from memory, "Do what you are told. Then remember what you've been told, and do it again the next time without being told. That is obedience."

"Right here, Excellency," Carlos said, and brought him the water. Emil drank it down, handed the bottle back and said, "Lift me out and into a chair."

Carlos and Gregorio lifted Emil from the box, each taking an arm and a leg, and set him gently into the folding chair. Emil sat, flexing his elbows and knees, and breathing deeply. His body needed to adjust after hours in the box, although this trip was comparatively easy. The hazmat barrel that got him from the prison to the airport, and from the airport to Italy, had been much more challenging. Because the lockdown had been so long, and the search for him so thorough, nothing had been allowed in or out of the prison until the next day. Emil's oxygen had gotten dangerously low by the time he was unsealed.

"Stand me up until I get my legs under me, and then get me to the restroom," Emil said. "You have my change of clothes?"

"Waiting for you in the restroom, Excellency," Carlos said.

"I'm ready to get this diaper off," Emil said, chuckling. "It's the most humiliating part of all this." He flashed to the barrel again. There had been no diaper for that trip. By the time the barrel was unsealed, Emil was squatting in a prison jumper filled with his own shit.

The restroom had been appointed with a shower and a dressing area. As soon as he walked in, Emil noticed that it was spotless and that it smelled of myrrh.

"Well done, Carlos," he said. "Just the way I like it."

"Excellency," Carlos said with a smile and a bow, "we will wait for you in the office."

"We've much do in a very short time," Emil said.

The office door opened. Gregorio and Carlos were wearing latex gloves. They had been cleaning the sniper rifle and sorting ammunition. The person who stepped through the door caused both men to pause, oil rags and gun parts in their hands.

It was an elderly woman. She wore a nun's habit on her head that wrapped her forehead and fell in creases to her neck. Her gray hair was visible only in wisps, and it was mostly hidden by the habit and the shawl draped over her head. The simple canvas dress fell to the tops of her feet, and it was drawn at the waist by a simple rope belt.

"*Buenos Dias*," the woman said in a deep voice that was anything but feminine.

"Excellency," Carlos said. "You look … like a nun from my village growing up."

"The clothing you got me is a work of genius, Carlos," Emil said.

"It was my brother Gregorio, Excellency, who came up with the idea, much as I would like to take credit."

"Gregorio, come to me," Emil said, and reached into a pocket of the dress. Gregorio dried his hands on a rag and knelt in front of Emil, head bowed. Emil could see that he was trembling. Emil placed a hand atop his head. "May you be blessed and richly rewarded for your service. Hold out your hand."

When Gregorio held his hand out, still bowed low, Emil placed in it a large bundle of bills with a rosary on top. "This rosary is the one I used to pray through my trip here. May it bless you with abundance, you and your entire family." He closed Gregorio's hand over the gifts and lifted him to a standing position. "Now give an old lady a hug."

All three men laughed and Emil hugged them both.

"Now, to business," Emil said. "Carlos, do you have the hat?"

"*Sí*, I mean, yes Excellency," Carlos said, and reached under the table behind him and brought up a round box.

"Is it precisely like mine?"

"It is, Excellency," Carlos said.

"Gloves," the Shark said, and held out his hand for a nitrile pair. He snapped them on his hands and lifted the box lid. Inside was an exact replica of the felt hat he wore last time he was in Rhode Island. The band even had a feather the same color as the one that now rested in its retirement in Venice, Italy.

"It's perfect," Emil said. "Carlos, come to me," Emil said, and reached into a pocket of the dress. The man kneeled before him. Emil pulled a wad of bills from the other pocket of his dress and placed it in Carlos's hand with the same blessing he had given Gregorio.

"See to it that it gets delivered as soon as possible," he said.

"Next item of business," Emil said. "I have a personal delivery to make. Since I will be in public, I need the best protection you can provide. I want the minimum number of security personnel, but they have to be your most trusted men and women. And your most skilled, in the event of trouble."

"When?" Carlos said.

"Tomorrow afternoon. Does that give you enough time?"

"We will make it happen," Carlos said.

"Next item of business," Bente said, "is our sister, Maria Sanchez. I am concerned, Carlos."

"Yes, Excellency. We are concerned too. We thought she might be part of the incident we had to take care of the other night."

"Yes, the incident. We will talk about that in a moment," Emil said. "Right now, I want to talk only about Maria. Was she involved?"

"She was not, sir," Carlos said. "I confronted her and was satisfied she had nothing to do with it."

"Good," Emil said. "I fear she is compromised by her … relationship with our friend, Captain Max Steele."

"We have solid surveillance on every area of her life. Her house is bugged and we have recorded every word. Her car is bugged. The clinic is bugged. We listen to everything, sir."

"And?"

"And we have been waiting to tell Maria Garza. She has been worried. Our report is that all of a sudden, the situation seems to be working itself out."

"What does that mean?"

"Perhaps it would be good for you to listen to the conversation Maria Sanchez and Captain Steele had last evening in her home," Carlos said.

"My time is precious," Emil said. "Is it worth my time to listen to this recording?"

"I believe it is, Excellency. It may diminish your concerns."

"Then let's have a listen."

"Now, sir?"

"Now," Emil said.

"Captain Steele is a confident man," Emil said, chuckling.

"He doesn't like you much," Carlos said, smiling.

"What a pity," the Shark said. "It does indeed sound as if Maria Garza had cause for concern. But you are correct. It looks like it is working itself out without our intervention. So far."

"Yes Excellency," Carlos said. "So far."

"After I leave on my errand, contact Maria Garza. Tell her I wish to speak with her about a reassignment."

"A reassignment for Dr. Maria Sanchez?" Gregorio said. "An extraction?"

"*Sí*, Gregorio," Emil Bente said. "You are as smart as you are efficient. Speaking of, have we pulled all of our people from the hospital at this point?"

"Yes Excellency," Gregorio said, and smiled.

"Good," Emil said. "Then let Steele enjoy himself tearing Memorial Hospital apart. I like having him busy looking in all the wrong places. We'll not have to deal with him directly unless he gets close again. Please keep me updated."

"One complication, Excellency," Carlos said.

"I'm listening."

"The FBI is following Maria Sanchez."

Emil started. "For how long? And why?"

"One car. Two days. And we don't know."

"What do they think they know?" Emil said. "Your opinion?"

"Don't know, Excellency. Could be they are grabbing at the wind. Maybe watching hospital staff who knew the, uh, victim, you know?"

"A guess, but possible," Emil said.

Carlos nodded. "We've been watching the watcher. One car. The agent seems bored. Never on his radio. Plays a lot of games on his phone."

"Not exactly readying himself to kick down her door?" Bente said, chuckling. "Okay."

"But we do need your guidance, Excellency," Gregorio said. "We've talked about what to do – watch, wait, act. It's not a simple decision."

"Explain."

"If we take out the watcher," he said, "we eliminate anyone seeing something they shouldn't at the clinic. But once we've taken him out, we've telegraphed to the Feds that there's something worth watching."

"I see," Emil Bente said.

"Maria's gone by the time the truck comes for pick up, which means the watcher is also gone."

"You sure?"

"We're sure."

"Then, for now, keep watching the watcher," Emil said. "If he becomes more interested, let's talk again. In the meantime, Maria Garza plans to visit Maria Sanchez."

"When?"

"Tomorrow," Bente said.

"I will alert Pablo," Carlos said.

"Now, I'm sorry to rush you, but I will not be here more than two days and there's much to attend to while I'm here."

"At your disposal," Carlos said.

"Okay, next item of business," Emil said. "The incident at the hospital. We need to mop that up," Emil said. "I want no trace left of that assassin."

"Hmm," Carlos said, and looked at Gregorio.

"A problem?"

"*Sí*, Excellency," Carlos said. "This assassin. He is a very … private man."

"You don't know who he is."

"No one knows," Carlos said. "We're checking. Looking."

"He's a loose end," Emil said, glaring. "Find him." He looked at each man for several long seconds. The intensity of his stare was withering, and he knew it. "Listen to me very carefully. Erase him. This operation succeeds or fails, lives or dies, on how we deal with loose ends. There is no more important work." He paused. "It is not enough to tie up some loose ends. Some need to be cauterized so the ends will never connect to us again. Am I making myself clear?"

Carlos and Gregorio nodded. He saw that beads of sweat had formed on both men's lips. Good.

"Cauterize him," Emil said. "Any assistants, too, if he has not already disposed of them himself."

"*Sí* Excellency," Carlos said, and looked to Gregorio, who nodded.

"Okay Carlos, let's talk about the incident at Miserericordia Clinic Tuesday. I want every detail. We're going to snuff this fire out before it gets going, and definitely before the FBI begins to smell smoke. You following me?"

"Following you," Gregorio said, and glanced at Carlos.

"We follow you," Carlos said. He detailed everything he had witnessed from the hillside and recounted how he and Pablo took the men out before they got inside the clinic. "Gregorio took the bodies back to the warehouse."

"Is that where they are now?" the Shark said. "May I see them?"

Carlos was silent for a moment. "Yes and no, Excellency. We disposed of the bodies that night."

"Acid?"

"With the acid, yes," Carlos said, nodding. "But we saved you the feet."

"You what?"

"Gregorio, get the dry ice."

Gregorio hurried from the room. He returned a moment later with a white Styrofoam chest. When he removed the lid, two clear plastic packages were nested in a smoking pile of dry ice.

"We wanted you to see," Carlos said.

"The feet," Emil said.

"The tattoos on the bottom of the right foot," Carlos said, nodding. "Same for both men." He lifted one of the bags by the clasped opening and set it on the table.

Emil watched Carlos as he snapped his stiletto open and sliced through the bag.

The foot was blue and red where it had been chopped from the leg, and the toes had turned a haunting shade of purple.

Emil snapped his fingers and motioned with his hand for gloves. He lifted a foot and turned it over. Tattooed on the arch was an upside down cross with a large viper coiled at the intersection. A skull hung from its mouth.

Emil crossed himself.

"*Sí*," Carlos said.

At that moment, a wisp of dry ice smoke wafted over the foot in Emil's hand. He dropped it like he'd been shocked. The fingers of his hand went rigid, and he sucked in a breath.

"See that?" Emil said, and shuddered. He looked at the two men. They nodded. As one, all three crossed themselves.

Silence hung in the room. Emil blinked, then blinked again. He felt the ache in his jaw begin again. He pointed at the foot and then at the ice chest at his feet. "Gregorio, to the acid. Quickly."

Gregorio nodded, grabbed up the foot and the bag in the plastic sheet, stuffed it in the cooler, and hurried with it from the room.

"So," Emil said, and took another deep breath.

"*Sí*," Carlos said. "You needed to see for yourself, yes?"

"Yes, for myself." Emil said. He stood and paced the room, still in his disguise.

Carlos wanted to ask him to remove the costume, wondered if God was angry with them because of it, saw the smoke and the foot in his mind again, and shuddered.

"Who are we dealing with?" Emil said, more to himself than to Carlos. "Who wants our business and thinks we're weak because of the FBI's takedown? Yes, who thinks we're ripe for a takeover?" He started to pace more quickly. "And then there's the how."

"The how," Carlos said, repeating.

"Yes, Carlos, the how," Emil said. "How does our adversary know so much about the operation? How would he know our trucks? And our cleaning business? Our routes and our pickup times?" He jammed a finger at Carlos. "And that, THAT, takes us right back to the who question."

"The who," Carlos said, not knowing what else to say. Gregorio slipped back into the room.

"Right," Emil said. "Who is feeding intel to them that's so secret that only a very small handful of us within the organization know it? You see what I'm getting at?"

"*Sí*, yes," Carlos said.

"So let's think for a second about who, in this small handful of people, it could be."

"And Friday is in two days."

Emil stopped pacing and stared at Carlos. "So?"

"So, Friday's a pickup day," Carlos said. "They might try again."

"I'll be gone by then," Emil said. "Can you handle it?"

"Oh, we'll handle it. No doubt about it."

"But right now, find the leak," Emil said. "Soon as you do, I'll come back and plug it myself." He slammed his hand so hard on the table that Carlos and Gregorio jumped. "Now, ready your men for the visit I need to make," Bente said. "You have the address?"

"I do," Carlos said.

"You and Gregorio are with me," Emil said. A moment later when Emil turned around, he was alone. Carlos and Gregorio had stood and left the room without making a sound. They were the only men Emil knew who could appear and disappear soundlessly, without even disturbing the air.

Emil straightened his robes. He was good at cleaning up messes, excellent in fact, but this was a big one. One misstep and the whole base of U.S. operations could be compromised. In his mind, he saw the bottoms of the feet again. The tattoo. His competitor was sloppy to etch an identifier like that onto his people. Sloppy. Or arrogant. Or – Emil didn't want to think about it – so lethal he didn't have to concern himself with anonymity. He might need help to deal with this adversary, perhaps more help than the Marias, Carlos, and Gregorio could provide. But not yet.

Office of Elizabeth Fenton, Director
FBI Headquarters, Northeast
Providence, Rhode Island

Director Elizabeth Fenton knew rot when she smelled it. She had developed a nose for it, a sixth sense. "There's rot behind the desk," she said.

"Beg pardon?" Chief Jeremiah Simone said, the late Timothy Parker's replacement as Kingstown Police Station Chief.

"It's a phrase we used … it doesn't matter … a long time ago," Director Fenton said. "Means we've got dirty cops somewhere in the system."

Simone gave a single nod. "My granddaddy used to say every ear of corn looks perfect 'til you pull down on the shuck. He'd point and say, 'See them rows? Nice and straight. See them ears, full and beautiful. But there's rot inside some of them ears. Some of them are just pretending.'"

The director nodded. "I can't tell if the rot's in your cornfield or mine. Anything's possible, I suppose," she said. She looked at the ceiling. "This is the kind of stuff that makes me want to surrender my badge, just slip into retirement in a cabin in the woods."

"Know what you mean, Director," Simone fidgeted in his chair.

"This whole … thing, system, department," she made a sweeping gesture with her arms spread wide, "is supported by the pillars of trust and teamwork. When you haven't got those, down comes the house."

"You can't tell who's who."

She nodded. "Bad guys make their living leading double lives. The best ones are good enough to hide in plain sight," she said.

Simone snuffed. "And how do you deal with the bad guys out there on the street, when you're looking at your own guys and wondering."

"So Parker was a shock?"

"Couldda knocked me over with a feather," Simone said. "I served as his assistant for seven years. Knew him for 20. He's godfather to my youngest son. How do you recover from a betrayal that deep?" He uncrossed his legs and leaned forward. "Now, I'm looking at my people, knowing I've got to deploy them, knowing I've got to depend on them, but I'm watching them from the corners of my eyes."

"Your man, Lester, at the hospital," the Director said. "Dirty?"

He shook his head. "Clean, pretty sure, but I still had to cut him from the squad. Very least, he's too stupid to be on my team." He sighed.

"Got a call from my Captain, Steele," Fenton said. "Know him?"

"By sight and by reputation only," Simone said. "Guy's a legend."

The Director continued, "Steele said he thought Lester was clean. No need to go the indictment route."

"Agree," Chief Simone said. "Shame, though. One of our good ones just lost his job."

"Couldn't have been that good. You just said he's stupid."

"You know what I mean, Director," Simone said. She watched the blood rise in his neck. "Every mistake's a learning experience, but some mistakes are terminal. They end your career."

"I apologize. I was being sarcastic," Fenton said. She ran her hand across her forehead. "What do you say when there's nothing to say?"

Simone looked at his hands.

"But something's up at that hospital," Fenton said. "I can smell it."

"I'd be taking a hard look at that prison, too," Simone said.

"Oh, we are," Fenton said. "We are looking at everything. Everyone."

"And meanwhile," Simone said, "the thousands of bad guys on the street get to keep doing all they're doing, because they've got us so busy looking for worms in our own corn."

"Brilliant strategy, don't you think?"

"I remember when cops were damn near incorruptible," Chief Simone said.

"No, you don't," she said. "Look at history. You just think you do."

"Guess I was naïve."

"No," she said, "you trusted people."

"And now I'm paranoid."

She laughed. "Right. It's the invisible stripe they sew on your sleeve when you get promoted."

"Lucky me."

"Lucky us."

The phone rang. Director Fenton lifted the receiver and listened. Replaced it. "My next appointment is here," she said. "I know you are reviewing every officer's file, and pulling out every desk and looking behind it, so to speak. Let me know if you find anything."

The Chief rose from his chair and took the hand extended to him across the desk. He nodded and turned for the door. A knock sounded as his hand reached the handle. He swung the door and found himself inches from the face of Lt. Bert Higgins. A stack of files bulged under the young man's arm.

"Well, now," Chief Simone said with a smile, "Good morning, Lieutenant." He shook Higgins's free hand.

"Every day's a holiday, Chief," Bert said.

"Yeah, on the Alcatraz calendar," he said, and laughed.

"She beat you up pretty good?" Higgins said, smiling and nodding at Director Fenton who still stood behind her desk.

"Nah, but think I'll go ahead and kill myself anyway," Simone said.

"Good plan," Bert said, and clapped him on the shoulder as he passed. Chief Simone gave a thumbs-up over his shoulder as he left. Bert closed the door and turned to Director Fenton.

"How well do you know him?" she said, sitting down and stacking together a pile of papers.

"Simone?" Bert said.

She shook her head. "Steele, of course. Focus, Lieutenant Higgins." She held her hand out for his files.

"Sorry, Director," he said. "Been up all night. Punchy, I guess."

"Go splash water on your face, fix your tie, and hit the coffee pot for two cups on your way back."

"Yes, ma'am," Higgins said, the smile long gone from his face.

"And if you ever come into my office like this again – looking like hell and speaking flip about me," she said, still not looking up, "there will be a letter in your file. We clear on this?"

"Yes, Director Fenton," the Lieutenant said.

"Go," she fanned with the back of her hand, "and get back here, stat, with that coffee. One of those cups is for me." She opened the file marked "Elizabeth Fenton, Director. Eyes only."

She heard the door open and close. "Such a bitch, Lizzie," she said, barely above a whisper. *That kid stayed up all night spying on his partner and the girlfriend, and you take his head off.* She thought about her conversation with Simone. You go from naïve to paranoid in this business. And if you get promoted, you get the privilege of becoming jaded, cynical, and an all-star bitch. Congratulations. You get your own small cell, with bricks in each wall that you stacked there yourself. No one gets in. And you can't get out. "Such a bitch," she whispered, and put her head into a nest of arms and elbows on her desk.

The Director's phone chirped and she jerked. Pain shot across her shoulders. It had returned. She lifted the receiver and listened. Her assistant was accustomed to the lack of greeting when Fenton answered, and said, "Lieutenant Higgins is back."

"Does he have coffee?"

"Yes, ma'am," the assistant said.

"Then he may come in."

When Lt. Higgins entered, the Director was impressed at the effort the young agent had put into his appearance. Much more presentable. "Thank you," she said, when he offered the coffee. "Take a seat." Higgins placed himself in one of the two chairs opposite the Director. "Let me ask you again," she said. "How well do you know Max Steele?"

"I'd say I know him well," he said. "We spend a lot of time together."

"At work?"

"Yes, ma'am."

"How about outside of work?" Director Fenton said.

"No, ma'am," he said. "Not so much."

"And how about Dr. Maria Sanchez?" Director Fenton said. "Do you know her well too?"

"I do not, Director," he said.

"Other than what you have been able to dig up about her in the past 24 hours?"

"Affirmative."

She had continued to scan the top folder. "Appears to be an impressive job of research," she said. "Why don't you hit the highlights for me? Anything stand out?"

"She used to be a Roman Catholic nun," he said. "That stood out."

"I'll just bet," she said. "What else?"

"I can't find any … documentation to suggest that she left the Order."

"So as far as you know, Maria Sanchez is still a nun?"

"As far as I have been able to document," Higgins said, "yes."

Elizabeth Fenton sucked air through clenched teeth. "Think Steele knows?"

"You need to ask him," Higgins said.

The Director blinked and looked up. The face of the young detective seated across from her was as red as if he had been scalded. "I don't NEED to do anything, Detective."

"Yes, ma'am," Higgins said, not looking at her.

"Look," she said. "I know this is difficult. It gives me no pleasure to assign you this task." She watched for a reaction. Got none. Bert Higgins stared straight ahead, his jaw muscles taught, his back straight and unmoving. "Let's proceed," she said. "Anything else stand out?"

"Only that I cannot trace Maria Sanchez all the way back, like to birth certificates and such," Higgins said.

"Say more."

"She appears in public records about the time she entered the Order," he said.

"Roman Catholic, you said?"

Higgins nodded. "In Italy."

"And what do you make of this … gap from birth to ordination, Lieutenant?"

"I'm not sure, Director," he said.

"Your hunch?" she said.

Higgins was silent for a few moments. "The question I'm asking myself," he said at last, "is whether she was adopted into an orphanage run by nuns and never registered as a citizen. We are, after all, talking about Italy."

"With a last name like Sanchez," the Director said.

Higgins nodded. "Yes, ma'am. That's what got me thinking she might have been orphaned and adopted."

"Where in Italy?"

"I beg your pardon?" he said. "Where what?"

"Where is her Catholic Order?"

"Venice."

"Take this file back," Director Fenton said, and handed it to him, "and keep digging. I want more."

"Yes, ma'am," Higgins said.

"Oh, and Lieutenant?"

"Yes, Director?"

"How would you characterize the relationship between Captain Steele and Dr. Sanchez?"

Higgins was silent.

"Lieutenant?" she said.

"With respect, ma'am, I'd like to request a transfer."

Director Fenton had been scribbling a note to herself. She stopped and put the pen down. When she looked up, she saw the same fixed stare across from her as before, and the same set jaw line. He was a man looking at nothing, and ready for anything. Present, but unavailable. She'd seen detectives bunker up like this before, and it was always to protect something they cared about. Deeply.

"Your request is denied," she said. "Look, Detective, some things about our work are … messy, but necessary, to get to the bottom of things. We have to set personal feelings aside."

Higgins was silent, as immovable as a statue. No, not a statue, she thought. A heavy rock, solid and silent. In her mind's eye, she watched Lieutenant Higgins place his partner behind him for cover.

"Let me assure you, Lieutenant," she said, "that I hold your partner in high esteem and would not want you to interpret my probing as an attack upon him."

Silence returned from the rock across from her. She had to admire his unwillingness to play the game with her. So many young agents would ransom their mothers to rise within the chain of command. She took in a breath and folded her hands in front of her on the desk.

"Let's try again, Detective Higgins," she said. "How would you characterize the relationship between Captain Steele and Dr. Sanchez?"

"I wouldn't have knowledge about that, ma'am," Higgins said, still not looking her in the eye.

"Fair enough," she said. "Continue the surveillance detail on Sanchez. I want to know where she goes and what she does."

Higgins was silent.

"You may go," she said.

After he left, she nodded to herself. *They are a good team, Steele and Higgins. Loyalty like that cannot be taught and it cannot be bought.* She drank from her coffee cup. *But it can cause temporary blindness. Like love.*

FBI Headquarters
Providence, Rhode Island

Lieutenant Higgins went looking for the two things he needed most: good coffee and his partner. He hadn't touched the coffee in his hands while seated in the Director's office. He took it with him when he left and poured it in the break room sink like it was poison. He dug his phone from his jacket pocket, snapped the ringer off silent, and dialed Max's cell. After several rings, it went to voicemail.

Bert heard the beep to leave a message and checked his watch, "Hey, Cap. They keep you overnight in Mantisto? Meet me for coffee at Lavish Lattes. If you hurry, I'll buy." He ended the call and looked at his phone. It was wet. He drew a hand along the side of his head and came back with sweat. He snatched a paper towel from the roll next to the sink, tucked the files under his arm, and headed for the exit.

Lavish Lattes Café
Kingstown, Rhode Island

Lavish Lattes was located on one of Kingstown's most popular streets. Parking was a problem. Bert had directed the air-conditioning onto himself for the entire forty-minute drive from headquarters back to Kingstown, and he was finally starting to cool down. On his way out of the building, he discovered that he had soaked through his shirt. He'd left the Director's office dry, but no sooner had he left than his body reacted like he'd been in a title fight.

He'd have to warn his sparring partner at the gym tonight. He had some things to work out with his fists and his feet. Get his head back on straight. He never knew how he was feeling or what he was thinking until he had punched and kicked and sweated for an hour or so. His last girlfriend had called him a "stuffer." She said he stuffed his stress into a trunk all day long, and sat on the lid. She'd been right. But when he got the gloves on, it was like standing up and letting the lid fly open.

Bert drew his lips tight across his teeth and shut off the car. Sometimes he still missed her. There weren't many people in life who really "got" you. She understood him like no one else had. No woman anyway. Max got him, and he felt that he got Max, too. But he wasn't about to tell that to Director Bitch. His FBI cadet instructor's words shot through his head, "You always, always, get your partner out with you, no matter what the threat or how bad it gets. You always get out together." They would. They'd get out together.

The line was long inside the coffee shop, stretching almost to the glass doors. The drone of conversation, and the scuff of ceramic on wood, created its own comforting noise in his head. It dialed down the war drum that thumped in there. The Director was declaring war on the mob, and she was looking for the enemy within her own ranks. That made her dangerous. Sometimes zeal distorts vision. You see what you are looking for instead of what's really there. He knew it, but he wondered if Max knew it, wondered if he should tell Max about his director's agenda. Could he do it while also steering clear of the confidentialities inherent in his "eyes only" investigation?

Bitch. What kind of leader would send a guy's partner to dig dirt on him and his girlfriend?

He ordered his coffee and snagged a small table near the window at the front. Now, to wait for Max. It wasn't like him not to take Bert's calls. And it wasn't like Max not to return a call within thirty minutes, even if it was merely a text to say he wasn't available, working on something.

Bert wasn't worried, not yet. Max was a big boy and could take care of himself. But this was a workday, and Max was always working. Unless he was in trouble. Bert took a distracted sip of his coffee and lurched forward as the scalding hot liquid scorched his tongue. He snuffed and shook his head. What next? And suddenly he was grinning. *Ain't nuthin' but a thing.* He snapped up his phone and called Max again. It went to voicemail. Something was up. He'd give it thirty more minutes and one, maybe two, coffee refills, and then he was going to hunt down his partner.

Residence of Captain Max Steele
Kingstown, Rhode Island

Bert knocked again on Max's front door. He thought he heard rustling noises inside. Max's car was in the driveway, so chances were good he was in there. Unless somebody had come and taken him. Or come and stayed, and taken him hostage, and perhaps was still here. When you are fighting the kinds of people Emil Bente employed, anything was possible. He drew his Glock 9MM from the shoulder holster and stepped to the side of the door. As he did, he heard the dead bolt slide back from the door jam. Only with his ear close to the wall would he have been able to hear it. He reached with his free hand for the door handle, and at the same moment, it turned and the door flew open.

Bert was in a full crouch before he had taken his next breath, and his eyes were over the gun sights. "FBI," Bert called in a loud voice. "Get on the floor. Now. On your face."

"For the love of God," a weary voice said.

"Max?"

"Get in here before you give somebody else a heart attack," Max said.

Higgins stood and peered cautiously around the door jam. Max Steele was standing fifteen feet inside with a gun in his hand and a lit cigarette hanging from his lips. In his underwear. When he saw Higgins stand, he turned and walked toward the kitchen. Higgins holstered his Glock and stepped inside. The place reeked of cigarette smoke.

"What the hell are you doing?" Bert said, scanning the living room as he headed for the kitchen. He found Max with his head in the refrigerator. Only his boxer shorts and his socks were sticking out from the door. He popped his head up and cigarette ash fell to the floor.

"Wanna beer?" Max said, and raised a bottle above the door.

"It's not even noon yet," Bert said, "and you don't smoke."

"Apparently I do," Max said, and spun the cap off the bottle in his hand. He tossed the cigarette into a pile of dishes in the sink and took several long swallows of his beer. A thin trickle escaped his lips, snaked its way down his chin through whisker stubble, and dripped onto his undershirt.

"I think I got the wrong house," Bert said. "I was looking for my partner, Captain Max Steele, veteran FBI agent, and all around badass." He jammed a finger toward Max. "Now, who the hell are you?"

Max had walked away mid-sentence when Bert began speaking. He snatched the pack of cigarettes from the kitchen table, lit one, and blew smoke toward the ceiling.

"Captain Steele quit," Max said. "Sure you don't want a beer?"

"Last I checked, it was a work day."

"Not if you quit," Max said, and slugged down the rest of his beer. With a cigarette once again dangling from his lips, he shuffled in his stocking feet toward the refrigerator. Bert intercepted him halfway there and slapped the cigarette from his lips. He pushed his face close to Max's.

"I'm about to kick your ass," Bert said.

"You might be one of the few who could do it, too," Max said. "Except I cheat." Max flinched with his free hand, and in the next instant, he was hurtling backward over a kitchen chair. He landed flat on his back.

"Not if I cheat first," Bert said, leaning over him. "You want more? Or are you gonna snap out of it?"

Max reached under his back and winced. "I think I fell on my beer bottle." When he drew his hand back from beneath him, it was bloody.

"Ah shit, Max," Higgins said. "I'm sorry. I'll call EMS."

"No!" Max sat upright, breathing hard through his nose. The lower half of his undershirt was blood spotted. "No EMS. No trips to the ER," he said, chugging air. "Don't want to see that bitch."

"Ah," Bert said. "Now I get it."

"You don't get shit," Max said.

"Enough with the bluster, buddy. Sit still and let me check your back."

"I need a beer."

"You need to shut up and hold still," Bert said. He moved behind Max and lifted the undershirt slowly until it was over Max's head and off. Two pieces of glass were stuck in his lower back. They had caused quite a bleed, and a pretty big mess, but Bert saw they had barely penetrated the skin. He sucked in a deep breath.

"You're lucky Max," Bert said. "We can patch you with a little gauze and tape. Then if you still want a beer, I'll get you one."

"You got a deal, partner."

Bert convinced Max to shower, shave, and dress. The wounds were easy to treat. When Max joined him again in the living room, he was looking much more like himself.

"Better?"

"Better," Max said. "Thanks for trying to kill me, asshole."

"You deserved it," Bert said.

"Remind me to be better prepared next time I piss you off," Max said.

"Next time, answer your phone," Bert said.

"Yeah, I should've," Max said, and sat gingerly in his recliner.

"Yeah, you should've," Bert said. "For all I knew, Bente had you in here with a cattle prod up your ass."

"I know," Max said, and shook his head as if to clear water from his ears. "I just didn't want …." He trailed off.

Bert waited to see if he was going to spill it, waited a full minute in the silence, but Max just sat there rubbing his face with his hand.

"So you had a fight with Maria," Bert said.

Max laughed.

"Something funny?" Bert said.

Max nodded and continued to rub his face. "Such role reversal." Max rolled a little sideways as he laughed and then grabbed at the cuts on his back. He sucked in a breath and winced. "I used to be in your shoes with my old partner, Bull Sullivan. He loved his wife. Adored her. But Italians. Good God, they knew how to fight!"

Bert smiled. "And they'd get in a fight and Bull would funk out."

"Right," Max said, his face suddenly brightening with the memory. "And Bull would be huffin' and blowin' …."

"And drinking," Bert said.

"Yup. The dumbass."

"Like you now," Bert said.

"Okay, yes," Max said. "And I'd have to talk him back down from the cliff."

"And what would you tell him to do?"

Max shot a look across the room. He knew he'd been played. He smiled. "I'd tell him to take his ass back over there and tell her sorry."

"Anything else?"

"And have sex," Max said. He laughed and rolled sideways again until he yelped in pain.

Bert was laughing now, too. "Did you really?"

"I did." Max laughed again and caused himself a coughing fit.

"You're an idiot, Cap," Higgins said.

"Why he ever took advice from the likes of me is beyond comprehension," Max said.

Bert laughed again.

"You laugh," Max said, "but that boy always came in the next day with the biggest grin on his face."

"Women love idiots," Bert said.

“Good thing,” Max said.

“So, Captain Idiot,” Bert said, “are you going to heed your own advice and go apologize to Dr. Sanchez?”

“I don’t think she cares for me, you know, like that,” Max said. “This is different.”

“I didn’t understand a word you said,” Bert said.

“It’s okay.”

“It’s only okay if you are okay, partner,” Bert said. “I need you at a hundred percent.”

Max nodded. “And you’ve got a right to expect it,” Max said. “My head’s clearing.”

“A suggestion?” Bert said, seeing his opportunity.

“Shoot,” Max said.

“Maybe give it a rest for a bit,” he said. “You know, give it a week or two.”

“Yeah, maybe so.”

“You still want that beer?”

“Nah, but a hot cup of coffee might do wonders,” Max said.

“Grab your jacket and let’s go.”

They both heard the ring, faint but distinct, from the other room.

“My phone,” Max said.

“So NOW you’re gonna answer it,” Bert said as Max pushed to his feet, wincing, and shuffled into the bedroom. Bert heard Max answer, heard muffled words, but couldn’t make them out. When Max reappeared, he was shoving arms into his jacket.

“Bodies,” he said, “at the harbor.”

“Who?”

“And a motorcycle with a bullet wound,” Max said.

“Our assassin.”

"Looks like it," Max said. "And his nurse."

"I'm parked behind you," Higgins said. "I'll drive."

"About time we got a break," Max said.

The man who snatched his house keys from the counter was not the same man Bert had seen when he first arrived. With the exception of severely bloodshot eyes, Max was back.

Harbor
Kingstown, Rhode Island

The harbor's breath was as foul today as Max had remembered the last time he'd been on these docks. It was when he and the forensics team had crawled all over them following a massive explosion. They'd found DNA that confirmed Bull's execution. They'd gathered enough evidence to confirm that the Bente Cartel had been there and were the probable perpetrators. The Shark and his men had not left behind enough evidence, though, to charge or prosecute anyone. Emil Bente was too careful. He let them find just enough to know what he'd done, and that he was too smart to be connected to it. Again.

It took Max a moment – a long moment – to process being back today in the very same place he'd first made his promise to avenge Detective Nate (Bull) Sullivan's murder.

Mercifully, the bodies they were looking at today were found near a dock several hundred yards away from where Bull was killed. But, as Max straightened up to stretch his wounded back, he could see the dock in the distance. In his mind, he saw it all again. He shook his head and looked back down at the crime scene before him.

"This one doesn't carry the Shark's signature," Max said.

"Found by illegal crabbers," one of the forensics team members said. "Naked and half covered in crabs."

Max winced at the visual image it conjured in his mind. "Both bodies chained to cinder blocks, right?"

"Correct," he said.

"One male, one female, both in their late 20s, early 30s?"

"Not the way I would describe them clinically, but correct enough for your purposes, Captain."

"Was that a Yes?"

That was a yes," he said. "The motorcycle was down there, too."

"How far out?"

"Couple hundred yards. See the buoy?"

"Sloppy, sloppy, sloppy," Max said, and walked over to the bike, now drying in the sun. Bert was already there, peering at the bullet hole in the odometer.

"Trajectory appears consistent with a shot fired from above the bike," Higgins said. See how it glanced across the face instead of obliterating it?"

"Lester's story checks," Max said. "That what you're saying?"

Bert nodded. "But nothing else does. You've always said the Shark makes people and things disappear without a trace – POOF – into thin air."

"Right," Max said, "I'd bet my left nut Emil Bente had nothing to do with this hit."

"Might as well bet with 'em, since you won't be using them any time soon," Higgins said, and grinned.

"Oh," Max said. He shot his partner a withering look. "The compassion. I'm underwhelmed."

Bert shrugged, "I'm an asshole."

"You are," Max said. "Please don't miss my point."

"I haven't. The Shark didn't do this," Bert said, and blinked. "But who else would?"

Max nodded, "Right. Who else indeed? And why?" He found the coroner at the end of the dock. "Harry, I need you to ID these bodies as soon as possible."

“Do our best,” Dr. Harry Drine said.

Max turned to his partner. “You like jigsaw puzzles, Detective Higgins?”

“Used to when I was a kid,” Higgins said.

“You’re still a kid,” Max said, and slugged Higgins in the shoulder.

“Wait. Is this like your fishing thing?” Higgins said.

“What do you do with puzzle pieces that don’t seem to fit anywhere in the big picture?”

“You leave them alone and find others that do,” Higgins said.

“Right,” Max said, “and then you come back to them later and try again.”

“And if you still can’t get them to fit?”

“Sometimes you find you don’t need them to see the big picture anyway,” Max said. “Contrary to popular belief, no crimes are solved so completely that there aren’t lingering pieces that don’t fit. Some pieces never fit.”

“They don’t teach that at the Academy,” Higgins said.

“They don’t want you to know that this work will drive you mad, if you let it.”

“Terrific.”

“You okay?” Bert said, as he glanced in the rear view mirror. The last glimpse of the harbor faded behind them.

“Yeah sure, fine,” Max said.

“Still want that beer?”

Max snorted. “Yeah, about that …. “

“Don’t worry, Cap,” Higgins said. “I don’t remember nothin’.”

“Thanks Bert,” he said. “Showed my ass.”

“I don’t remember nothin’.”

“Okay,” Max said, “I owe you one.”

"Matter of time until I collect, too," Bert said. "Shit happens, Max. Nobody's immune."

"Especially when a woman is involved."

"Copy that," Bert said. "Sure you don't want to get those cuts looked at? I can drop you at the ER."

"Thanks, but no thanks, asshole."

Bert laughed. "You were pretty funny about that."

"Go ahead and laugh," Max said, and wiped a hand across his mouth. "I can still taste those damned cigarettes."

Bert grew sober, "Glad you're okay."

"Thanks," Max said. "Wonder how long my place is gonna stink."

They were approaching Max's house. Bert pulled into the driveway.

"Need help cleaning up?" Bert said.

"I got it," Max said. "Thanks for the ride." He got out with a wave. Bert watched until his partner had disappeared through the door. The files he had shared with Director Fenton were tucked away in the trunk. It was dinnertime, but Bert had lost his appetite. He backed out of the driveway and headed for Headquarters. Time for a little more betrayal.

Residence of Captain Max Steele
Kingstown, Rhode Island

Max opened every window in the house, and set about sweeping up glass. He smiled, remembering how Bert had knocked him clean off his feet. It was the kind of thing guys smiled about.

His thoughts turned to Maria. Her words echoed in his mind. "We're just fucking, Max." *Really? Was that all it was? Was she just some horny chick wanting to get it on with a cop?* He shook his head and kept sweeping. He should just forget about it, forget he ever met her, forget she ever mattered. He carried the dustpan of broken glass to the trash bin. “Like this,” he said, and dumped it. And the next instant, he’d dropped the dustpan, snatched his keys off the counter, and headed for his vehicle. “I’m an idiot,” he said muttering. He’d just drive by, see if she was home. He backed the car out of the driveway. Yeah, see if she was home, is all. He didn’t want to talk to her.

Like hell.

Residence of Dr. Maria Sanchez
Kingstown, Rhode Island

Maria’s apartment was on the other side of town. Max Steele drove through her neighborhood until he had come within a block of her place. But, as he approached the last cross street, Max hit the brakes and pulled to the curb. What the hell?

He circled the block to be sure. Yup. He’d know Lamby’s car anywhere. Max parked two blocks away and walked. He could get a better look on foot. He approached the Detective’s Eric Lambowski’s bureau car from the rear. The side windows were tinted, but he could tell Lamby was in there. He stopped next to the driver side window. It lowered.

“Lamby,” Max said.

“Evening Captain,” Lambowski said. Max noticed that his trademark smile was absent tonight.

“So, what’s up?” Max said. “You selling drugs out here? Buying? What?”

“Official business, Max,” Lamby said, and shifted in his seat. Max watched him reach for the clipboard beside him and turn it over.

“Yeah?” Max said. “Official business? Like what, exactly?”

"Come on, Max," Lamby said. "Give me a break."

"Sure thing, Lamby," Max said, still smiling, although he could feel his teeth start to bare into a snarl, "soon as you tell me what the hell you are doing on stakeout, on this street. Wouldn't be watching Dr. Maria Sanchez, would you?"

"Cap," Eric said, holding both hands up in front of him, "I just do what I'm told."

"That's what I'm asking, my friend," Max said, emphasizing the last two words. "Who put you on this detail? Who?"

"Talk to Higgins," Detective Lambowski said. "That's all I'm gonna say. I gotta get back to …."

"Higgins?" Max said. "As in my partner, Higgins?" Max slapped his hands on his thighs, turned on one heel and stomped back to his vehicle. *Great. Just. Great.*

Fifty yards away, and two stories above Detective Lambowski's vehicle, two soft shutter clicks sounded. The lens zoomed in further until his face filled the frame. One more click. The lens zoomed back out to the man striding away. Two more clicks, and the shooter headed for the fire escape.

Chapter Seven

Neighborhood of Dr. Maria Sanchez
Kingstown, Rhode Island

Max slammed his bureau car door, put the key in the ignition, and stopped. His head began to spin. *Wait just one minute.* Dr. Maria Sanchez was under surveillance by the Federal Bureau of Investigation and Captain Max Steele, who had been in Dr. Maria Sanchez's apartment as recently as last night, knew nothing about it. But Captain Max Steele's partner, Lieutenant Bert Higgins, knew a lot about said surveillance and even appeared to be directing it. Meanwhile, said partner spends the day with Captain Max Steele at the harbor, and does not say one word about it. WHAT THE HELL? Why was Dr. Maria Sanchez under surveillance by the FBI in the first place? Whether or not he knew about it, and he damn sure should have, what was this surveillance supposed to reveal? Dr. Maria Sanchez is an Emergency Room doctor at Memorial Hospital. Is this because of Nina's death, and if so, why wasn't he, the lead investigator, let in on it? None of it made any sense, and all of it was pissing him off.

His cell phone buzzed in his jacket, and he snapped it to his ear without even looking to see who was calling.

"What," he said.

"Max?" a familiar voice said. He yanked the phone from his ear and looked at the caller ID. Sure enough, it was Vanessa Sullivan, his deceased partner's widow.

“Van, sweetie, how are you?” Max said, his glare melting into a smile. “I’m sorry I haven’t called.”

“Max,” Vanessa said, “I need you to come over right now. Right. Now.”

“What’s up?” Max said. “You okay? The boys?”

“Now, Max,” she said. “Not on the phone.”

“10-4. I’m *en route*,” he said. “Just tell me you’re safe.”

“We’re safe, but scared.”

“Twenty minutes. Lock the doors. You got your Glock?”

“In my hand,” she said, “but I’m shaking.”

“Eighteen minutes.”

The line went dead. Max tossed the phone into the passenger seat and stomped the accelerator. Vanessa Sullivan was a very strong woman. Tough. Capable. Independent. Rock solid. To hear her voice quake like that set off every alarm in his body. He wasn’t sure what he was walking into, but it would be with his gun drawn. He patted his rib cage to assure himself it was there.

He made it in fifteen minutes. When he rounded the corner onto her street, blue and red lights shot like sparks from the top of several squad cars. Good. She had the sense to call the cops, too. Max came in too fast and had to slam on the brakes to keep from hitting the first squad car. He leapt out and was surrounded immediately by four officers. He knew them.

“What’ve we got?” Max said.

“Dunno, Max,” Sergeant Bolo said. “She said we can’t come in until you get here.”

“Let’s go,” Max said. He pushed past them and headed up the walk. The porch light blazed like a beacon amid the flickers of blue and red that bounced off the house. He motioned with a backward palm for the officers to stay back while he approached the door. He drew his Glock and brushed off the safety.

“Vanessa?” he called to the door as he approached. He stepped to one side of it. He heard the locks draw back, and then the door swung wide.

"Max," Vanessa said.

"Van," he said, taking a quick glance around the door jam, "for your safety, I need you to put the Glock on the floor next to the front door. Then you and the boys get flat on the floor in the kitchen. The guys need to secure the house."

"Okay," she said, and he heard them rustling.

"You down?"

"Yes," she said.

Max looked back to the sidewalk and motioned with his arm. "Let's go." He straightened his arms into a shooter stance and rushed through the door. He heard the quick stomp of feet behind him.

"Van, is there a basement? I forget," he said.

"Yes," Vanessa said from the kitchen floor. Max glanced in as he passed. Her twin sons were on either side of her. He let the barrel of his weapon lead the rest of his body to the right. From other sections of the house, he heard officers shouting, "Clear." He approached the basement door and hesitated. His training officer's face flashed in his mind, and he heard the words of warning in his head. "Rats like holes. If they're waiting for you, it's behind the basement door." Max positioned himself on the opposite side of the door's swing radius, wishing he had a flashlight. He placed his hand on the doorknob and sucked in a breath.

"Wait," a voice behind him said.

Max recognized Sergeant Bolo by his voice without needing to take his eyes off the basement door.

"We got enough dead heroes," Sgt. Bolo said.

"Got a flashlight?"

In response, he saw a brilliant cone of light illuminate the door. He glanced back, careful not to look at the beam directly. Bolo's flashlight rested atop his weapon.

"Ready," Bolo said.

Twisting his left hand backward to turn the doorknob, so he could keep the Glock in his right, Max yanked the door and it swung wide. The beam from the flashlight flooded the top of the stairs.

"Clear?" Bolo said.

Max nodded.

"You want me first with the light?"

"Toss me the light," Max said. The stairs went dark and Sergeant Bolo passed the flashlight to Max. The calls from officers in the rest of the house had stopped. By the murmur of voices he heard, Max guessed they were getting Vanessa and the boys out.

Max flicked on the flashlight and nodded to Bolo without taking his focus off the basement steps. Max pivoted around the door jam and hurtled down the steps. He heard the thudding of Bolo's boots close behind. Max scanned the basement with the light. Both washer and dryer had heaped baskets of dirty clothes crowning them, and the basement was cluttered with toys, but he saw no one. He heard Bolo radio for another flashlight.

"Have somebody hit the light switch at the top of the stairs," Max said.

"I'll get it," Bolo said.

"Bolo," Max said. "Call it out. You stay here and cover me."

"Right," Bolo said.

Max moved to the far exterior wall, flicking the flashlight back and forth in an arc. The floor overhead creaked and groaned, and he flinched. Instinctively, he flicked the flashlight up to the unfinished ceiling. Brown papered insulation bulged and drooped in lazy waves. He lowered the light and continued to scan. Suddenly, the whole basement was filled with light and Max could see instantly that the basement was empty.

"Clear," he called.

"Clear," Bolo said in echo. "I hate basements."

Max returned his weapon to the shoulder holster. "Squawk upstairs. Make sure they're out," he said to Bolo. "And why didn't somebody give me a radio?"

Bolo was murmuring into his shoulder mic. Max hadn't expected an answer anyway. His own damn fault charging in here without getting set. "Get your ass shot one day buddy," he said under his breath and shook his head. His eyes continued to scan, and then they stopped. He flicked the flashlight back on and shone it toward the far basement window. No glass. He moved closer. Jagged edges, and broken glass. He shone the light on the floor. Glass shards. He took a step back.

"Forensics here yet?" Max said.

"Um, no."

"Get 'em here. B & E," he said. He heard Bolo relay the message. "Look at this, Bolo. Why in hell do they make basement windows big enough for a man to get through?"

"Coal," Bolo said.

"Come again?" Max said, looking at him.

"Coal chutes," Bolo said. "Especially older houses like this. Used to heat them with coal. Delivery truck would back up, attach his chute to the basement window hole, and dump it in. Lots of people had coal rooms."

"You're making it up," Max said.

"I'm not. My granddad had one."

Max returned the beam to the floor and then to the window for another careful look. "Let's talk with the lady of the house," he said, and they headed for the stairs.

Outside, the front lawn was dotted with officers and gear. A fire truck and EMS ambulance had joined the gaggle of vehicles choking the small residential street, and two small knots of neighbors had gathered to watch from a distance. One was recording with her camera. Of course.

Max spotted Vanessa and the boys by the fire truck, each wrapped at the shoulders in an emergency blanket. He motioned for Vanessa to step away from the boys to the side lawn, away from the radio squawk and engine noise and young ears. She walked quickly to him, still clutching the blanket to her chest. Her dark chocolate hair fell into her face, covering one eye.

"Did you see it?" she asked and swiped at her hair. Her eyes were wide. It reminded him of the look a terrified bunny once gave him when he surprised it in the woods.

"The basement window? Yes," Max said, scanning the scene around him distractedly.

"What basement window?"

The one … wait … let's back up," Max said, and looked intently into Vanessa's face. "Did I see what?"

"My bed," Vanessa said.

"Your bed?" Max said. "No."

"Oh God, Max. I nearly died."

Max took her by the shoulders and lowered his head to look directly into her eyes, "Let's slow down a second, sweetie."

Vanessa blinked, and then nodded.

"Okay, now what's this about your bed? No one has said anything."

"That's because you can't see it," she said, and turned away from him. "I think I'm going to be sick." Her words were followed by a splash of vomit as her stomach emptied itself on the ground. Max looked up to see EMS techs striding in his direction. Max was steadying her by the waist. Within seconds, he was replaced by one of the techs.

"I want her checked," he said, and turned away, but then immediately he turned back and took the tech by the arm. "On second thought, let's transport her." The tech nodded. "Bolo," Max said in his loudest megaphone voice. He watched every officer's head snap toward him, and then Bolo broke from the group and trotted over.

"I need the nicest guy you've got here," Max said.

"You're looking at him," Sgt. Bolo said, and grinned.

Max clapped him on the back. "Yeah, but I need you as my right hand man. We're going back in for a minute." The Sergeant nodded. Max pointed to the twins. "I need a really good guy to take those scared boys out for the biggest hamburger and shake combo they can find. And then meet us at Memorial ER in, say, ninety minutes, two hours. Tell them Mom's fine. She'll meet them there."

Bolo was already nodding. "That would be Dweeb."

"Dweeb?" Max said, and couldn't suppress the laugh.

"Officer Duwheat, over there picking his nose. See him?"

Max looked. Sure enough, a young officer twenty yards away had a finger buried up his nose to the second knuckle. Max lurched with laughter and instinctively reached for his own nose.

"Don't YOU start," Bolo said, and Max bent over again.

"Killin' me, Bolo," Max said, and yanked a wallet from his jacket. He pulled out a fifty-dollar bill and handed it to the Sergeant. "Tell Dweeb to get himself something, too. Obviously, he's over there digging for something to eat."

Sergeant Bolo closed his eyes, shaking at the shoulders. He snatched the bill from Max's hand and headed back across the yard.

Max turned to see more EMTs bouncing a wheeled stretcher across the front lawn. Vanessa was holding a plastic oxygen cone to her face, but saw him look her way and motioned for him. Her arm was outstretched toward him and when he got within range, she grabbed him with surprising force and pulled him to her. Lowering the oxygen mask, she said, "My bed."

"Yes," Max nodded. "We're going to check it."

"Under the covers," she said, and then staggered.

"I got it, Van," Max said. "Now would you cooperate with these nice people, please, and let me get to work?" He helped keep the oxygen tube from getting tangled as they positioned her on the stretcher. He leaned down and kissed her forehead. "We're getting the boys dinner and a cop car ride. We'll all meet you at Memorial. Cooperate. That's an order." She gave him the thumbs-up. He turned, still looking back and smiling at her, and nearly crashed into Sergeant Bolo.

"Mission accomplished, Captain," Bolo said.

"Thank you, sir," Max said. "Now, how 'bout we head back inside for a minute?"

"Forensics is grumbling about coming for a simple breaking and entering," Bolo said.

"You tell them whose house it is?" Max said with more heat than he intended.

"Take it easy, Cap. They're coming."

Inside the house, Max paused at the base of the stairs to the second floor and turned to the sergeant.

"Bolo," he said, "Vanessa says there's something in her bed up there."

"Oh, great," Bolo said. "Alive or dead?"

"Under the covers," Max nodded.

"If it's a snake, Steele, I swear," Bolo said.

"Do you need to be reassigned, Officer Pussy?" Max said, and slugged him in the shoulder.

"I notice you ain't in any hurry to get up there," Bolo said.

Max climbed the stairs, smiling. Bolo followed, muttering.

The master bedroom was off to the left and a few steps from the top of the stairs. The room itself was so neat and tidy, it looked like a showroom floor display. The king bed was made. The comforter was a deep shade of royal purple. It draped the bed from the edge of the pillows at the head to the footboard. If he hadn't been looking for it, Max might never have seen that the comforter was raised slightly and that something under it formed a small lump.

"I swear, I'll shit my pants," Bolo said behind him.

Max turned and saw that Bolo had his gun out of the holster and was holding it with both hands in a shooter stance.

"Maybe we should wait for forensics," Max said. "If we mess up evidence . . . ."

"Yeah, let's wait," Bolo said.

"You're about to blast the evidence to kingdom come anyway," Max said. "Get a grip, Bolo."

"I'm getting a grip Max," Bolo said, "a two-handed grip."

"Tell you what," Max said. "I'll go downstairs and wait for Forensics. You stay up here and watch to see if it moves." Max barely got the last words out of his mouth before he doubled over laughing. If only he had able to keep a straight face, he would've witnessed a grown man shit his pants.

"You're not serious," Bolo said.

"I'm not serious," Max said, and doubled over again.

"It's not funny," Bolo said.

"It is so funny."

"I guess it is," Bolo said.

"Put that pea shooter away, as they say in the cartoons."

"No way," Bolo said, his stare still locked on the lump in the bed.

"Okay," Max said, wiping his eyes. "I suppose if something does slither out from underneath those covers, I'll be glad you're ready to blast it."

"Damn straight," Bolo said.

"If you can pry yourself out of that shooter's stance for a second, radio somebody to bring me a talkie with an earpiece, please."

As Bolo spoke into his lapel mic, Max stepped to the window and took in the scene below. The twins were gone. He hoped Dweeb was showing them all the gadgets in the squad car that young boys like to see. The fire truck and ambulance were gone too. Max sucked air through his teeth. There would be no getting around it: he was going to have to go to Memorial's Emergency Room. And he was probably going to run into Dr. Maria Sanchez. How would he be when he saw her? What would he say? What was there to say? Maybe she wasn't at the ER. His thoughts turned to Maria's street and to the surveillance. What the hell? The surveillance could mean nothing, or it could mean … what? Something. His partner knew something, apparently. The son of a bitch. *Thanks for telling me. Might be time for me to knock you on your ass, Bert.* Max could feel his eyes narrow, felt his hand ball into a fist. Later. He'd talk to him later. When he wasn't so pissed.

He felt the hand on his shoulder, and he whirled around with his hand still wadded into a fist.

"Whoa, whoa, whoa," Sergeant Bolo said, and stepped back.

"Sorry," Max said. "Guess we're both a little jumpy."

"Think I just saw my life in review," Bolo said, lifting his eyebrows.

Max laughed. "I'm a danger to myself and others."

"Well, your radio's coming, Captain Danger."

"Has the snake moved?" Max said.

"I wish you wouldn't say that," Bolo said.

Max heard boots on the stairs. An officer entered holding a handheld with microphone and earpiece. Behind him, carrying sizable duffels, was the forensics team. Max nodded to everyone, inserting his earpiece and clipping the radio to his belt.

"That's better," he said. Into the mic he said, "Radio check."

"10-2," a voice said into his ear. He glanced at Bolo, who nodded.

"Loud and clear," Bolo said.

"I know what 10-2 means, Sergeant," Max said. He turned to the lead forensics tech, a man he'd known for a fist full of years, and stuck out a hand. "Randy."

"You interrupted my dinner," Dr. Randall Jacobs said, shaking Max's hand. "Tell me why I'm here."

"Did you know my old partner, Bull Sullivan?"

"Only by reputation and the occasional passing encounter, years back," Randy said.

Max pointed to the bed. "His widow saw something under there that scared her shitless. She's getting checked out at the ER."

"So, really shitless?" Randy said.

"Puking," Max said.

"Okay," he said, snapping on gloves and turning to his team. "Let's find out what's so terrifying."

"Oh, and if it's a snake, toss it to Barney Fife over there," Max said, pointing to Sergeant Bolo, who returned Max's grin with a middle finger.

Within minutes, Randy's team had scanned the bed and determined that whatever was under there was inanimate. "No snakes," Randy said, and grinned. A member of the team inserted a tubular micro-camera under the top edge of the comforter to get a look at what was underneath. "No wires," Randy said, as he peered over the tech's shoulder at the display screen. "No plastique," he said, and straightened up. "Time to clear the room and peel the covers back," he said. "Everyone to the front yard, except you and you," he said, pointing to two forensics team members.

"I think we just got kicked out," Bolo said in a low voice as he and Max descended the stairs.

"Yep," Max said.

"I'm just as happy," Bolo said, "This shit makes me jumpy."

"Do tell."

The night air had gone crisp. Max stood near the mailbox and stared at the upstairs windows. This forensics team was good, but they were not fast. Probably what made them so good.

He didn't know how long he'd been standing there with his hands tucked into his armpits, but at last Randy appeared on the porch. "All clear," he said. "You'll want to have a look." Max was already moving toward the house. Inside, he took the stairs two at a time and hurried into the bedroom. The purple cover had been pulled back, and what Max saw sent a fresh chill through his body.

Money. Lots of it. In shallow stacks and in perfectly straight rows, forming a rectangular shaped pile. And resting on top was a diamond-studded rosary left in the shape of an S.

"Bente," Max said, and heard the growl in his voice. He turned to Randy, "Note? Was there a note?"

Randy shook his head and pointed to the bed. "Just what you see."

The silence that ensued held Max. It was as if he was suspended by wires he couldn't see, over a cliff of emotion whose power frightened him. Rage. Dark, murderous rage. An urge so strong.

"Max … I," Randy said.

"Leave me," Max said loudly. "Just leave me alone." He felt his chest rise and fall, heard the huffing sound in his ears, felt the words squeeze from his lips. "I. Will. Kill. You."

High overhead, a four-propeller drone whirred quietly. Its infrared lens focused on the house and the front yard. It transmitted images wirelessly to its controllers. They wished they could also listen in.

Memorial Hospital
Kingstown, Rhode Island

Dr. Maria Sanchez saw her from across the Emergency Room. The elderly woman looked small and frail, and she clutched her purse with both hands, looking first one way and then the other. Maria dropped her clipboard onto the counter and hurried to the outer area.

"Nettie," she said, and saw Nettie Spruill's shoulders slump in relief.

"I … I didn't …," Nettie said, as Maria threw both arms around her. There were no words. Tears fell from both of their eyes. It was the shared language of broken hearts. They held each other for a long time and wept.

"He …, He …." Nettie said at last.

"Shhh," Maria said. She felt a tap on her shoulder. Linda Turnbill, the charge nurse, was motioning her to the back. "Use my office," she mouthed. Maria nodded. She led Nettie into the nurse's office, sat her in a chair and closed the door. She pulled the desk chair around and sat next to the rumpled woman. She put the box of tissues in her lap. Both of them reached for tissues.

"Where is he?" Nettie said, and dabbed her eyes. "And thank you for calling me. I'd never have known."

"Upstairs," Maria said. "And you are welcome. We'll go see him in a minute."

"Is he hurt?"

"Physically he's fine, Nettie," Maria said, reaching for another tissue. "God, I'm a mess today. I'm sorry." Nettie patted her hand and Maria took it, and held it.

"Nettie, Jeremy has had some sort of mental … incident."

"What does that mean?" Nettie said. "A stroke? Has he had a stroke?"

No, thank God," Maria said. "Physically, there's been no trauma. I'll let his attending physician explain it to you in more detail, but since I am going to take you to see him, I wanted to prepare you."

"Prepare me for what?"

"He's comatose," Maria said. "Breathing on his own, his body functioning normally under the circumstances, but mentally …."

"Mentally, he's run away somewhere and shut the door," Nettie said. "I had an uncle who … well never mind. Please, may I see him?"

"If you're ready, I'll take you," Maria said.

She helped Nettie from the chair, noticing how small she was. Nettie Spruill's personality had always made her seem larger. Her strength had made her seem substantial. Now Maria watched a frail, trembling, elderly woman with hair that had not seen a comb or brush, shuffle toward the elevators. Maria wrapped a hand under Nettie's arm, just in case.

The hospital kept the fourth floor locked, mostly so that those who wandered would not wander far. Many of the patients on the psychological ward either walked the hallways aimlessly, or walked them with great purpose and intention, headed somewhere only they knew. But there was a lot of activity on the ward, and the staff encouraged it.

It was a new experience for Nettie. Maria felt the tension seize the woman as she looked through the tempered glass in the door.

"It's okay," Maria said. She pressed the buzzer and looking up into the camera nested in the corner of the ceiling.

"Help you?" came a voice from the wall speaker next to the door.

"Visitor for Tittle," Maria said. The door buzzed and Maria pulled it wide for them to pass. They made their way to the nurse's station. Before Nettie could speak, Maria greeted the nurse. "I'm Dr. Sanchez. How you doing? I've got the guardian for Jeremy Tittle here. Please put Dr. Nettie Spruill on the approved visitor list."

The nurse nodded and wrote in a folder she grabbed from the tray.

"Who's the attending? And are they here?" Maria said.

"It's Dr. Marks, Dr. Sanchez," the nurse said, "And she's here somewhere." The nurse did a flap with her arms.

"I understand, believe me," Maria said. "I'll catch up with her sometime. Right now, I'm taking Dr. Spruill to see the patient." She hurried Nettie away from the desk.

As soon as they were out of earshot, Nettie turned and whispered, "But I'm not his guardian, dear."

"You are now," Maria said, "and don't let on otherwise. Until we can make contact with his family, you are the closest person in his life."

Nettie nodded. "He needs someone."

"Right," Maria said, and opened the door to Jeremy's room. Nettie hesitated at the door, and then rushed inside. The man in the bed lay motionless. His eyes were unfocused and his jaw was slack. Only the color of his skin and the rise and fall of his chest, showed he was alive.

Nettie slowed as she approached the bed. She picked up his hand, careful not to disturb the IV taped onto the back of it. Maria saw her mouth open, but no sound came out. Then she laid her head slowly, gently, onto

Jeremy's chest and Maria watched the old woman's back tremor as she wept over him. It was too intimate, and Maria was too raw. She backed out of the room and closed the door.

Maria turned and went to find Dr. Agnes Marks, the attending doctor and the hospital's resident Southern belle. Her nickname, for obvious reasons, was Groucho, but only to her friends, and Maria was one of them. She found her in the break room.

"Hiya, Groucho," Maria said, dropping into a chair on the opposite side of the table. "How's the coffee?"

"More bitter than my mother," Agnes Marks said, "but I saved some for the next victim."

Maria waved her hand.

"You look like hell," Agnes said.

"Nice to see you, too," Maria smiled without mirth.

"Long night?"

"Long night."

"Here?"

Maria shook her head. "And if you ask me any more questions, I'm going to start crying again. And I might have to kill you because I've got a job to do downstairs." No sooner had Maria spoken the word "cry" than her eyes filled with tears and the rest of her words had come out in squeaks.

"Aww, baby girl," Groucho said, and rushed around the table, kneeling next to her friend. Tears splashed down Maria's lab coat.

"Please tell me this isn't about Hunka Hunka Boom Boom," Groucho said softly.

Maria nodded, her lips contorted to hold back the torrent. She snatched napkins from the holder on the table.

"Oh, baby girl," she said, and wrapped her friend up in a hug. Maria chugged sob after sob into Agnes's shoulder. "You love that boy, dontcha."

Maria nodded into Groucho's shoulder and convulsed again.

"Shhh," she said, and clutched Maria tighter. "Love always wins, baby girl. Love always wins." Groucho knew it wasn't true, but sometimes hope was the only elixir the grieving could keep down.

Residence of Vanessa Sullivan
Kingstown, Rhode Island

"I knew it," Max said. "I could feel him. That's why I called for forensics." He waved his hand as if swatting a bug. "Not that you'd find more than a trace of him. But I knew it wasn't a simple break-in."

"He's really messing with your head," Dr. Randy Jacobs said.

"He's as brilliant as he is diabolical," Max said, as if he hadn't heard a word Jacobs had said. "He will show up like this and make it unmistakable that he's been here, yet leave no trace of evidence to link him to any of it. He makes his presence apparent, but without leaving any real evidence that he's been here. Does that make sense?"

He looked over into the passenger seat of the bureau car at Dr. Jacobs, who was holding his paper coffee cup with both hands.

"Perfect sense," Randy said. "I was the Lead when he left the rosary on the Ondolopous woman's chest in the hospital, remember?"

"I remember," Max said.

"He spares no expense making whatever statement he is making," Randy said.

"Okay, here's what completely messes with my mind," Max said. "The guy seems to care. Look at all that money. It's not hard to figure out that the money's intended to make sure those boys and their mother are taken care of, provided for. And that rosary. I'd bet my house those are real diamonds. See what I mean, Randy?" Steele fixed on him with raised eyebrows. "Close to a half million dollars in cash and another hundred thousand dollar piece of jewelry, just to make a statement of his presence? I don't think so. He acts like he cares what happens to the families of the people he kills. I mean, you were also at the crime scene when we took him down, at Brother Lawrence's place, right?

"Never forget it."

"Chopped that guy into bite-sized pieces," Max said. "Bente's a monster."

"The heartless monster, who has a heart," Randy said.

"Right," Max said, "Maybe he's more than one person housed in a single body. He would be less frightening, you know, if he had a mental disorder."

"God knows," Randy said.

"My fear is that he doesn't," Max said.

"That's what you suspect."

"It is."

Mantisto State Prison
Kingstown, Rhode Island

Vinnie Bontecelli had taught himself to listen while he slept. He remained one inch below the surface of wakefulness at all times. It kept him from unwanted surprises. It also meant he never slept hard or got any deep rest.

He heard them coming. Three sets of feet. One pair of slippers and two sets of jackboots. Two guards, one inmate. He sat up on the edge of his rack. Waited. The feet stopped outside his door. The food slot slid open two inches. A small flashlight beam scanned his cell and then fixed on his face. Vinnie squinted but said nothing. The slot closed, and the door opened far enough for one person to slip through, and then it closed again.

Vinnie's eyes were accustomed to seeing in the dark. He spent much of his time in darkness. But he had just had a flashlight shone in his eyes, and so he was unable to see details of the person who'd entered. He could make out slippers and a jumpsuit. The head was hooded, and it covered the face. An inmate who wanted to remain anonymous. Interesting. He decided to push it.

"Got a name?" Vinnie said.

"Whisper, Comrade, only whisper," came the whispered voice so soft he barely heard it.

"Got a name?" Vinnie whispered. "Comrade?"

He heard a soft chuckle from across the cell. "You are funny. It's a sign of intelligence. That will serve you well, if you choose to be smart."

"I'm listening," Vinnie whispered. "Don't waste my time."

"That is funny, too," the hooded man whispered. "All you have is time."

"Not for you, unless you have something for me."

"Fair enough," the man whispered. "We may be able to arrange your departure from this place."

"Dead or alive?" Vinnie said.

"That depends upon you," the man whispered. "The plan is very dangerous. Your safety will increase greatly if you do precisely what we say."

"Are you for real? And who is we?" Vinnie whispered. "Who am I working with?"

"We are the wind that rustles through the trees. You do not see us. You only know we have been here by the trembling of the leaves."

"What kind of bullshit is that?" Vinnie said in a loud whisper.

"Do not shout," the small voice across the room whispered, "or we are done here."

"I don't trust people I don't know," Vinnie whispered.

"Then you do not understand trust," the voice said. "Trust is reserved for people you do not know. Or it isn't trust. It is something else."

"What kind of horseshit you peddling, Comrade?" Vinnie said in a regular voice.

"Perhaps you are not ready for your journey to freedom," the voice whispered and tapped the door lightly beside him.

Vinnie heard the door unlatch.

"Wait," Vinnie whispered, but the figure slipped through the door and it locked behind him.

Vinnie leapt to his feet and pressed himself against the door, listening. Three sets of feet moved down the hall, the same two sets of jackboots and one set of slippers. The sound faded until there was nothing. Vinnie strained against an insufferable silence. And then he roared and cursed and screamed until spittle ran down his chin. "Who are you? What do you want from me? I'll kill you. I'll kill you. Hear me Comrade?" He felt it building within him, building until the top of his head burned like it had been scalded. He backed away from the cell door, and then rushed forward and threw himself against it. He wadded his fist and punched the solid metal door. Punched it as hard as he could, bone against immovable metal. Punched it again. And again. And again. He heard the bones break, felt the cartilage snap. Looked at his hand spurting blood. Bones spiked like jack-knifed tractor-trailers along the roadway of veins on the back of his hand. He punched the door again. And then everything went black and was no more.

Chapter Eight

Private Airport
Kingstown, Rhode Island

"Change of plans," Emil Bente said to Gregorio. "Inform the pilot we will be delayed."

He held the secure satphone to his ear. "I am grateful for this news, Warden, and you were right to call me directly."

"I'm relieved," Al Antonetti said. "I wasn't sure."

"Your timing is perfect," the Shark said. "A special gift will be delivered to you."

"Thank you, sir, and if there is anything else …."

"Are you arranging hospital transport, or will you take him yourself?" Emil said.

"I was going to arrange for hospital …." the Warden said.

"No," Emil said sharply. "Do not let Bontecelli out of your control for any reason."

"Then we will transport him, sir."

"Excellent." Emil terminated the call. Gregorio returned, the radio still in his hand.

"Where is Bird One?" Bente said to him.

Gregorio switched channels. "Base," he said, "this is Outpost Two."

"Go ahead," the Base dispatch operator said.

"Where is Bird One?"

"One returned to Base two mics ago."

"10-4. Standby." He looked at the Shark.

"I heard," Emil said. "Returned two minutes ago." He was pacing the length of the storage facility's back office. He stopped and pointed at the men. "We need supplies. Listen carefully."

Carlos hurried to the desk and grabbed a pen.

"Not you, Carlos," Bente said. "I need you to cover Maria Garza when she visits. She will be exposed."

"Yes, Excellency, but I can help you here first," Carlos said.

Emil was already shaking his head as Carlos spoke. "Go now. I'll feel better if you are early. Gregorio will assist me here."

Carlos nodded, tossed the pad and paper to his brother, and vanished from the room like a wisp of smoke.

"Gregorio," Emil Bente said. "Where is the nearest Catholic church?"

Gregorio had been fumbling with the radio and the pad. He froze, "Excellency?"

"Where? Find out," Emil said. "We need prayer cards. Quickly."

Misererecordia Clinic
Kingstown, Rhode Island

The morning was crisp. The sun was impotent against winds that swirled up the hillside to Misererecordia Clinic. Maria Garza stroked the false distention strapped to her midsection and gathered the heavy shawl closer around her head. She had arrived early on purpose, hoping to be first in line when the clinic opened. But she had underestimated the zeal of the cocaine mules anxious to discharge their loads and be loaded again. She was fourth in the line of women, all of whom, like her, appeared great with child. She didn't speak. None of these women had ever seen her face. None of them knew her name or knew she directed the Base of Operations. Their only points of contact with the Bente Cartel were with the Hispanic fisherman who unloaded and loaded them in darkness at the dock, and with Dr. Maria Sanchez when they made their drops. Twice a week they came, for which, along with their silence, they were paid a substantial wage.

Not even Carlos, Gregorio, or his men knew Maria Garza by face or knew the Base's location. They knew only her voice. It was by design, and it had worked flawlessly, until this past year. Maria Garza lowered her head and fumbled with the plain beaded rosary hanging from her neck. Maria Sanchez must be returned to the fold. Maria Garza prayed for her sister's meekness, repentance, and return. It would happen immediately, please God. If it did not, Maria Garza would kill her. She had grown up with Sister Sanchez in the cloisters, had made vows with her, loved her like a sister, and trusted her with her life. *Todo está bien.*

She glanced down the hill toward the road and saw several more pregnant Hispanic women waddling up the driveway. She saw Pablo watching from the shadows, leaning against the great oak tree. Presently, Dr. Maria Sanchez emerged from her car and pulled a lab coat closed against the wind. Good. Maria Garza fluffed the top of her shawl until her face was hooded completely. She heard muted greetings, heard the clinic door open and shut, but she did not raise her head. Best to make this visit a surprise. She knew Bird One was overhead with Carlos at the controls, watching. She wished she could see what he was seeing. As the Base operator, she could track every move in real time. Now, she was part of the ground operation, and it felt strange. She was vulnerable, exposed, and blind. *Please God, let this line move quickly.*

At last, Maria Garza was at the wooden steps leading to the clinic door. She patted the syringe pen beneath her robes and prayed she wouldn't have to use it. A small Hispanic woman opened the clinic door, descended the steps, and made her way to the path down the other side of the hill.

It was time. Maria Garza drew in a deep breath and entered. She closed the door, and locked it. Dr. Maria Sanchez was emerging from the back storage area of the trailer. She carried a laptop and looked up from the screen only long enough to nod and receive the code. Maria Garza knew the code, of course. She had been in on the discussion determining what the coded signal would be. Maria Sanchez nodded and motioned for the woman to enter the examination room.

"*Inglés o Español?*" Dr. Sanchez said, still pecking at the laptop.

Maria Garza peeled back the shawl and smiled, "English will be fine, Sister."

"Maria!" Dr. Sanchez said. She dropped the laptop on the examination table, and threw her arms around Maria Garza's neck. The basket attached to Garza's midsection pressed between them.

"*Todo está bien,*" Maria Sanchez said.

"Is it? Is all well, Sister Maria?" Maria Garza said into her ear as they continued to embrace. She felt Maria Sanchez tense, felt her body go rigid. Maria Sanchez released her from the embrace and took a step back. The two women eyed each other.

"You are here on business. Have you come to check up on me?" Maria Sanchez said.

"I bring greetings from his Excellency," Maria Garza said. "We missed you at the meeting."

"Is that what this is about?" Maria Sanchez said. "I told you it wasn't safe for me to be away right now."

"So you said," Sister Garza said. "A wise decision under the circumstances. His Excellency understood. But we still missed you."

Silence rested upon the examination room. Tension crackled between them.

"Your presence delights me," Maria Sanchez said at last, "and it frightens me."

"Excellency is … concerned," Maria Garza said. "The threat to this operation seems to come from every direction, no?"

"Yes, two men tried …." Maria Sanchez said.

"*Sí, Sí,* my sister," Maria Garza nodded. "Carlos briefed us."

"Carlos is an asshole," Dr. Sanchez said hotly.

"You have adopted the language of the street, I see."

"Can you blame me? He accused me of trying to steal from the Cartel."

"Your communication with each other was direct," Maria Garza said.

"You could call it that," Dr. Sanchez said. "But God knows what he is telling you about me. And you don't get to hear my side."

"Why is that, do you think?"

"I am too close to …."

"Now we're getting to it," Maria Garza said.

"Now we are getting to what?" Maria said, and took another step back.

"The cause for our concern, Sister Sanchez. You have gotten very close to Captain Max Steele, have you not?" Maria Garza said with a force in her voice that surprised even her.

"Those were my instructions, were they not?" Maria Sanchez said, mimicking her.

"Indeed they were," Maria Garza said, "but it is the manner in which you have engaged your target that brings me here today." She leveled a fierce look at Maria Sanchez. "Since it is the language of the street that you now speak, let me be clear that we know you are fucking him."

Maria Sanchez froze, her mouth hanging open and wordless. Then her body began to rock. In the next instant, she toppled like a tree felled in the woods. Her forehead smacked against the counter with a terrifying crack. Blood spat from the wound even before her body had finished falling to the floor.

Maria Garza shot from the examination room and wrestled to unlock the clinic door. She bounded down the steps waving her arms and shouting to the women lining the side of the trailer. "Go," she said. "The doctor is injured. All of you must leave. Quickly." She heard the women speaking rapidly in Spanish as Maria Garza ran back into the trailer.

A growing pool of blood surrounded Maria Sanchez's head. Maria Garza called her name, but got no response. She grabbed a towel and held it tightly against Maria's forehead. This wasn't good. EMS would have to be called and she would be seen. The authorities might not know who they were looking at, but her face would no longer be anonymous.

Some things couldn't be helped. Sister Maria, whom she loved like blood, needed her. It was a risk she would take. She wished she could speak to Carlos up the hill, warn him not to overreact. If he misunderstood and started shooting from the hilltop .... No. He would not be so foolish.

She felt for a pulse.

Mantisto State Prison
Kingstown, Rhode Island

Vincente Bontecelli had lost a lot of blood by the time they found him on the cell floor. The shift Sergeant had notified the Warden, who dispatched a team to rig a stretcher between the seats of the prison bus. The Warden had insisted there was no time to arrange for a secure ambulance. They rushed Vinnie without fanfare to Memorial Hospital, except that the Warden doubled the guards. Because of the sensitive nature of the patient's identity and underworld connection, they bypassed ER and took Bontecelli directly to intensive care where he could be isolated while they prepped him for surgery.

Memorial's orthopedic surgeons were world-renowned, especially their hand surgeon, Dr. Hiram Bluacre. Because of the hour, they reached him at home. The staff would need the patient stabilized, have an EKG strip done, x-rays taken, and the operating room prepped before he arrived. The ICU staff and surgical team were in high gear when Bontecelli was wheeled in.

A corrections officer with a shotgun walked in front of the stretcher, and another armed officer walked behind. The surgical lead took one look at the officers and began to shake his head vigorously.

"Oh, hell no," Dr. David Fleischer, Surgical Lead, said. He stabbed an index finger at the officers. "You two need to get back, way back, out of the way."

"Our orders," Officer Drucker said.

"Yes, yes, your orders," he said, "but this isn't the prison. This is Memorial Hospital and you follow my orders, all of them, got that?"

Both officers stared fixedly at the man in blue pajamas, but slowly, reluctantly, they moved to the opposite wall.

"Thank you," Fleischer said, "And by the way, I read faces and I am okay with you thinking I'm an asshole. But I promise you: your prisoner is safe. Not one patient on this wing can even get out of their bed, let alone harm your inmate or assist in his escape. And in about three minutes, I am going to let you watch me give Mr. Bontecelli enough happy juice that he won't move either. Nurse!"

A young man in scrubs stepped forward.

"Take a drink and food order for these gentlemen," he said, motioning toward the officers. "Anything they want." Dr. Fleischer nodded toward the guards and then hurried around the corner. He poked his head back around the corner, "And get them each a decent chair to sit in."

Vehicle

Kingstown, Rhode Island

Rotten luck. The Cartel had just pulled all of their people from Memorial Hospital. Unfortunate timing to pay a visit now. Emil Bente glanced at Gregorio who now was clothed head to toe in hospital scrubs.

"Make sure Bird One and Bird Two are overhead," Emil Bente said, "by the time we get there. Post Birds Three and Four a quarter mile away."

"Already done, Excellency," Gregorio said from the driver's seat of the delivery truck.

"I worry the caliber of their weapons is too small," Bente said.

"Too much weight and they cannot fly with them, "Gregorio said. "Should be fine, Excellency."

Bente glared at him. "How many times, *Amigo*? How many times have I said it? Over prepare."

"Yes, Excellency," Gregorio said. "Over prepare. We tested them."

"Yes," Bente said, "accurate only at short range?"

"Yes, but we will be in and out. Quickly. And before the police can respond."

Emil nodded. "And then you get me on that plane," Emil said. "If it goes badly, remember, we meet at the plane. You fly with me if necessary, and then sneak back into the States later."

"We won't need to …," Gregorio stopped himself. "We are prepared, Excellency."

"Radio the pilot," Emil said, "I want him 'engines hot' just in case." He ran his hands along the folds of the habit on his head and smoothed the brown skirt. His feet hurt in the ugly shoes he knew most nuns wore. Soon enough, they would be off his feet.

He imagined himself leaning into Vincente Bontecelli's ear, the man he considered his real brother. He would apologize *mano-a-mano.* He would promise to make it up to him, to make it right, all of it, even if it took the rest of his life. Vinnie would spit on him, if he could. And Emil would deserve it. He would take it and not wipe it off. And then Vincente would see his love, and his remorse, and he would forgive, please God.

"Approaching," Gregorio said. He checked the ID badge clipped to his pocket and touched the Glock concealed against the small of his back. Emil slipped into the rubber-lined cloth gloves that would hide his masculine looking hands and protect him. He gathered the tiny cloth bag he would carry with him.

"May God be with us," Emil said. Both he and Gregorio crossed themselves. "If you are caught, well …." Emil trailed off. "Don't be caught."

"*Sí*," Gregorio said. The satphone buzzed between his legs. He snatched it up. "*Sí*?" His head snapped toward the Shark, and he handed him the phone. "Carlos. The clinic."

"Be quick," Bente said into the phone. He was silent for a full minute, listening. Gregorio watched the side of his face.

"Burn it," Bente said. He threw the phone on the vehicle floor and glared at Gregorio.

"Excellency?" Gregorio said.

"We must hurry," he said. "It gets more dangerous by the moment."

ICU Unit
Memorial Hospital
Kingstown, Rhode Island

The surgery on Vinnie's hand took longer than expected because of the complexity of compound fractures. By the time Dr. Bluacre snapped off his gloves and headed for the coffee machine, everyone was tired. During the surgery, the ICU team retrofitted the isolation room to serve as Bontecelli's recovery room. It was off by itself on a short hallway in the ICU wing. Officer Drucker was already positioned in a chair by the door. The other guard, Officer Burns, had stationed himself outside the operating theatre. He followed behind the bed as it was wheeled from surgery, a shotgun still draped across his thick forearms. Once the bed passed into the isolation room, he sat on the opposite side of the door. He stopped the nurse as she emerged through the door.

"Ask if we can handcuff him to the bed," Burns said to her.

She was already shaking her head as she listened, "Not on that right arm, I can tell you," she said.

"One side will do," Burns said.

"I'll check," she said, and hurried off.

"The gun scares her," Drucker said.

"Should," Burns said, and patted his shotgun. He jerked a thumb at the door. "Ain't afraid to use it. This asshole ain't gettin' away on my watch."

"Oh, hell no," Drucker said.

"He's a slippery dick, what I hear," Burns said, and jerked his thumb at the door again, called toward it dramatically. "Try me."

"Ha," Drucker said, nodding. His phone buzzed and he snapped it from his shirt pocket.

"Drucker." He listened and reflexively straightened himself in his chair, glancing at his partner. "Um, yes, sir, Warden, sir. Yes, I got one." He patted the flashlight on his duty belt. "Right away, sir." He ended the call and looked across the door front.

"We are handcuffin' this guy," Drucker said shaking his head. "Even in the ICU. Care what they say." He stood. "Cuz I got to go. Warden wants the bus inspected and guarded so we don't get hit goin' back."

"Makes sense I suppose," Burns said. "If I'm by myself up here, we are definitely handcuffin'."

His partner nodded. Both men entered the room. One held Emil's left hand while the other snapped the cuffs to the bed railing. The patient stirred, turned his head and smiled groggily.

"Evening, Ladies," Vinnie said. His eyes were slitted and his speech was slurred.

"Evening, Asshole," Burns said, and shook the handcuffs to test them. He turned to Drucker. "Now take my cuff key and go," Burns said, "I'll deal with the flack up here." They opened the door. On the other side stood the nurse. Drucker pushed past her and headed for the elevator.

"Wait," the Nurse said.

He didn't.

"Wait!"

Ecclesia Seminary
Kingstown, Rhode Island

Most spring days are pleasant, but some exude the splendor of creation in all its richness. The beauty is partly in the incompleteness, in the longing for, and the promise of, new beginnings. The birds are calling, urgent for a lover and a nest. The daffodils are stretching green spires toward the sun in hopes of flowers that trumpet the joy of new life. The trees are forcing life back from the center of their trunks, where it has hidden through the long winter days and nights. Now is the moment, when life surges back into the branches to feed the still-bundled, expectant buds.

Sometimes Rev. Victoria Nile found her spring walks would become more like spring stands, because she found herself standing in the midst of all that was reaching and hoping around her, and she dared not move lest she miss a moment of it. She stood now in the half-light cast by the seminary chapel and turned in a slow circle, breathing deeply, and feeling all of it, surging.

She glanced at the chapel doors and pursed her lips. Seemed there was more church out here in the incompleteness than there would ever be within the hallowed walls of the place one considered sacred. Still, human beings needed a place to gather and to worship. But her passion, her sacred, and secret, reason for being at Ecclesia Seminary, was to raise up leaders who would teach that real worship happened out here, surrounded by miracle upon miracle of life in all its becoming.

She turned and ascended the steps, fumbling for keys as she climbed, and then remembered it was not locked. It had been her first order of business as the new dean: to insist that the front door of the chapel never be locked. The risk of vandalism and theft was far outweighed by the fact that broken and hopeless people would find an unlocked door. The power of a perpetually unlocked door still clogged her nose and filled her eyes. Like now.

After all, what was one soul worth? What was easing the pain of a broken life worth? Was it worth all the silver and gold within those chapel walls? Was it worth the repair cost if something broke? Was it even a question for lovers of God? She wiped her eyes and continued up the steps.

She stepped inside, and took a breath as the door eased shut behind her. She let her eyes adjust to the darkness and her ears to the stillness. The air was charged and she glanced around. She could feel she wasn't alone. As her eyes adjusted, they took in a small shape in the front pew. As she neared, a weathered and wrinkled face turned and smiled. It was a weak and joyless smile pasted across a face Victoria Nile had seen before.

"Dr. Spruill?" she said. "I recognize you from the reception."

"Please call me Nettie, Dean Nile," Nettie said.

"Only if you will call me Vickie," Dean Nile said.

"Yes, it was a lovely occasion. I hope you felt welcomed."

"May I join you for a minute?"

Nettie patted the pew cushion next to her. The two sat in silence for several moments.

"How are you settling in, Vickie?" Nettie said.

"Boxes," Vickie said. "I swear they breed."

"They say every move provides a welcome opportunity to lighten your load."

"I committed to giving a third of my possessions away with this move, and failed," Vickie said. "I fear I am a work in progress."

"Me, too," Nettie said, "but my possessions are the least of my problem."

Dean Nile waited, and the silence returned. She learned long ago not to reach for the burdens people carried on their backs, even though you fear they may collapse beneath the weight of them. Those who wished to unburden must hand them off themselves.

"With all your new responsibilities," Nettie said, "you don't need the woes of an old woman."

"Sometimes we can be transfer stations for each other. You share your struggles with me, and I with you, and together we can transfer them to the altar where they belong."

At the words, Nettie convulsed and her body seemed to lose all strength. She slid off the pew and crumpled face first onto the carpet. Dean Nile shoved off the pew and settled next to Nettie. Mercifully, the old woman's descent had been gradual and the landing was soft.

"I'm a killer," Nettie said into the carpet. Her slender frame seemed frailer now than when she sat on the pew.

Vickie placed her hand in the middle of Nettie's back.

"I try so hard," Nettie said, and hiccupped, "to help, you know. Just to help. And they keep dying."

"Who keeps dying Nettie?" Vickie said softly.

"Every man I've tried to love," she said. The words came haltingly, one at a time. "I'm poison."

"What's happened?" Vickie said, "Has something happened?"

The back of Nettie's head bobbed and Reverend Nile heard sobs muffle from the carpet. Sometimes the hardest part of ministry is to be present, and silent. Vickie, the human being sitting next to Nettie, wanted information, craved it, as if to fill the information void was to equip the minister. But healing seldom came by information, either by the giving or by the receiving of it. Presence with Nettie's tears. Silence with Nettie's pain. Love sent without words to surround her. It took all of Reverend Nile's focus.

“It’s happened again,” Nettie said pushed herself into a sitting position.

“What’s happened, Nettie?” Vickie said, leaning down to look through strands of Nettie’s ashen hair for her eyes. They were swollen and red. “Do you want to tell me?”

“Now Jeremy,” Nettie said, making no move to clear the hair that fell in dark gray tangles, or to wipe the tears from her cheeks.

“Jeremy,” Dean Nile said, “Tittle? Jeremy Tittle?” She knew she was pressing for information but couldn’t help herself.

The woman’s silent nod froze Vickie for a moment and her mind reeled. She focused on her breath and took a slow inhale through her nose. And waited. Waited a full minute in the silence and then she could wait no more. “Has Dean Tittle passed? Is that what you’re telling me?”

“Into another world,” Nettie nodded, “to get away from me.”

“How did he die, Nettie?” she said.

“He didn’t,” Nettie said. “I did.”

Vickie took the woman’s boney hands. Nettie’s skin was paper thin and nearly translucent. “And yet, look at these hands,” she said. “You’re still here, and very much alive.”

“I wish I weren’t,” Nettie said.

Dean Nile swallowed the words, “You mustn’t” before they erupted from her lips. *Presence, Vickie.* She watched the elderly woman, noted the expressionless face, the unfocused eyes. Held her boney hands. Waited.

“Will you go with me to see him?” Nettie said at last and looked into Dean Nile’s eyes. “Vickie?”

“Of course,” she said. “Where are we going?”

“Memorial.”

Hillside Above Miserericordia Clinic
Kingstown, Rhode Island

"Get her out," Carlos said into the radio, "Quickly. And the product in that trailer."

"*Sí*," Pablo said.

"And tell Maria Garza to vanish. Hurry."

"*Sí*," Pablo said. He was already climbing the driveway in long strides. He burst into the trailer, reached across the counter, and began snapping latex gloves onto his hands.

"*Vamanos*," he said to Maria Garza who held a bloody towel to Maria Sanchez's head.

"No," Maria Garza said. "She is my sister."

In the next instant, Pablo's huge fist closed around the thick layers of cloth between Maria Garza's shoulder blades. He lifted her until her feet no longer touched the ground and walked her to the back door. He kicked the door open and placed her on the step outside.

"*Vamanos*," he said, and slammed the door.

He returned to Maria Sanchez, grabbing a fresh towel from the shelf. He gathered her gently into his arms. Snatching her purse from the counter, he kicked the clinic's front door open and carried her out. At the bottom of the hill, he laid her across the trunk of her car. He stuffed his hand into her purse and felt for the keys, unlocked the car, laid her across the front seats, and set the purse on her belly. Then, as if a magician had waved a wand, he was gone.

High atop the hill, Carlos adjusted his elbows on the truck cab, watching through binoculars. "Go," he said, and tried to shoo the fire truck and EMS vehicle with his arms. "Go!" The loaded rifle lay in its foam-lined nest at his feet. It seemed only moments before that he had had it trained on Sister Maria Garza as she stood on the back trailer steps. She disappeared down the back trail the other women used.

An investigation would begin soon, law crawling all over this hillside. Soon.

He slammed the binoculars onto the roof. It was all out of control. And whenever it was out of control, someone ended up dead. Maybe they would all die. God help Maria Garza. And God help him for what he was about to do. He reached for the satphone and punched in Gregorio's number.

Hillside Above Misererericordia Clinic
Kingstown, Rhode Island

"Outpost 1 to Outpost Three," Carlos said into the radio.

"*Sí*," Pablo said.

"You okay?" he said.

"*Sí*," Pablo said.

"Have you called for the ambulance?" Carlos said.

"No."

"Excellent. I knew I could rely on you."

"*Sí*."

"Sanitize it. Remove what you can. Understand?"

"*Sí*."

"*Fuego*," Carlos said. "Petrol. Lots of it," Carlos said. "How long will it take?"

"Fifteen minutes," Pablo said.

"Too long," Carlos said.

"Ten minutes."

"Five. I will call EMS as soon as the smoke reaches my nose up here. Let me know when you are ready."

Durante Preparar. Over prepare, even if it meant Dr. Maria Sanchez had to wait for medical attention. It was their only hope of surviving this moment.

Carlos lit a cigarette. His eye caught motion to the left. On the Sound, a frigate was passing a barge making its lazy way to port. He smelled the stench of rotten fish and fuel oil. It had been the perfect spot for the operation. Sanchez had seemed the perfect operator. So close to the harbor, and yet remote in its own way. He took a long drag. The salt wind snatched his exhale and scuttled it across the ridge. He grabbed the hair atop his head into a fist and squeezed until it hurt.

It would be months before they could have the operation running again, months before they could build another safe spot, with safe people. Carlos squeezed his hair again. The Shark was going to be so pissed. He reached down and snapped closed the rifle case, gathered extra clips for his 40 caliber Smith & Wesson nested in the back of his jeans. Wondered if Pablo needed help down there. He didn't dare risk driving down to the clinic. He jumped off the tailgate, his boots landing hard upon the rocks. Checked his watch.

It would be one hell of a fire.

Chapter Nine

ICU Unit

Memorial Hospital

Kingstown, Rhode Island

"Wait! Wait just one minute here!" the ICU nurse said.

Corrections Officer Drucker had continued toward the elevator. It dinged and the door opened.

"Have fun," Drucker said under his breath. He was smiling as the elevator door closed again. Poor Burns.

Dr. Fleischer heard the raised voices all the way at the ICU nurses' station. He dropped the papers in his hands and they scattered on the floor. He ran for the isolation room around the corner.

"Give me your keys," the nurse said, her voice somewhere between a howl and a shriek.

Officer Burns had retreated from the room and now stood beside the doorway with his hands across his shotgun, jaw set and silent.

"What's going on here?" Dr. Fleischer said.

"He had no right," she said, jamming a forefinger in Burns' face. Then she wheeled on Dr. Fleischer. "You see my patient in there? You go look at his left arm and tell me what you see."

Dr. Fleischer entered the room. Vinnie was jangling the handcuffs noisily against the railing and humming to himself.

"Are you okay, sir?" Dr. Fleischer asked.

"Those kind ladies brought me jewelry," Vinnie said, clanging the cuffs.

"What la-," Dr. Fleischer pivoted and stabbed an index finger like a knife. "Off," he said to Officer Burns.

"No can do, Doctor," Burns said, grinning.

"Keys," Dr. Fleischer demanded, his hand outstretched. "Give me your keys."

"Don't have them," Burns said. Besides, we unlock nothin' and nobody without a direct order from the Warden."

"This is not the prison. This …."

"I listened to that the first time," Burns said, cutting him off. "This isn't the prison, but those are prison cuffs. You got no say."

"We'll see about this," Dr. Fleischer said. He and the nurse stormed past Burns and disappeared around the corner.

"Hoo," Burns said, and sat himself down again next to the door.

A man in surgical scrubs had just emerged from the elevator, followed by a stooped, elderly nun. The doctor walked quickly around the corner and headed toward the nurse's station. The nun seemed to struggle keeping her balance. She limped her way slowly along the corridor. Burns watched her approach, saw her reach into a small, flat bag. He smiled when he saw the prayer card emerge in her hand. Recognized it.

"Sister," he said.

The nun seemed not to want to approach too closely, keeping a safe distance, and Burns relaxed. She held the card outstretched toward him. He shook his head no, but she wasn't looking at him.

"For the poor patient," the nun whispered. "Please. Have mercy and give it to the poor patient."

Burns rolled his eyes, leaned half off his chair toward her, and took the laminated card with Jesus, and the heart, and the bright light behind him. He sat back down and stared at it in his hand. Something was off. Jesus was moving on the card, swaying, and the card was going in and out of focus. Officer Burns started to rise and then toppled headlong onto the floor. At that same moment, a horn blew and the intercom crackled to life, "Code Blue, ICU6. Code Blue, ICU6." Gregorio had done his work well down the hall. The prayer card was next to the unconscious guard. Emil snatched it up and returned it to his pouch. No longer hunched or limping, he sprang into the isolation room and shut the door.

"My brother," he said to Vinnie.

There was a pause, as Vinnie appeared to be focusing his eyes. Then Emil saw the eyes harden. "You are no brother of mine," Vinnie said hoarsely. "I figured some shit was up."

"I had to see you."

"You come to kill me?"

"No," Emil said, and shook his head. The habit swayed. "And if you knew my heart, you would never ask the question."

"Thought I knew your heart," Vinnie said. "If I knew anyone in this world, thought I knew you. *Bastardo*."

"I betrayed you," Emil said. "I risked coming here to look you in the eyes, so you could see these eyes, these eyes you've known all your life. I wanted you to look into these eyes when I tell you how sorry I am. I have no excuse. Vincente. Brother. I have sinned against you. I beg your forgiveness. Please Brother."

Emil watched the man in the bed tremble and saw his eyes well with tears.

"Let me come close, close enough for you to spit on me. It is what I deserve." Emil leaned his face close to Vinnie's and whispered. "Then I will make it up to you. And that is what I promise." Vinnie screwed up his mouth and spat directly into Emil's face. Emil made no move to wipe it off. Vinnie was shaking as if beset with spasms.

"I am so, so sorry, my brother," Emil said, as tears mixed with spittle on his face.

"I," Vinnie convulsed and then righted himself. "I could not bring myself to hate you."

"Please forgive me, Vincente," Emil said. "I beg you."

"It is finished," Vinnie said. "We will not speak of it again."

"Say it," Emil said. "Have mercy and say you forgive me."

"I forgive you, Emil Bente," Vinnie said as a tear spattered onto the pillowcase. "My brother."

At the words, Emil dropped his head onto Vinnie's chest. Then he rose.

Vinnie tried to reach for Emil's hand and the cuffs clanged.

"I cannot touch you with the gloves," Emil said.

"Ah," Vinnie said. "You are the spider who paralyzes its prey, no?"

"An old trick," Emil nodded, "but still effective." He gathered himself. "I must go."

"Take me with you," Vinnie said. "Please brother."

"I can't," Emil said. "You are hurt too badly. But now," Emil pointed at himself, "now you know I will come for you. And when I return, you will come with me."

"Heard that before," Vinnie said, still hiccupping with sobs.

Brother, look me in these eyes. Look," Emil said, and waited until Vinnie had locked eyes with him. "I promise."

"I used to think your promise was unbreakable," Vinnie said.

"So did I," Emil said. "I am a wretched man."

"So am I," Vinnie said. "I admit."

"I beg you, brother, forgive this wretched man who bows before you."

"I forgave you already, Emil my brother," Vinnie said. He shook his head. "I said we will not speak of it again."

Emil leaned over and kissed Vinnie's feet, one at a time. And then he did it again. "Until we are together again," he said, and hurried from the room.

Outside, people rushed from the elevator and pushed down the hall toward ICU6. Emil hunched and knelt over the unconscious officer, as if attending to him, and motioned for them to move along toward the Code.

He thought about taking the stairs but the optics wouldn't be right for a frail old nun. He righted himself slowly and limped to the elevator, pressing the down button. With his hands still gloved, he pulled another card from the pouch. He wiped the card over every surface of each glove. Just in case. *Over prepare.*

Bureau Vehicle
Vanessa Sullivan's House
Kingstown, Rhode Island

There is no more debilitating force in a man's life than woman trouble. He'd been sitting in front of Vanessa's house, knowing he was going to have to face it, knowing that his next stop was going to be Memorial Hospital's Emergency Room. But twenty minutes had passed and still Max Steele had not started the engine. The hell of it was, he couldn't even blame this paralysis on Maria. She wasn't responsible for his circuits being jammed. She didn't have her hand on his, preventing him from starting the car. Much as he had liked the protection, as a younger man, of pointing the finger at the woman, he knew better now.

It was inevitable that he would see her, unless she had called in sick or asked for a vacation day, but both were too much to hope for. Why did she make him feel so – what was this thing in his chest? Why were his hands sweating? He rubbed them absently on his pant legs in the bureau car.

Glancing to the rearview mirror, he reached up and adjusted it down until he could look himself squarely in the face. *Max Steele, you are a grown man. You're a grown man in love with a woman. If she does not love you back, or love you the way you love her, then you're just going to have to deal with that square on. There's nowhere to run, so running away is not an option. There is no way to hide, so let's get that out of our head too, shall we? And circumstances have aligned so that you're going to have to cross paths with Maria Sanchez. Suck. It. Up.*

He banged his hands on the steering wheel, reached down, and turned the key. The engine sprang to life. He yanked the bureau car into a tight turn and headed for the hospital.

His cell phone chirped. Snatching it from his coat pocket, he looked to see who was calling. Lieutenant Bert Higgins. Course. Perfect timing. Max declined the call. Bert could leave a message. And go back to spying on his partner.

Emergency Room
Memorial Hospital
Kingstown, Rhode Island

Max Steele parked deliberately near the perimeter of the hospital lot to give himself time to walk off the jangle coursing through him. He stood outside the bureau car for a moment and scanned the area. Detective habits die hard. He noticed the lot was about two-thirds full. It would be busy in the Emergency Room. His eyes took in the Mantisto State Prison bus in the far distance as he began to walk and he wondered what was up with that. Filed it in a mental drawer and kept walking.

The Emergency Room's glass doors parted. For a brief flash, they looked to Max like the jaws of a great beast. He blew breath through his teeth and kept walking. He had been right: the ER was as frenetic tonight as if it was the weekend. His eyes scanned the waiting room for any familiar faces, and especially for Bull's twins. He nodded to the receptionist and headed to the back.

Linda Turnbill, the charge nurse, was the only one at the desk, but the clatter and clank of utensils and the swish of curtains opening and closing between beds, gave evidence of a fully engaged staff.

"Excuse me, Nurse Turnbill," Max said. Max had known her for years, knew her to be tough and no nonsense. She could kill you with one look.

"Captain Steele," she said with a frown. She held a file suspended in each hand and stared hard at him.

"What?" he said.

In response, she turned away to the other side of the rounded desk.

Terrific. Just what he needed. He wanted to go back to the vehicle, just leave, go anywhere, be anywhere but here. His feet wouldn't move. His throat went dry and he licked his lips. He shoved his hands in his pockets and stared at the floor. The cacophony assaulting his ears was almost more than he could bear.

When he looked up again, Linda was back, still glaring at him. *Terrific.*

"Linda, Nurse Turnbill …," he said.

"I don't want to get involved," she said, holding up a hand.

"Then don't," Max said. The words came out much harsher than he had intended. The nurse dropped the file she was holding. Her hands balled into fists, and they went to her ample hips.

"That's not what I meant," Max said, pulling his hands from his pockets and placing them on the counter. "Look, I came to …. Look, I'm sorry …."

"Spit it," she said. The fists were still on the hips. Max would rather have been facing down a charging rhino.

"Give me a break, will ya?" Max said.

"Break? Break?" Linda said, "Quite the choice of words, young man, after you broke that poor girl's heart."

Max's eyes retreated to the floor. Seldom in his life had he felt so cornered. But if anybody could do it, Battle Ax Linda could. He took a deep breath and blew it out slowly along the buttons of his shirt.

"I need to look in on Vanessa Sullivan," he said, still avoiding eye contact with the heated mother hen across from him.

"Slip 4," she said. "Gave her something to settle her stomach."

"Okay, thanks," Max said, and shuffled his feet in the direction of Slip 4. The bed was shuttered by curtains, and Max whispered a silent plea to the

Universe, or God, or whoever might be taking calls at the moment, that Maria wouldn't be on the other side. He parted the curtain. Vanessa was alone, staring at the ceiling. She jumped, and then fell back on the pillow.

"Thank God it's you," she said.

"Van, Jesus, Van," Max said. He sat on the side of the bed and wrapped both arms around her. He could feel her heart thudding fast against his chest. "It's all over, Sweetie."

She broke from his arms and looked into his eyes. "Is it? You promise?"

"I promised Bull I'd look out for you and the boys. I will keep that promise, whether it's over or not."

"I know," she said. "Where are the boys?"

"I have a grown boy with a big gun guarding and entertaining them. Don't worry. They're perfectly safe."

She grinned. "They love everything to do with cops and taking down bad guys, even after what they've lived through."

"Chips off the old block," Max said.

"Nate would be so proud of them," she said.

"Bull Sullivan IS so proud of them," Max said. "Don't think for a minute he isn't smiling down at them, and you, from his heavenly deer stand."

Vanessa laughed, and her eyes filled with tears. "God, he loved to hunt."

"He loved you most."

"Sometimes I still make myself sick missing him," she said. "Then I remember what he told me the last time I kissed him, and I know I've got to keep on living."

"Want to share?"

She shook her head.

"Understand," Max said.

"I just know I've got two boys to raise and I need for them to be safe."

"When someone breaks in like that," Max said.

"Yeah, and beats that security system Bull had installed. You see that?"

"I saw," Max said.

"Max, I know you've already got a lot on you, but I need to ask a personal favor."

"Anything."

"Take that man off the grid. I don't care what you have to do, but I want that man rotting in hell. You got me?"

"Van, I . . . ."

She grabbed him by both shoulders and locked her eyes on his. "You got him once. You get your hands on him again, you finish him. No more prison. No more prison breaks. Finish him Max."

The curtain slid open behind him, and Max whirled. FBI Director Elizabeth Fenton stood between the two sheets of fabric.

"May I come in?" she said.

Max shot to his feet before the thought of standing even entered his conscious mind.

"Come in," Vanessa said.

"I'm Lizzie Fenton," the Director said, moving to take Vanessa's hand.

"I remember you," Vanessa said, "from the funeral."

Director Fenton nodded. "And how are those boys?"

"Full of burgers, fries, and shakes," Max said. "And playing cop with one of Kingstown's finest."

"Having the time of their lives, I'm betting," Vanessa said.

"Perfect," Director Fenton said, "an event no doubt orchestrated by the brilliant and talented Captain Steele."

"Oh boy," Max said, and shook his head. "She wants something."

Fenton smiled and shook her head at him. "Not at the moment." She paused. "Mrs. Sullivan, you feel up to talking about a couple of things?"

"Sure," Vanessa said, "I'm feeling better."

"Splendid," she said, "Max shot me a brief summary of what happened, and I've checked in with forensics. It appears you got a personal visit from Emil Bente himself."

Vanessa nodded.

Max nodded too. "The rosary is his personal calling card, as you know."

"Indeed I do," she said. "A good chunk of money, too." She looked from Vanessa to Max, "But no note?'

"Nope," Vanessa said.

"You looking for something, Captain Steele?" Director Fenton said to Max, who had kept glancing toward the parted curtains as she talked. "You seem distracted."

"Um, no, Director," Max said, "Sorry." He walked over and drew the curtains together.

"So," the Director said, turning to Vanessa, "priority one for me and my team is to ensure that you remain safe. I've already sent the directive to post an agent outside your home, 24/7, for the next couple of weeks at least."

"Thank you," Vanessa said, "I can take care of myself."

"No doubt, Mrs. Sullivan," she said, "but this office takes care of its own. Period."

"Well, thank you and I accept," Vanessa said, "although I don't think Bente meant me any harm."

Director Fenton and Max glanced at each other.

"And perhaps just the opposite, in his own twisted way," Fenton said.

"My thought exactly," Max said.

"But if he shows up again, I'm gonna waste him," Vanessa said.

Director Fenton laughed. "Spoken like a true agent's spouse. The only people finer and more courageous than my agents are their spouses." She grew serious again, "May I also arrange for the boys to be escorted to and from school for a while?"

"Yes, thank you," Vanessa said. "I'm grateful for the support, and glad you are taking some of the load off Max's shoulders. You know he would be trying to do all of that by himself."

"Yes, I do," Fenton said. "And we need him out there hunting." She took Vanessa's hand again. "Anything else I can do for you, anything, you pick up that phone."

"I will," Vanessa said.

"And now, Captain Steele, would you be kind enough to escort me to my vehicle?"

"It would be my pleasure, Director," Max said, grinning at Vanessa. He hugged her gently. "I'll call you."

They walked through the clatter and rush of personnel, until at last they were through the exit doors and into the parking lot. Elizabeth Fenton didn't speak until they were at her vehicle.

"Get in," she said.

Max opened the passenger door and adjusted the seat all the way back to give himself legroom. He closed the door and waited.

Director Fenton got behind the wheel and closed the door. She stared straight ahead for a full minute, and then said to the windshield. "Please don't quit Max, or ask for a transfer, or be completely pissed off at your partner. It's my fault. I let it get away, without putting you into the loop soon enough. I owe you an apology." She turned and looked at Max, whose mouth had dropped open slightly.

"Of the two or three things that I thought you might say to me just now, this was not one of them."

"I'm sorry, Max."

"Lambowski called you," Max said.

"No," she said. "Lambowski called Higgins. And Higgins called me. And how."

"And how?"

"Yep. Higgins called me everything but a bitch. Even though I would have deserved it, he still would've lost his job if he'd used the B word and both of us knew it. Let's just say he communicated the same message in so many words."

Max was shaking his head, but a small curl appeared at the corners of his mouth. "He's still young, Director," Max said, "but he is one tough *hombre*. I'd pick him to cover my six anywhere, anytime."

"If you ever doubted his loyalty to you, don't," she said. "He put his neck on the line standing up to me."

"Thank you for telling me," Max said.

"Figured I'd better straighten this out before you put each other in the hospital. I need you both."

"You figured right," Max said.

"Thought so."

"Okay, explain it to me," Max said. "The rest of it."

She paused and her eyes returned to the windshield. "It started as a simple background check of visitors to Nina Ondolopous Bente at Memorial. Dr. Maria Sanchez was on that list several times, even though she is an ER doc and had no official business in that room, to our knowledge. I knew about your relationship with Sanchez, and I should have told you then that we were running a background check on her and the reason why. I didn't. I didn't think it would matter. Turns out it does."

"Wait, turns out what does?" Max said. He felt his heart flip in his chest and adjusted himself in the seat.

Director Fenton paused. "Mind you, we don't have the full picture yet because the background check was incomplete. But so far, we have traced her back to Italy."

“Wait. Italy?” Max said.

“So you don’t know any of this, right Max?”

“Any of what?”

“That answers my question,” Director Fenton said.

“You’re speaking in riddles,” Max said.

“That’s because I’m so uncomfortable right now. I’m not sure how to share what I think I know,” she said. “God help me, if I am wrong, I will have made a messy situation exponentially messier. But Max, I think you are being played.”

“Played? I just got done with a crime scene where I felt like I was being played by Emil Bente,” Max said. “And before that, I was out on the sidewalk by Maria’s place, feeling that I was being played by my partner and the department. So, pardon me, Director, but who’s playing me now?”

“Dr. Maria Sanchez,” Fenton said.

“How’s that?” Max said hotly. “Don’t tell me. She’s an assassin.” He blew air through his teeth.

“Or should I say, Mother Maria Sanchez is playing you?” Elizabeth Fenton said, and looked at Max.

Max scoffed. “Mother? MOTHER?” he said loud enough to be heard outside the vehicle.

“Mother,” Director Fenton said, nodding. “Maria Sanchez is a Roman Catholic nun.”

“Forgive me, Director, but I KNOW that’s not true,” he said.

“Really? And how do you know, Captain?”

Max was silent. He closed his eyes.

“Because you slept with her?” Fenton said.

Max's mind flashed to Maria's naked body atop his frame, pounding down onto him, screaming and writhing.

"Max?" Director Fenton said. "Are you okay?"

Max shoved the car door open and climbed out, shutting it behind them. He walked away. Didn't care where, as long as it was away. Far away. From the hospital. From his director. From his partner.

It was all bullshit, and everyone was full of it. "I don't give a shit," he said to the robin that eyed him from around a tree trunk. He crossed a two-lane road. And then another one. He felt surge after surge of adrenaline course through his body. He wanted to run. And he wanted to hurt somebody. God help the hapless bystander who gives him any shit right now.

He wasn't sure how long he walked, or where he was, but he happened upon a small park and sat on the bench. The night belched its cool blackness across the landscape. A lamppost fifty yards away shed the only light. Max welcomed the darkness, with its musky scent of pine bark.

His eye picked up movement and he glanced toward the light post. A lone figure walked slowly in his direction. Something dangled from each hand, but Max couldn't make it out. He squeezed his bicep against the shoulder holster. The Glock was still there. Slowly, he draped his arm across his lap, closer to it.

Keeping his head facing forward, he watched the stranger from his periphery, getting closer and closer. There was something about the stranger's gait, though, that was familiar. And then the man spoke.

"You still want that beer?" Bert Higgins said. He held up a bottle in each hand.

Max smiled. As jacked up as everything was, he couldn't help it. His partner had gone to a lot of trouble, and that meant something.

"Is it cold?" Max said.

"Barely," Bert said, "We'd best be drinking it." Bert sat on the bench, twisted off the bottle cap, and handed Max the beer. Then he opened his own. "Here's to lying, stealing, cheating, and drinking."

"Appropriate," Max said.

"When you lie," Bert said, "lie to save a friend. When you steal, steal a young maiden's heart. When you cheat, cheat death. And when you drink, drink with me."

They clinked bottles.

"I'll drink to everything except the maidens," Max said.

"Fair enough," Bert said.

They drank in silence, sitting next to each other, not looking at one another and not saying a word. Sometimes it's the best thing. Sometimes it's the only thing.

When they had drained their beers, Max looked at his partner.

"She call you?" He said. "Fenton?"

"Yep," Bert said. "Then all I had to do was find you out here. In the dark. Good thing you're microchipped."

"Ha," Max said. "You saying I'm a dog?"

He and Bert were silent again. At last Bert glanced at him and said, "Can I give you a lift home?"

"I guess," Max said. "Nowhere else to go."

High overhead, a four-propeller drone whirred quietly. Its infrared lens focused on the men, watching them stand up from the bench, relaying the video feed wirelessly to its owner.

Residence of Captain Max Steele
Kingstown, Rhode Island

Bert Higgins and Max Steele rode in silence most of the way to Max's house. Max appreciated Bert's discipline to let him talk when he was ready.

A less mature man would have been blathering. They were pulling into Max's driveway when Bert said, "Get a good night's sleep."

"Thanks," Max said, staring ahead through the windshield. He opened his mouth to speak again, and froze. "What," he said, "is that?" He pointed toward his front stoop. A round box sat on the mat in front of his door. The automatic porch light's beam glinted off a gold ribbon tied in an ornate bow on the top.

"Smart remarks are flooding my brain," Bert said.

"Not now," Max said. He glanced quickly in both directions and then behind through the back window. "Something's off."

"Off good, or off bad?" Bert said. Then he shook his head. "Sorry. I just slapped myself."

"Off, as in let's not get killed," Max said. Both men drew their weapons. Bert killed the engine, while Max kicked open the side door and crab walked to the back of the vehicle. "Go," he said, and Bert slipped from the driver's side door. Max covered his retreat to the back of the vehicle.

"What we got?" Higgins said, scanning with his eyes over the top of his gun.

"Could be anything," Max said, "Could be nothing."

"Could be embarrassing if you call it in, and it's nothing," Bert said. "I know what you're thinking."

"Exactly," Max said. "God, this day!" Max said, "And us with beer on our breath."

"I can hear it now," Bert said.

"But better than dead," Max said. "Imagine the headline if I go up there and get my ass blown away, 'Detective Max Steele, FBI Dumbass, lost his life in an obvious setup, because he was too proud to take a little ribbing in the squad room.'" He glanced at Bert and then back over his gun sights toward the house. "Damn it! Call it in."

Within minutes, the street in front of Max's house was alive with flashing lights and armed officers. A small bomb retrieval robot crawled its way across the lawn toward the stoop.

Randy Jacobs had just arrived and slipped next to Max.

"We've got to stop meeting like this," he said.

"All I wanted was my lawn manicured," Max said, not looking at him. "My partner says, 'I got an idea. Let those clumsy forensics dicks tear the shit out of your front lawn and then the Department will have to pay for the redo.'"

"Brilliant strategy," Randy said.

"My partner's a genius."

The robot had the lid off the box and was in the process of tipping it over. Max wasn't far away, but he used the binoculars around his neck anyway. He focused on the rim of the box and followed as it toppled. Something moved inside it, and he tensed.

Out flopped a felt hat with a small feather in the band.

The lawn had grown quiet, but now it exploded into chatter and clatter, as a cautious relief swept through the crew.

Not Max. His face contorted into a snarl.

Bert came running over, his cell phone pressed to his ear, his other arm waving.

"Can I call you back?" Bert said. "Yes, ma'am. One minute, no more." He ended the call, grabbed Max by the sleeve, and directed him away from the noise.

"That was Fenton," he said.

Tell her I'll call tomorrow, first thing, with a full report."

"Negative," Bert said. "You want to call her right now." Bert's eyes were wide and intense.

"Ah Jesus, Bert," Max said.

Bert pressed the call button, handed Max the phone, and said, "It's about Bente."

While Max spoke with Director Fenton, Bert jumped in his vehicle and did a three point reverse from the driveway, narrowly avoiding one of the forensics vans. He saw Max end the call. Steele ran to the passenger side door. In one motion, he had it open, had himself in the seat, and had the door closed again.

"Memorial," Max said, "lights and flashers. Let's go."

Bert already had his foot mashed on the accelerator. The bureau car leaped forward, tires squealing. "Anyone we can call there?" he asked.

"Thinking," Max said. "Fenton has dispatched units to meet us there."

Bert had both hands low on the steering wheel in perfect 4 o'clock and 8 o'clock positions for rapid turns. "What do we know?"

"Not a hell of a lot," Max said. "That's how they wanted it."

"They," Bert said

"Yes. THEY, whoever the mess THEY are," Max said. "If we ever get the list of THEY's, we'll bring the whole Cartel down. We seem to be guessing all the time. It's starting to piss me off."

"Wait," Higgins said, and took a corner hard. The tires complained. "Did you just say, 'What the mess?'" He snorted.

"Trying not to say 'fuck' anymore. Used to be one of my favorite words. Not anymore." Max was silent for several long moments, his eyes fixed on the dashboard. "Will you let me focus, please."

"Roger that, Cap," Higgins said with a quick nod of his head. "You said we seem to be guessing all the time."

"It's like that mother spider and her babies," Max said. "Have you seen that video clip?"

Bert was silent, eyes fixed on the road. "So this is what focusing looks like? Spiders?" The bureau car continued to gobble asphalt before him.

"She's carrying her young on her back," Max said, ignoring him, "but you don't notice the baby spiders right away because they are so well hidden. Then you poke Mama, and hundreds of those little suckers scatter in every direction."

"Nice," Bert said.

"Bente," Max said, ignoring him, "and the Cartel are like mama spiders. You get hold of one, and a hundred more scatter into the woodwork. Pisses me off that we only catch one at a time, if any."

Bert took another tight turn and the tires squawked. "So there's more than one mama spider, you say?"

Max was shaking his head. "I'm not so sure anymore. More I know, less I know." He snatched the phone from the console and punched it with his finger.

"Director, yes ma'am," Max said into the phone. "Forgot to ask." He listened for a moment and rolled his eyes. "Yes, ma'am. Fast as we can. Yes, ma'am." He pulled the phone away from his ear for a moment, glanced at Bert.

"Ma'am," Max said, "Called to make sure you dispatched a helicopter. We need every eye." He listened for a moment. "Okay, good. Any idea what we are looking for? Copy that. Yes, ma'am, I will." He ended the call. "Bitch," he said to the lifeless phone.

"We got eyes in the sky?" Bert said.

"Yes," Max said, nodding. "Sherman, not Billings."

"Where is Tex when we need him?" Bert said.

Max smiled, remembering the colorful pilot who helped them capture the Cartel's Number One and Number Two men last year. "He only flies the big boys. Can you imagine him in a bubble-headed dragonfly like the one we got coming tonight?"

Bert smiled and pressed the accelerator to pass two vehicles on the interstate. "ETA eight minutes." He glanced at Max. "You going to call Maria and warn her something's going down at Memorial?"

Max was silent for a long moment. He drew in a breath and blew it out. Shook his head. "For all I know, she's in on it."

"Think?" Bert said.

"Not sure what to think, partner."

"Hear that. Me neither."

"Okay, let's focus," Max said.

"Like we're not, Cap?" Bert said, and then immediately regretted the sarcasm.

"The intel we have," Max said. "Let's go over it. Fenton says Memorial called. Caller unknown. Bontecelli was transported there for a surgical procedure on his hand, and nobody told the FBI squat about it. Fenton's hot about that, but that's not intel."

"Okay," Bert said.

Max held up a hand, "Post-op, Bontecelli is secured in ICU. Then all hell breaks loose. A Code on the other end of the wing from where they've got Bontecelli sends everybody running there. They come back, the corrections officer guarding Bontecelli is face down on the floor, unconscious, but alive."

"And Bontecelli's gone," Bert said.

"And Bontecelli," Max said, "is not gone. Get this. Bontecelli is handcuffed to his hospital bed and very much still there."

"Kidding me," Bert said. "Then why the lights and sirens, and backup and helicopter?"

"Not done," Max said. "The second corrections officer is out by the bus and says he saw a doctor in scrubs and a nun running for a truck."

Bert shook his head. "Can't make this shit up. He stop 'em?"

"Nope," Max said. "Says they were in and gone before he could blink."

"What truck and where's it now?" Bert said.

"That's where we come in," Max said. "And Sherman."

"ETA on our backup?"

"Negative," Max said, "but I'm betting we get there first." He raised the radio to his lips. "Units 3 and 8, what's your ETA, Memorial?"

"Unit 3," the radio squawked, "We are 10-76 from HQ. ETA 13 mics."

"Unit 8?' Max said.

"8," the radio crackled. "Northeast, 16 mics out."

"Shit," Max said. "Everybody's late to the party."

"Last minute invite," Bert said.

"Yeah, why is that? Better believe we're going to get some answers."

Bert hit the exit ramp and mashed his brakes. "Hate to ask, Cap," he said, "but where's Maria?" He heard another deep breath next to him.

"Better find out, huh," Max said.

"Better."

Max knew he could text her, but what would he say? Maybe he should call Battle Ax Linda in the ER. But she was so pissed at him, she wouldn't give him anything.

Max felt a tap on his arm. Bert's hand was outstretched toward him. "Maybe I better do it," he said. Max nodded and handed him the phone.

"Hey there and howdy," a voice sounded through the radio. Both men recognized the voice. Max raised the radio to his lips,

"What is it with you fly boys?" Max said. "Think you're above using radio code."

"Hey Captain," Sherman said from the helicopter. "I am 10-23 at Memorial. What are we looking for?"

"Tell him we are ETA 3 mics," Bert said.

"Looking for a truck carrying a doctor and a nun, possibly a nurse as well," Max said. "We are ETA 3 mics." He heard the mic click.

"Sounds like a bad joke," Sherman said. "Description on the truck?"

"Not much," Max said. "Dark panel truck. That's it. I know: there's a million of them on the roads."

"10-4, Captain Steele," Sherman said. "I hope you're noticing my radio etiquette."

"Noted," Max said, and shook his head. Glanced at Higgins. "Think it's the altitude?"

Bert laughed. "You going to give me the phone?"

"Oh," Max said. "Right. I'll dial it for you. What number you want?"

The radio crackled to life, "What the ...?" Max grabbed the radio just as it squawked again, "Not alone up here, Cap," Lt. Sherman said. "Taking evasive measures!"

"From what, Sherm?" Max said.

Bert stomped the accelerator. "Almost there, Cap."

"Sherman, you all right?"

"Incoming! Taking fire!" he heard the helicopter pilot shout.

Max had the radio pressed to his lips and was ready to speak as Higgins rocketed the car into the Memorial parking lot and slammed on the brakes.

Max lurched forward, and kicked the door open.

"What? Where are you?" Max said.

"Mile due North of Memorial. Taking fire," Sherman said. "UAVs. Two." The sound of gunfire sounded through the radio's receiver, metal on metal, a stuttered plinking and the whine of the engine.

"Mic must be jammed open," Max said. "Sherman. Sherm!" Max yelled into the radio, even though he knew with the mic open, he wouldn't be able to transmit.

His Glock in one hand, and still holding the radio in the other hand, Max craned his neck and scanned the sky through the windshield.

"Heading north," Bert said, and mashed the accelerator again. Max opened his window and let his arm fall outside with the Glock firm in his hand. Soon, he heard the thwacking of the helicopter blades above and craned his neck. He saw the under lights winking against a starless night. As he watches, small streaks of flame, lots of them, chased each other across the sky. They seemed to come from two spots ahead of where he was looking. He heard a popping sound, and dread roiled his gut.

Through the radio, he heard Sherman scream. It was a mixture of pain and terror. And then the sky bloomed with a bright fireball. The explosion shattered the darkness and filled the night air. It was directly overhead. Bert slammed on the brakes and both men dove from the vehicle as debris rained down over a mostly empty mall parking lot.

Max rolled close to the Bureau car and aimed his Glock where he had seen the streaks of flame. He fired off a full clip, ejected the magazine, and dug in his pocket for a fresh one. Something hot fell next to his head and he rolled beneath the vehicle. Then came the smoke, bilging, billowing rolls like witches hair, curling in and around and under the car.

"Back in the vehicle," he shouted. He rolled out from underneath the car, holding his breath until he was inside and the door was shut. Bert was throwing himself in from the other side and their heads collided.

"Ow," Bert said.

"You hurt?" Max said.

"Nah," Bert said, rubbing his temple and wincing.

Max tried the radio. It was useless. He patted himself down for his phone. Bert handed it back, and Max dialed dispatch.

"Base, we were …."

"We heard," Dispatch said. "Fire and EMS are rolling. Units 3 and 8 are almost at your 20."

"10-4," Max said, breathless. He heard himself panting.

"You hit?" he said, looking at Higgins and then patting himself down.

"Couple of burns," Higgins said. "Small." He looked at his partner who was sticking two fingers into a burn hole in his tweed jacket. "Please tell me you didn't inhale."

Max shook his head, then rested it back against the seat rest and closed his eyes for a long second. Then he rolled his head sideways toward Higgins, "You heard him say UAV?"

Higgins nodded. "Two."

"Weaponized UAV's? What is this? War zone?"

"Apparently."

"Sherman," Max said, "never stood a chance."

Memorial Hospital
Kingstown, Rhode Island

Emil Bente had watched in rapt attention as Gregorio positioned Bird One and Bird Two to intercept the FBI helicopter. The intensity of the explosion knocked out the night vision camera feed in both UAVs, but they were still flying. They had performed with precision. Emil Bente shouldn't have been surprised that the FBI found out about their hospital visit. Steele was good. Very. But it was a shock to see, through the UAVs' night vision cameras, that the FBI had dispatched a helicopter. It was why Bente over prepared.

"Return the Birds to Base," he said. Everything had worked perfectly. He got an opportunity to test the Birds, and he got the distraction he needed to make his escape from the area and onto the plane.

Gregorio was coordinating the Birds via remote feed from a controller inside a metal briefcase. The Shark had been forced to take the wheel. He rolled along the road, observing the speed limits and traffic signals, not attracting attention. Gregorio balanced the briefcase on his legs.

"The machine gun is mounted below the video camera, yes?" Emil said.

"Yes," Gregorio said, not taking his eyes from the screen. "Because of its weight, we had to use a small caliber. Means we had to get very close."

"So, targets will see them clearly," Emil said. "And if the target is armed . . . ." Emil said.

Gregorio nodded and made the sound of an explosion. "We risk the UAVs every time we discharge their weapon," he said. "We must get close. And the weapon gets very hot and can melt the camera and even the propellers above. Even the heat rising from it affects flight."

"It is a developing technology," Emil said.

"At this level, *Sí*," Gregorio said. "The multi-million dollar military UAVs are another thing entirely."

"Let's get a couple of those," Emil said, and smiled. "Radio Base. Have them prepare to receive the Birds."

"10-4," Gregorio said, and smiled. He picked up the radio, "Base," he said. "This is Outpost Two. Birds almost home."

"Copy that, Outpost Two," Base said.

He pushed the button and leaned back. On the screen, Gregorio watched the UAVs make a lazy turn and head up the screen.

"Mission accomplished," the Shark said. "Now get me on that plane."

Chapter Ten

Bureau Car
Memorial Hospital
Kingstown, Rhode Island

"Dial it," Higgins said.

Max had just finished briefing Director Fenton. His finger was still on the button ending the call. "Dial what?"

The large, high-powered, light beam they had called for, arrived atop a semi-truck and was already plugged in and ready to go. When they switched it on, a cone of light shot into the sky. The beam rotated slowly in a 360° arc, and many eyes searched the dark night for any sign of the drones Sherman had seen before he was blown from the sky. Max expected that the drones would be long gone, but they couldn't take that chance. What if the drones returned and turned their attention upon the hospital and all of the innocents inside?

"The Emergency Room desk," Higgins said. "Then give me the phone." His voice was hard as stone. Max searched the number, dialed and handed the phone over. After a moment, "Dr. Maria Sanchez, please," he said. After a pause, "Lieutenant Higgins. Yes, ma'am. I need to speak with her directly." He shifted the phone to the other ear. "I see, and when did she leave? I see. Thanks so much. No, thank you, I will deliver my message in person."

"That sounded menacing," Max said, as Higgins ended the call.

"What?"

"I will deliver my message in person."

He shifted toward Max in his car seat. "She's gone for the evening," he said. "Guess when she left?"

Max jerked his head in question, then threw his hands up and said, "Let me guess."

"Yep," Higgins said.

"Time for a little chat," Max said.

"Not you," Bert said.

"Yes, me," Max said. "Lying bitch got one of my men killed."

"We don't know that."

"Don't be an ass," Max said.

"Don't take it out on me."

Max grabbed his own ears and wrenched his head. "Ah, Bert, I'm sorry. I'm just so mad."

Bert was silent, staring through the windshield at the mayhem in the parking lot. Some of these people would be here all night.

Max muttered something under his breath.

"What's that?" Bert said.

"I said, I'm the one who's an ass."

"Just let me go talk with her, Max, please. Then you can talk with her. Later. Isn't that what you'd tell me if the places were reversed?"

"The phrase is, 'if the roles were reversed,'" Max said, and punched him softly in the arm. He looked at Bert. "You sure are having to do a lot of cleaning up after me."

"Sir," Bert said, grinning and pointing to the passenger side door, "would you please step out of the vehicle. I have official business to conduct."

"Negative," Max said. "Much as I'd like to know just how deep in this thing she is, it'll have to wait. We need to prioritize, and our priority is Bontecelli."

"Roger that, Cap," Higgins said. "Let's go kill him, I mean, talk to him."

"Don't tempt me," Max said.

Floor 4
Memorial Hospital
Kingstown, Rhode Island

Dr. Nettie Spruill and Dean Victoria Nile were buzzed through the door onto the locked fourth floor. They made their way slowly along the crowded hallway to Jeremy Tittle's room. The door was slightly ajar when they arrived. Nettie knocked and pushed it gently. A nurse was attending to the IV bag hanging behind Jeremy's head. She was speaking softly to him as she moved back and forth between the IV stand and the port on Jeremy's wrist. She glanced at the visitors and smiled.

"Jeremy, you have visitors," she said, and then turned to leave. As she passed Nettie, she squeezed her arm and whispered. "He's doing much better today."

Nettie nodded, but her attention was riveted upon the elderly man in the bed with tussled snow-white hair. His slack mouth was closed, and he squinted toward her and Rev. Nile. The last time she had seen him, his jaw had hung slightly sideways and his eyes had been unfocused. Progress indeed.

"Jeremy?" Nettie said. She staggered slightly. When Vickie Nile caught her around the waist, she could feel the woman's frail body trembling.

"Jenny, is that you?" Jeremy said. "I've been waiting for you all morning."

Nettie moved closed to the bed. Jeremy held a hand out toward her and she rushed to hold it.

"Do you recognize me?" Nettie said.

"Course I do, Jenny," he said. "Man knows his own wife when he sees her."

Nettie leaned over and kissed his forehead, still holding his hand in both of hers. Jeremy's face broke into a grin.

"And who's your friend?" he said, nodding toward Dean Nile, who had positioned herself at the foot of the bed.

"That's our friend Vickie," Nettie said. "Remember her?"

Jeremy squinted and shook his head, "Must've gotten a nasty bump on the head, Vickie," he said. "Having a little trouble getting the old engine running again." He tapped his head with his other hand.

"Quite alright, Jeremy. I am happy to see you."

"Happy to see you, too, and course Jenny here. Been waiting all day to see her lovely face," he said.

"And Jenny is very happy to see you too, dear," Nettie said, and smiled. She glanced at Rev. Nile and nodded. Nile's smiled had faltered a bit, but she recovered herself and applied it again on her face.

"You are doing so much better, dear," Nettie said.

Jeremy nodded. "Gas up the RV, girl. Let's take that trip we always talked about."

"Soon as the doctors say so, we'll pack it up," Nettie said.

"That'll be great," Jeremy said. He glanced at Nile. "Jenny here is a whiz bang organizer. She had to be with all our kids. They were a handful." He patted Nettie's hand.

"Where will you go," Nile said, "on your trip?"

Jeremy patted Nettie's hand again, "Tell her, Honey," he said.

Rev. Nile saw Nettie stiffen. She looked at Vickie, and then back at Jeremy. Her mouth opened but no words came. Vickie saw the grin fade from Jeremy's face. He looked at Nettie.

"I'm sure wherever you go, it will be fabulous," Nile said quickly, but Jeremy was looking soberly into Nettie's face.

"Have you changed your mind?" he said.

"Of course not," Nettie said, "I just prefer my husband to be the one to share news that big."

"Oh," he said, and looked back to Nile, "In that case, we are going to the Grand Canyon. It's all we've talked about for years. Right, Honey?"

"You know it," Nettie said, patting his hand.

"I think that's perfectly wonderful," Vickie said, and nodded slowly. She folded her hands and dropped them in front of her. "And if you will excuse me, I promised to look in on another friend. But I will be back in a bit to collect you, um, Jenny."

"I'll walk you out," Nettie said, and slipped her hand from Jeremy's. "Be right back," she said, and kissed his forehead again.

Floor 3
Memorial Hospital
Kingstown, Rhode Island

Lieutenant Bert Higgins and Captain Max Steele exited the elevator and stepped into the third floor. After a brief search, they located the prison guard. He was raised in the bed almost to a sitting position. Oxygen tubes snaked from his nose to portals in the wall behind him. Bert tapped on the door and they entered.

"Officer Burns," Max said, "Steele and Higgins, FBI, reporting for duty, sir." Max grinned and faked a salute.

"Yes, sirs," Burns said. He extended his hand for a shake, and Higgins reached for it.

Max slapped it away. "Don't!"

Bert recoiled like he'd been shot.

"Don't touch him, please," Max said, "and for God's sake, don't shake his hand."

Instinctively, Higgins clapped his hands behind his back.

Burns fiddled with the oxygen tubes. "Mother Mary tried to kill me."

"Did indeed," Max said, nodding.

"Can you get me outta here?" Burns said.

"I think you're hanging here until old pajama bottoms says you can go."

Burns laughed and then coughed. "Which one?" he said. "They're all wearing 'em."

Max nodded. "Taking orders from a person in pajamas is a little tough, isn't it."

Burns nodded dramatically and grabbed at the oxygen tubes again. "Where's Drucker? You see him?"

"He said – if I remember correctly – that if I'd guard your sorry ass, he'd stay with the prisoner."

"Sounds like him. Asshole," Burns said, but a grin spread across his face.

"He called the Warden," Max said. "Briefed him."

"Told him we didn't lose the prisoner?" Burns said.

"Reckon that was one of the first things out of his mouth."

"Good," Burns said, and laid his head back on the pillow.

"So while we're waiting to get you out of here, and for the benefit of my partner here, run me through what happened."

Burns nodded and then told them how the old nun had limped over, handed him a prayer card, and that was the last thing he remembered.

"What did the nun's voice sound like?" Bert said. "Can you describe it?"

"Just whispered, that was all, whispered about havin' mercy or pity or something, on the poor patient and gave me the card to give him." He shrugged. "I didn't think nothing of it."

"Course not," Max said. "Why would you?"

"Thank you," Burns said, nodding again. "Didn't do nothing anybody else wouldn'ta done."

"Right," Higgins said, "and Captain Steele, let's make sure we tell the Warden we would've done the same thing as Burns here."

"You bet we will," Max said.

"Thank you," Burns said.

"You get a look at her face?" Max said.

Burns shook his head. "She was wobbling, looking at the floor like she was trying not to fall over, you know?"

"Okay," Max said. "She look up at you when she gave you the card?"

"Nope, just whispered toward the floor, but I knew she was talking to me."

"How's that?"

"Cause I told her no, I didn't want no prayer card, and that's when she started in on the mercy on the patient and all at stuff."

"So you took it."

"I've seen 'em before. It's them Catholic ones with the Jesus and a heart and all that."

"So nothing special about the card itself?"

"Nope."

"You see anybody else?" Bert said. "Anybody with the nun?"

"Nope," Burns said.

"Okay," Max said, "Appreciate your help and glad you're okay."

Bert nodded, "And good job hanging onto that prisoner."

Burn's face lit up into a smile, "Ha, yeah, we handcuffed his ass to the bed. My idea."

"Brilliant," Max said, waving and moving toward the door. "Mind if we look in on your prisoner?"

"Excuse me," Burns said, obviously enjoying himself, "but you the mu-fukin' FBI. You don't need my permission."

"Out of respect, I'm asking," Max said.

"Yes, sir," Burns said, and saluted, "Permission granted."

Floor 3
Memorial Hospital
Kingstown, Rhode Island

Higgins and Steele stepped into the hallway. When they were a few steps from the door, Higgins turned to Steele. "That's the nicest you've been with someone you're interviewing."

"That guy about got killed," Max said. "Know how much corrections officers get paid?

"Let me guess," Higgins said, "Not enough to risk their lives every day."

"Twelve bucks an hour."

"Shittin' me," Higgins said.

"Not."

Higgins shook his head. "Worst plumber I ever called was making fifty an hour, and he didn't deal with half the shit those guys do."

"Now you see why I showed some respect and appreciation?"

"Poor bastard," Higgins said, "Almost lost his life for twelve dollars an hour."

Max nodded and headed to the elevator. "Next," Max said.

The elevator lifted them to ICU. They exited and headed to the ICU nurse's station.

"Yes, Director Steele?" an attractive nurse said as they approached.

Bert laughed into his hand and covered it, clearing his throat.

"Thank you, ma'am, but I am just a Captain," Max said, and smiled.

"Okay, Captain," she said, "How may we assist you?" Max noticed that her words were directed at him, but her beautiful smile was directed at Higgins.

"Ma'am?" Max said, suppressing a grin.

"Hmmm?" she said.

"Ma'am, are the labs for Burns available?" Max said.

"Oh, um, let me check," she said, and hurried away.

Max turned to Bert and raised his eyebrows. Bert laughed and shrugged. "Don't look at me, Director Steele."

Max shook his head. "Be sure to include that in the report to Director Fenton."

"Aye, aye, sir," Higgins said. Then his face grew serious. "Something on the prayer card I assume."

"You assume correctly," Max said. They swabbed his hands, fired it to the lab. I'm not expecting anything toxic. Bente is thorough. If he'd wanted that officer dead, we'd be visiting him in the morgue."

"How generous of him," Bert said. "Shame he didn't show the same level of compassion to Sherman."

"Or to Bull Sullivan," Max said, and felt his hands wad into fists. "I'll see that son of a bitch in hell."

"They, um, find him? Sherman?" Higgins said, and pointed. "Out there?"

"Probably gonna need a shovel and a trash bag," Max said, and looked down, pinching the bridge of his nose. "Poor bastard got blown to bits."

“So who’s the nun, you think?” Bert said.

“Let’s go ask Vinnie,” Max said, “No doubt it was all about him.”

“No doubt,” Bert said.

Max took his sleeve as they walked, “I’ll send YOU back to the desk in a minute to get the tox results. I’m certain that nurse would be happy to smile for you again.”

“Stop right there,” Higgins said, “Director.”

“Oh, no,” Max said, shaking his head dramatically, “you’re not gonna deflect with that Director crap. You, sir, are a hound. Here we are, on the job, and you’re making googlie-eyes at the nurses.”

“I was not ….”

“Oh, don’t even try Higgins,” Max said. “I looked over and you were shining right back at her.”

“Shining?” Bert said, “You’re such a romantic.”

Max laughed.

“And speaking of,” Bert said, “we need to sit down and talk as soon as we’re done with Bontecelli.”

“Maria?” Max said.

“Maria,” Bert said, nodding.

Max stopped 10 yards from the door to the isolation room. “Do you believe this? All this?”

“No,” Bert said, shaking his head. “One minute I’m so pissed off I can’t see straight, and the next I’m laughing, and then next I’m getting a lump in my throat.”

“Same,” Max said, and nudged him.

“You have no feelings,” Bert said, and punched him lightly.

“I wish. Still can’t believe Sherman’s gone.”

“We’ll get this bastard, Cap.”

"Let's go talk to Asshole's former second in command," Max said, "and by the way, a working hypothesis is that the nun couldn't have been Bente because either Bontecelli would be dead or would be gone."

"Sounds right," Bert said. "But with Bente, you never know."

"Just in case, Bert, when we go in there? Don't touch the guy."

"Roger that."

Max looked toward the isolation room door. A large uniformed corrections officer stood in front of it, cradling a long barreled shotgun. Max and Bert pulled their creds and approached, and the officer nodded. "Yes, sirs," Officer Drucker said.

Max patted him on his thick shoulder. "You've done a fine job here, Officer Drucker."

"Thank you, Director Steele," Drucker said. Bert Higgins turned with his head and took two steps toward the elevator door. "What's wrong with him?" Drucker said, nodding in Higgins' direction.

"Bad cough," Max said. "He'll be back."

"He ain't contagious, is he?" Drucker said, and cocked his head.

Max laughed and shook his head. Bert was making his way back, his face a mottled red.

"Shall we go in, Director?" Bert said.

Drucker was watching Higgins closely and stepped back to give him a wide berth as he and Max passed into the room.

Vinnie's bed was parallel to the door, and the patient was looking away when they entered. At the sound, he turned his head.

"Hello ladies," Vinnie said without mirth. "Been expecting you."

"Vinnie," Max said, and nodded. Bert positioned himself in the far corner. Watching everything. Expecting anything.

"Who's the pussy willow in the corner?" Vinnie said, and tried to motion with his good hand. The handcuffs jangled.

"Not sure you know my partner, Lieutenant Higgins," Max said, unsmiling.

Vinnie fixed Steele with a long stare, and then turned his eyes to Higgins. Silence bloomed in the room like a mushroom cloud.

"I knew your old partner," Vinnie said.

Higgins saw his partner twitch, and the look that covered his face. Max's eyes blazed hotly toward Vinnie. Bert wouldn't have been surprised if Vinnie's clothes caught fire.

"You killed my old partner," Max said.

"That why pussy willow's jammed in the corner over there? Scared I'll get him, too?"

"I'd just as soon kill you as look at you," Max said.

"Thought you said you needed me, last time we talked," Vinnie said, and chuckled. His eyes were glazed from the pain meds. "Hey Steele, I was there when he died. Your old partner. Did you know that? You wanna know how we did it?"

Bert's eyes shifted to Max, whose eyes never left Vinnie's, but whose right hand moved into his jacket.

"Max," Higgins said quietly. Max ignored him and continued to reach into his jacket where the Glock sat nested in the shoulder holster.

"Yeah, Bontecelli, why don't you tell us," Max said. He drew his Glock from the holster.

"Max," Bert said. "Stop."

"Wait. Wait, just a damn minute," Vinnie said, stammering. Bert saw drool trickle from the side of his mouth.

"Tell us just how you murdered my partner, you piece of shit," Max said. He pushed the 9MM close to Vinnie's eye.

"You can't do nothin' to me," Vinnie said, but his eyes and heaving chest betrayed the false bravado. Max jammed the muzzle into his eye socket.

"Max," Bert said, and started to move toward the bed.

"Back Higgins, or I swear …."

"Wait," Vinnie said, his voice thinning to a squeal.

"You have two seconds to tell me who came to see you today," Max said in a growl and jammed the Glock further into Vinnie's eye. "One."

"Jesus, wait," Vinnie said, pressing the back of his head into the pillow.

"Two."

"Bente," Vinnie said through his nose. "It was Bente."

"What'd he want?" Max said. "What'd he say to you?"

"He said sorry," Vinnie said. "Put that thing away, you crazy …."

"Bullshit," Max said. "What'd he say? What'd he want?"

"Swear to God, Steele," Vinnie said. "He wanted to say sorry, wanted me to forgive him."

"You're about to die," Max said.

"Max, for Christ's sake," Bert said, catching on, "Don't do it."

"Yeah, don't," Vinnie said. "I can still help you."

"You piece of shit, this is for Sherm," Max yanked the Glock from Vinnie's eye and slammed the gun down hard onto Vinnie's bandaged hand.

Vinnie screamed, a long, chilling scream. Then another.

In one fluid motion, Max holstered the Glock and stepped away from the bed. "Get the doctor," he said in a loud voice.

Bert started toward the door, just as it burst open and a doctor and two nurses rushed in, followed by Officer Drucker with the shotgun.

Vinnie screamed again. Max had moved to stand next to Higgins. The doctor whirled on them. "You two, out. Now." Drucker had already whirled and was passing back through the door into the hall. Steele and Higgins followed close behind.

"Hell happened in there?" Drucker said.

"No idea," Higgins said. "We were talking, and the next minute, the prisoner was screaming." Max nodded. Bert had pulled a pad of paper from his pocket and was scribbling. He tore it off and handed it to Drucker. "Here's my cell phone number. Call and update us when you know something. We've got another emergency."

Drucker nodded. Bert and Max headed for the elevator.

ICU

Memorial Hospital

Kingstown, Rhode Island

"He thought you were gonna kill him," Bert said as the elevator descended.

"I thought I was gonna kill him," Max said.

"I believe you," Bert said. "It was all over your face."

"Did you smell it in there?" Max said, "Just before we left?"

"Did I – what?" Bert said.

"Smell it?" Max said. "Just before we left?"

"Now that you mention it," Bert said.

Max nodded and smiled. "Vinnie shit himself," he said, "scared him so bad, he shit himself."

Bert rolled his eyes. "Feel better?"

"Much," Max said. Bert watched his partner's eyes take on the thousand-yard stare. He gave Max the moment he needed. "Won't bring Bull back," Max said finally.

"Might hear about this later," Higgins said. "Upstairs I mean. Docs aren't stupid."

"Our word against the convict's," Max said, and glanced at Higgins.

"I didn't see anything," Bert said.

"I didn't either. Had my back turned. Musta tried to hurt himself."

"Nobody's gonna buy that."

"Nobody's gonna press it either," Max said. "Slip and fall rule."

"Heard about that," Higgins said. "Academy rumor mill."

"Law enforcement brass understands that sometimes pedophiles and other scum slip and fall a few times on their way to lock up. Accidents happen and people get hurt."

The elevator doors opened to the first floor.

"How about a decent cup of coffee?" Bert said, "Lavish Lattes, my treat, anything you want."

Max locked eyes with Bert. "We really need to stay and get …."

Bert held up a hand. "We really need to have that coffee."

"Right," Max nodded. "You really buying, you cheap bastard?"

Bert nodded.

"Ho ho," Max said, and headed for the exit, "This is going to cost you big."

Lavish Lattes Café
Kingstown, Rhode Island

True to his word, Max ordered a five-dollar cup of coffee, grinning like he'd won the lottery. Bert ordered a dark roast, black. The coffee shop was packed, as usual, and they had to wait for a booth. It was the price you paid at Lavish Lattes. The shop could have chosen to fill their space with small tables and crammed lots of chairs around them. It would have doubled, and perhaps even tripled, their seating capacity. But what made the place so luscious, so luxurious and intimate, was its large booths running down both sides. The booths were separated by padded, partial walls, and were virtually soundproof. Unless someone was passing by in the aisle, guests could speak privately with each other.

At last, Max and Bert were seated. They sat opposite each other and sipped their coffees.

"You keep dinging me like that," Bert said, pointing to the cup in Max's hand, "and I'm gonna need a raise." The smile on Max's face was worth the price of the coffee.

"This stuff is liquid gold," Max said.

"That stuff is liquid sugar," Bert said, and laughed.

"You believe people drink this stuff so late?" Max looked at his watch.

"Thank God they're still open," Bert said. He took a long sip and then sat back. "Okay, let's empty our pockets of all the marbles, spread 'em on the table, and talk 'em through."

"Nice image," Max said. "And because you bought me this fabulous coffee, I'll refrain from suggesting you've lost yours."

"Too kind," Bert said.

"I am," Max said.

"I'll start," Bert said.

"And don't worry if you repeat stuff I already know," Max said. "Let's look it all over."

"Works for me," Bert said. "Some of it is gonna piss you off."

Max nodded, but said nothing.

"Fenton ordered me to do a confidential background check on Dr. Maria Sanchez because her name had shown up three times on the visitors list for Nina Ondolopous Bente. I felt like shit about it, about not telling you, but Fenton ordered me to tell no one but her."

Max opened his mouth to speak, but Bert held up a hand. "Just listen, Max," he said, and continued, "I traced her background to Italy, where it appears she was raised and trained by an order of nuns, the Order of Mary. I tried to research the Order, but it turns out that St. Mary is a very popular lady and there are hundreds of Orders of Mary. I'm not kidding. Hundreds." Higgins stopped and stared in silence at his partner.

"Fenton already told me," Max said. "She's a nun."

Bert nodded, "Is a nun, or at least was a nun. Don't forget, she's also a physician, so the trajectory of her life could have led her in a number of directions."

"Think she was an orphan?" Max said.

"I do," Bert said, "but that's a guess. You wouldn't expect a last name of Sanchez, born in Venice, Italy, of Italian parents, but I suppose anything's possible. The strange thing is I can't find a birth record. All of that could be cloistered in some confidential file protected by the Order of Mary, but that, too, is a guess."

Bert paused for a long sip of coffee. "The last thing I wanted to do was conjure a witch-hunt out of hunches and speculation instead of facts. The facts about Dr. Maria Sanchez are few and far between." He held up his hand again when Max tried to speak. "There are more marbles, Max. Just listen."

Bert waited until Max nodded, then continued, "I've found nothing that would tie Maria to the death of Nina Ondolopous Bente. Her visits appear random and well documented. If she had had malicious intent, she could have avoided detection easily. My guess is that, because she was in the Emergency Room when the woman first came in, she cared enough to check in on her, even though she was no longer in charge of her care. Again, speculation, okay?"

Max nodded. Bert noticed that Max hadn't touched his coffee the entire time Bert had been speaking.

"You and I know, regardless of her past, we need to find out where she was tonight, find out if she has had anything to do with Bente and his operation."

Max nodded. He laid his head on the table, the crown of his head barely touching his coffee cup.

"I know, right?" Bert said. He laid his hand on the back of Max's head and gave it a tussle.

Max picked his head up. "So is she a nun, or isn't she?" he said.

"All I know," Bert said, "is that she was."

"And how long has she been at Memorial?" Max said.

"Two and a half years. And before that, a hospital in Mexico for eight."

"What the mess?"

Beret blinked at him and then grinned. "Still trying to get used to your new word."

"We need answers," Max said, ignoring him, "and I want to talk to her, confront her. But another part of me doesn't want to talk to her." He stared at his partner. "Can I ask you a question, kind of off point but also not?"

Bert laughed. "I'm not sure I understood a thing you just said, but go ahead, shoot."

"What is it about women that scares the crap out of grown men?"

"I've always wondered," Bert said. "Never had the balls to ask another guy."

"So they scare you, too?"

"Are you kidding? Course. Can't talk, can't think."

Max nodded. "It's like you're a sweatshirt that's turned inside out and all your seams are showing."

"It's more like your belt gives way, your pants drop to your ankles, and you can't get them back up."

"Yes!" Max said. Then he grew sober. "You know I'll kill you if you mention any of this, to anyone else, ever in your entire life."

"Back atcha," Bert said.

“So,” Max said, “you done?”

“I’m done,” Higgins said. “We good?”

“We’re good, partner,” Max said, and sipped his coffee. “Back to the crime scene? We can take our coffees with.”

“Memorial?”

“Memorial,” Max said, “by way of Dr. Maria Sanchez’s apartment.”

“I’m talking to her,” Higgins said. ”Not you.”

“Good by me,” Max said, and punched his partner’s shoulder. “You can lock me in the trunk where I’ll be safe.”

“Chicken shit,” Bert said.

“Are we still talking about that?”

“We are not,” Bert said, shaking his head. “Most definitely not.”

“Thank you,” Max said.

They drove in silence to Maria’s apartment and Bert climbed out. Max sat in the passenger seat, his eyes riveted to the apartment door. He watched Higgins knock. No one opened the door. Higgins continued to knock and wait. Then he watched the door while Higgins returned to the vehicle.

“I don’t think she’s there,” Bert said, dropping into the driver’s seat. “You know how you can feel it most times when someone is there but not answering?”

Max nodded.

“I got nothing.”

“Then let’s find out where she went when she left Memorial,” Max said.

Bert put the vehicle into gear and aimed it for Memorial Hospital.

Chapter Eleven

Emergency Room
Memorial Hospital
Kingstown, Rhode Island

Charge Nurse Linda Turnbill looked at the radio in disbelief. Dr. Maria Sanchez was being transported by EMS with a head wound.

"If this doesn't beat all," she said, and threw wadded fists up to her hips. She turned around to the semicircular desk and jerked.

Don't startle me like that," she said, glaring into the faces of Captain Max Steele and Lieutenant Bert Higgins.

"Like what?" Max said. "We just walked up."

"Well, please just walk away again," Nurse Turnbill said.

"Whoa, Whoa, Whoa," Max said, and held up his hands as if to deflect a blow. "You can't kick us out of here."

"Guard," Linda shouted to the uniformed man sitting by the Emergency Room door. The elderly security officer rose and walked to the desk, his hat tipped back on his head. "What's the trouble here, Miss Linda?" he said.

"These gentlemen were just leaving," she said, and pointed an index finger toward the exit.

Max was digging in his coat pocket. He produced his badge and ID, flipping it open and shoving it in the officer's direction. "Captain Max Steele, FBI, at your service."

The guard nodded and stroked his chin. "Don't appear Linda here appreciates your service," he said.

"And the FBI appreciates your opinion, sir, but we aren't going anywhere until we get a few questions answered." He whirled back to the desk and glared at Nurse Turnbill. "You may as well holster those fists on your hips, Miss Linda, Nurse Turnbill, because you will cooperate with the FBI," He paused for effect, "either here or downtown. Do you understand?"

The guard's eyes were wide. He stared first at Max and then at Linda. Then he turned and walked slowly back to his seat by the door.

The charge nurse's face was rose-colored and her eyes were bloodshot and narrowed into a squint. "I've got work to do here," she said, and spittle shot from her lips as she spoke. "A trauma patient is *en route* as we speak. Now, if you want to interfere with the proper care and treatment of a trauma patient, then you'd best get a pair of handcuffs and muster a good explanation for both our bosses."

"Cap," Higgins said, and touched the sleeve of his partner's jacket. Max shrugged him off.

"Where is Dr. Maria Sanchez?" he said, spitting words back at her.

"She happens to be our trauma patient," Linda said, her voice rising to a shrill scream, "Now get the hell out of our way so we can treat her when she arrives."

Max had his mouth open, prepared to speak. He shut it. After a moment, he opened it again, and then he shut it. He felt Bert's strong hand close around his bicep and he allowed himself to be muscled away toward the exit.

When they were outside, Max whirled on his partner, "What just happened in there?"

"Knock me over with a hummingbird," Bert said.

"You're an idiot," Max said.

"You're a hothead," Bert said, and shoved Max's shoulder.

"Damn it, Higgins," he said. "That woman vexes me."

"Let me guess," Bert said, "She reminds you of your mother."

"She reminds me of the dog that bit me when I was six years old. Bit me right through the cheek while I was screaming," Max said.

"Sounds like you should get over it," Higgins said.

"Sounds like you should shut up, Lieutenant," Max said, and shoved him back.

"I think we're having a guy moment," Bert said. "I feel uncomfortable."

Max's fierce look dissolved. He paused and then he bent over in a paroxysm of laughter. "You know just what to say, dear." They both laughed, and the tension melted.

At last Bert spoke, "Think the old Battle Ax was lying? About Maria I mean?"

"I say we hang out and see," Max said, the scowling returning to his face. He looked at his watch.

Emergency Room
Memorial Hospital
Kingstown, Rhode Island

Eight minutes later, Max Steele and Bert Higgins watched the flashing EMS truck nose over the storm grate, kill the lights, bend into a tight, U-shaped turn, and reverse.

Bert's attention shifted to his partner. Max had stiffened. He took two steps toward the EMS vehicle. Then he pivoted, jammed his hands into his trouser pockets, and returned.

"Easy Cap," Higgins said.

"What? I'm fine," Steele said.

The EMS personnel had stepped from the vehicle and were pulling the stretcher out. The woman's face was almost completely covered with a red cloth, but the white lab coat provided the unmistakable tell that it was Dr. Maria Sanchez. One of the techs was pressing a cold pack to her head as they wheeled her through the doors.

Max never moved, but his eyes followed the stretcher through the doorway and continued to fix there long after the glass doors had slid closed. Bert approached the EMS tech standing near the vehicle, writing on a metal clipboard. Bert flashed his creds.

"What we got?" Bert said.

"The young woman glanced at Higgins's badge and ID, then looked up and smiled.

"I remember you, Lieutenant," she said.

Bert nodded, searched around, but found no words.

The tech went back to writing on her clipboard.

"You going to make me waterboard it out of you?" he said, grinning.

"How about we just splash in a kiddie pool together?" she said, and winked. Her smile revealed perfect teeth and there was a playful dance in her eyes. Bert snuffed a laugh and pinched the bridge of his nose, looking down. As he did, he took in the near-perfect curves hiding beneath the EMS tech's uniform.

"Whatever it takes," he said. "I've deployed on more dangerous missions."

"I'm not sure you have," she said, lifting her chin slightly and showing him her teeth again. Her auburn hair was tied into a modest twist behind her head and small gold hearts glinted in her ears.

Bert could feel his tongue begin to swell, as it always did near attractive women. Soon it would tie itself in a knot.

"I, uh, was asking …."

"For my number?" she said, grinning. "I was just writing it down for you." She shoved him playfully in the shoulder. "You are much too cute not to have a ring on that finger, so I figured you must be shy."

"Painfully," Bert said, smiling toward the ground. Try as he might, he could not bring himself to make eye contact. But he took the slip of paper when she handed it to him and buried it deep into his pocket.

"Now Lieutenant Bert Higgins – yes I know your first name. It wasn't hard to get from the girl network."

"The girl network?" Bert managed.

"Oh yeah, we all talk about the good looking guys."

"About the transport …." Bert said, glancing to the ER doors and back.

She nodded toward Max. "By the looks of old paleface over there, you already know it's Doctor Sanchez."

Bert shot a glance at his partner, and Max was indeed pale. Bert brought his gaze back and met her eyes. Green. Oh my, God. Emerald green. He looked down again. "What's your name?" he said.

"It's on your piece of paper, Lieutenant," she said. "Now concentrate."

"Having trouble," Bert said, and grinned, feeling his tongue twisting into a pretzel.

"Obviously, and I'll take that as a compliment," she said. She patted her clipboard. "Patient suffered blunt force trauma to the temple, and is stable but unconscious. Is that what you walked over here to ask?"

Bert nodded. She laughed and turned away, speaking over her shoulder. "You two make a fine pair. He's pale as a shaker of salt and you are red as a bottle of hot sauce." Her truck door slammed closed and she pulled away. Bert walked back to where Max was standing.

"What just happened over there?" Max said.

Bert chuckled and waived him off with his hands.

"She was shining at you like a full moon," Max said.

"Stop," Bert said, grinning, and waived him off again. "Maria hit her head or something. Stable but unconscious."

"Blood loss? Light, medium, heavy?"

"Didn't think to ask," Bert said.

"Were you able to think at all, partner?" Max said. "Looks like she scrambled your eggs pretty good."

"Takes one to know one, Paleface,"

"What?" Max said. "Who?"

That's what she called you," Higgins said, and laughed.

"What? I'm fine."

"So you say," Higgins said. "May want to tell your face."

What?" Max said, rubbing his chin.

"You want to go in?" Higgins said. He reached in his pocket and fingered the slip of paper. He glanced toward the EMS parking field.

"You want to stay out?" Max said, watching him.

"Let's go, Paleface," Bert said, and started for the ER doors before his partner could hit him with a comeback.

"Hey," Max called after him, "Battle Ax Linda may be waiting inside to belt us with a bed pan."

"I'm armed," Bert said. He was already angling toward the nurses' station. Linda Turnbill was not at the desk. No one was. That was all the permission he needed. Max caught up with him halfway down the corridor of curtained examination slips.

"You're breaking protocol, Lieutenant" Max said, grinning.

"Law enforcement officials are allowed to use the break room to get coffee and do their reports," Higgins said. "That's where we're headed if anyone asks, you copy, Captain Steele?"

"Damn, you're good," Max said, "and if we happen to see or hear anything, interesting, along the way...."

Higgins nodded. "Besides, she's part of our official investigation. All personal relationships aside."

They didn't see or hear anything.

Emergency Room
Memorial Hospital
Kingstown, Rhode Island

"Now what?" Max said when they were in the break room. He looked around, remembering the first time he had set eyes on Dr. Maria Sanchez. It was in this very room.

"You're the Captain," Higgins said to his partner, but it was clear from the thousand-yard stare that Max was somewhere else.

Bert gave him a moment, distracting himself by making coffee. Strong coffee. When it was brewed, he poured two cups and set them on the table. He pushed one toward Max, who nodded.

"You look terrible," Higgins said.

"Thanks, partner," Max said. He sipped coffee and winced. "This," he pointed to the cup, "is terrible."

"You're welcome."

Max blew across the top of the cup and took another sip.

"What's going on," Bert said, pointing to Max's forehead, "up there?"

"Race track," Max said. "Cars going both ways."

"Sounds right," Bert said.

"It does?"

Higgins stared at him for a long moment. "You have reason to suspect, at least, that Maria isn't telling you everything about herself. At most, she could be playing for the other team." Bert arced his left fist slowly from his left ear around to the front. "And yet you care for her, maybe a lot, right?" He arced his right fist from his right ear around to the front, toward his other fist. "And now she's injured and you don't know how or why." He crashed the two fists together.

Max blinked, jerked his head in acknowledgement, and said nothing. The silence between them was broken by Nurse Linda's loud, shrill voice in the doorway.

"Steele," she said, her face blotched and her lips trembling. Max started to rise from the table. Before he had gotten halfway to his feet, Linda lunged forward and slapped him hard across the face. The crack of her palm against Max's cheek echoed off the breakroom walls, and startled Max so much that he sat down hard again in his chair.

"You bastard!" she said in a shriek. "It wasn't enough for you to break that poor little girl's heart. No. You had to go and get her knocked up, too. I oughtta beat you to death right here and now." She was sucking air in through her nose like an old vacuum. Her hands were balled into fists and both arms were trembling.

"Now wait. Wait, what?" Max's eyes went wide.

Bert had stood. Now he positioned himself between Linda and Max. Linda hit Bert hard on the chest with both fists and forearms.

"You get outta my way," she said. She screamed and then collapsed against his chest, sobbing. Bert put a reluctant arm around her shoulder, not sure if she was through attacking them or just resting between rounds. After a few moments, he felt her body relax and he guided her into a chair across the table from a cow-eyed Max Steele. Bert wet two paper towels and gave one to each of them.

Linda mopped her face and the back of her neck, while Max sat frozen with the dripping towel in his hand. "Is she okay?" he said softly, almost as if he were in a daze.

"Fat lot you care," she said.

The comment brought the flint back to his eyes, "You don't know a thing about it. Now where is she?"

"You're not on the approved visitor list," she said, and sniffed.

"Dammit Linda, I love that woman," Max said, standing and towering over her. "Now you tell me where she is or I will tear this place apart until I find her."

"THAT," she said, "is what I wanted to hear." She pointed to the door. "Bed 11. Still unconscious, but she might be able to hear you."

Max shot through the door like a halfback lunging for the goal line.

Bert rubbed his chest and smiled at Linda. "You're pretty tough," he said.

"I'm … sorry," she said. "I'm partial to that girl."

"Let me guess," Bert said, sitting down, "X-rays were ordered and the precautionary pregnancy test was administered because the patient was unconscious."

She nodded.

Bert blew out a breath, and closed his eyes. He knew he had to make the call, and he hoped Director Fenton had brought a change of underwear to work with her.

That was two calls he needed to make, one now, and another at some point. Bert Higgins wasn't sure which one unnerved him more. He leaned back in his chair enough to wedge a hand into his pants pocket. The hand came out clutching the folded piece of paper. He opened it. In beautiful handwriting was the name, Kristin Muldoon, and a telephone number. Each "I" in her first name had been dotted with a heart. Very feminine. He liked that. He wondered if she had been right: that he never would have had the balls to approach her for a date. Probably right.

"Hey, Handsome," a voice said from the doorway. Bert looked up into those same perfect teeth smiling at him and he shot to his feet, bumping the table and spilling both cups of coffee. Each stream of hot liquid ran in a different direction. Linda leapt to her feet, and both she and Bert rushed for the paper towels. Bert thought he heard laughter behind him.

He and Linda sopped up the coffee, and then Linda rushed off muttering something about the front desk. Bert grinned and shrugged.

"You can't make this stuff up," Kristin said, leaning now against the door jam. "I come to tell you something official, and I find you looking at the piece of paper I gave you. You get major points, Mister."

"I, uh," Bert said. "Something official?"

"Yeah, thought you might want to know the scanner chirped and two ladders were dispatched to that clinic where we picked up Doc Sanchez."

"It's on fire?" Bert said.

"Big time, what I hear," EMS Muldoon said.

Bert was already moving toward the door, and she stepped back to let him pass.

"Hey, thanks Kristin," Bert called over his shoulder as he ran, reading the numbers hanging over the curtained beds.

Higgins slowed as he approached bed number 11. He peeked around the corner of the curtain. His partner had pulled the chair close to the bedside, and he was hunched toward it, holding Maria's hand. An IV tube was taped to it and her head was bandaged so that only half of it was showing. Max Steele looked up and leaned back when he saw his partner's face.

"Sorry to disturb, Boss," Higgins said, "but I need a word."

Max nodded and rose, kissed Maria's cheek, and then slipped through the curtained opening. He raised his eyebrows at Higgins.

"Clinic's on fire," Higgins said.

"Let's go," Max said, and the two ran for the exit.

Kristin Muldoon had been walking back from the break room and paused at the ER desk.

"My, my," she said to Linda Turnbill, "I do love watching a man's butt when he's running," she said.

"Not you, too," Linda said, and scowled. "I swear, you girls will be the death of me."

Misericordia Clinic
Kingstown, Rhode Island

By the time Captain Max Steele and Lieutenant Bert Higgins arrived at Misericordia Clinic, the fire was mostly under control. The wind whipping up the hillside from the harbor was blowing burning embers onto other combustible materials. Two of the four responding fire trucks were working to contain the spread, while the other two doused the clinic. It appeared the structural fire was almost out. Smoke billowed high into the air, where gusts grabbed it, making garish shapes and streaks. The landscape was crawling with firefighters and ribboned with hoses. The access road was choked with police vehicles and rescue units.

They parked several hundred yards away and exited the bureau vehicle. "Be a while before we know anything," Max said, and looked over at his partner. Bert Higgins was craning his neck skyward and turning in a slow circle.

"What's up?" Max said.

"That's the right question," Bert said, continuing to scan. "Checking to see if there's anything up there."

Max began to look too. "Like a UAV you mean," he said.

"Like a UAV," Bert said.

"Good call partner."

"Wouldn't put it past him, would you?"

"Not at all, especially not after last night," Max said, "and because this clinic was torched. Likely."

"Thinking arson?" Bert said.

"Ten bucks says it was."

"Don't take that bet, young man," a voice said behind them.

They turned to see the smudged face of Kingstown's fire chief.

"Hey, Chief," Max said, and extended a hand. Chief Blanchard's demeanor was always gruff and all business. Bert kept silent and stepped back.

"Torched for sure, Steele," the Chief said, shaking his hand stiffly. "Boys said they could smell the gasoline soon as they rolled up."

"Anybody inside?" Max said.

The Chief shook his head. "That's how I got this war paint," he said, pointing to his face. "Wanted to look it over myself."

"See anything else we might want to know?"

"What I saw," Chief said, "was next to nothing. That always tells me something."

Max bobbled his head. "Me, too. If it's too clean, it's too clean."

"Right," Chief said. "And it was." He turned on his heel and walked away.

"Okay," Higgins said, "feeling like a rookie again here."

"You are a rookie," Max said.

"Yeah? You think so?"

Max clapped him on the back. "Less and less every day, partner. You're smart, you pick stuff up quick, and you've got great instincts."

"Aw shucks, coach," Bert said, and grinned.

"And you're an asshole," Max said, smiling. "But you are my kind of asshole." He shot him a thumbs-up. "And … you are still learning. Like now. First, you see anybody watching? Any sky watchers?"

"No."

"Me neither, and now I know why."

"I'll bite. Why?" Bert said.

"Because the show's over. Nothing to see," Max said. "That's what the fire chief was saying. Let's go sit in the car." They returned to the vehicle. Higgins started it and began backing out.

"Let me guess," Max said.

"Yep," Bert said.

“Haven’t you had enough coffee for one day?”

“I spilled it,” Bert said. He held up a hand. “And I am taking no questions about the matter at this time.”

Max laughed, “Please learn from us and not from the politicians. And despite my use of the word please, that is an order, rookie.”

“10-4, Cap.”

“Okay, you drive us to the coffee, I will explain. You know how every fire tells a story.”

Higgins nodded.

“Right,” Max said. “You piece the story together with the clues or ‘tells’ that are left behind. No doubt you listened to plenty of boring lectures about this topic. What they didn’t teach you is that there are two scenarios in particular where the story that the fire has to tell you is not much use. The first scenario is where the fire is too dirty, meaning that the perpetrator has intentionally thrown in a bathtub worth of ‘tells’ that send you chasing your tail round and round, getting nowhere.

The second scenario is where the fire is too clean, like this one. That means the people who started this fire picked the whole place clean of usable evidence before they started it. In this case, all we are likely to know is that there was something here that would have told us something about them and whatever they had going here. You follow?”

“I follow,” Bert said, pulling off the side of the road and putting the car in park so he could look Max in the eye. “And if this fire’s too clean, then there must have been something going on at Maria’s clinic they didn’t want us to know about, like, really didn’t want us to know about.”

Max was quiet for several moments. “You’re thinking there’s a very good chance Maria Sanchez is dirty.”

Bert looked at his hands. What was there to say? Then his eyes went wide and he looked again at Max. “We have go back,” he said. “Immediately.”

Emergency Room
Memorial Hospital
Kingstown, Rhode Island

Clergy of every stripe were in and out of Emergency Rooms like worker bees to a hive. People in crisis often wanted their minister or priest to come to the Emergency Room.

So, no one would think twice about the nun who entered. Everyone would assume she was called by a family member of someone being examined and treated here. This particular nun placed two fingers in between the hanging sections of curtain surrounding each bed. The privacy curtain parted just enough for her to look in. When she came to Number 11 and inched the curtains apart, she glanced slowly in both directions and then entered.

"Maria," Maria Garza said to the unconscious frame of Maria Sanchez. "I've taken great chances coming to see you. But I am here, sister, because you have taken great chances of your own, haven't you?" Maria Garza reached beneath her robes. Her hand returned with what looked like an ordinary pen. Gripping the thin cylinder with both hands, she pulled it apart, revealing a long syringe needle protruding from the bottom half. She leaned over Maria and continued in a low voice, "Excellency warned me that this day might come, and so it has. Sister Maria Sanchez, you have dishonored the Name and now …."

"Stop!" a voice said so loudly behind Maria Garza that she nearly fell on top of Maria Sanchez.

"Oh," Maria Garza said, dropping her hands by her sides so the robes shrouded them, "You gave me such a fright."

"What are you doing in here?" Linda Turnbill said, her fists firmly planted on her hips.

"Why, saying prayers over this dear soul," Maria Garza said.

"You need to stay right where you are until the police get here," Linda said.

Maria Garza stood very still and smiled. "Oh, and how shall you keep me here, dear?"

"Like this," Linda said, and took two steps toward the nun. In a flash, Maria Garza swung the needle up and into Linda's neck. The effect was instantaneous. Maria Garza let the nurse's body collapse across Maria Sanchez's legs. Then she left, slapping the drapes closed behind her. Instead of heading for the exit, though, the nun headed the other way, burrowing herself deeply into the belly of the hospital until she could make her way out again.

ICU
Memorial Hospital
Kingstown, Rhode Island

Vinnie woke, groping his way through a thick pharmaceutical haze. After Steele had left, the doc had shot something for pain into his IV. He remembered screaming in pain, and then nothing. He opened his eyes and saw that the dressing on his hand had doubled in size. He peered around the room. He'd always been able to feel when someone else was in the room, and he felt it now. At last, his eyes focused on a figure crouching in the opposite corner, clothed in all black. Even his head, face, and neck were covered by a black mask.

"Hell are you?" Vinnie said in the raspy voice he'd had since waking from surgery. "And where is my guard?" When he had closed his eyes, the prison guard had been standing just inside the door.

The next sound he heard snapped him awake. The voice. Vinnie knew that voice.

"So glad to see you again," the man said, and pushed himself up. "Comrade."

"You," Vinnie said. It was all he could manage. His throat had gone dry and felt like it was closing.

"We were sorry to upset you the last time we spoke," the man said.

"You were the only one in that cell with me," Vinnie said.

The man had moved to the side of the bed opposite Vinnie's bandaged right hand and approached the bedside. Vinnie tried to pull away, but his left hand was still cuffed to the bed rail.

"Pity about your hand," the man said, shaking his head. "Temper, temper."

Vinnie could only see his eyes and mouth through the slits. His eyes were the darkest brown he had ever seen. Nearly black. No pupils.

"Still not answering my questions," Vinnie said, and glared at him. He heard his heart pounding in his ears.

"Still trying to take control of the conversation, I see," the man said. He held very still. Dangerously still. Reminded Vinnie of a pit viper that gets deathly still before it strikes.

"Come to kill me?" Vinnie said. "My people won't like that."

"Kill you? No," the man said, still without moving. "We talked about arranging your escape, remember?"

"I remember everything," Vinnie said.

"You remember everything," the man said, "so you remember that I won't answer your questions. Yes? So why don't you shut up, Vincente?"

"I'll kill you," Vinnie said, and choked on some spittle.

"You've done us a favor, harming yourself and coming here," the man said in the same monotone he had used the other night. "The helipad makes transport so much easier."

"Helipad?" Vinnie said.

The man nodded in a single down stroke of his head. "We are taking a trip together."

"And where are we going?" Vinnie said. "Can you at least answer that?"

The dark figure paused for a long time, and then he spoke. "Good thing you're Italian." He turned and strode soundlessly from the room.

Vinnie looked after the man for a long while. He felt movement on the bed, and looked back at the outline of his legs under the thin cotton bed linens. They were trembling. Was Emil keeping his promise? Getting him out of that godforsaken prison? Taking him back to Italy? For what? To heal up so he could be useful again to his friend and the Cartel? Vinnie shook his head. Didn't make sense that he'd send a man such as this. This was not Bente's way. And it wasn't the way the Feds operated either, even their black ops boys. Vinnie had studied their ways. Had to over prepare. Know everything. Know how everybody operates. Anticipate every move.

The dark figure was not one of Bente's men. And he wasn't FBI.

Popping sounds echoed from the corridor. Men's voices were shouting. Vinnie heard at least five different voices. He heard the slap of hard-soled boots on the floor. And suddenly his room was filled with black-clad figures wearing helmets and goggles, and carrying automatic weapons. Two of them laid their weapons on the bed between Vinnie's legs.

"Eh," Vinnie said as loudly as he could, "Eh! Get them things off me. They're pointing right at my balls." One of the men was working to undo the IV bag from its metal tree, and Vinnie heard him chuckle.

"Somethin' funny asshole?" Vinnie said, and choked again from straining his neck backward to look at the man. The man stopped and moved beside the bed. In the next instant, Vinnie saw a gloved hand coming toward his head, and he heard a loud smack. A bright yellow light bloomed before his eyes. Somewhere in front of him he heard words whispered in his direction. "Call me asshole again and I will break your legs. Capisce?"

Vinnie felt the blood spill from his slack jaw. In the distance, he heard more popping sounds.

"Let's move," a voice said.

Chapter Twelve

Misericordia Clinic
Kingstown, Rhode Island

Bert shot a look into the rearview mirror and pulled the vehicle onto the road.

"We have to go back immediately?" Max said, feeling his head pressed into the headrest by the acceleration.

Bert was nodding his head vigorously. "Hospital," he said. "And have Kingstown PD on a Code Red to Signal 8 with us there."

Max was already punching numbers into the phone. "I must be missing something here and I assume you're going to tell me."

Bert started to speak, but Max held up a finger and spoke with Kingstown Police. He ended that call and punched numbers for the Director's cell. After he requested backup and ended the call, he looked at his partner and said, "Now, what's this about?"

"Something you said about the scene being too clean," Higgins said. "I'm thinking to myself, okay, so the bad guys are doing a 'walk away' from whatever they had going on, and they're torching the place to cover any trace. And then I'm thinking what, or rather who, started the clean up and walk away operation to begin with. Right? Probably Maria's injury at the clinic, and the need for her to be transported to the hospital, which would spark some kind of inquiry or investigation of the location where she was hurt."

"Oh no," Max said.

"Right," Bert said, "These shit bags are nothing if not thorough."

"They make people disappear as soon as they become a liability," Max said. "And, besides them, who was left after the fire, to roll over on them? Sanchez."

Bert could feel his partner's eyes boring into the side of his head. "I'm hurrying," Bert said, "Call the ER."

Max snatched up his phone, and then smacked it back down on his leg. "I don't have the number."

"You're kidding."

"You always call," Max said.

Bert dug in his jacket, extracted his phone and tossed it to him. "See if you can find it."

"Just get us there."

Floor 4
Memorial Hospital
Kingstown, Rhode Island

Outside Jeremy's room, Nettie and Vickie walked slowly down the corridor. Neither of them spoke. Then Vickie put her arm around Nettie's small shoulders and squeezed.

"He's so much better," Nettie said, and swiped a tear from her cheek. "He's come a long way back from wherever he was."

"He thinks you are his wife," Vickie Nile said. Nettie shrugged and nodded. "His wife died years ago."

"So I understood from talking with him while I was being vetted as his replacement." She stopped walking and turned toward Nettie. "That has to be hard for you."

Nettie gave another small shrug and looked down the hall. "He loved her dearly." When she looked back, she lost her balance again. "Are you okay?" Vickie said, catching her. "Guess I got my wish," Nettie said, and lowered her eyes. "I wanted to die. And I have." She looked up into Vickie's eyes. "To the man I love, Nettie is dead, and Jenny is alive again."

"Nettie," Vickie said, and drew her into a hug. "My heart weeps for you."

They hugged for a long time and then Nettie drew away. "I've got to get back. He needs his Jenny."

"But you are Nettie."

"I am whomever he needs me to be," Nettie said. "Right now, it's Jenny." She turned and made her way toward Jeremy's room.

Reverend Nile went to find Jeremy's doctor. As she headed toward the nurse's station, a nun clad in full habit shuffled past. She thought about approaching her to ask if she'd look in on Jeremy from time to time and pray with him, but she decided it could wait. First, the doctor.

Sister Maria Garza followed the smallish woman shuffling along the hallway and sized her up. It might work, if she worked it right. She needed a change of clothes. Right. Now.

Sister Maria Garza had put on her best smile for the door camera outside Floor 4, and she'd been buzzed through to the locked wing. She made her way casually down the hall and slipped into the room she had seen the elderly woman enter moments before. The man in the bed was turned toward the window, and his eyes were closed. She heard water running in the bathroom and assumed it was the woman. She would have to be quick. She clutched the cincture rope tied around her waist. It was a symbol as much as it was a belt to secure the robes at the waist, meant to remind the clergy that they were yoked to Christ. She untied the knot and slipped the rope from her waist. She hurried to the opposite side of the bed. She doubled the thick rope and held it taut between her two hands. Then, in one violent motion, she slapped the rope across the man's face and crammed it into his mouth. He gasped and his eyes shot open. Maria Garza pulled the rope behind his head. The rope jammed between his upper and lower teeth and gagged him.

"Breathe through your nose," she whispered loudly in the man's ear as he jerked and flailed his arms at her. She tied the rope tightly behind his head and double knotted it. Then she grabbed the pillows from behind his head and yanked off the pillowcases. She tied each arm to the bed railing. The man was wheezing and bucking in the bed, and Maria Garza knew the noise would reach the woman in the bathroom.

She looked at the side table and smiled. There, the Holy Bible sat in its hard-sided cover. She picked it up and hurried around the bed, positioning herself behind the bathroom door. She had hardly gotten herself set, when the bathroom door opened and the gray-haired woman stepped out.

"Jeremy!" she said, just as the Bible came rushing into her peripheral vision. Maria Garza hit the woman in the temple with as much force as she could muster, and she crumpled to the floor. Maria Garza dropped the Bible and set to work taking off the woman's clothes. And her own. If someone came into the room right now, it would be over, so she had to be fast. The man was still struggling against his restraints in the bed and making muted grunts behind the rope. In less than two minutes, Maria Garza was dressed in the woman's clothes, except for the shoes. Her own would have to do. She had dressed the woman in her nun's habit and had lifted her into a chair next to the bed. She pulled the shawl up over her head to shroud her face.

Maria Garza pulled the jacket hood over her head, stooped as best she could in imitation of the woman, grabbed the woman's purse and slipped from the room. She walked as briskly as she thought she could get away with and not attract attention. Once she had been buzzed back through the door, she bypassed the elevator and headed for the stairs. Four floors to freedom.

By the time she reached the ground floor, Maria Garza was panting. The sign affixed to the emergency exit door to her left warned that an alarm would sound if the door were opened. Time for a quick decision. She took a few moments to catch her breath, and then she pushed through the door. The blare of the horn over her head was deafening. She lowered her head and slowed her pace. The concrete walk rose slightly, and eventually it joined the main hospital sidewalk along the drive lane.

A covered enclosure next to a bus stop sign sat about 30 yards away, and a transit authority bus was pulling up to it. Maria Garza walked to the bus as rapidly as she thought might look credible to anyone watching, and she boarded. She fished in the woman's purse and found a wallet with enough money for the fare and more. She waited her turn behind the others, not daring even to risk a glance behind her. At last, she paid and made her way to a seat in the rear of the bus. She hadn't bothered to see where it was going, and she wasn't about to ask. What did it matter? Her head and eyes remained downcast, but presently she heard the bus doors hiss closed and they were away.

Maria Garza felt her shoulders slump and she let out a long breath. She had escaped the immediate threat, but she would not feel secure until she returned to Base. She wondered how long it would take, and whether she was even heading in the right direction. She needed to talk with Carlos. And, of course His Excellency would expect a detailed report. She shook her head. It would be a report of failure. She had failed to deal with Maria Sanchez as she had been instructed. She had failed to complete her mission, failed to prepare adequately for all eventualities, failed to over prepare. And she had left behind evidence of her presence and clues as to her identity by having to eliminate a nurse and incapacitate two people in order to escape.

She must prepare to be sacrificed, for the good of the Order. It was the cost, if you dishonored the Name, and no one was exempt.

Emergency Room Entrance
Memorial Hospital
Kingstown, Rhode Island

Lieutenant Bert Higgins and Captain Max Steele's bureau car crashed over the Emergency entrance storm grate and bounced into the horseshoe shaped drop off area. They burst from the vehicle and ran inside. No one was at the desk. They sprinted for Slip 11. Max tore the curtain aside and both men stopped.

"Get help," Max said. Bert sprinted away, mashing buttons on his phone.

"Max could see that Maria was still breathing, so he focused his attention on the body slumped across the bed on top of Maria's legs. He put two fingers to Linda's neck. No pulse. Her skin was already cold, but he lifted her and set her down onto the floor to begin CPR.

Within seconds, a crash cart could be heard rumbling and clattering across the floor. People in scrubs and lab coats appeared one after the other and set immediately to work.

They trached her and got oxygen flowing, shot several things into her arm, and then they shocked her with the PDA paddles.

After a few minutes of frenzied effort, they sat back on their legs and shook their heads. Linda Turnbill was dead.

One of the physicians who arrived was examining Maria. After a minute or two – Max could not perceive time right now – the doctor turned and gave him the thumbs-up sign. Then he returned to Maria. Max pivoted on one leg and launched himself toward the corridor, smacking headlong into his partner coming up behind him. Both men bounced and grunted. Neither lost the look of concentration.

"Who saw something?" Max said to Higgins. "Somebody must've seen something."

"Still checking," Higgins said.

"I want a list of everyone on duty the past four hours. Everyone," he said. Higgins nodded and strode away. Max grabbed the sleeve of a white coat walking by.

"Captain Steele, FBI," he said, and reached into his coat for his ID.

"I know who you are," the doctor said.

"Max winced, "Yeah, we've had to be here a lot this year, huh."

"Crazy," the doctor said, shaking his head. "What do you need?"

"I need a hospital administrator to lock this place down. I need staff at every door immediately, checking everyone who comes in and especially everyone who goes out. Just until we can get enough of our people here to cover."

"I'll see what I can do," he said, and headed for the nurse's station.

Max grabbed his cell phone from his jacket pocket and dialed Director Fenton. He got her on the first ring.

"Details," she said, dispensing with any greeting.

"Ever been nearby when someone hits a hornet's nest with a stick?" he said, not waiting for a reply. "That's what we've got here."

"Here, where?" Elizabeth Fenton said.

"Need help. Memorial. One dead. Locking it down now. Send every available," he said. "And Miserericordia Clinic got torched."

"Just heard about that," she said.

"And Dr. Sanchez is unconscious."

"Attacked?"

Max was shaking his head, and then realized Fenton couldn't see him. "No, ma'am, least not as far as we can tell. Looks like a bad fall. Head trauma."

"Stable?"

"Stable."

"Tell me about the homicide," she said. "No wait, you need help. How many you need me to send?"

"Many as you got," he said. "There's a chance the perp is still in the hospital or on grounds somewhere."

"Call you back," she said, and the line went dead.

Max had to hand it to her. She was a calculating bitch, but she was damned good in an emergency. Max stowed the cell phone and went to look for Bert. He found him standing with the security guard near the Emergency Room exit.

"This officer knows every exit in the hospital," Higgins said to Steele. "Has to check them on his rounds."

Just then, an alarm sounded. It was faint and far away, but distinct enough for all three men to hear.

"That's a fire door," Officer Durbin said. "Goes off if someone opens it."

"I know what a damned fire door does," Max said. Then he sucked in a breath and squeezed his eyes shut for a moment. "Sorry, Officer. Can you tell which door?" Durbin shook his head. "All have the same sound. We just need to follow the noise. Gotta hurry. These doors go quiet again once they shut."

"They're not supposed to," Max said.

Durbin shrugged. Bert was already sprinting away and Max followed close behind. "Stay on this exit, Durbin," Max shouted behind him.

The two agents ran in the direction of the sound. At several points, they had to burst through heavy, double doors. At one set of doors, they toppled a cart full of food trays. Food and cups and silverware sprayed across the hall. The sound continued to get louder and then, in an instant, it went quiet.

"Where are we?" Max said to Bert.

"No clue," Bert said through gulps of air.

"Where's the nearest exit?"

"Same answer."

"Nearest elevator? And set of stairs?"

"Same answer."

"Dammit," Max said. The two men continued to jog, and came upon a junction of hallways. The hall to the right was relatively short. The one to the left showed 50 yards of hallway leading to a set of double doors and the promise of more hallway beyond.

"You go right and I'll go left," Max said. "Meet back here." Bert nodded and set off.

"Watch your ass," Max called after him and sprinted left. He wondered how much help was on the way and when it would be here. He hoped they weren't too late. He saw a woman walking toward him in a lab coat, and he called to her.

"Nearest staircase? Exit?" he said.

The doctor pointed behind her. "Around the corner."

Max got to the corner, and his entire body locked up. A deep sense of dread swept over him. Panting hard, he fished for his cell phone and dialed Higgins.

"Go," Bert said after the third ring.

"Who did we leave to guard Maria?" Max said.

"Shit," Bert said.

"And no one to call," Max said. "Dammit!"

"I'll go," Bert said.

"Call me." Max listened to the silence that ensued and then looked at the phone. Bert had ended the call. He turned the corner and aimed for the stairs. There had to be an emergency door there.

He found the stairway door and burst into the stairwell. Directly across the space was an emergency exit door. He burst through it and the horn began to scream. Max hunched his shoulders and continued to run up the walkway to the road. He looked left and right. Not a soul in sight. In the distance, though, he heard sirens. They were gradually getting louder. He decided to wait for the men to arrive so he could be in on deployment decisions. He hoped Maria was still safe in the ER.

He and Bert were so hell bent on catching these guys that it was clouding their judgment. It was his fault. All of it. He was the leader. He shook his head and then squinted down the drive lane while he waited. In less than a minute, two hundred yards of drive lane were littered with marked and unmarked vehicles from which poured both uniformed and plainclothes men and women. Max found himself waving his arms and shouting like an officer on crossing duty. The faint ring of his phone found its way through the din, and he grabbed for it, turning away from the crowd huddled around him.

He glanced at the number, and then put it to his ear, "What's the word?"

"Safe and sound, thank God," Bert said.

Max craned his neck and arched his back, hearing his neck pop and complain. "Super news," he said. "Now I want her placed in protective custody, stat, but not removed from the premises."

"I'm on it," Bert said.

"And soon as she's secured, get to ICU and make sure nothing happens to Bontecelli."

"Copy."

Max opened his mouth to speak, but heard the silence again and looked at his phone. His partner had hung up on him again. Had to admire the kid's focus. They would have to work on expanding it to more than one thing at a time. He turned back to the clutch of people helping him direct assets. Max began speaking again as if he had never turned away. "Soon as the building exits are covered and the exits at the property perimeter are closed, I want officers to go floor by floor."

"Who are we looking for?" one team lead said. "Description?"

Max shook his head. "Not that simple. Stop and question anyone who appears out of place or out of their area. And stop every priest and every nun. Doctors, nurses, aids, and volunteers, too. If you get anything, call it out."

"Jesus," another lead said.

"Yep," Max said. "If you see Jesus, stop and question him, too." The agents chuckled and dispersed.

Delivery Vehicle
Memorial Hospital
Kingstown, Rhode Island

The escape from Memorial was a thing of beauty. The drones did all the work. Less than two miles from the hospital, the dark truck jerked and bounced into the salvage yard, where a white utility van sat, waiting. Emil shot a look at Gregorio.

"Fresh gloves," Emil said, "Put them over the ones you already have on." He himself had donned two pairs over the drug-soaked gloves he wore.

Gregorio spoke to the salvage owner. The two nodded and shook hands. Then Emil and Gregorio were in the panel van and away again. With the drones secured, Gregorio had resumed as driver. Next stop: the harbor. It seemed like an hour, but in less than fifteen minutes, Gregorio sped onto the darkened dock. He cut the lights next to a sedan with darkened windows. Even before they stopped, a crane was in motion from the docked barge, and a boom was lowering toward the van. The transfer to the car was seamless and silent. Then they were away again, this time to the airport.

Emil broke the silence. "Too easy," he said, staring hard at his men. "Makes me nervous."

"You say over prepare," Gregorio said, "we over prepare."

Emil nodded. His smile was a flicker so brief that it was gone as soon as it had appeared. "I am leaving you and your brother with unfinished business." He tore the nun's habit from his head and threw it on the floorboard. So much unfinished business. He needed to remain. No one could take command like him. No one could clean up a mess like him. He loved a challenge, especially loved a tough one. But the risk was too great. Agent Steele had captured him once. And then there was his competitor. Emil Bente stared at Gregorio for a long moment. "Where is Maria Garza?"

Gregorio shrugged. "We saw her last at the clinic."

Emil held out his hand toward Gregorio. "Satphone. Let's call her." He saw the man start, and then his chin dropped.

Gregorio shook his head. "Forgot it."

"Not at the hospital, Gregorio."

"No, Excellency," Gregorio said. "Never packed it."

Emil glared at him. "Prepare, then over prepare, Amigo."

Floor 4
Memorial Hospital
Kingstown, Rhode Island

The fourth floor nurse's station was a beehive of activity. Like most hospitals Reverend Victoria Nile had been in, and she had been in a lot of them, five people were tasked to do the work of nine. It seemed the height of insanity to run an operation this way when lives were at stake. People who were this overtasked and overloaded, no matter how experienced or skilled they were, made mistakes and patients suffered. When patients suffered because mistakes were made, they filed expensive lawsuits. If she were a betting person, she'd bet the cost of litigation, and the legal fees to cover the hospital against the threat of lawsuits, was far greater than it would have cost the hospital to staff a nine position department with nine people.

With a pang of guilt for distracting these poor, beleaguered souls, she called one of them to her. "I am Reverend Victoria Nile and I would like to have a word with Dr. Jeremy Tittle's physician. Tittle's in Room 416."

The woman in yellow scrubs smiled, made a flicker of eye contact, and then nodded. "She's on rounds."

Nile smiled. "And no doubt playing hide-n-seek with the rest of the people wanting to speak with her."

The nurse smiled and made full eye contact.

"Oh, I get it," Rev. Nile said, "Been a participant in Catch-that-Doc more times than I can count. Just give me a name and say 'Go.'" The nurse laughed.

"Dr. Marx, last seen heading to the opposite end of the wing," the nurse said, and grinned.

"Say it," Rev. Nile said, and cocked her head playfully.

"Go," the nurse said, and laughed.

Vickie pretended to charge away down the hall, laughing. Might be the only laugh that nurse – perhaps either one of them – would get today.

She headed for the end of the wing. She would wait for the first white coat to appear from a room. If it wasn't Dr. Marx, she'd wait for the next white coat. Persistence was the name of this game. Nettie would be all right for a while in Jeremy's room. Or Jenny. The scene in Jeremy's hospital room flooded her mind. Without a blink, Nettie had become Jenny, for Jeremy's sake. For love's sake. She blew out a long breath. Was she still capable of such love?

Dean Nile ended up standing sideways to the large plate glass window at the corridor's end. She saw her reflection and winced. People like her sat in seminary offices, conceptualizing about the love of God and how human beings can live out that love in the world. Then there were people like Nettie who answered the question with the way she lived her life. Who was the real minister?

A flash of white caught her eye and she turned to see a woman standing outside a room thumbing through a chart. Nile set off toward her.

"Dr. Marx?" she said.

She saw the doctor's shoulders jerk inside her lab coat, but the woman didn't raise her eyes from the chart. Rev. Nile positioned herself so close to the woman that it had to be invading her comfort zone. She glanced at the lab coat and said again, "Dr. Marx, a word?"

"I'm really ...." the woman said, looking up and flicking away a lock of curly blonde hair.

"Two minutes," Nile said, "And not two minutes that turn into ten, promise."

The doctor stared at her, and Rev. Nile continued. "I'm the new dean of Ecclesia Seminary, and Dr. Jeremy Tittle in 416 is both my predecessor and a member of my congregation. There is an elderly woman in his room right now who loves him to pieces and feels responsible for his condition.

I just need a little help here so that I can help them both." She stopped, and bit her lip.

"Wow," Dr. Marx said. "Seems like they're pretty lucky people, you going to bat for them like this." Her face softened into a smile. "Kind of thought you were going to tackle me there for a moment."

"Only if I had to," Nile said, and grinned.

"Please don't. They've got no one to replace me if I go down." Dr. Marx closed the file in her hands. "Clergy still have privilege in my book, despite what the HIPPA Nazis say, so I'll tell you this much. Dr. Tittle has suffered a psychotic break, but I think he's going to be one of the lucky ones who finds his way back again. He is already talking and eating on his own."

"He thinks the woman in there is his dead wife," Rev. Nile said.

Dr. Marx nodded, "I said he is going to be one of the lucky ones, because he's coming back, with the help of some very sophisticated pharmaceuticals." She snatched at more errant hair in her face. "But he's not home yet."

"How can I help him? Them?"

"Him? You can help by talking to him as much as possible, engaging him. Come see him as often as possible for the next couple of weeks." She paused, "Her? Promise her that he's on his way, that he's coming home to her."

To her surprise and slight embarrassment, Dean Nile's eyes filled with tears.

"What's this?" Dr. Marx was looking into her new acquaintance's reddening face.

"Nothing at all," Nile said, "and my two minutes are up." She touched the doctor's arm. "You would make a fine minister."

"I already am," Dr. Marx said, and turned toward the door across the hall. She waved a small hand behind her.

Nile dug into her shoulder bag for a tissue. The words sounded in her ears. "Promise her that he's on his way, that he's coming home to her." A fresh wave of tears overflowed and spilled. The love of her life had never returned. She started back down the hall, blotting her eyes and blowing her nose. It's not about you, Vickie. She reached Room 416, knocked softly and pushed through the doorway into the room.

For a moment, her head spun and she staggered, clutching her chest. Jeremy was on the bed, bound and gagged, and a nun was sitting in a chair next to him with her back to the door. Nile spun and shot back through the door. She ran to the nurse's desk.

"Need help," she said over the counter. "Call the police." She hadn't noticed the man in the charcoal gray suit next to her until he touched her arm.

"Federal agent, ma'am," he said, and flashed his wallet.

"Room 416," she said, and staggered against the counter. "Quickly."

"Who's in there," he said, "besides the patient?"

"A nun," she said, "Only saw her from the back. Patient is gagged though. I don't even know if he's still alive. I just ran."

"Anybody else in the room?" he said.

"I," she paused, "didn't look."

She heard the agent murmuring into a small button dangling from his ear. "I need Steele, and backup." Then he straightened and turned to the staff. "Everybody please back up. And clear this hallway. I need everyone behind a closed door until we come get you."

People began scattering in every direction.

"I'm 416's doctor," a voice behind him said.

The agent nodded and pointed at Dean Nile, "Take her with you and get behind that counter." He pointed to the nurse's station. "And I mean down under. Right now."

"You," he grabbed the nurse in yellow who had spoken with Reverend Nile earlier, "get that locked door to this wing unlocked and prop it open. Go." The nurse ran down the corridor to the door. A man and a woman with guns drawn pushed into the hallway as soon as she opened it. Seconds later, several others followed behind them.

Captain Max Steele was in the lead and arrived first. He pointed at the agent crouched beside the door. "You been in?" he said, jerking his head sideways toward the door.

The agent shook his head, "When I heard there was a nun in there …."

Max was nodding his head. "Could be Bente," he said in a voice so low it was almost a whisper, "but it could also be a nun. Ready?" He didn't wait for an answer. He motioned the agents to form a wedge shape behind him. "When my arm goes down," he said quietly, "we go in. Pass the word back." A low murmur ensued as the agents in front relayed the message behind them. Max's body was crouched in front of the door and his arm was raised high in the air. He glanced at the agent next to him, who nodded, and then he glanced quickly at the men behind him. In one motion, he dropped his arm and crashed through the door.

"FBI. Get on the floor," he shouted. "On the floor. On the floor. Now!" His eyes took in the room, but his gun remained fixed on the back of the nun's head seated next to the bed. No one and nothing moved. The nun remained absolutely still, and Jeremy Tittle looked unconscious, at the very least.

Max shot a finger toward the closed bathroom door, but the lead agent was already moving in that direction. He and two agents directly behind him flung open the door and pushed in.

"FBI, get on the floor," they shouted.

Max kept sweeping the rest of the room with his eyes, ready for the slightest motion. There was none.

"Clear," the agent called from the bathroom.

Max heard the heavy breathing of agents behind him, smelled the adrenaline and gun oil, and knew he was well covered. He took two steps toward the seated nun, letting his gun barrel lead him. Then he reached for the shawl, grabbed a handful of it and the hair beneath it, and yanked the head backward as he shoved the muzzle of the gun into the side of the person's head.

The blotched and slack face of Nettie Spruill gaped garishly back at him.

"Left is clear. Right is clear," he heard officers say.

"Clear," he heard again from the bathroom.

Max felt his body relax, "Get medical in here, stat." He felt Nettie's neck for a pulse. Found one. He blew out a breath. "Crime scene everyone," he said without looking away from Nettie or Jeremy. "Everybody out." Then he snapped his fingers, "Gloves." Someone handed him a pair of black latex gloves. "Seal the wing," he said. "Search every room." He heard someone pull the door and bark orders. Max snapped on the gloves. After a few moments, a white lab coat appeared in his peripheral vision. "Any crime scene techs yet?" he said, again without taking his eyes off the scene in front of him.

"Rolling," a voice said.

"Shit," Max said quietly. "We can't wait." He pointed to Nettie and Jeremy. "THEY can't wait."

"I need photographs," he said to the lead agent. "Quickly. Use your phone." Max continued to hold his Glock outstretched. "Doc?"

"Right here," a level female voice said beside him.

"I know you need to attend to them," he said. "Give us two minutes to document what we can. While we're doing that, you get two beds to put them in. These people need your help, and I need them out of here. The bed in here stays."

"On it," Dr. Marx said.

"I need your best people," Max said over his shoulder. "Can your people move them without touching the bed or the chair?"

The doctor touched his shoulder.

"Colonel Marx, United States Marine Corps, retired, at your service, sir," she said.

"Thank God," Max said, "the cavalry."

"Storm trooper and certified badass," she said.

"Even better," Max said. "Get to work, Colonel."

"Yes, sir," Dr. Marx said, "but I need the vics, stat." She was already shouting orders to the hospital staff by the time she reached the mouth of the room.

The lead agent flashed photos with his phone as he moved about the room. Max moved close enough to Jeremy Tittle to see a slight rise and fall in the sheet covering his body. His face was pale but not deathly white. Through the gloves, he felt for a pulse, and found one.

"Ready for me to take the rope off?" Max said to his photographer. "You got enough up here?"

"Affirmative," the agent said, and kept flashing around Nettie and the chair.

As gently as he could, Max reached behind Jeremy's head and untied the double knot. He unwound the doubled rope, carefully extracting it from between the man's teeth. Even after the rope was out, Jeremy's mouth remained open. It looked as if his teeth were bared.

"Colonel," Max said loudly. He stood beside Jeremy's head and peered toward the door.

"Here," he heard her call.

"Gloved and booted?" Max said.

"Affirmative, sir," Dr. Marx said.

"Let's move them," Max said. The medical team hurried into the room. "Don't touch anything but the bodies. Especially metal bed railings and chair surfaces."

"Roger that," Dr. Marx said next to him.

The medical team had Jeremy and Nettie out and onto rolling beds in under a minute. Max had to admit, he was impressed. He followed the second bed through the door into the hallway.

"Where you taking them?" he said to Dr. Marx. She had been joined by several other white lab coats. They were leaning over the bodies and calling out orders.

"ICU. I think it's best," Dr. Marx said.

"Negative on that," Max said. "It's still on lockdown with a prisoner."

"Good Lord," Dr. Marx said.

A man in a dark suit hurried to Max. "All rooms cleared," he said.

"Whole floor?" Max said.

"Whole floor, every room."

"Good work."

"Colonel," he said, turning back to the doctor. "What's your next best alternative?"

Dr. Marx was silent for a moment, "Surgical theatre I suppose."

"Get it cleared," he said, and she ran toward the nurse's station. Rev. Nile was standing, but staying behind the counter, out of the way. Dr. Marx lifted the phone and leaned against the shelf behind the counter. Then she tossed the phone down and ran for the beds.

"Hang that up," she called to Rev. Nile as she passed.

"Theatres 3 and 4," she called to the medical teams at each bed, and immediately the two scrums of people began moving toward the exit.

"Go with them," Max said to the lead agent, "and take a team." The man pointed to four agents, and they followed Dr. Marx.

"Figures," Max said. He watched the forensics team pushing their way through the door into the hall at the exact moment the beds were pushing their way out. If the situation hadn't been so serious, it would have been comical. He saw Dr. Marx's hands go up in some sort of gesture and she was nearly bowled over by the forensics team, who moved like one giant snowplow through the gaggle of people.

As the team broke free into the hallway, Max saw Randy's face in the lead. Randy was not smiling.

"I understand part of my crime scene has left and that they've had, what, fifty people in and out of it so far?" Randy said. He stepped aside to let the rest of the team pass into the room.

"Easy, buddy," Max said. "I'll take full responsibility."

Randy shook his head and followed the rest of his team.

Max's phone buzzed. He looked at the number, expecting to see Higgins calling. He took a deep breath. Director Elizabeth Fenton.

"Director," Max said.

"Sit rep," she said.

"Situation report is that our assassin is still at large, whereabouts unknown. Higgins was dispatched to guard the prisoner, Bontecelli. I assume by now he has the entire ICU on lockdown."

"You assume?" she said.

"It's Higgins, Director Fenton," Max said hotly.

"Call and make sure. We don't assume. You copy that, Agent?" Fenton said, matching hot for hot. "Then call me back." The line went dead. Max pulled the phone away from his ear and flipped his middle finger at it.

Max called Higgins. He heard ring followed by ring. No answer. Voicemail. He hung up on it and dialed again. Voicemail again.

Chapter Thirteen

Memorial Hospital
Kingstown, Rhode Island

Max called Director Fenton back.

"Sit rep," Director Fenton said without preamble.

"Negative contact with Agent Higgins," Max said.

"Keep trying," she said, "Thoughts about the assassin?"

"GOA, ma'am," he said.

"Catch me up on the agent-speak, Steele," she said.

"GOA. Gone On Arrival," he said. "These people are ghosts."

"Then we damn well better figure out how to become ghostbusters, Detective Steele, and I'm not being clever. You follow me?"

"Director Fenton, If you've got a better agent for this assignment, then I will standby here until my relief arrives," Max said.

Silence followed for a time as both of them breathed into the phone.

"Continue sit rep," Director Fenton said finally.

"Three victims, one deceased and two unconscious and being attended to. I am familiar with the identity of all three. The deceased was the ER charge nurse. We called her as we were making our way back to the hospital, on a hunch that Dr. Sanchez might be in danger. By the time we arrived, she was dead and the perp had fled. Our two unconscious victims were attacked on the fourth floor."

"Wait," Director Fenton said, "isn't that a locked ward?"

"Very good, Director," Max said. "It is indeed."

"Christ," she said.

"That may be who opened the door," Max said. "Keep listening. The former dean of Ecclesia Seminary is here. Suffered a psychotic break of some sort. They found him unconscious and gagged with a clerical waist rope. A retired professor friend of his was found in the room, also unconscious. She had had her clothes stolen and was wearing a nun's habit, sans clerical waist rope. And just to crowd the circus ring further, the new seminary dean was here on the floor, too."

"So what do we have?" she said. "One perp with a lot of help, or more than one? Please tell me we are not headed back to that God-forsaken seminary."

"Can't tell yet," Max said. "I intend to interview that new dean shortly."

"But your gut is telling you the perp has left the premises."

"Yep," Max said, "and I hope to hell one or both of our victims is going to wake up and ID that bitch."

"Don't you have three?" Director Fenton said, and Max noticed a shift in her tone of voice.

"Three," Max said. "One is dead."

"Okay, but three living victims," she said. "How is Maria Sanchez?"

A protracted silence hummed like electricity on the line. Finally, Max spoke, "Unconscious," he said, "and almost certainly involved in the Bente Cartel."

"I'm sorry," Fenton said, "truly."

"She's in protective custody," he said. "Soon as she wakes up, I'm requesting to be excused from her interrogation."

"Of course."

"And that, Director Fenton, is the end of my situation report."

"Is that all you got?" she said, and chuckled. Max was too pissed off to laugh. "Hang in there, Captain. Because I know you so well, I know you are crazy frustrated. But Bente and his thugs will screw up. When they do, you'll take them down once and for all."

"Do we need to discuss my resignation?"

"Because of Sanchez?"

"Yes, ma'am."

"We do not," Fenton said. "These people are brilliant in their deception. I have already cleared you."

Max waited.

"Find Higgins." And then there was silence on the line. Director Fenton had ended the call without so much as a good-bye. As usual. He hadn't told her Maria was pregnant. He closed his eyes and a long sigh escaped his lips. He pocketed the phone and headed to the nurse's station. He needed to talk with Dean Nile and find out what her connection was to this crime scene. And he needed to find his partner, even though he knew Lieutenant Badass could take care of himself. At the counter, Max stopped. No one was behind the desk. Dean Nile had disappeared.

Terrific.

ICU

Memorial Hospital

Kingstown, Rhode Island

Vinnie heard the brakes pop loose on the bed wheels and he opened his eyes. Only half his vision had returned. The other half was still a bright yellow haze from the blow he'd received. The bed moved pivoted and moved toward the door the door. Vinnie's eye caught sight of the prison guard's crumpled frame. They must have propped him in the corner behind Vinnie's bed. The front of his shirt was stained dark with blood. They'd cut his throat.

As the bed passed through the door, a fresh round of gunfire erupted. Instinctively, Vinnie tried to raise his arms to shield himself, but both hands were secured to the bed. He was helpless. So this was how it would end. He had faced death many times, and he'd always survived. The joke was he would die slipping on a bar of soap in the shower. But maybe not. Maybe today was the day, shot while helpless, tied to a hospital bed. Humiliating.

The helmeted men rolled his bed to the elevator, and that's where he remained, listening. After a minute or two, he pieced together enough words to understand that they were waiting for keys. They wanted keys for the door to the roof, and for the elevator's rooftop access. They were also patting themselves down for a handcuff key. Not long after, they wheeled him into the elevator and several men packed in with him. One brandished a handcuff key and held it in front of Vinnie's face.

"We make you happy before we make you sad," he said.

"Whatever that means," Vinnie said, and coughed. The men chuckled and Vinnie saw two of them clap the third on his massive shoulders. He was a full head taller than the other two and twice as thick. Vinnie didn't ask any more questions. They weren't going to answer anyway. His right hand throbbed. They unlocked his left hand. A thought flickered. If he could reach one of the guns still between his legs, he could take out one or two of them and then die like a man. As if the men could read his mind, one of them took hold of his free hand and clamped it in a tight grip.

The elevator slowed and stopped with a soft chime. He was rolled into the hallway near the stairway door. "Prop the elevator door with the bed. Post at the top of the stairs until the extraction signal," the large man said. Then he moved to the bed and grinned at Vinnie. "Only one way to the roof, my friend, when you don't have the elevator key," he said, as the other man pulled Vinnie into a sitting position. "Guns," he said, and one man grabbed the weapons from between Vinnie's legs. He looked at Vinnie. "This will hurt," he said.

The man grabbed Vinnie's arm and pulled him toward the edge of the bed. He lowered his shoulder and in one jerk move, tossed Vinnie's body onto his shoulder in a full body lift. Vinnie screamed in pain. The man carried him like a sack of coal into the stairwell and began to climb. The other men had preceded them and now hurried ahead up the stairs. By the time the large man stopped climbing, the others had worked the door open. The man stepped with him onto the roof. Vinnie was in so much pain he felt he might pass out. He heard the soft whine of the rotor as the helicopter blades started to move.

The man set Vinnie on a thin mattress on the helicopter floor, and the door closed. The man who had crouched in the corner of the room, the same man who had visited him in his prison cell, leaned over Vinnie from his seat, "You in pain, Comrade?" he said. He stripped off his ski mask and smiled. "It is nothing compared to what we have in store for you." The engine noise increased, and with a sideways jerk, Vinnie felt the helicopter take flight.

"Who do you work for?" Vinnie said through a heavy fog of pain. His hand throbbed. The man did not reply. Vinnie closed his eyes. Italy and torture were a terrible combination. Some of the worst butchers – the ones who could keep you alive while most of your parts lay in pieces around you – were Italian. Sometimes you get to live, and it is a blessing. Sometimes you get to live, and it is a curse. Death is not the ultimate punishment. Suffering, relentless and merciless, is the unspeakable horror.

"Emil Bente will see you dead," Vinnie said as loudly as he could. His words felt impotent and weak. They elicited only the faintest grin from his captor.

"We're going to a great deal of trouble to extract you in such a way that it is right under Emil Bente's nose," the man said. "He won't even know what he is seeing. Until we tell him." He reared back his head and laughed.

At last, the helicopter set down. The large man appeared and gagged Vinnie. He picked him up like he was a doll and jumped from the side of the helicopter onto the ground. Vinnie howled in pain through the gag.

Another man was waiting in a modified golf cart with a rear seat and high-set, knobby tires. The men tied Vinnie into the seat. The large man situated himself next to Vinnie in the back. He leaned over and whispered in Vinnie's ear. "Going to the airport," he said, "The back way." He laughed. "We're gonna wave to your pal on our way out." Vinnie would have spit on him if he could. He felt tears drop from the sides of his eyes. Pain. Pain that screamed with the impotence of the damned.

Memorial Hospital
Kingstown, Rhode Island

His phone buzzed. This time it was Higgins.

"What's your 20?" Max said.

"ICU," Higgins said. "Get down!"

"What?" Max said. "Bert? Bert?" His partner had ended the call. Immediately, his phone chirped with another incoming call. Damned Director again.

"Live shooters in ICU," she said without preamble.

"Copy," Max said, and started running for the stairs with the phone still pressed to his ear.

"Wait, Steele," she said. "I can hear you running. Wait! Wait for help! FBI Tactical and SWAT are rolling. Max? Max?"

Max jammed the phone in his outer pocket and took the stairs two at a time, his Glock bouncing in the shoulder holster.

"Holy Shit, holy shit, holy shit," a male voice said above him as Max continued to charge up the stairwell. He heard muffled pops and recognized them immediately. He drew his Glock.

"FBI," he said in a loud whisper, slowing, listening, but still climbing the stairs. "Get on your face."

"Holy shit," the man said. "It's Security. Security!"

"On your face," Max said, and peeked around the railing where the stairs turned halfway between floors. He watched the elderly man flop onto his face on the concrete landing. The bill of his security cap speared the floor and popped off his balding head.

Max rushed up the final steps. ""Get up," he said. "You're good."

"Holy shit," the man said, wheezing. "Shots fired, other side of that door."

"Somebody call you from ICU?"

The man nodded. "Don't know what they expected me to do about it, but here I am."

"You armed?" Max said.

The security guard snorted and shook his head. "They don't even give us squirt guns. Freakin' ridiculous."

"How much do you get paid?" Max said.

"Ten dollars an hour," he said.

Max shook his head once. "Not enough to go into harm's way, even with an AK. How about you get back downstairs and guard the patients in the operating theatres."

"10-4," he said, and stood with a wince.

Max slapped him on the back as he scuffed past him down the stairs.

"Holy shit, almost forgot," the man said, turning back and grabbing his pocket. "You ain't getting in there without a key. This door's locked stair-side." Three loud pops sounded from the other side of the door and both men ducked reflexively. He fumbled for the key ring, his hands trembling, and gave it to Max. Then he grabbed the railing and started down again.

"Holy shit, forgot my hat," the man said.

"Leave it. Get downstairs," Max said, turning his full attention to the door. He stared at it for a moment, wishing he could see through to the other side. If SWAT and FBI Tactical are rolling but not here … who was putting up the fight? Higgins? By himself? He needed intel. How many shooters? What kind of weapons? Where were the bad guys placed?"

He imagined opening the door and being cut down immediately by a guy waiting on the other side. If they were organized, and if there were enough of them, they would have a guy on this stairway door. It's what he would do. Maybe he should wait. His mind filled with the lower teeth of his instructor at the Academy. The guy always stuck his jaw out when he talked and you couldn't help but focus on the lower row of jagged, yellow teeth. "Remember the 3-30 Rule," he used to say, "Waiting three minutes for backup can add thirty more years to your life."

Trouble was, Max was not a waiter. He was a stormer. Tear in like a tornado and suck up the bad guys while they're still trying to figure how anyone could be so stupid as to run straight at them. He fingered the keys in his hand and began to slow his breath. He tried the keys quietly, one at a time, until he found the right one. He left it in the lock while he patted himself down for his spare clip. He was patting his sport jacket pocket at the very moment it buzzed and vibrated. He jumped, and then grinned. What were the odds of that happening? Make for a great story to tell the grandkids, if he got those 30 years. Grandkids. His mind filed with Maria's face and he thought about the baby growing inside her. His cell buzzed again. He dug for it and looked to see who was calling. If it was Fenton again ….

It was Higgins. Max answered, and whispered into it. "Go."

"Where are you?" Higgins whispered back. In the next instant, a loud pop exploded through the phone.

Where are you?" Max whispered. "You okay?"

"ICU," Higgins said.

"I'm here," Max said. "Stairwell."

"Freakin' hospital and I can't even find gauze," Higgins said.

"Hurt?" Max said, and felt his whole body tense.

"Just a nick," Bert said, "but bleeding like a sumbitch."

"Location?" Max said. "Yours and bad guys?"

"Back of nurse's station, metal lateral files."

"I'm coming," Max said.

"Wait for backup partner," Higgins said. "There's a bunch of them."

"How many?"

"No idea," Bert said, still whispering, "but the guy that winged me was a pro. Moved like a cat. Full tactical."

"No shit?" Max said in a whisper.

"No shit."

"I'm coming," Max said.

"Don't be a dumbass," Bert said.

"How many? Approximately?"

"Can't see. Lots of feet pounding the halls."

"Stay put," Max said.

"You're kidding, right?" Bert said.

Max hung up, his mind racing. Are these Bente's men? Someone else's? Did they come to terminate Vinnie Bontecelli? Rescue him? Who needs him dead? Who needs him alive? The questions would have to wait. His partner was pinned and hurt. He'd already lost one partner. Whatever else was going on, Bert Higgins was first priority.

Max began to grid the ICU in his mind, visualizing each hallway, trying to remember where the stairs were in relation to the nurse's station. To the right of the elevator. Yes. And that meant the station would be around the corner and about thirty yards down the hall. So, eight to ten seconds away, depending what happened when he opened this door. The popping of gunfire had ceased, but he heard muffled shouts coming through the door. Thirty more years be damned. He was getting Bert out.

Max crouched on the landing, readied the Glock, and reached for the key. He focused on his breath again, let his jaw hang loose, and breathed through his mouth. He turned the key until he felt it unlock. Then, he yanked on the handle, and stormed through the door. A heavily armed figure stood ten feet from him, facing sideways to the door. In an instant, Max assessed his target. The man was dressed in all black, wearing a tactical helmet and goggles, heavy flack vest thick with hardware, and holding an assault rifle. Max knew he had one second either to live or die. The man had jerked when Max opened the door, and he was swinging his weapon when Max, who was already in his shooter's stance and sighting over the end of his Glock, squeezed off two rounds. He saw them crash through the man's goggles. The Glock's discharge was deafening as it rang throughout the hallway and into the stairwell. Max would have to proceed on sight alone because the ringing in his ears was drowning out all other sound.

He swung his arm parallel to the elevator door, and his eyes and body followed. What he saw next sucked the air from the hallway. Two thick muzzles and partial helmets appeared around the corner fifteen yards away, one about six feet up the wall and the other below it a few feet. Max whipped his body back into the stairwell as a barrage of automatic weapon fire sounded. He leaped halfway down the first flight of stairs and then vaulted his body over the railing onto the second flight. His feet skidded on the concrete steps, despite the rough surface. He was slipping down the next flight when the stairwell exploded with the sound of automatic weapons and the slap of metal rounds into concrete near his head and neck.

Max threw his body down the next flight of stairs, and then the next. The explosions stopped, but that could mean any number of things, the worst of which was that they were in pursuit and positioning themselves for a kill shot. And he couldn't hear shit.

3-30. He should have waited for backup.

Harbor
Kingstown, Rhode Island

Maria Garza took a circuitous route to the harbor. It was strange to see the harbor in daylight. She'd been accustomed to getting to Base under cover of night to avoid detection. Today, she would have to approach the access vessel in broad daylight. What choice did she have? She approached the taxi stand a hundred yards away from the dock, blending in and watching for anything unusual. The harbor teemed with activity. Trucks rumbled past, bilging exhaust, and smacking thick tires through ruts along the access lanes. Taxis and buses made loops looking for fares. Lots of people walked. She could tell the foreigners because they arched their necks to take in the crane booms inching into place over cargo. They stood out from the majority of walkers, whose bent shoulders and downcast eyes told stories of impoverished lives, dangerous work, and runaway addiction.

Maria Garza's thoughts were interrupted by the presence of two men standing close to her, too close, one on each side. The taxi stand was not crowded. She took an exaggerated look up and down the access lane for taxis, assessing the men from the periphery of her vision. She flexed her fingers. She and the other Marias were sixth degree black belts, and they were trained in street level mixed martial arts. In her younger days, she was a force to be reckoned with. Now, her muscles didn't stretch like they used to and every joint ached.

The men were Hispanic, but too well dressed for dockworkers. And they didn't smell like the docks – another important "tell" that they didn't belong. They were not looking at her, but that meant nothing about the threat they posed. She would have a half-second advantage at most. Two backward strikes with her fists to their groins and both would be on their way down. But what if they were harmless men with no sense of personal boundaries? And the scene it would cause, the attention to herself, had to be weighed. Invisibility in the crowd was her best defense. She decided to move to the other side of the taxi stand away from them.

As she took the first step away, she felt the jab beneath her left shoulder blade, quick and sudden, gone as soon as it had come. Even as she looked, the man on her left was turning and striding toward a black, unmarked vehicle, pulling into the taxi stand. Every window was tinted. Not good. At all. Then the docks began to quiver, and she couldn't feel her legs. She told herself to run, but her legs wouldn't move. She felt a muscled arm lock around her shoulders supporting her weight and she was walk-dragged to the black car.

"*Sí, Sí, Madre*," the man said loudly, "*Vamos a llevarte a casa*."

Taking their Mama home: very clever. But as she was being folded into the back seat, she knew, wherever she was going, it wasn't home. She tried to speak, but her mouth wouldn't move. The men were speaking rapidly in Spanish, and several times she heard "*aeropuerto*." Maybe they were an extraction team and she really was going home. His Excellency was so kind. And merciful. She had made a mess of things. She felt bumps in the road as the car pulled away, but her eyes wouldn't move and her head was tilted back. Then she saw teeth in front of her eyes, teeth bared wide in a smile. "We heard you are a nun," the teeth said in a thick Latino accent. "Yes, let it be so. Satan will be so pleased."

She saw the point of the stiletto move close to her eyes and she tried to shut them. Couldn't. She tried to scream, but she heard nothing. The point of the stiletto moved upward away from her face, and she saw the brown fleshy fist that held it. Then the point rushed toward her eye, rushed with great speed, but Maria Garza watched it in slow motion. Watched the fist fill her vision completely, watched the blackness approach and then surround her, until she was alone, enveloped in a great stillness.

Then, as if the knife had pierced a balloon swollen with tiny fractures of light, Maria Garza saw brilliant explosions. Sparks and bursts of intense light surrounding and enveloping her. She floated into it, as if weightless in the twinkling glitter mist. She stood and extended her arms, which worked perfectly now with no stiffness. She twirled and twirled. The air was chocked with prisms of spectral light, and it was filled with sound. It was laughter, delicious, joyful, and child-like. Her voice was back and she added hers to the chorus.

She was home.

Memorial Hospital
Kingstown, Rhode Island

Max Steele jumped the final set of stairs to the first floor landing, and threw himself against the exit door. The alarm screamed but Max barely noticed. He tucked his shoulder and rolled out onto the sidewalk. And then he was up, legs pumping, his feet eating up the sidewalk toward the hospital access road and the tall trees that lined it. His chest heaved and his lungs burned. He lunged behind one of the large live oaks, rolled again, and came up in a crouch. He fixed his eyes on the emergency door, waiting for his pursuers. His Glock was gone from his hand. His best defense now was to hide until backup arrived.

None of his pursuers appeared from the emergency door. Max continued to chug air, his lungs slowly recovering from the exertion and adrenaline. In his mind, he replayed the scene in the stairwell, and shuddered. At least a hundred rounds, and maybe twice that, had come his way. Only one of them would have done the job. He felt the pressure on his ears before he heard the growing sound of helicopter blades beating the air. He looked to the roof and could just see the rotor tips flashing in the sunlight. Then his eyes caught a rush of motion to his right. Vehicle after vehicle squealed around the corner and sped up the lane. The good guys. Max stepped out. and waved his arms to flag them down. The large, boxy, SWAT van was first to brake in front of him. Men dressed in gear that looked remarkably like that worn by the ones shooting at him, spilled from the back doors like a tipped bucket of fish.

Max had his creds out and held them at arm's length to the men striding toward him. Sounds mixed inside his traumatized eardrums, and he was having trouble hear and even thinking. He opted for a mix of words and pointing. "Chopper. Roof," he said pointing, and several heads whirled to look up and behind them. "Unknown. Follow it. Can we?" He watched two men peel off the scrum surrounding him. One held a cell phone to his ear, while the other lifted a radio.

"Whose is it?" one man dressed in SWAT gear said. Max assumed he was the Commander. "Whose?" Max indicated his hearing loss with his hands. The man nodded, and spoke into the phone.

In the next moment, personnel were running and diving and shouting. The words were a jumble in Max's ears, but as the SWAT commander drove his shoulder into him, and he felt himself crashing to the pavement, two words finally penetrated his ears. "Shooter. Incoming."

Chapter Fourteen

ICU

Memorial Hospital

Kingstown, Rhode Island

Lieutenant Bert Higgins had heard the bursts of automatic weapon fire around the corner, and he prayed that his partner hadn't done something foolish. Now, as he strained to hear every sound, heard only silence and the soft shifting sounds of people huddled with him behind the lateral files. His training told him several things. Silence did not mean they were safe. Or alone. Silence did mean that every sound they made was easier for someone else to hear. He pressed his index finger to his lips and rotated his torso, making eye contact with the others. He remembered he had turned his phone to silent mode, and he fished it out of his pocket. He'd had a missed call from Headquarters, but no word from Max. Where are you, Max? Please be alive.

He looked over at Dr. Fleischer. The doctor's neck was craned to watch the monitors and LED readouts of his Intensive Care patients. Bert imagined some were in need of immediate attention. Perhaps some were in their final moments before death, and the people who would be caring for them were huddled here, at least until he gave the word that it was safe. The weight of that responsibility was heavy, and it overwhelmed his instinct to remain hidden and protected. His Glock was still in his right hand, and with his left, he motioned for the others to stay. With a deep breath, he crawled out from behind the metal cabinets. He went flat on his belly and wormed his way to the opening between the side of the nurse's station and the wall. He peered up and down the hallway. Clear.

He rose to a crouch and took another deep breath. Most moments in a federal agent's life were mundane, procedural, and clerical. But the majority of their field training was preparation for moments like this one. When it was time to act, an agent was trained to assess the risks, and to take action in spite of them.

Bert sprang into the hallway and ran for the corner near the elevator. If there were hostiles, they would be here, and he was going to take them out or be taken out. It was as simple as that. He transitioned into a shooter stance and hurled himself in a roll around the corner, coming up ready to fire. His vision was at its widest angle and he took in the area in that first millisecond. He saw one black clad figure lying motionless near the wall opposite the stairway door. Half of the man's face was missing and the wall was spattered with brain matter and blood. The elevator was closed. The rest of the hallway looked clear, but he ran to the end of it and back, punching himself and the Glock into each room. Then he ran back around the corner and repeated the search past the nurse's station to the end of that corridor. Clear.

Next decisions: Guard the elevator and staircase, and release the doctors and nurses to attend to their patients? Or was that too risky for them should a firefight break out again? Where was his partner? He paused. Max might be pinned down somewhere and need help. Should he leave the civilians in their hiding spot and reconnoiter? He ducked into the doorway of the isolation room. It gave him a good view of both the elevator and the stairwell door. He grabbed his phone and glanced again at the readout. There was a text from Max.

"Shooter on roof. Bird on helipad. Stay where you are. Ordering you."

Bert Higgins snorted, more in relief that Max was alive than anything. There was nothing funny about any of this. But in this moment, his partner's style made him laugh: tell him where the bad guys are, where the focus of the action is, and order him to stay away.

"Right," Bert whispered to himself, "Like that's what you would do, Cap!"

He texted back, "Your 20?"

He waited for a reply, alternatively watching for movement in the hallway and glancing at the phone.

"Outside. Pinned down. Roof shooter."

That did it. Bert straightened to his full height. He ran to the black clad figure and began searching him down for weapons. The automatic weapon was gone, but he found the man's side arm still clipped in its holster. Fifty caliber. He grabbed it. He also found two flash bang canisters clipped to the man's duty belt. He stuffed them in his jacket pocket. Two pistols, two flash bangs, and a bad temper. He could feel the fighter in him rise up. He grabbed one last item from the man's body, and it was a critical one: earplugs. He twisted the man's head from side to side, plucking first one plug from the man's ear and then the other.

He ran back to the lateral files and poked his head behind it. "Give me ten more minutes, and I'll be back with the all clear," he said, smiling. And lying. "Don't move, and don't speak." Then he sprinted for the stairwell.

Time to kick some ass. He plugged up his ears, slipped through the stairwell door as soundlessly as he could, and began to climb the steps. The roof was several floors up, and though Bert could hear no sound, he knew these guys were pros. There would be someone guarding the top of the stairs. Probably just one, but armed to the freaking teeth. He needed a plan. Didn't have one. Kept climbing anyway.

He staggered on a step and almost launched himself face first into the stairs. It was awkward climbing with both hands holding weapons and trying to step silently.

Overhead, he felt the vibration of metal clinking against metal. His target had just bumped the railing. He was in full fighter mode, and the vibration penetrating his ear plugs made him grinned. You give yourself away so easily, my adversary.

He continued to climb, the hunter stalking his prey. He holstered the Glock and pulled one of the flash bang canisters from his pocket. It was going to be devastating in the tight, concrete stairwell. Devastating for both of them. There was no avoiding its impact. At least his throw didn't have to land perfectly. In this echo chamber, close was going to be close enough. He would take a hit. It was no different from an MMA fight. When you go in for the kill shot, you are going to get hit. Hard. You can't care about that. You absorb it and keep moving in. It was OOO time. Overwhelming force. Overwhelming violence. Overwhelming indifference to pain.

Bert slowed his climb, but continued to creep closer to his prey. By now, the man up there will have heard him coming. He will be waiting. He is waiting. Listening.

Bert readied the flash bang in his throwing hand. "O, O, O!" he said at the top of his lungs and hurled the flash bang onto the landing one-half flight below the top. He hunched himself into a ball in the corner away from the next set of steps. The man at the top of the stairs let loose a hail of gunfire, and then Bert heard him yell. The flash bang erupted with chest caving force. Pieces of concrete and dust flew in every direction. Immediately, Bert uncurled his body, grabbed a pistol in each hand, and sprang up the steps. He began firing both handguns even as he turned the corner. The bullets slammed into the wall and rose up the steps as he continued to pivot and fire. The bullets found their mark in the man who was still trying to recover from the impact grenade. His body bounced as round after round hit him. And then Bert was on him, smashing his windpipe with the Glock and shoving the 50 caliber against his nose. He pulled the trigger, yanked the man's body around, and hurled it down the stairs. He felt the vibration of the man's body tumble to the landing, but he never looked back. He opened the roof door and threw his body through it.

As he came up in his shooter's stance, two targets presented: a black helicopter already fifty feet in the air and beginning to angle away, and a black clad shooter prone and firing an automatic weapon over the roof edge. The shooter heard the explosion and commotion, and he was rolling onto his side and bringing the muzzle around. Bert ignored the helicopter and emptied the remainder of both magazines into the shooter. The helmeted figure bounced, jerked, and then lay still.

Bert sucked in a breath and fell onto his side. He hadn't realized he was holding his breath, and now he heaved and coughed. Spittle ran from the side of his mouth and he tasted blood. He rolled the rest of the way over and fished in his pocket for spare magazines. Reloaded. Crawled on his belly behind a brick pillar. Kept heaving air into his lungs. Time to assess. The helicopter was gone. The roof was clear. He grabbed his phone. The glass was cracked, but it appeared to be working. He texted Max. "Roof is clear."

Immediately, Max texted him back. "You OK?"

"Ok."

"Good. You disobeyed a direct order. Much obliged."

Bert leaned against the bricks, and breathed. He watched blood drip from his chin onto his chest. He yanked the plugs from his ears and listened. He wasn't sure how much time passed before he heard FBI Tactical and SWAT clearing the stairwell. It was a noisy process. Lots of shouting and banging of metal. Bert lay down onto his back and placed the open wallet with his FBI creds on his chest. He splayed his arms and legs. He wasn't about to survive all of this only to be shot mistakenly by an over-zealous good guy. At last, he felt boots hit the roof and heard the approach of pounding soles. A large caliber muzzle came into his peripheral view.

"FBI, FBI," Bert said.

In the next second, seeming to come from nowhere, and everywhere, Bert was surrounded by goggled, helmeted men.

"Roger that, and thank you, Captain," one set of goggles said.

"Ooh Rah," another said.

"It's Lieutenant," Bert Higgins said, "and damn glad to see ya."

"Captain in my book," a loud voice said over him. He squinted up into his partner's smiling face.

"Captain Steele," Bert said. "Always a pleasure." He made no effort to move.

"You hurt partner?" Max said. "Don't answer that. And don't move. I need a medic here, stat."

"*En route*, Captain Steele, sir," the man kneeling closest to Bert said. He murmured into his headset and then nodded toward Steele. "One click, sir. Elevator was stuck."

In less than a minute, Bert heard the clatter of a rolling cart. He turned his head and saw a face he recognized pulling the stretcher toward him. It was a pretty face with green eyes.

"You look great in red," Kristin said, and knelt over him. Bert could feel her ample breasts dragging across his chest as she gathered his opposite arm back to his chest. He wondered if that had been on purpose.

"What are you doing up here?" he said.

"I'm happy to see you, too," she said.

"That's not what I meant," he said.

"To answer your question, it's all hands on deck around here for a bit. Everybody's doing what they know how to do."

"Max," Bert said.

"Right here, pal," Max said loudly.

"ICU. They . . . ."

"Taken care of," Max said. Bert noticed Max dabbing at his ears with a wad of gauze and it was red.

"You know you're shouting at me," Bert said.

"Ears," Max said loudly. "Burst a sumpin, sumpin in there."

"Is that a technical term?"

"10-4," he shouted. "How's the nose?"

"What?" Bert said. "Is my nose broken?"

He saw Max lean toward one of the men, knew he probably meant to mutter it, but he said it so loudly, Bert heard him say very clearly. "Shock." Two other EMTs were inching Bert onto a stretcher and lifting him to the cart.

"Going for a little ride, sweetie," Kristin Muldoon said.

"Need something to wipe my face," Bert said.

"Not just yet," she said.

"What's wrong?" he said.

"Couple of sumpins in your mug," Max said, shouting over him. "Damn, son, you are some kinda badass."

Bert raised a fist as they wheeled him toward the elevator. He glanced at the fist. It was trembling. Badly.

"Max," Bert said, trying to look behind him.

"Right here," Max said. "Not going anywhere, buddy."

"Okay," Bert said. "The helicopter?"

"We're chasing it, Lieutenant. Now stand down."

"Tex at the wheel?"

"Tex," Max said, positioning himself next to the cart as the elevator doors closed them in.

"Okay, that's enough, handsome," Kristin said. "Be a good patient and hush." She wrapped a blood pressure cuff on his arm. The elevator slowed to a halt and the doors slid open. The hall was alive with sound. People were hurrying in both directions. One doctor narrowly missed walking straight into Bert's bed as he hurried with his head down, brow furrowed in concentration. He passed, white lab coat flapping open behind him.

"That's your man," Kristin Muldoon said, "I think."

"My man?"

"Your surgeon," she said.

"Wait a sec," Bert said. "What surgeon?"

"Couple of stitches," Max said, still dabbing his ears.

"I love scars," Kristin said. "So sexy."

Bert watched the ceiling as the bed travelled down one corridor and then several others. He had no idea where he was. At last, the bed slowed and Bert glanced at the wall next to large double doors. "Pre-Op." He felt Max's hand on his arm and looked.

"I'm off to chase bad guys," Max said loudly, pointing, "You. Cooperate. I'll see you on the other side." He patted the arm and hurried out of Bert's view. Bert closed his eyes. When he opened them again, he was being backed into a curtained area, and several people were rushing around the bed hooking things up. An IV stint was being inserted into the back of his hand. The same doctor, who had hurried past them in the hallway, bustled in and slipped the curtain closed.

"Okay, Lieutenant Higgins," the doctor said, "we've got two ahead of you."

"Who? What?" Bert said.

The doctor was silent, staring at him, his brow furrowed. "Let's have a quick look." He leaned close to Bert's face, focusing on the left side.

"Somebody gonna tell me what's wrong?"

"Sure," the doctor said. "You have two concrete fragments lodged in your face, both on the left side. One is angled up along your ear, and the other is very close to your left eye." The doctor pasted a smile, but it came across as a thin line of taut lip. "Might throw in a nose job for free. Feel any pain?"

"Nope," Bert said. "Is that bad?"

"Let's get them out as soon as possible."

"The other two," Bert said, "ahead of me. They okay?"

"We'll see," the doctor said. He turned and slipped through the curtain. Bert started to raise his hand to his face, but a strong hand gripped his wrist. "Uh, uh, handsome," Kristin said. "No touching."

"Don't you have to scamper off and save somebody else?" Bert said.

She shook her head. "Strict orders from the FBI. You are my prisoner. I am to 'watch you like a hawk.'"

"Max," Bert said, and started to smile. A bolt of pain shot through his face and he froze.

"Don't smile, sugar," she said. "Can you talk without pain?"

"Let's find out," Bert said, squinting at her.

"I was thinking we could pass the time getting to know each other," she said. Her smile warmed Bert in all the right places.

"Great idea," Bert said. "You start, and I'll rest my face."

"What a model prisoner you are," she said. "Let's see. I was born in heaven because I'm an angel."

Bert smiled and then yelped and started to grab for his face. Her strong hand held his arm in check.

"I will tie you down if I have to," she said.

"Might be fun," he said, and then couldn't believe he had just said that.

She laughed. "Bad boy."

"Please don't make me smile anymore," Bert said.

"I'm so torn," she said, stroking the arm she had been restraining. "I like it that I make you smile."

"Are you flirting with me?" Bert said.

"Duh," she said. "Are you flirting with me?"

"Duh," he said. He liked this woman. Cute, fresh, smart. And strong.

And that was the last thing he remembered. Kristin knew they wanted him quiet. She had watched them inject his IV line. Now, she patted his limp arm. "No more flirting for now, handsome. But I'll be here when you wake up."

Getaway Sedan
Kingstown, Rhode Island

Mistakes. Even the little ones could cost you big.

"I'm sorry," Gregorio said, "There is a satphone at the hanger."

"Yes, yes," Emil Bente said. "Nothing to be done until we can contact our people again."

The sedan had cleared the gate at the private airport and was approaching the hanger. "Everything ready?" he said to Gregorio. "And will your brother be waiting for us in the hangar?"

"*Sí*, Excellency," Gregorio said, lifting his hand. Emil saw that it was trembling. Fear was an effective control mechanism, as long as it was measured. Too much fear and its venom left the person paralyzed. It was the last thing he needed.

"You have done an excellent job," Emil said, forcing a smile. The man remained downcast. For a brief moment, a mental flash, Emil saw himself escorting both men into the hanger and executing them. It was likely the Cartel would have to fold operations here in the Northeast. Too much had gone down. The hospital. Maria Sanchez. The fire. And the unknown whereabouts of Maria Garza. She may have been captured, for all he knew. Was the operation's Base secure? Only when Emil opened his eyes did he realize he'd closed them.

"One week," Emil said. "Tell your brother."

"Excellency?" Gregorio said.

"You have one week to clean everything up," he said. "I will make you a list."

"Clean up," Gregorio said. "And then what? Shut down? What about the Marias?"

Emil nodded. "Shut down the operation. Leave Base operational, unless it gets too hot. Then call me." He pointed at Gregorio, "And yes, *Amigo*, the Marias. A delicate matter I prefer to handle myself. Send Maria Sanchez and Maria Garza home to me."

"Home?" Gregorio said.

Emil lifted a hand toward him. "I'm not finished. Home. To Venezia. Try to send them alive."

"And if we cannot," Gregorio said, "send them alive?"

"Then send the bodies to me," Emil said.

"*Sí*, Excellency," Gregorio said, his brow furrowed.

"Something?" Bente said.

"No more mistakes, Excellency," Gregorio said, "on my honor." Carlos had slip open the large hanger door and Gregorio pulled in.

"Okay, I go," Emil Bente said, and reached for the door handle.

Gregorio leapt from the vehicle and hurried to his brother. They embraced. "*Todo está bien,*" Gregorio said. Carlos nodded. His face was taut, and his eyes flashed. "To work," Carlos said. The hanger walls were lined with locked cabinet doors and a locked shed. Gregorio unlocked one after the other. Inside the shed, two off road dirt bikes gleamed in the overhead lights. The cabinet next to the shed held a weapons panel. An AR-15 and four AK-47 automatic machine guns were secured to it by heavy Velcro straps.

"Gregorio, join us at the acid barrel," Emil said. Carlos was prying the metal lid. All three men stripped off their clothes and tossed them in the barrel. Emil Bente was especially careful when removing his gloves and prayer card pouch. Identical light colored track suits awaited Carlos and Gregorio, who were speaking rapidly with one another in Spanish. Emil donned the black tracksuit and checked the oxygen tank and tubes in his transport box. The main bottle and its backup nestled at the far end atop the mattress. Emil eyed it distractedly while he dictated the list of action items for Carlos and Gregorio into a micro-recorder. He snapped it off, handed it to Carlos, and climbed into the box, donning the oxygen mask. As if choreographed, all three men crossed themselves. Then Carlos and Gregorio secured the lid and sealed it.

The plane's engines were loud in their ears as they wheeled the box from the hanger. They loaded the box and were latching the side of the plane when they noticed twin beams of light appear on the runway seventy-five yards across from the hanger access lane. Carlos and Gregorio ran for the hanger. Carlos mashed the radio to his mouth and yelled to the pilot.

"Go, Go!" he said.

"Roger that," the pilot said. The plane swung onto the access lane and rolled toward the runway access a quarter mile away. "Headlights from an aircraft," the pilot said. "Anybody we know?"

Gregorio had run to the cabinet next to the shed, and now he cradled the AR-15 in his arms. He positioned himself in the dark at the corner of the hanger and set up the tripod. Carlos ran for the breaker box and killed power to the hanger lights. Then he grabbed an AK-47 and hurled his body prone on the opposite corner of the hanger opening. His right hand still clutched the radio, and he raised it to his lips. "Hanger B to Tower."

"Tower," the voice said, the radio crackling noisily.

"Thought the airport was ours for the night," Carlos said. "You got an ID and a flight plan for the aircraft on the runway?"

"Standby," the radio said. Carlos picked up the machine gun again. The radio crackled and the voice said, "Tower to unknown aircraft, exit the runway and identify yourself. We need your flight plan." Carlos watched the headlights coming closer. The plane was accelerating. "Tower to unknown aircraft, you are not cleared. Repeat, not cleared, for takeoff. Power down and exit the runway." Carlos grabbed the radio, and then looked at it. What was there to say? He called to his brother, "Wait, Gregorio. Wait and see first." Gregorio nodded and then returned his focus to the scope.

The plane was racing down the runway and was almost parallel to the hanger. Carlos squinted through the darkness at it, looking for any identifiers. The aircraft was small but large enough to carry cargo. It looked dark, probably black, and bore no insignia. No registration numbers either that he could see. It shot past them, its wheels lifting from the tarmac. Carlos looked at Gregorio, who was looking at him.

Chapter Fifteen

Private Airstrip
Kingstown, Rhode Island

Carlos raised the radio, "Hanger B to Tower," he said.

"Standby," Tower said. The next sound Carlos heard through the radio stopped him in mid-breath. It was laughter, raucous, taunting laughter. The radio crackled again. "Hey there, assholes. You are as stupid as you are ugly," the voice said.

Carlos snapped his fingers at Gregorio, and mouthed, "Tower." Gregorio nodded and ran into the hanger toward the interior shed. He grabbed one of the dirt bikes, kicked it to life and raced from the hanger with the light off. It was a tiny airport. He could be there in less than a minute.

"Tower, did you find their flight plan?" Carlos said. Keep him talking.

"The plan is to fly my ass into your face," Tower said.

"Come again?" Carlos said.

"Oh, we'll come again. In the meantime, tell your boss in the box we've got his pal, Bontecelli. Oh, and tell him to enjoy his trip."

"Hold on," Carlos said.

"Something I can do for you, Carlos?" Tower said.

"You can start by telling me what's going on here," Carlos said.

He heard more laughter. His satphone buzzed. When he answered, Gregorio said, "Tower is secure. Found our Controller. Dead. They snapped his neck. You've been hearing a radio patch."

Carlos snarled and picked up the radio. "Hanger B to Shitballs. Suck my dick," he said into the radio. He heard more raucous laughter, and then one loud scream. He breathed in the dark. Listened. Silence. He lifted the satphone. "Gregorio?"

"I'm still here," Gregorio said.

"Come back. Quick. We gotta clean up and get outta here." He grabbed the top of his head like it had a spike in it. He needed a cigarette. His satphone buzzed again.

"Guess I'm clear for takeoff?" Bente's pilot sounded through the phone.

"Go," Carlos said. "And good job. Smart to stay off the radio and call on the phone."

"Roger that," the pilot said, "And excuse me, but what the hell just happened?"

Carlos ignored the question and asked his own. "Any chance you could catch that plane?"

"Negative," the pilot said. "You see the biceps on those arms?"

"The engines? Barely."

"I might as well be in a glider."

"Okay," Carlos said, "Just get Excellency out of here fast. And watch your back."

"Roger that."

Carlos ended the call as Gregorio came riding up on the dirt bike. The controller's body was draped across the gas tank. Carlos let him park and offload the body. Then he walked to his brother's side. "How we gonna explain that?" He pointed to the body.

"We're not," Gregorio said. "We're gonna make it disappear."

"And when his family calls the cops and they come looking for this guy, they will be crawling all over this place," Carlos said.

Gregorio nodded. "But if they find him, Excellency kills us." He closed his eyes. The two men were silent for a time. "Okay, how about this?" Gregorio said. "You drive his car to the salvage yard with the acid barrel. I follow on the bike, and bring us back here. Body goes in the acid, and we dispose of the barrel as dry cleaning waste at the plant. Family then reports him as a missing person."

Carlos began to grin as he listened, and then tipped an imaginary hat to his brother. "Not perfect, but good enough," he said.

In Flight
En Route to Italy

In the box, Emil Bente tried to relax and breathe normally through the oxygen mask. He hoped leaving was the right decision. He hoped leaving Carlos and Gregorio in charge was the right decision. He hoped Maria Garza was safe – or dead. He hoped Maria Sanchez was with her, either in hiding or in paradise. He hoped, he hoped, he hoped. When events and people are out of your control, you are left either with anxiety or with hope. He chose to hope and to clear his mind of every trouble. It was a long journey to Venezia, and the hours ahead would give him lots of time to rest, and to think, and to plan.

He shifted his legs slightly and thought he felt something move. Yes. Something moved. He was sure of it. He shifted his legs again, and he felt it again. It wasn't a jerking motion. It was smooth, like string pulling through a closed hand. What. The. Hell? Emil felt his pulse quicken, his heart beating faster and faster in his chest. Nothing was moving now. Had he imagined it? His eyes were open now. Everything within him wished he could look, but because of the tightness of the box, he was unable even to raise his head. There it was again. Something moved and then stopped near his thigh. It started to move again, and Emil felt pressure against his navel. He heard a yelp escape through the oxygen mask. His eyes darted from side to side, and he turned his head as much as he could.

What was it? And how on earth? He felt a smooth, heavy, slickness drag up his sternum, felt its weight, knew it must be headed for his face. And then it stopped. Emil was panting now and beginning to hyperventilate. He wanted to run! To fight! But he couldn't move. He was helpless. Maybe if he exhaled all the air from his lungs, he could reach a hand to his belly.

Then he felt it. Against his chin. A soft flick. And then another, light, like a brush of air. His feet were kicking involuntarily and his breath came rapid and shallow. With a deep breath, he blew the air completely from his lungs, constricted his gut muscles, and grabbed a clawed hand at his middle. His fingers closed around a cold, smooth, mass of skin and muscle, and his worst nightmare was confirmed.

Snake.

Chapter Sixteen

Memorial Hospital
Kingstown, Rhode Island

By the time Max Steele left his partner at pre-op and rejoined the investigation team, several groups had divided up and they were sweeping through the hospital. Director Elizabeth Fenton was coordinating. She waved Max to her. "Let's reverse roles a moment," Director Fenton said without greeting him, "and let me give you a sit rep. We've got teams blanketing the interior and exterior. Anybody we want who is still here will be detained. In the meantime, Tex is back."

"He catch anything?" Max said.

"Nix. They ditched him good."

"They're pros," Max said.

"So it would seem," she said, "and they don't mind sacrificing personnel to get things done, either."

"Anybody alive to interview?"

She shook her head, "None of these bad guys."

"Are there other bad guys?" Steele said.

You tell me, Captain," Fenton said, and looked at him. "Dr. Maria Sanchez is awake."

The two stared at each other for a long moment.

"Yep. She's one of the bad guys," Max said, and broke eye contact.

"Likely," Elizabeth Fenton said, her voice low and soft, "but she's carrying one of the good guys."

Max snapped his head back around. She was nodding.

"I couldn't figure out how to tell you," he said.

"Don't worry about it," she said. "I wouldn't have told someone in my position yet, either. Oh Max."

Steele blew out a long breath.

"Congratulations," she said, and reached for his hand.

Max lowered his head. When he looked up again, he made no attempt to hide the tears. "I'm sorry boss."

"Hey, life's a bucket of shit with a few buried diamonds. Babies are the diamonds." She squeezed his hand, "We'll figure this out. Don't you worry."

"Now," she said, dropping his hand, "I order you to go visit the prisoners."

"Yes, ma'am," Max said. He got a few strides down the hall, turned and ran back. "What about the other two, Spruill and Tittle?"

"Yep, everybody is awake," she said. "Interview them when you're done."

Surgical Theatre
Memorial Hospital
Kingstown, Rhode Island

Agents in dark suits formed a protective semi-circle outside the surgical theatre. They nodded as Max approached, and parted wordlessly to let him pass. He stepped inside the scrub room and stopped. He saw an agent seated just inside the door. A second agent sat against the opposite wall. The theatre was drenched in powder blue paper-cloth and crowded with pieces of equipment. His eyes fixed upon the petite woman in the center of the room, propped up halfway in the bed with her hands across her stomach. His gut lurched at the sight of her.

He stood for a long while, looking at her through the plate glass window. He was behind her, but he sensed she knew he was there by the way she kept shifting in the bed and glancing around. Who was this woman? What was this woman? Doctor, nun, lover, liar, drug dealer, mobster, mother? How could he hate her and love her at the same time? How could he feel so betrayed that he wanted to hurl her away from his life forever, and yet long just to hold her hand or brush his fingers through her hair.

He felt tears sting his eyes, and he swiped them away with a vicious chop to his cheek. Damn this woman. Damn her. She carried his child, so there would be no way of shoving her out of his life. Even if they were not together, and they would never be together again, their lives would remain connected because of the child. He wanted to talk to her, and he never wanted to speak to her again.

And here he was. For what? To do – what? Wrest the truth from her at last? Would he ever get to the truth? Would he trust what she told him? No, he would let others gather the truth as best they could, not him. So. Why are you here, and what will you say? Max wiped his palms on the front of his jacket and stepped toward the agent at the doorway. A wordless nod from each of them, and he was in the room. He waved to the agent against the wall, and then pointed a finger to the door in a silent request to be alone with Maria Sanchez.

He positioned himself at the end of the bed. On purpose. Any closer and he would wrap her in his arms, and he knew it. He gripped the bed's metal footrest with both hands. He waited until both agents had left the theatre before he looked at her.

Their eyes met, brilliant blue locking onto rich chocolate brown. The side of her face was wrapped in a large wad of bandage and gauze. The swelling had slitted one of her eyes.

"Damn you," Max said.

"It's too late," Maria said, "I'm damned already."

They were silent, staring into each other's eyes.

"Anybody read you your rights?"

She nodded. "First thing."

Neither of them blinked. The silence between them was absolute, but there was nothing but noise in Max's head. He struggled to form a thought.

"You hate me," Maria said.

"I wish," Max said. "I don't know why I would even care enough to hate you. Like you said, we were just fucking, right? Sister Maria?" He felt his eyes harden.

Maria Sanchez shook her head and looked down, "I was lying."

"And fucking me over good, right Sister Maria?" Max said, ignoring her words.

"Yes, lying," she said, "and then lying again to cover up the lies."

"There's a shock," he said. "Everything from your mouth's been a lie. Everything about the life you led here was a lie. Everything!" He was squeezing the footboard so hard, his fingers were going numb. "You tell Bente, 'Nice try' when you see him in Hell." He let go of the bed, and turned.

"Is he dead?" she said, looking up into his face.

"Not yet," Max said. "Matter of time, though. We'll take all of you down."

"I'm dead already," she said. She rubbed her hands absently across her belly. "They came for me. They will come again."

"They did," Max said. "And they will. But we will protect you for the same reason they will try to kill you."

Maria broke eye contact and looked down. She had swallowed back the tears, but now they came in a torrent. Sob after sob burst from her lips. "Our baby," she whispered. She looked up again and her face was twisted in a look Max had only seen a couple of times in his life: agony. She was blubbering through spittle and her nose dripped onto her chest. "Max, please don't let them kill our baby." Maria's body wracked as if it were being struck by bolts of lightning, and the cries leaking from her twisted mouth sounded more like they came from a wounded and dying animal.

Max wasn't sure when it happened, or how, but when he came back to himself, he was bent over the side of the bed with Maria Sanchez wrapped tightly in his arms. "Oh God have mercy on me," she wailed. "I love you Max. I've loved you from the moment we met. I am so lost. And I am so sorry. I want to die. But I want to live. Our baby, honey. Our baby." A fresh wave of convulsions shook her frame and Max rocked her gently. "Our baby."

Tears splashed from his eyes onto her shoulder. He felt horrible. And he felt wonderful. He hated her. He loved her. He was going to be a Dad. It was everything he'd dreamed of, encased within a nightmare with no happy ending. It was so beautiful. It was so horrible. And it was so damned sad. "It'll be okay honey," he heard himself say.

"No, it won't," Maria sobbed, gripping him tighter. "It'll never be okay."

"I know," he said into her neck. He wanted to pull away, wanted to cast her away. She was a criminal. She was the woman he loved. And she carried the baby who would bear his name. He was in heaven, and he was in hell. And he couldn't let go: of this woman, or of his love for her.

When Max emerged from the surgical theatre, the small group of agents was still crowded around. Max's head was lowered, but he knew they were all looking at him. By now, everyone knew. A couple of them clapped him gently on the back as he passed. Max emerged from the other side of the crowd and turned to face them.

"I know the jokes are coming," he said, "but today's not the day, okay?" The men nodded. "We lost a witness, and we gained a witness. They've already tried to take her off the board." He stared hard at them. "They will try again. Nobody gets within fifty feet of Dr. Maria Sanchez without an escort. I mean it. I want one hand on your gun and another on their butt.

You got me?" The men nodded. "Soon as she's well enough, we get her to a safe house. Do we have one yet?"

"I'll check with Director Fenton," a deep voice in the back said.

"I vote we get out of this hospital, soonest," someone else said. "This place is a house of horrors." Others muttered their assent. He heard nervous shuffling of feet.

"I'm out," Max said. "Off this part of the investigation. Director Fenton will establish a new chain of command for witness interrogation and protection." He looked each agent in the eye, slowly, individually. "I owe each of you an apology. I compromised us, and I own that. I will live with it rest of my life." He lowered his eyes to the floor.

"You didn't know, sir," an agent said.

"Shit happens," another said quietly.

"Truth is," Max said, not looking up, "these assholes are making us look like idiots. I'm the chief idiot, but our whole department looks inept. We had the number one and number two operators in the Cartel in custody. Now, we've lost them both. Unacceptable." He looked up again into grim faces. "Sorry, didn't mean to turn this into a meeting. Director's in the building, as I'm sure you're aware. Take your orders from her. I'm off to interview the vics." He started to turn, and then paused, "Let's get our shit together and kick their ass," he said. Some low growls erupted from the group. Max turned and walked down the hall.

He headed to the second surgical theatre where he expected to find Nettie Spruill and Jeremy Tittle. He wondered whether Bert was in surgery yet, wondered whether the surgeon could save the eye. The way that concrete chip was lodged, Max knew it had to be close to the optic nerve. If Bert lost the eye, it would wash him out of active duty. He didn't even want to think about it.

He found three people in the second surgical theatre. Nettie Spruill and Jeremy Tittle were in hospital beds. Dean Victoria Nile sat between them on a wheeled stool.

"Mind if I come in?" Max said as he passed the suits seated in the antechamber door.

"Join the party," Rev. Nile said.

"We have a party going on?" Max said.

"We do, indeed," she said. She turned to Jeremy and smiled. "Please tell Agent Steele who that sweet woman is in the bed right here, Dr. Tittle?"

"That is the sweetest rose in the flowerbed," Jeremy said, and smiled. His cheeks were purple from the corner of his mouth to each ear from the rope.

"Indeed she is," Dean Nile said, "and what is her name?"

"Her name is Dr. Nettie Spruill, of course" he said, "but from now on I think I'll call her Rose." Both Victoria Nile and Nettie Spruill applauded and grinned at each other.

Dean Nile turned to Max, "Jeremy Tittle is getting better, and we are thrilled."

Max smiled and took a seat on another stool. "How did you know I needed some good news about now?" he said. He looked at Jeremy, "How's your face and jaw?"

"Jeremy rubbed at it softly, "They won't give me a mirror yet, but I feel pretty good. Didn't lose a single tooth."

"And you?" Max said, looking to Nettie.

"I'm a tough old yard bird," she said. "Little headache is all."

"A concussion is all," Nile said, "but the doc says she's good to go home as long as the young lady who lives with her is there. Sarah's bringing clothes."

"Good news, He said. "You've been through a lot. All of you." He smiled into each face. "Okay," Max clapped his hands together softly, "got a minute to brief me on what happened?"

Jeremy detailed the appearance of the nun and her gagging him with the cincture. Then he detailed her assault upon Nettie with the Bible. "Took Bible bashing to a whole new level," he said, glancing at Nettie, "you poor thing."

"Never saw it coming," Nettie said. "And she stole my clothes."

"I saw her leave," Rev. Nile said, "though I didn't know what I was looking at. Saw what I thought was Nettie walking away down the hall, and I remember thinking the shoes were different, but my mind didn't connect the dots."

"Why would they?" Max said, nodding.

"Yeah, I know," she said, "but I darn sure wish they had. I'd have loved to tackle that nun."

Max raised his eyebrows and grinned. "You were where? When this all went down?"

"Up the hall, having a word with Jeremy's doctor," she said.

"I see," he said.

He turned back to Jeremy, "Sounds like you are the only one who got a good look at her. Can you give me a description?"

"Nettie's size and shape, oddly enough," he said. "But Hispanic. Nun in full habit. Scary eyes."

"How so?"

"Like a caged animal, you know?" he said. "I was seeing stars and feeling like I was going to pass out, so I didn't get a real good look at her. Then it all went black." He shook his head. "I don't know where Jenny went. Would help to know if she saw anything."

Max paused and held his gaze upon the battered looking man in the bed. At last he said, "Yes, when you see her, find out if she has anything to add to what the rest of you saw."

Jeremy Tittle nodded, but his brow had developed deep furrows and his eyes lost their focus. Max looked at the women and saw a knowing look pass between them.

"She get away?" Rev. Nile said at last, "Our nun?"

“Afraid so,” Max said. He planted his hands on his knees and stood. “Well, I am glad you all are safe and recovering. Thanks for the time.” He waved and made his way to the door.

“Captain Steele?” Jeremy said, raising his arm, his eyes coming back into focus.

Max turned.

“It may not mean anything, but she was muttering to herself,” he said. “The nun.”

“What was she saying?” Max said.

“Funny. It wasn’t English, but it wasn’t Spanish either,” he said. “Sounded like Italian.” He frowned. “Mean anything?”

“Yep,” Max said. He flashed Jeremy the thumbs-up sign and left the room. Now, to find Tex.

Chapter Seventeen

Cafeteria
Memorial Hospital
Kingstown, Rhode Island

He found Tex Billings in the cafeteria.

"Shouldda known you'd be stuffing your face," Max said.

Tex wiped his broad, square chin. "Do you know this hotel doesn't serve beer? What's up with that?"

"Looking to drown your sorrows?" Max said.

"Boy howdy," Tex said.

"I'll take that as a yes," Max said.

"Sumbitches lit outta here in a Ferrari of a chopper, and they gave me one of them little freakin' go-karts. I never even saw their tail feathers."

"How about drones?" Max said.

"Nary a one that I could see," Tex said, "and after what happened, you can bet I was lookin'."

"How's everybody handling it?" Max said. "About Sherm?"

"We're pissed," Tex said.

Max nodded. "We are, too. And embarrassed."

"We been joked, poked, and pissed on," Tex said.

Max sat back in the chair and laughed, running both hands through his salt and pepper crew cut. "Tex, we should call you 'The Professor.' Nobody can put into words how we're doing quite like you." The two men bumped fists. "I'm so ready to kick some ass."

"Me too, Cap," Tex said.

"I've got an idea," Max said. "It's so new, yours are the first ears to hear it."

"Go," Tex said.

"I say we get out of reaction mode and take the fight to them," Max said. "Ever fished with a net?"

"Now don't start with that net throwing thing," Tex said. "Higgins told me all about it."

"Starts with finding the fish," Max said, ignoring him, "and I may know where they're hiding."

Tex fixed Max with a long stare. "I've seen that look in your eyes before, Max. I believe we were blowin' shit up at the time."

"How's your Italian?" Max said.

"Italy?" Tex said.

The two were interrupted by the approach of a man Max recognized, both by the surgical scrubs and by the knitted brow. "They told me I'd find you here," the surgeon said by way of greeting.

Max shot to his feet. "How's our boy?"

"Lucky as hell," the surgeon said. "Missed the optic nerve by 1.5 millimeters."

Tex gave a low whistle.

"Will he keep the eye?" Max said.

"Guy must have angels," the surgeon said. "Eye patch for a couple of weeks to rest the area. There's a ninety-five percent likelihood he'll make a full recovery."

Max blew out a breath. "You're a whiz, Doc."

"We got lucky on this one." He turned to go.

"Doc," Max said, "what about the nose?"

The surgeon shrugged. Cartilage was damaged. He'll have a lump once the splint comes off."

"So, an eye patch and a nose splint?" Tex said. "We can sell tickets to the freak show."

Max laughed. "My partner's a badass. I'd watch myself."

Tex laughed and both men shook the surgeon's hand, whose brow relaxed momentarily, before resuming its furrow. Without another word, he hurried away. Max put his head down on the table.

"Relieved, partner?" Tex said.

"Was holding my breath for that kid," Max said.

"Wouldda washed him out if it'd gone different," Tex said.

"Totally."

"So," Tex said, "this thing we're planning. Junior Badass gonna get to come with?"

"Absolutely," Max said, rising from the table. "To be continued. I have to sell the Director, so I'm going to find my ducks and get them in a row."

"I take it we're not leavin' today," Tex said.

Max shook his head. "Few weeks."

Tex stood. "So, while you're getting' your ducks in a row, I'm going to find me a bottle of beer and wring its neck."

Memorial Hospital
Kingstown, Rhode Island

Compartmentalize. Give everything a drawer in your mind, and lock it away until it's time to focus on it again. It was the only way Captain Max Steele could continue to function. If all of the drawers opened at once, Max knew he would explode. But the locked drawers exacted a price. Each added 20 pounds to his backpack, at least. He was feeling the weight.

As the elevator doors closed on the hospital cafeteria, he pondered which drawer to open next. He needed to talk to Director Fenton. Now that the flashpoint of this crisis had passed, there were details to circle back on, items to deal with, and a trip to plan. He looked at the elevator buttons and had no idea which one to push, no clue where Fenton might be. He snorted a laugh and was grateful he was the only passenger. He imagined if the elevator had been full, and the person in the front looked at him and asked him which floor he wanted. He supposed an answer like, "Pick one," would attract some looks. He pulled his cell phone and called her.

"What's your 20?" Director Fenton said by way of answer.

"Was about to ask you the same," Max said. "Need to Signal 8."

"Outside ER entrance," she said.

"10-76," Max said and ended the call. The elevator doors had reopened and he searched for the button to close them. Finally, feeling completely inept, he punched First Floor and the doors closed. When the elevator stopped, he made his way to Emergency. Once through those doors, he emerged to a dark sky. He'd lost all sense of time. The lights made the Emergency entrance area brighter than it was during the day.

He found Director Fenton pacing in the shadows at the perimeter of the EMS parking field. Smoking.

"You don't smoke, ma'am," he said.

"I do now," she said, her face serious and taut.

"Got another one?" Max said.

"You don't smoke either, Captain," she said.

"Sounds pretty good right now."

She shook her head. "Bummed this one. And I'm not sharing."

"Wouldn't dream of asking," Max said, and grinned when she shot him a look.

"What do you want?" she said.

"You mean, what will it take for me to leave you alone?"

"Affirmative," she said. "I need to think."

"I'll be quicker if I can speak plainly, Director," Max said.

"Let's have it."

"I need you to crash that Warden at Mantisto," Max said, "and I mean good. I want him indicted for murder and hung by his nuts."

"That's plain enough," Director Fenton said, nodding. "You know the chain of causation is going to be difficult. He's a slippery one."

"Tying him directly to what happened here?"

"Precisely."

"If we can't indict him, then I'll kill him with my bare hands," Max said.

Director Fenton was grinding out the cigarette with the toe of her black shoe. "Please don't say stuff like that to me," she said. "The less I know about your violent tendencies, the better."

"Roger that," he said.

"I'll call the Prosecutor and get her teeth lodged in his ass. Will that satisfy you?"

"For now," Max said. "*Adios.*" He waved and started back for the entrance.

"Where are you going?"

"Gonna check in on Lieutenant Badass."

"He is that," she said. "Give him an atta boy from the boss."

Max nodded and left at a trot.

Max found Kristin Muldoon in the post-op waiting room.

"Here to relieve you, ma'am," Max said. "Thank you for your service."

"Ha," she said, and grinned. "I live to serve, Captain. But I'll accept your offer and rotate off post. I'm going to get my butt roasted and served to me on a platter if I don't get back to work."

"Give me your supervisor's name and number," Max said, and reached into his pocket, but his hand returned with his wallet instead of the phone. He pulled a twenty-dollar bill. "I'll call your super, soon as you agree to go downstairs and eat some supper." He pressed the bill into her hand and grinned.

She took the money and bowed. "Do you know how many cheese fries I can get down there for twenty bucks? Whew!" She gave him her supervisor's name and number.

Max punched it in his phone and waited to push send. His smile turned serious. "I hear Bert got lucky," he said to her.

She nodded. "That surgeon looks so serious and intense, but he's actually a nice man. Came and filled me in."

"Found me all the way in the cafeteria," Max said. "Good man." Max eyed her. "He tell you the boy's gonna look like hell for a while?"

"I'm EMS, don't forget," she said. "We see ugly every day."

Max stood and she did, too. "You know it's against protocol to hug people," he said, wrapping the young woman in his arms. "Thanks for looking after my partner."

"A pleasure, sir," she said, hugging him back.

"Now scoot," he said.

"He has my number," she said, backing toward the hallway. "Tell him to call me, or else."

"Yes, ma'am," Max said, and waved her toward the door. He pressed send and praised EMS Muldoon up and down for her service to the FBI. The supervisor was stunned and thrilled that someone on his staff had assisted an FBI operation. Max recommended a promotion and a raise, and ended the call.

Pocketing the cell, he approached the man behind the sliding glass window, explained who he was, and asked permission to sit with his partner in recovery. The man said he'd check. Max knew what that meant and settled in for the long wait. He wondered about Bert's family, his parents. Had they been called yet? Were they on their way? And would he get to meet them? Max wondered what it was like to be a parent, to raise children, and release them into the world. He was about to find out. He opened that drawer a crack, and then slammed it shut again. Later. He would think about it later.

His cell buzzed in his pocket and he pulled it. Director Fenton. Max stood and hurried into the hallway before he answered.

"Steele," he said.

"I don't give a rat's ass, she said loudly. "You get him back here, stat," Director Fenton said to someone within shouting distance, her voice loud and raspy. "Steele!"

"Yes, ma'am," Max said.

"Northeast parking field, stat," she said. "Call me from there." The line went dead.

Max heard the thwack of helicopter blades overhead as he sprinted across the parking lot toward the gaggle of bureau cars and flashing lights. As he approached, two men in SWAT gear stepped from the crowd of people. One carried an armload of gear. The other motioned to Max. The helicopter was beginning its descent to the parking field and the noise was fierce. The two men motioned with hand signals for Max to extend his arms straight out at the shoulder. Max had sense enough to put his cell in one fist before they began, so he'd be able to call the Director and find out what was going on. The men systematically outfitted him with flak jacket, helmet, gloves, and goggles. They motioned for him to pocket the phone.

Into his arms, they laid a large assault rifle. They helped him into the chopper's passenger seat, and the two men who had dressed him hopped in the rear.

"Ready to bust some broncos, Cap?" Max saw Tex's smiling frame at the controls.

"Let's go," Max said, taking off the helmet and a glove. He fished out his cell and dialed the Director. The helicopter jerked and they were away.

"Private air strip," Director Fenton said when she answered. "Anonymous 911 caller said to tell Max Steele to come get Bente's nun, and gave an address."

"They actually said my name?" Max said. "And Bente's name?"

"Shut up and listen," the Director said. "Hanger fire at the location. EMS and two engines taking fire from overhead."

"Drones?"

"You tell me when you get there."

"Police?" Max said.

"Casualties among the first responders. Backup *en route*," Director Fenton said. "EMS pinned. Can't get to them."

Max pressed his phone to his chest and called over the rotor noise to Tex, "ETA?"

"Three clicks."

Max put the phone back to his ear. Director Fenton had been speaking and Max caught the tail end of her sentence.

"... upside down on the hanger door."

"10-9 your transmission," Max said. "Didn't catch it."

"Naked body," she said. "Nailed upside down, crucifixion style, on the hanger door."

Max heard himself suck in a breath.

"Burning," she said. "EMS helpless. Watching."

"We're three clicks from scene," Max said, "I'll advise when I can." He ended the call even though he heard the Director speaking. Max slapped the helmet on his head and noticed for the first time that a small microphone protruded from the helmet. "Radio check," he said.

"10-2, cowboy," Tex said through the earphones embedded in the helmet. "Standing by," another voice said. Max glanced back to a thumbs-up sign from the men seated behind him.

"Okay, listen up," Max said. "Airborne hostiles, number unknown, possibly drones. Tex, do not get our asses shot down."

"Roger that, Captain," Tex said.

He pointed to the man behind his left shoulder. "You are One." He pointed to the man on the right. "You are Two." More thumbs-up. "I want you Night Sight. Lock and load." Both men slapped the night vision goggles over their eyes and readied their heavy caliber weapons. When he looked forward again, Max saw the tiny glint of the hanger fire in the distance.

"We've got officers down," Max said. "And another vic spiked to the hanger door."

Tex shot him a look. Max nodded. "Hooey," Tex said, "how I love a dog fight."

"Let's take out the hostiles and then we'll hunt the pricks at the controls," Max said. He hefted the heavy machine gun in his lap and flicked off the safety. "One and Two, I'm staying off NV so I can be our eyes for the bright stuff." Max knew the bright flashes from the hanger fire would blind the men wearing night vision goggles.

"Approaching," Tex said. "Suck yer nuts up boys and stow 'em away."

"One has TA," the SWAT officer on the left said.

"Roger that, One," Max said. "Target Acquired. Go."

The helicopter bucked repeatedly as One squeezed off a burst. Max watched a stream of white slashes hurtle away from them into the night sky.

"Hang on," Tex said, "taking fire." He threw the helicopter into a steep left bank. Max felt his gut slam into his spine, and he panted against the centrifugal force.

"One," Max said through gritted teeth, "report."

"Standby," One said.

"Splash, Splash," Two said.

Max saw a large ball of fire in the distant sky. Good.

"Incoming," Tex said, and the windshield exploded in a blast of shards.

"Report," Max said. His face stung like he'd stuck it into a nest of mud daubers.

"One is clear."

"Two is clear."

"Tex is pissed," Tex said, and spat a piece of glass from his mouth. "Bastards." Max saw blood around his mouth.

"Tex?"

"All good," Tex said. "Time to rodeo."

"One has TA," the man on Max's left shoulder said.

"Dammit," Two said.

Max understood. Shooter Two wanted the second kill.

Max said to One. "Target Acquired. Go." The chopper bucked and rattled as One sent two streamers of fire toward the target. Since the hostile fire was just left of center to the helicopter, Max got to watch the rounds all the way there. They found their mark and the sky flashed with a bright pop and then faded out. Max saw orange entrails descend to the earth.

"Splash, Splash," Tex said. "Hooey, that's some shootin' right there."

"More Targets, Two? One?" Max said.

"Checking," Two said.

"Take us around, Tex," Max said.

"Roger that," Tex said. The helicopter banked. Air blasted through the front of the shattered windscreen. A chip broke loose from one of the edges and smacked Max's goggles. It hit with enough force that, without the goggles, he would have lost the eye. He'd have to tell Higgins.

"Clear," One said.

"Clear," Two said

"Set her down, Tex," Max said.

Tex swooped in and dropped onto the landing strip a safe distance from the burning hanger.

"Two, reconnoiter the area," Max said. "Find me wreckage of those drones."

"Tex, get the medics to look at you."

Tex was already shaking his head, "Finer than a frog's hair, Cap. Whatcha need?"

Max looked at the pilot, thought about arguing, knew it would do no good. "Once you've checked your bird, you and One head back up and scout for our drone operator. I reckon a five-mile range for those birds. Needle in a haystack, I know, but just in case."

"Why dontcha leave me your pea shooter, too," Tex said, pointing to the assault rifle. "Just in case."

"Good call," Max said, and hefted it over. He wrestled his way out of the shoulder straps and leapt to the ground. The officer on the left, One, moved forward into Max's seat and strapped in. Two was already trotting across the airfield.

Max looked left and saw a long stream of flashing lights bouncing along the road to the airstrip. He walked toward the hanger door. He couldn't get close because of the heat, even though firefighters had begun dousing it. But he got close enough to see the charred and smoking remains of a female body splayed on the metal door. She had been hung by spikes upside down with the feet crossed. Her arms were outstretched and attached with spikes through the hands. The torso was held by two strategically placed spikes, one through the pelvic area and one through the chest cavity. Max put his gloved hand over his mouth and stepped closer. At that moment, the top of the skull gave way and a chunk fell to the ground. Liquefied brain matter oozed down the door. Max turned away, and wretched. When he wiped his mouth with his glove, it came back wet. And red. He bent over and wretched again.

Hands on his knees, Max Steele watched the slow drip of blood from his face with a curious detachment. Shouts and clatter and engine roar washed over him in waves, but in his mind there was a stillness, a bubble of silence in a vault full of drawers. Captain Max Steele, compromiser of operations and world's worst catcher of bad guys. He really should surrender his shield, for everyone's sake. The next moment, Bull Sullivan's face bloomed in his mind and Max heard his words as clearly as the day he had said it, using his beer bottle to point at Max's nose, "You'll know it's time to quit when your boot is grinding the bad guy's face into the dirt. Not before." It was the last beer they'd shared. Then Max saw his new partner's face, thought of the last beer they had shared, and knew he couldn't quit on either one of his partners. A voice sounded in his ear, and Max jumped. It was Tex coming through the helmet. "Go for Steele," Max said, straightening up.

"I got nothing, Cap," Tex said, "and I'm smelling petrol."

"Set it down, Tex. Now. Set it down," Max said quickly.

"Yeah, not up for the roman candle thing," Tex said.

Max craned his neck and turned in a slow circle, until he saw the winking light beneath the chopper. Tex brought it down, fast and hard, on the runway several hundred yards away. Max stepped away from the light behind him and dropped the NV goggles on his helmet over his eyes. The bird's rotors were spinning down and he saw two figures sprinting away from it. Tex, the king of understatement. Smelling petrol indeed. He was running like a man expecting that bird to blow any second.

And it did.

As if on cue, Max's goggles filled with a blinding flash, and a moment later, he felt the kick of the concussion blast. He began motioning to the closest fire engine, with his arm in a roundhouse. "Go, Go, Go."

"Tex, report," he said into his helmet mic.

"Dammit," a Texas accent drawled, "She was a good girl."

"One, report," Max said.

"Checking, sir," One said.

Max held his breath.

"Shoulder dislocated," One said.

"Whose?" Max said.

"Mine," Tex said, "and I lost my erection."

Max began to laugh, and soon, he was roaring with laughter. He couldn't even respond. Tex. One of a kind. Max was so glad he was still alive.

Sometimes tears come as laughter, and they are a lot more pleasant.

Chapter Eighteen

Private Airstrip
Kingstown, Rhode Island

Max turned back to the smoldering hanger. His eyes had large yellow spots in front of them from the explosion, but if he looked from the side, he could make out some of it. Constructed of noncombustible materials, the hanger's frame was largely intact. He watched several firefighters with air tanks on their backs enter the structure. Others fanned out around its sides.

They were entering the after action phase. Assessment. Medical. Data gathering. Securing evidence.

"Tex, One, Two," Max said into his helmet, "I'm going dark on this mic."

"Roger that," One said. "We're good here."

Max took off the helmet and let the night air cool the top of his head. He wondered how long he'd have to wait before he could see. With the spots still glowing in front of his eyes, he couldn't even navigate on foot.

"Steele," a voice said from a distance.

"Yep," he said.

"Thought that might be you," the voice said, closer now, "but couldn't tell under the commando shit." Max laughed. Randy Jacobs.

"Whoa, buddy," Randy said as he neared, "we need to get you cleaned up."

"I guess," Max said. "Can't see shit. Flash blinded. How about you give me an elbow to hold?"

"Sure thing," Randy said. "I swear, man, you are a full-time job."

"Kiss my ass," Max said, "sir."

Randy led him, barking warnings about the ground beneath and ahead of Max's feet. The noise around them was increasing steadily and the air seemed alive with words and sounds. Randy seated Max on the back bumper of an EMS vehicle. Bright beams of light were shown on his face. He saw a metal object approach and heard the words, "Just a little pinch" and he knew what that meant. He braced for the needle stick.

"Please tell me I'm gonna get a badass scar out of this," Max said, and started to smile. His chin was already beginning to feel like a rubber ball.

"Uh huh," a woman's voice said. "No smiling. And sorry, no scar even approaching the level of badass."

"Like your style, Doc."

"Friend of Randy's," the voice said. "He said I should euthanize you."

"Please do," Max said.

"And miss all this fun?" she said.

"Okay. Write me a script for two months rehab on the beach."

"See what I can do," she said. Max felt a pat on his shoulder. "Be back in a few with my pliers."

"Wait, what?" Max said, but got no reply. He fought the urge to touch his chin. It felt like a lump of silly putty. He closed his eyes and listened. Over the din of orders being shouted, and scuffling feet, and ripping paper and Velcro, he heard a man shouting. He recognized the voice.

"You put this damned thing back in, now, or I'll run my shoulder into the side of your truck. Then I'll kick your ass."

Tex. Always the cooperative sort. Max pursed his lips to keep from smiling.

"Sit rep," a voice next to him said. Max twitched and ducked reflexively. "Easy soldier," Director Fenton said.

"Couldn't stay away, huh?" Max said.

"You didn't answer your phone," she said. "I came to collect your body."

"Hilarious," Max said, feeling suddenly weary. Post-adrenaline sag.

"I'm not joking," she said. "Vision improving?"

Max realized his eyes were still closed. He opened them, and the two white orbs in front of him had shrunk by half.

"Better," he said. "They told you."

"Yes," Director Fenton said.

"Getting our asses kicked, Elizabeth," Max said. It was the first time he had used her given name, and frankly, he didn't give a shit about rank right now.

"It's not even halftime," she said. "Long as my team's still alive, I'm winning."

"Careful," Max said, "you're starting to sound like a human being."

"My people are hurt, and it's pissing me off," she said, ignoring him. "Think that's our nun hanging on the door?"

"I do," Max said.

"Sadistic bastards," she said.

"Satanists, I'd say, by the positioning of the spikes," Max said.

"Inverted crucifixion?"

Max shook his head, and a pain shot across his forehead into his aching ears. He took a deep breath. "That's not necessarily satanic. St. Peter was crucified upside down," Max said. "Begged them to do him that way. Said he wasn't worthy to be crucified like his Lord."

"How do you know that?" Elizabeth Fenton said. "Max Steele, you amaze me sometimes. Honestly."

Max shrugged. "I know stuff."

"I guess!"

Max continued, "Placement of the other two spikes, though, does suggest cult. One in the vulva, and one in the heart. Life and death."

"Makes me want to cross myself, and I'm not even Catholic."

"How's Captain Amazing?" the doctor's voice said. Max saw her smiling eyes above the piercing white balls centered in his view.

"Director Fenton," Max said, "meet Dr. Pliers."

"If you will excuse us, Director," the doctor said, "our commando here has to lay back for me."

Max felt the press of her hand on his sternum and he complied. "See this lens on my head, Max?" she said. "Bright light. Bright, bright light. So I recommend you close your eyes and keep them shut. Can you do that for me?"

From somewhere near his feet, he heard Director Fenton's voice. "I'm gonna go for a look see."

Max nodded.

"Uh huh," the doctor said, "Here's how it is, Captain Steele. Good boys who hold still get the glass pulled out and get to stay. Bad boys who can't hold still get transported to Memorial and we do it there."

Max raised a gloved thumbs-up sign next to his head and closed his eyes. He felt something lay atop his mouth and nose, and told himself to relax. He heard sirens blip and knew ambulances were beginning to transport.

"Good news, and not-very-bad news, Captain," the doctor said after a time from somewhere overhead. "Good news is you got speared with a narrow shard, so the surface puncture is small. Not-so-awful news is it went deep. That's why it was such a bleeder. Plus the fact that it was your face. Facial wounds bleed a lot." She touched his arm. "I got the big piece out, and now I need to dig around in there to make sure nothing broke off and is hiding from me. You let me know with a raise of your thumb if you feel any pain, okay? DO NOT NOD. Thumb only." Max raised his thumb.

"Good, I like to tell you what I'm doing so you can help me. For this next part, don't move. At. All." Max held very still. She hadn't told him she might be probing near some nerve endings that, if damaged, could collapse portions of his face. He already knew. God knows how he knew. His head was full of useless information.

"I had a feeling," she said. He heard the clank of metal on metal, and then he felt liquid snake down the sides of his neck. "I'm finger painting with surgical wash. It comes off eventually." She ripped and tore at packages, and soon Max felt the cover lift from his nose and mouth. "Think you can sit up?"

Max raised a thumb.

"Good," she said. "I have to mummify you a bit because the bandage is in a tricky spot and it will fall off. Be sure to take a couple selfies." She laughed. "Do not smile." Max raised a thumb. This woman was fabulous. No wonder she and Randy were friends. He saw her headlamp turn off from behind the shuttered lids of his eyes. "You may open your eyes," she said.

When Max opened his eyes, the spots were pinpricks of light. He looked at the doctor's round face and gray hair. He raised a thumb.

She laughed. "Oops, forgot. You may also speak. But if you grin, you could open that sucker back up. You have three internal stitches and two external."

"Thanks, Doctor Pliers," Max said.

"Scratch and dent specialist, at your service," she said, and trotted away.

Max scooted his way to the edge of the bumper and stood. He ached all over. He reached for his chin, but then he thought better of it.

"Steele," a voice called above the din. Max turned, looking, and saw two arms motioning to him. Randy and Director Fenton stood at the front left corner of the hanger. He made his way carefully through the crowd of rescue personnel and their equipment.

"Whatcha got?" Max said when he was within a few yards of them. If the looks on their faces were any indication, they had something important.

"What we've got," Randy said, "is a live one. Barely." He turned and started around the side of the hanger toward the back. Steele and Fenton followed. He stopped next to a prone figure. An oxygen mask was on the man's face, and the doctor who had worked on Max was tending to him. His black clothing was charred and the stench of gasoline rose from his body. Max watched the attending medics cutting the man's clothes off his body.

"Meet your torch," Randy said. Director Fenton covered her nose against the smell.

"Looks like he tried to set himself on fire, or somebody else did," Randy said. "His body was still smoking when they found him. First responders came to process the body and found a pulse."

"So he was in there," Max said, pointing toward the gaping elephant doors at the back of the hanger.

Director Fenton nodded, "Got interrupted."

"Doused himself?"

"This guy was shot twice in the back," Randy said. "He might have doused himself, or he might not have been alone and his buddies doused him, thinking he was dead, and left the body to be burned up in the fire."

"So we're speculating," Max said. "Point is he's still alive."

"For now," Randy said. "Dr. Vance is one of the best trauma docs we've got."

Max stepped over to the body. "Dr. Pliers," he said.

"Captain Glass Jaw," she said, not looking up.

"Oh, that was good," Randy said behind him.

"Our friend gonna make it?" Max said.

She shrugged. "I wouldn't bet on him. These rounds take most of the body parts with them when they leave," she said, and pointed. "My medic said you should look at his foot."

"The foot?" Fenton said, moving up beside Max.

Max had already squatted down. "Randy. Flashlight?"

"There's one on your belt, soldier."

"Been a long night," Max said, reaching for his side. He slapped out the flashlight from its Velcro sleeve and shone it on the man's bare feet. "Tattoo on one of them."

"So I was right," Fenton said. "Cult."

Max held the light steady on the bottom of the foot. Upside down cross, snake coiled in the middle with a skull in its mouth. "What the mess?"

"Pardon?" Director Fenton said.

Max snorted but said nothing.

"Explains the body on the front hanger door," Fenton said.

"But nothing else fits," Max said. "Who? And why?"

Doctor Vance had been leaning over the body, but now she sat back on her feet, placing gloved hands on her ample thighs. She glanced at Max and shook her head.

"Shit," Max said.

"Tag him and bag him," Dr. Vance said to Randy. He nodded.

"I need photos of that foot," Max said.

"Course," Randy said. Fenton and Steele left them to their work.

"I'm betting the prints we lifted from Jeremy Tittle's hospital room match the fingers on our hanging body out there," Fenton said.

"No doubt in my mind," Max said. "And what do you bet the ownership of this hanger is untraceable."

"Emil Bente," Fenton said. "The man who leaves no trace."

"Ever hear the phrase, 'The enemy of my enemy is my friend?'" Max said. He glanced at her. "Bente has an enemy. Satan himself, by the looks of it."

"So Satan is our friend," Fenton said, and snorted.

Max chuckled, but it was mirthless. "You know what I mean."

"I do," Elizabeth Fenton said, "Whoever did this is teasing us with clues about Bente's operation."

"Clues they want us to have," Max said. "Suggests Bente not only has an enemy, but also a rival."

"Takeover?"

"I'd bet on it," Max said. "I need to talk with my partner."

"Let's go see him," she said. "It'll be hours before we know what we've got in there." She pointed to the smoldering hanger. "I haven't had time to be horrified."

"I don't think I want to sleep anytime soon," Max said.

"Nightmares," she said. "They come as aftershocks, don't they, like with earthquakes? It's all over, and then it's all back in our dreams."

"What has been seen, cannot be unseen," Max said, "and cannot be flushed. It waits, like monsters under the bed. Crazy huh."

"I feel less crazy knowing it happens to you, too," she said.

Chapter Nineteen

Bente Residence

Venice, Italy

She wheeled herself to the low mantle, her gnarled hands skimming the tops of the wheelchair tires. In order to replace the votives when they burned low, Mother Maria had first to blow them out. She hated that part. She had votives for her sons and for each of the Marias. It was wrenching to use her breath, the very sign of life within her, to blow out the light that represented the lives of those she loved. Her hands trembled, making it more difficult to replace the candles quickly and get them lit.

Today was worse than usual. There was trouble. She felt it. Sister Maria Milagra would be here soon, and the Holy Mother would drink deeply from her trusted source of information. Maria Milagra was the best kind of mole for the former Cartel head. Senior to all, and much like the eldest sister, it wasn't considered strange when she checked in on the other sisters, and even with Emil, gathering intelligence she would then pass along to the Holy Mother.

At last, the candles were lit. The Holy Mother clutched at the rosary around her neck and began fingering the beads and murmuring prayers. She prayed for blessings. She prayed for protection. One life at a time, beginning with her sons. Such troubled souls, each one. And such enmity between them. It was a mother's heartbreak.

She heard Maria Milagra's characteristic tapping on the wooden archway leading into the room, and she turned her chair.

"*Bene, Bene, Molto Bene, mio Maria Milagra,*" Mother Maria said.

"Mother," Maria Milagra said, "I pray you are well."

"Come," Mother Maria said, "let us sit by the fire."

"For a moment only, Mother," Maria Milagra said.

"Oh? Is something the matter? Has something happened?"

"Yes, Mother, and I must meet His Excellency's plane as soon as it lands," she said.

"What has happened, child?"

"I do not wish to tell you," she said. "Please do not make me."

"Something terrible," Mother Maria said.

"Terrible," Maria Milagra said. "I must go."

"You must sit. Now," Mother Maria said, her voice rising and growing stiff. "Tell me this instant."

Maria Milagra burst into tears and dropped to her knees in front of the only mother she had ever known. She buried her head in the old woman's lap and wept. Mother Maria held her head and rocked her gently. Finally, she raised Maria Milagra's face in her bony hands, and looked into her eyes.

"Someone is dead?" she said softly.

"Yes, Mama," Maria Milagra said, "your daughter, Maria Garza."

The Holy Mother blinked, and then dropped Maria Milagra's face back onto her lap and raised a hand to her forehead. "Yes, go quickly and get Emil," she said, barely above a whisper. "Bring him to me directly."

Maria Milagra pushed herself up and hurried away, her fist halfway in her mouth.

Mother Maria turned to the votive candles, hot tears streaming from her eyes. Through the blur, she reached for Maria Garza's candle and held it in her lap. It flicked and flickered beneath the woman's breath as she sobbed and breathed and prayed. And then she raised the candle to her mouth and blew out the flame. It resisted her breath for a moment, and then smoke rose in a thin ribbon from the wick. Suddenly, at the base of the wick, she heard a popping, sizzling sound unlike anything she'd heard before. The hair on her thin arms stood straight up and she dropped the votive from her hand. It tumbled from her lap and crashed in an explosion of shards on the stone floor.

Aeroporto di Venezia
Venice, Italy

Aeroporto di Venezia, better known as Venice Marco Polo Airport, was located 4.3 nautical miles north of the city. A boat service ferried passengers to and from the airport several times a day. The Roman Catholic Church owned a hanger for the exclusive use of senior Cardinals. Several decades ago, the Church was granted permission, quietly and privately, to construct a second hanger for "storage and miscellaneous use." It remained unmarked and unidentified by letters or symbols, and soon the airport registry of hangers contained no listing of it.

Once cleared, Emil Bente's aircraft taxied to this hanger and nested itself in the center of the cavernous space. The hanger was cavernous, except for an enclosed office, a few rolling carts, half a dozen tool chests, and a modest Fiat sedan parked near the rear doors. The pilot leapt from the craft and hurried to block the wheels, slide the hanger door closed, and open the cargo space. He fetched the long cart and slid the coffin-sized box onto it from the cargo hold. The tools he needed to undo the lid were waiting for him on the cart's lower tray. He set to work.

At last, the final screw was out. The pilot slid the lid off the box and manhandled it to the wall nearest the office. He turned back to the box. Typically, Excellency would be sitting up and calling for water, but the pilot saw no movement. He rushed to the box. Inside, the man laid very still, the oxygen mask still over his nose and mouth. The pilot peered in, and gasped. In Bente's right hand, he clutched a dark colored snake just behind its head. Its triangular mouth was open and dried blood formed a jagged blotch on the cloth interior of the box. Its eyes had gone milk white.

"Excellency!" the pilot said, "*Oh mio Dio! Stai bene*?" The pilot crossed himself, and then leaned over the still unmoving body. He reached two fingers to Emil Bente's neck to check for a pulse. A powerful hand grabbed the back of his arm and yanked him down. "Excellency, I …." the pilot said. Emil's right hand was on the pilot's neck, followed immediately by his left. He squeezed and the pilot began to writhe and flop against the side of the box. Still Emil held him, crushing his windpipe, until he felt the man's body go limp.

Emil Bente sat up and shoved the pilot's body off him. It crumpled to the hanger floor. He tore the oxygen mask from his face and gulped in the mid-morning air. He grabbed the limp, but surprisingly dense, body of the snake and examined it in his lap. It was a pit viper, with prominent holes on either side of its triangular head. The mouth wasn't completely closed, and he pried it open until he heard a crack. The whitish interior of the mouth was ribbed and muscled, but the fangs were missing. The snake was toothless. Someone intended to terrify Emil, but not kill him. It was a message, a taunt. He wanted to hurl it across the hanger, but then he thought better of it. He would keep it. Might come in handy when he expressed his appreciation to the son of a bitch who did this to him.

He laid the snake atop the oxygen bottles at the end of the box and climbed out. His legs wobbled with his first few steps. He had been accustomed to the pilot's assistance, the same pilot who prepared the box he travelled in, that bastard. He went to the office and grabbed two bottles of water. He drank one as he walked back to where the pilot lay. He opened the second bottle and poured it onto the pilot's face until the man's consciousness returned. He sat up spluttering and gasping for breath. Emil grabbed him by the front of his shirt and dragged him to one of the tool chests. He opened the bottom drawer and pulled out a large aircraft wrench. The pilot's eyes went wide at the sight of it.

"Tell me about the snake," Emil said, and raised the wrench over the man.

"I don't know, Excellency," the pilot said. "I didn't know. He …."

"He? Who?" Emil said, and chopped the wrench down onto the man's right shoulder. The crack of bone echoed against the hanger ceiling, and the pilot screamed.

"He, he say, he," the pilot said, spluttering. Spittle fell onto his chin and his face was contorted into a garish mask. His breath came shallow and fast.

"Who?" Emil said, "Who did this?" He raised the wrench above his head again.

"I didn't know," the man said. "I didn't …."

The wrench slashed down again, striking the left shoulder at the joint. The pilot's arm dislocated, and the pilot opened his mouth to scream but Emil swung the wrench into his jaw, shattering his teeth into the back of his throat. The pilot's eyes rolled in their sockets and he slumped forward, unconscious. Emil cursed and stomped into the office for more water. He grabbed two bottles in his free hand and returned.

"Emil," a woman's voice said, and his head snapped up. Standing near the tool chest was Maria Milagra, her hands outstretched toward the pilot's body. "In the name of all that is holy, what is this?"

"You shouldn't be here," Emil said.

"You look at me with hate in your eyes," she said.

"*Silenzio*," Emil said. He felt his mouth curling into a snarl. "Leave me."

Maria Milagra hesitated for a moment, staring at Emil and the bloodied wrench in his hand, and then she turned her back. "You treat me like dirt," she said over her shoulder. "I am nothing but your whore." She hurried to the rear exit and disappeared.

Emil watched her go, and then set the wrench on top of the cabinet. He unscrewed the cap to the water and poured it onto the pilot's face. Then he kicked him with his foot and poured the second bottle over him. At last, the pilot groaned and rolled onto his back.

Emil grabbed the wrench and leaned over him. "Who?" he said. "Who did this?"

"Yeeooo brrrrrr," the pilot mouthed through blood and bits of teeth.

"Again," Emil said. "Who? Tell me."

"*Brutta,*" the pilot said, wheezing.

"Brother?" Emil said, his voice rising to a roar. "My brother?"

The pilot nodded. Emil raised the wrench and buried it in the man's throat. The pilot's body lurched and twitched for a full minute while Emil watched and drank the remaining water. When the pilot's body went still at last, Emil raised his foot and stomped his face. "Rot in hell," he said, and spat on him.

Chapter Twenty

Memorial Hospital

Kingstown, Rhode Island

Nothing prepares you to see someone you care about, with tubes attached to them, and with their head wrapped entirely in gauze and tape. Even the beeps and ticks of equipment surrounding the bed take on a different sound. Max stood at his partner's bedside, looking. He imagined Bert's face beneath the bandages, imagined the wounds and the stitches and the nose splint. Without thinking, almost as if he couldn't help himself, he took Bert's hand and gave it a gentle squeeze.

"Max?" a voice said beneath the bandages.

"Shhh," Max said. "Mummies only speak in horror movies." He patted his partner's hand.

"Anybody else there?" Higgins said.

"Why, you want to talk bad about your Director?" Elizabeth Fenton said from the chair next to the bed.

"Not anymore," Higgins said.

"Doc said don't make you laugh," Max said, "and don't let you talk. So shut up."

"I want a Philly cheesesteak," the mummy said.

"On me as soon as you can eat it," Fenton said. "I'm proud of you, son."

"Thanks, Mom."

"I didn't mean it that way, you goof," Fenton said, and swatted the air.

"Doc said shut up, so shut up," Max said. "I need to tell you some stuff anyway. Unless you're too tired or too sore. If you want me to brief you, give a thumbs-up.

The hand rose from the other side of the bed with a vertical thumb.

"Okay," Max said, "Director Fenton and I have just returned from an air strip. We think we're putting a couple of puzzle pieces in place, finally. Embarrassing to admit, but we didn't earn the pieces. They were presented on a silver platter by what looks to be a Cartel competitor. They served up our rogue nun, but sadly, only after they crucified her upside down. Nailed her to the door of an airplane hangar they torched. Bente's hanger by the looks of it. That must be how he's getting in and out of the country. By the time we arrived, the hangar was a fireball, and there were two drones buzzing overhead like angry bees after their nest's been whacked by a stick.

"Dayum," the voice said inside the gauze.

"Shut up," Max said. "Doctor's orders, and Doc's only 'condition' for letting me hold this briefing with you and the Director." Another vertical thumb appeared from the bed.

"Wait," Director Fenton said, "in and out of the country? Where?"

"I'll get to that," Max said, waving his hand. "First, I want to tell my partner something he's gonna love to hear. Tex and the boys shot both drones down."

Bert raised a fist in the air. Max nodded. "Got the bastards. Damn good shooting. Serious killing machines, though, those drones. Shot up Tex's bird pretty good, but he got out before it blew."

"Blew? Whoa, Tex," the mummy said.

"He's okay, Bert," Max said, "and shut up. Last time I tell you. Tex got out with only a dislocated shoulder. Probably giving EMS a run for their money right now." Max paused. "And did I say shut up already?" He smiled, and glanced to the chair where Director Fenton sat. She wore a rare, if wry, smile on her face. Max continued, "Our techs are gonna have a field day with those drone carcasses. If we're lucky, we can tie a string between manufacturer and purchaser."

He shifted from one leg to the other, but didn't let go of Bert's hand. "Point is we got 'em, and we got one of the guys who'd been playing with matches. Same crew you encountered on the roof. Same ones who snatched Bontecelli."

"It wasn't Bente returning for Bontecelli?" Fenton said.

"Nope," Max said. "I put a quick call in to the Coroner when I was in the head."

"Um, that's too much information, thank you," Fenton said.

Max grinned. "Asked him to look at the feet of the men in tactical gear we killed. Same tattoo, same foot, every one of them. Now, who they are, and why they want Vinnie, are open questions. But it wasn't Bente's men you were battling, Bert. These are some dark hombres."

"Cult maybe," Fenton said from the chair.

"Beginning to think so," Max said, nodding his again. "Getting good, huh partner?" Max patted him and received another vertical thumb in return. "Thought this stuff might encourage you to heal a little quicker. I need help running this stuff down."

"Please don't listen to this man," Fenton said. "Do exactly what your doctors tell you."

"But hurry," Max said. "This thing is getting both clearer, and more complicated, by the minute. When you can see, I'll bring in a flip chart. We need to draw this one out, check and challenge what we think we know. And speaking of, the only clue we've got to the identity of these guys is the tattoo on the bottoms of their people's feet. Seems they all have them. I'm sure I don't need to ask our fine Director over here for an assist with requisitioning research into the tattoo and who it identifies."

He paused, and she gave him a thumbs-up sign. He laughed. "Director Fenton gave us the thumbs-up, buddy, so you are off the hook on that research project." He paused again, and then continued more slowly. "We need to know who they are and where they are. Gonna pay a visit and ask them pretty please to give us our star witness back. Must say I admire them in a twisted sort of way, the way they've been handing Bente his ass. Better than we've done."

"Maybe the best person to kick an asshole's butt," Elizabeth Fenton said, "is another asshole."

"Why Director," Max said, "such wisdom." They laughed and another vertical thumb rose from the bed.

"Now listen up partner, 'cause I'm getting to the good stuff," Max said. "Your previous research is turning out to be important." He paused and glanced at Fenton. "One nun is a coincidence, Bert, and you traced her identity well."

"Sanchez," Fenton said, and then added, "I'm sorry Max, go ahead."

"Sanchez. Right." Max took a deep breath. "One nun is a coincidence, Bert. Two nuns is a tell. Tie those strings to each other, and then tie them to the rosaries the Shark has been dropping." He let that sink in for a moment. "Now tie those strings to the Order of nuns Maria Sanchez comes from in Italy."

Bert jerked and started to sit up, but Max was quick with a hand to his shoulder. "Easy boy, but I had the same reaction," Max said. He looked at the Director. "Ma'am, we may have discovered Bente's base of operations. Once my partner and that grizzled yard bird, Tex, are healed up, we request permission to pay a visit to Italy. Venice, Italy to be exact."

Fenton grabbed her head with both hands and squeezed. "Granted."

"Holy shit," the gauzed face said.

"Indeed," Max said. "Now shut up. And get better."

Memorial Hospital
Kingstown, Rhode Island

Captain Steele and Director Fenton stepped from Higgins's hospital room into the corridor.

"Now what?" Steele said. "Besides the mountain of paperwork? We need a stenographer to document all that's gone down here."

"I'll give you a new box of pencils," Fenton said.

"You're all heart."

"By the way, before I forget," the Director said, "I have already made some calls about our Warden at Mantisto Prison. I'm launching a full investigation."

"Thank you," Steele said. "The prison lost a man upstairs, you know. Drucker. What do you bet that prick, Antonelli, isn't even here?"

Director Fenton was quiet while they walked. They rounded the corner to the elevator. When the doors parted, they found themselves looking at the over-sized frame of Kingstown's Chief of Police, Jeremiah Simone. He nodded.

"Chief Simone," Elizabeth Fenton said.

"Director," he said with a thin smile. "Good to see you under these unfortunate circumstances."

She nodded.

Chief Simone turned his attention to Max Steele and extended a hand, "Captain Steele, I know you by face, but I think this is the first time we've met."

"Max took the man's hand in his. "My pleasure. How you settling into the new post?"

"I don't think I've sat down for more than five minutes since I took it," he said, still shaking Max's hand.

Max felt the solid mass of metal in the man's grip and glanced down. Chief Simone saw the look and grinned.

"Didn't pinch ya with it, I hope," Simone said.

Max shook his head. "Nope, just noticed it."

"Hefty sucker," Simone said. "Bigger than a damn super bowl ring and a pain in the ass, but it belonged to my grandfather. I never take it off."

Simone had dropped his hand to his side, but now raised it for Max to see.

The elevator doors slid closed. In the muted light of the elevator, Max looked at the ring. It appeared to be solid gold in the four-sided shape of a diamond.

The end